When Tag raised his head up out of the crisp cool stream, the sound of muffled laughter raised the hair on the back of his neck.

He wiped his eyes and ran his fingers through his too-long hair, pushing it away from his face and glanced from one side of the hidden alcove to the other.

No one.

He shook his head and tapped at his ear. Lack of sleep and decent conversation had obviously played with his mind and he was hearing things.

Giggle.

There it was again. He flicked his head toward the bushes where he'd lain his clothing. Two very young boys, wearing mischievous grins, met his eyes—one held his trousers, chaps, and boots, and the other his shirt, vest, and drawers. Something in their eyes reflected an image of him and his twin brother, Levi, at their age, all full of trouble.

He shook his head and motioned forward, but the youths disappeared behind some shrubbery before he could reach them, leaving a very naked Tag with nothing but his sopping bright blue handkerchief and a bar of his mother's soap to save his pride.

Tag treaded through the water toward the bank, but stopped just short of emerging from the river at the sound of a woman's voice.

"Everett Hanson and Gandy Stevens, where did you get those things?"

The boys muttered something he could not hear.

"What do you mean there's a man swimming in my alcove?"

My alcove? It couldn't be. He'd been told that the Scott's hadn't had any children.

Tag flicked his head from one side of the inlet to the other, searching for a place to take cover, but short of leaving the water and hiding in the trees, he was out of luck.

"It's not funny, Charlie," the woman continued. "What have I taught you boys about taking things that don't belong to you?"

A splash of purple filled in the slits at the bottom of the trees and moments later, a woman, much younger than he'd anticipated, stepped through the bushes and into view as she continued to chastise the boys, his clothes in her arms.

"Stay put and I'll handle this," she told the children.

There was nowhere for Tag to go to protect the woman's sensibilities. With one hand, he made small ripples around him. At least the movement of the water would serve as some sort of covering and he still had the handkerchief in his hand he could use for cover.

"Where did you get th…" her words faded as she searched the alcove until she met his eyes.

She obviously hadn't expected him—especially in this state of undress, although she did hold the evidence of his obvious vulnerability in her hands. Her face filled with color as she cleared her throat and spun away, facing the brush from which she'd appeared.

"Who are you?"

REDBOURNE SERIES, BOOK SIX
TAG'S STORY

KELLI ANN
MORGAN

inspire books

Inspire Books
A Division of Inspire Creative Services
937 West 1350 North, Clinton, Utah 84015, USA

THE WRANGLER

An Inspire Book published by arrangement with the author

First Inspire Books paperback edition July 2018

ISBN-13: 978-1-939049-39-1
ISBN-10: 1939049393

Printed in the United States of America

ACKNOWLEDGEMENTS

To all of you who have waited so patiently for Tag's story to be released and have remained fans. I can't express well enough how much I appreciate having you along for the ride.

To my wonderful beta readers—Jennifer, Darcy, Kathy, and Janene—who have lost sleep as they read to provide insights in making this story what it is. Thank you!

To my amazing copyeditor, Rocky. Thank you for catching even my silliest mistakes!

And, to the two biggest heroes in my life—Grant and Noah—your support and encouragement mean everything to me! I would have never finished this book without you!

To my big little brother, Steven, who doesn't always appreciate it when I correct his grammar. Love you, kiddo!

REDBOURNE SERIES, BOOK SIX
TAG'S STORY

CHAPTER ONE

Redbourne Ranch, Kansas, March 1871

Taggert Redbourne awoke with a nagging feeling in his gut. The sun had not yet peeked over the mountain tops, but he could not go back to sleep. He ripped his blanket from on top of him and bolted upright. Rather than lie in bed for another hour, warring with his thoughts to allow him some peace, there was plenty of work to be done with several new horses that had come to the ranch.

He sniffed at the air. The savory aroma of meat cooking wafted through his room, enticing Tag downstairs. The cold of the Acacia wood floors sent shivers up his back and down his arms and he scrubbed his extremities briskly as he made his way to the kitchen.

A warm cushion of savory scents engulfed him as he entered the kitchen to find Lottie, the family's cook, humming as she stirred a large pot of cocoa over the stove.

"Good morning, *querido*," she said with a smile. "*No podias dormir?*"

"No, I couldn't sleep, Lottie, but who could when you're in the kitchen?" He flashed a smile of his own and bent down to kiss her on the cheek before reaching out and snatching a piece of bacon from the plate.

The Spanish woman giggled. "You are incorrigible," she said as she placed one of Rafe's ceramic mugs in front of him, full to the brim of steaming hot cocoa. He admired the craftsmanship of his brother's creation a moment before clasping it in his hands.

"Do I smell bacon?" Cole, the youngest of Tag's six brothers, stood in the doorway, one eye open, his arms stretching toward the ceiling.

Lottie laughed. "Come in, *mijo*. *El bacón* will be ready *en un momentito*."

"What are you doing up so early?" Tag asked. Generally, it was like dragging a pig through the mud to get Cole up before the sun.

"Couldn't sleep. Just a feeling—"

"In your gut?" Tag finished for him.

"Yeah, why? You too?"

Tag nodded as he heated his hands on his cup and took a sip of the cocoa. He closed his eyes as the warm, rich liquid drained down his throat. It was just what he'd needed.

The door opened. Their father stepped in, bringing with him a chilled morning breeze.

"And here I thought I was the only one crazy enough to be up before ol' Jasper." Jameson Redbourne shot a look between Tag and Cole with a raised brow, then smiled. The man had a commanding presence. He clapped his gloves together, placed them on the bench behind the door, and hung his hat on a protruding peg.

As if on cue, Jasper, the family's rooster, crowed.

They all laughed.

Cole spit out the sip of cocoa he'd just taken from his mug as he tried to contain an ironic chuckle and Tag pounded him on the back.

"You all right there, little brother?"

Cole nodded, wiping the liquid from his chin and the corners of his mouth.

It wasn't long before they were joined by several others sitting around the table eating their breakfast. Bacon, eggs, biscuits, and bottled peaches filled their bellies as they chatted about nothing in particular.

"Am I late?" Leah Redbourne asked as she walked into the kitchen, putting another pin into her quaffed hair.

Jameson stood. "Not at all, my dear," he said as he placed a quick kiss on his wife's lips. "Your boys and I just made it an early morning is all and Lottie was inspired, as always," he winked at the cook, "to get a head start on the day as well."

Lottie brought Leah her mug, colored with vibrant hues of green and blue, and placed it in front of her.

"You are a godsend," their mother praised as she lifted the cup to her mouth and blew back the vines of steam that rose from its contents.

"Tag?" His father looked up from his food. "I understand that you have a few new horses to work with today, but I'd like a word sometime this afternoon."

"Yes, sir. Is everything all right?"

His gut churned again.

"Of course. It's just something of business that I'd like to discuss with you."

Tag's eyes narrowed slightly and his brows scrunched together. Usually, his father talked all things business with his brother, Ethan, who'd taken over the day-to-day duties at the ranch.

"I'll make some time," he confirmed.

His father nodded and took another bite of his biscuit.

"Did Raine sleep in town again?" Cole asked.

Their oldest brother was the deputy sheriff in Stone Creek and sometimes that required him to be away from the family for days at a time.

"'Fraid so. They're holding the Hollyhock Gang until the territory marshal can make it out here. Raine doesn't want to take any chances they'll get away again."

Knock. Knock.

They all looked to the door as it opened.

"I'm sorry to interrupt," Handy, the newest hire at the ranch, removed his hat as he stepped inside and twisted it in his hands, "but I'm afraid we need Tag out in the stables. There's a problem with one of the new horses."

"What kind of problem, son?" Jameson asked, concern lacing his brow.

Tag wiped his mouth, stood to kiss his mother on her forehead, then took his dish to the sink.

"I'll be right there," he told the man before turning to their cook. "*Gracias*, Lottie. *Fue delicioso.* It was delicious," he added the English translation for his father's benefit.

"I know what it means!" Jameson protested a little too loudly. Though his father knew Spanish nearly as well as any of them, it had taken him twice as long as any of his children to learn the language.

Tag smiled to himself as he heard the laughter from those still left at the table. He ran upstairs to pull on his boots and collect his hat before heading out to the stables.

This last little herd had just come in yesterday and he imagined they would have plenty of unique problems. The group consisted of fifteen horses—four mares, ten geldings, and one stallion, all Morgans in a variety of colors and markings, except one—a Belgian.

Handy caught up to him as he made his way toward the new horses.

"It's the Belgian, Tag. She's pacing and has started to sweat. I thought maybe she was colicky, but then she started trying to kick at her abdomen, like she's got a bellyache or something."

Tag nodded.

"I still cain't hardly believe someone could have been so cruel as to have just left them behind for so long without so much as a word to anyone." The ranch hand worked to keep pace with Tag.

The horses had been rescued from an abandoned farm a few counties over and it irked Tag to no end that they'd been completely abandoned. The eccentric city slicker who'd moved into the old Mackabee place had only been there a year before he'd given up and hightailed it back to whatever rat-infested hole he'd climbed out of. Folks like that had no business working with animals—especially the non-vermin kind.

Tag slammed his gloved hand against his leg, then balled it into as tight a fist as he could manage.

"Three weeks," he muttered under his breath.

"What was that, boss?" Handy asked.

Tag cleared his throat and adjusted his hat. "Eh...I just imagine those horses were cooped up in that blasted corral for nearly three weeks. If it had been any other farm, they would have broken through the gate after the first day, and by the looks of that corral, they tried, but Xavier Mackabee was nothing if not good at fortifying his fences."

"Yes, sir," Handy said.

Tag shot a glance sideways, his brow raised. The young cowpoke hadn't been around long enough to know the Mackabees, but he figured the kid knew enough about ranching to spot a good fence or two. His brother wouldn't have hired him otherwise.

"By the looks of it, though," Handy said, "I reckon a horse or two got out."

"Very possible. We'll have to keep an eye out." When Tag and his men had rescued the horses, he'd noticed a few of the upper slats had been splintered and broken through on the corral. He hoped any horses that may have broken through were not hurt too badly.

Why the man hadn't at least turned the horses out to the fields was completely asinine. After that amount of time, the grasses had been eaten to the dirt and, now, the horses appeared emaciated.

There are plenty of folks around here who would have been happy to take on a few extra healthy head, but now…

"I guess it's lucky there's been so much rain lately. At least they had something to drink."

"Yeah, lucky." Tag snorted. If he ever got his hands on that rancher, he'd have a few things to say. Tag shook his head and blew out a deep breath. There was nothing he could do about the past and somebody else's mistake, all he could do was make sure these horses received the best care he could provide them. His work had already been cut out for him with this bunch, without any additional complications.

He shook his head again and clenched his teeth, his jaw flexed as he walked through the stable doors and back toward the stall that housed the Belgian.

The restless mare paced nervously about in one of the larger compartments.

Snap!

Handy jumped back with a startled grunt as the horse kicked at the side of the stall, the wood splintering, but not cracking through.

The mare shook her head wildly, then bent down, biting at the flesh on her side.

Tag attempted to approach the large horse, his hands raised as he spoke in soft tones, but was quickly warned away as she switched her tail, so he struggled to do a visual once over, but the stall was still pretty dark in the early morning hours.

"Open all the windows," he commanded, though his voice never reached much louder than a gentle plea.

As light plunged into the stable, the mare screamed in protest as she lay down, then stood up again, obviously agitated. Her belly shifted and the realization of her situation struck him. All the signs had been there and he cursed himself for having missed them last night.

By the time the herd had arrived well into the late hours, it had been too dark to examine them completely, but he had taken the time to visit personally with each of the horses for a few minutes, making sure they had plenty to drink and had been brushed down properly before he retired. Some of them had been a little skittish, but they'd warmed to him quickly enough. All but the Belgian.

"She's foaling," Tag said, disgusted with himself, as he climbed up onto the stall gate to give her a little room.

When a whoosh of water splashed to the floor, it confirmed for him that the animal was indeed in labor.

"Lord, help us," he muttered, dropping his head low. What would normally be a joyous occasion at the ranch, now carried a weight with it. The malnourishment the expectant mare had experienced in this last month would surely affect the ease of delivery. She could die.

"Grab a couple fresh bundles of straw," he told the new ranch hand. "All we can do now is give her space and make sure that the stall is as warm and comfortable as possible."

Handy slapped the top of the gate and nodded as he pushed off and headed out.

There was plenty of room in the young mare's stall and once they'd covered the floor in straw, the only thing that would be left to do was wait.

"Tag! Tag!" Hannah, the youngest of the Redbourne clan at nineteen, and his only sister, came running into the stables. "It's my goat! I think she's having her baby. Come quick." Her voice held a combination of anxiety and excitement as she waved her hand wildly in a beckoning motion.

What are the odds?

"Come on!" she cried anxiously. "She's out in the field. Her back and tail are arched and she won't stop pacing back and forth along the fence. Those are the signs, right?"

"Hannah," he said in a tone he hoped would help soothe her fears, "just come here for a minute," he said, less worried about the goat that had been kept under the vigilant and watchful eye of his little sister.

"But…"

"You won't regret it. And then I promise to check on Sally."

With a grunt of resignation and a slight pout, Hannah joined him at the stall gate.

"What's so important?"

"Look." He pointed to the mare who had now lain back down, one leg of her foal protruding.

"Ahhhh," Hannah gasped. "I didn't know one of the new mares was expecting." She climbed up onto the gate and straddled the top. "And the Belgian too? She is the most beautiful of them all."

Hannah had been with them the day they'd discovered the herd and had taken an instant liking to the mare. The large draft horse was somewhat of a novelty around Redbourne Ranch. Most of the horses they bred and trained were Appaloosas, Morgans, and Quarter Horses. Cole's black Arabian had been the largest deviation from those until now.

"Tag?" Her voice trailed as her brows slowly furrowed together. "Is she going to be all right? Handy said that those horses hadn't eaten in days, maybe weeks."

"Honestly, I don't know enough about her yet. I hope so, but we'll just have to wait." He wanted to offer some consolation, but the truth was, anything could happen and he didn't want her to be disappointed if things went south. He placed his arm around her shoulder and squeezed.

She hugged into him.

"You can stay with the mare," Hannah said with finality. "I think she needs you a little more than Sally does right now."

"You know it takes goats a lot longer to kid than horses, right?"

"I know," she whispered. "You've told me before. Can I stay?"

He looked down at her, hardly able to believe how much she'd grown up. "I don't know," he teased, "you sure you wouldn't rather be with your goat?"

Hannah thought for a moment, then shook her head, her

anxiety quelled for the time being. "She'll be okay."

Handy returned with the straw and the three of them worked around the mare, careful not to cause her too much more stress as they spread it throughout the stall. Before they'd finished, the foal's head and shoulders had emerged.

"It won't be long now."

After another few minutes, the foal was out. It was smaller than Tag had expected a Belgian's young to be, but it was breathing and crawling forward. A good sign.

The mare was still restless. She stood up, then lay back down again, nickering and still biting at her sides. This concerned Tag as the mare should have been ready to rest by this point.

"Something's wrong," he said quietly.

"What?" Hannah's brows creased with concern. "Should I go get Doc Cooper?"

"There isn't time. We need to do something now." Tag feared that in the mare's apparent agony, she might kick out at the little filly which had already lifted her chest up off the ground. He jumped down into the stall and slid the foal to the opposite end, noticing that she was significantly smaller than even the most average of newborn foals.

Premature. It was the only thing that made sense.

The mare released a loud whinny and squirmed awkwardly on the floor, pulling Tag's attention back to her dilemma.

Maybe if I can get her to her feet, Tag thought as he gingerly approached the mare, but he was caught off guard at the sight of another foot protruding from the new mama.

"We've got another foal, Handy!" he called out as he hopped back up on the railing to give the mare some space.

Twin births in horses was dangerous business—especially with a malnourished mare. He'd never known a set of twin foals to be born alive, let alone survive. He glanced over his shoulder at the young newborn filly struggling to push herself to her feet, amazed at the strength it was demonstrating in light of the situation.

"I know you're tired, girl," he cooed to the dam, "but just a little longer and you can rest, I promise." He kicked a leg up over the gate and hopped down on the other side, propping his arms on the top to keep a close eye on the situation.

"We're going to have twins?" Hannah asked excitedly.

Tag's heart hurt as he glanced down at the hopeful look spread across his little sister's face. "It's not likely they'll survive, sis," he told her, shaking his head solemnly. It was best not to make light.

Her smile fell. "What? Why not?"

"Hannah," Marty, the foreman, called from the open stable door, "Sally's kidding right now and Cole thought you'd want to be there."

Hannah looked conflicted and she glanced up at Tag.

"Go on," he encouraged. "I'll come by and check on her in a little while."

"All right," she conceded. "But, you stay!" she demanded with a firm nod. "You need to be here right now," Hannah told him. She rushed into his arms and hugged him tight before turning and heading outside with Marty.

Another twenty minutes passed before the second foal was completely out of his mama. It was even smaller than the first and while it was moving, it didn't make much of an attempt to free itself from the birthing sac and Tag feared that it was too weak. He grabbed a saddle blanket from the closet and rushed to the foal, ripping open the sac and kneeling down next to the newborn, briskly rubbing the blanket over its belly in an attempt to spur breath.

Nothing.

He tried again, still to no avail. He used the blanket to clean off the nose, then tried toweling him off again, this time a little more vigorously.

"Come on. Breathe, damn it!" he said under his breath.

Still nothing.

He leaned back to sit on his feet, raising his head heavenward, his jaw clenching as he fought the anger that coursed through him. Had the mare been well cared for, the twins may have had a chance. He closed his eyes and with resignation, glanced back down at the still little colt.

CHAPTER TWO

The mare had calmed down enough, her energy spent, that she no longer protested Tag's presence in the stall with her and her babies, and she turned to nudge the sickly foal. She licked his face and down his neck. It never ceased to amaze Tag—the instinct for a mother to care for her young and a new wave of regret washed over him.

"I'm sorry, girl," Tag said, pulling the blanket from the lifeless colt. "I did what I could." He stood up and unlatched the gate, his head low as he watched with awe and a twinge of sadness. How was he going to tell Hannah?

Another few minutes and the dead colt would need to be removed, so the mare could bond with the filly.

"The kid is here!" Hannah's sing-song voice could be heard flittering on the breeze outside.

Timing.

"It's a girl and she is beautiful," his little sister sputtered with excitement as she burst back into the stable.

Tag managed a smile. "You've taken great care of your goat, Hannah. You should be proud of that. Congratulations."

"Thank you," she said with a slight curtsey. "And how are the foals?"

Tag stared at her a moment before shaking his head. "The colt didn't make it."

Hannah's smile dropped. "No!" She ran to the gate and peered inside.

He'd lost foals before, so Tag didn't understand why this one had affected him so strongly, but for whatever reason, he felt a deep sense of sadness that the young colt hadn't even had a chance at life.

"He's moving!" Hannah exclaimed with reined excitement.

"Hannah, it's just the mare. She's nudging him, trying to bond."

"But, he's lifting his head. That foal is alive, Taggert Redbourne, and don't you try to tell me otherwise. Look!"

Tag rushed to Hannah's side and sure enough, the young colt squirmed beside its mother. Tears threatened and he cleared his throat to regain control.

He's alive? He's…alive!

Silence passed between them a few moments before Tag was collected enough to speak. "We'll have to watch him real close," he said quietly. "He's not out of the woods yet, little one."

The new filly had found her footing and awkwardly made her way over to her mother, who began immediately sniffing and licking the first-born foal.

Tag released the breath that had been stuck in his chest. He folded his arms on top of the gate and leaned in, watching the miracle with a renewed sense of wonder.

"I think you, little sis, are a good luck charm," he said with a wink as he pushed away from the gate.

She beamed up at him.

"I'm going to make sure we don't have any more surprises this morning. Would you like to stay with the mare a while?"

"Yes, please."

While Hannah was certainly no longer a child—as had been proven by the many potential suitors who'd come to call on her lately, at nineteen, she still seemed so young, so innocent, and full of wonder. He hoped she would never lose that quality.

"I'm going to start checking on the other horses, but I will be back shortly to check in on them and make sure they are progressing."

Hannah nodded, but did not take her eyes off the little filly that was still working to gain her footing.

Tag left to attend to the other horses, satisfied that Hannah would stay with the new mother and her babies.

By the time he returned to the Belgian's stall nearly an hour later, the filly had already discovered how to eat, but the young colt still had not gained enough strength to push his chest up off the ground.

"Hannah," Tag said, placing a hand on her shoulder so as not to startle her, "I need you to go and collect some of Sally's milk for me. Can you do that?"

"Sure, Tag, but why?"

"I have a feeling this mare won't have enough milk for the two of them and as weak as the colt is, I think it's best that we feed him."

"Can I do it, Tag? Please?"

He laughed.

"Yes," he said with a bow of his head. "I have plenty of other things that need to be done today. It would actually be a great help if you would."

She jumped down from the gate and ran out of the stable.

"I heard we had a little miracle out here."

Tag turned to the voice. His father grabbed a rope from the side wall and joined him next to the stall.

"Honestly, I'm hoping for a few more. The colt is very weak, but at least his mama hasn't rejected him."

"How are the rest of them?" His father motioned down the row with his chin.

"I've only had a chance to look over two others this morning and I won't lie, it's not pretty. It looks like they haven't eaten properly in weeks, but I am optimistic that with a little proper care and attention, they'll recover."

"You have always been able to work miracles, son."

A moment of silence passed between them.

"About that business…"

"Yes, sir?" Tag turned to his father and gave him his undivided attention.

"We've been given a business opportunity to have a continuous supply of horses and cattle from Texas." Jameson scratched his chin. "I'm afraid your mother isn't very pleased with me at the moment for what I am about to say, but I can't think of anyone else I trust."

"To do what exactly?"

"Well, we need good, solid, trained horses that can be bred to be stronger, faster, and more durable in ever-changing climates. There are a lot of good, strong horse breeds in Texas and I think with a little…miracle-working," he cleared his throat, "we could easily produce the best stock around, combining the best qualities of different breeds. What do you think?"

It wasn't like his father to beat around the bush and that twinge in Tag's gut returned. He picked up his grooming kit and started toward the stall with a large grey roan gelding. Jameson followed.

"Haven't we already been doing that?" Tag asked. "We run two or three drives up from Texas every year, mixing in a few Spanish breeds with the others each time. I'm already working more hours than most. I'm not sure what more you expect."

"That's just it. This would be different. Think expansion, son. We are functioning near capacity here, and I couldn't be more proud of the work you do…"

"But?" Tag unfastened the leather bag and retrieved his brush.

"But nothing," his father said.

Tag opened the stall where one of the Morgan geldings he'd

examined earlier stood and set down his grooming kit at the far edge. He moved to the front of the horse where he ran his hand down the animal's leg and gently squeezed. The gelding lifted his foot and Tag leaned into his shoulder, picking rocks and debris from the hoof.

"I think it only makes sense," Jameson cleared his throat, "that we would want to have a foot so close to the market." He moved around the stall into Tag's view. "I mean, if we could expand Redbourne Ranch to include a training facility at a Texas location, we could be a jump ahead of anyone else."

"I'm not sure what you are trying to say and I've never known you to beat around the bush like this, so what's going on?"

"You're right. The fact is, expansion may not be the right word. I'd like to *partner* with the Oak Meadow Ranch near Austin. And Ethan agrees."

Tag looked up from the horse. "Okay, so, you're going to partner with some Texas rancher, but what does that have to do with me?" He released the foot and moved to the other side where he started to repeat the process.

Jameson snorted breathily, then stared at Tag expectantly a moment before continuing. "You're a great wrangler, son, and I appreciate all the work you do around here, but ever since Levi found Cadence, and he's been away so often, you've seemed a little…"

Tag paused and looked up from his task. "A little what?"

It was true, Levi getting married had set him to thinking and he'd realized it was time for him to move on. To do something more. He'd been patiently watching for the right opportunity to leave Redbourne Ranch and start a place of his own and had saved a sizeable nest egg to assure that he would get the kind of place he wanted—a place with a river running through it, wide open fields, a view of the mountains, and close enough to town that lumber would be easy to come by. But, he'd not told a soul. He hadn't wanted to see his father's disappointment.

"Lost."

Tag didn't know what to say, so he just looked down and returned to his work, a little more vigorously than he had before.

"I know you've been itching to find your place in the world. It's no secret you're ready for a place of your own."

Tag dropped the hoof and stood up straight, his brows knit together, his head tilted slightly.

How? He should have known. His father knew everything. He didn't know how, but he always did.

"The Oak Meadow is for sale and I told the owner that I knew just the right man to buy it."

Tag stared at his father, his eyes narrowed.

"You, son. I want to go into business with you."

It took a moment for his words to sink in.

Texas? Me?

He shook his head slowly. While he had been thinking about his future lately, this was not what he'd had in mind, and he had to quiet the voice inside of his head that was a constant reminder of the sense of adventure he'd had before the war. He'd grown up since then and just wanted a quiet, simple life on a small ranch where he could breed and raise horses of his own. Running a large operation was not the opportunity he'd been waiting for.

"Son?"

"I'm a wrangler," he said simply as he walked around his father to retrieve a brush from his kit, "not a businessman or a foreman."

"Correction," Jameson said, "you are the best wrangler I have ever known."

Heat radiated from beneath Tag's collar at the appraisal.

"And, you are smart. I've seen Marty consult with you on numerous occasions."

Their foreman had often inquired of his opinion on things, but his contributions to the business side of things were certainly not praiseworthy.

"Ethan," his father continued, "well, he looks up to you. He feels like we are under-utilizing your talents. I know it would be a big change from Redbourne Ranch and I know that it might be difficult to leave..." Jameson scratched his head as if trying to recall something, "...uh, Florence Hipple," he said, obviously pleased with himself for remembering her name, "behind, but..."

It was Tag's turn to snort. He'd walked Flor home one day after church and it was like the whole town had already considered them as good as married. If the truth be told, it was the Mayor's daughter, Janie Walters, he was sweet on. He'd had every intention of walking Janie home from church that day, but her cousins had been in town and she'd ridden home in the wagon with them. Flor had simply been there with a question about one of her horses and the rest had taken on a life of its own.

"...you are the right man, Tag. I know it. I feel it in my—"

"Gut," Tag finished for him with a nod. He felt like a spoiled child. His father's offer was a once in a lifetime opportunity—one that could change the course of his life forever—yet he hesitated.

"It wouldn't have to be forever if you didn't want it to be," his father continued. "Just long enough to get the place running properly. A few years maybe. I know Cole also has hopes of running his own ranch one day and we could start grooming him to take over once it's on its feet, making a profit, and running seamlessly."

No pressure. Redbourne Ranch was as streamlined as they came, but even its operation was never seamless.

"Why not just offer it to Cole now?"

"He's still a might young for such a responsibility—not that I wouldn't trust him to do it, but I've just had the feeling that this opportunity belongs to you. If it's about the money..."

"It's not about the money," Tag countered. He hadn't wanted to rely on his family's wealth to make his way, so he'd saved nearly every penny he'd earned over the last ten years or so, but he'd always imagined he would purchase land near Stone Creek, where he'd be close to home, to family.

He ran the brush in lengthy strokes along the horse's neck. "It's just an…unexpected offer," he said, aware of the silence between them.

"I understand. So, how about if, after a while, you decide Texas is not the right place for you, I'll buy you out, no questions asked, and you can move home. Cole may be ready at that point to take over." Jameson placed a hand on Tag's shoulder. "You could always marry the Hipple girl *before* you left if you wanted. What do you think?"

Tag stopped mid-stroke, dropped his head, and chuckled. He didn't recall ever having heard his father speak so quickly. "First," he said, collecting himself enough to resume his task, "there is *nothing* between me and Flor Hipple. I walked home with her *one day* after church. End of story. Second," he said, raising the brush momentarily and looking at a spot on the wall, "I appreciate the confidence you have in me for something so…so big, but—"

"This would be a great opportunity, Tag. For all of us. I would help finance the operation of it, of course, at least until it starts making a profit on its own." Jameson raised a hand. "Don't answer now, son. Take a day or two to think on it." He stepped backward, heading toward the door. "Oh," he said turning back to Tag, "you remember Josiah Scott?"

"The rancher from Round Rock?"

"That's the one. His boy, Peter, was killed in a tragic accident last year. He owns the Oak Meadow. He's the one selling. The property is located in a small town about twenty miles from Austin. It sounds like the perfect location and while I'm told it's been neglected since his son's passing, it should fit our needs nicely. A contract has already been drawn up and is in my office. It has your name on it, but if you decide against it, I will buy the property and make it work—though, of course, that would not be my first choice."

Tag nodded. His father didn't waste any time when he had his mind made up to do something. He was a very difficult man to say no to.

Jameson rested a hand on the door. "Regardless of what you decide, son, we still need to pick up a herd and drive them back. I would like you to take Cole with you to collect a small remuda and several hundred head of cattle.

This would be the third drive this season, but Tag was always up for buying new horses to work with.

"Keep in mind that while I believe Josiah Scott to be a good, honest man, I'd also like you to survey the property before any final decisions are made. We need to make sure we're getting exactly what we expect. And I expect it to be ripe with opportunity." He winked at Tag, then pulled open the door. "If you decide the property is worth what we're offering, don't hesitate."

"Yes, sir," Tag said, then blew out a strong breath. "Thank you, sir," he added as his father slipped outside.

It took a few moments for their conversation to really sink in.

"Move to Texas to run a ranch?" he said aloud. "Me?" He shook his head. In the back of his mind he'd always considered what it would be like, but to be provided with the opportunity so out of the blue, he wasn't at all sure it was what he wanted. It was too fast. He needed time to think it through. The drive would do him some good.

After he finished brushing the roan Morgan, Tag went back to the Belgian's stall to check on the new mama and her two foals. The smaller of them still lay next to his mother, but wasn't moving much.

"Will this do?" Hannah asked as she bounded into the stable holding out a large glass bottle topped with a rubber teat full of the white liquid.

"Perfect timing." Tag opened the gate to collect the foal,

but the moment he bent down to pick it up, the mare snorted a warning.

She had obviously bonded with the babe, and was feeling protective of it, but unless they did something now, that colt was not going to survive. The last thing he wanted to do was to agitate the new mama after everything she'd been through, but he didn't have much of a choice. He glanced at Hannah, who'd developed a look of worry, then back at the mare and an idea struck.

"We don't have a lot of time to allow her to get used to you, but I am hoping since you were here through a lot of her labor and while she was breathing heavily, she will recognize you or at least your scent. Give me your ribbon."

Without hesitation, Hannah untied the back of her hair and handed him the pale blue band.

He leaned forward and slipped the tie around the colt's foreleg, then backed away. The mare lay her head on the ground, apparently too tired to put up much of a fight.

"That should give her a moment to get used to the combined scent," he said as he strode from the stall. "I'll be right back." He headed out to the storage shed to fetch a new bundle of straw.

Within minutes he had a place for his little sister to sit in the stall adjacent to the mare's where she could hold and feed the colt and still be close to the foal's mama without being in harm's way.

"Are you ready?" he asked as he opened the gate once again.

She nodded.

He reentered the stall and slipped his arms beneath the colt, its slight weight even more of a surprise than he'd expected, and then transported it into the compartment where Hannah had sat down in the corner of the shared wall between the two. He placed the foal next to her on the fresh straw.

"If you need me, call out. I'll be in and out of here all day, examining the others. Let me know if you can get him to eat anything."

"We're going to be just fine, aren't we, Whisper?" she said.

Heaven help him—she'd named the foal.

Please, Lord, he prayed, *let that colt live.*

CHAPTER THREE

"So, I hear you've got a new adventure on the horizon."

Tag looked up to see his oldest brother, Raine, standing in the frame of his bedroom door. He pointed at the other bed in his room and motioned for him to sit down. The room had been a lot quieter since his twin brother, Levi, had gotten a job with the railroad and had gone off and gotten himself hitched.

"How's the jailhouse bed?"

Raine laughed. "Hard."

"I guess the marshal made it to town."

"And none too soon. Another day and I would have shot Sly Hollyhock myself."

Tag whistled.

"So, Texas, huh?"

"I keep asking myself if ranching is really what I want to do with my life."

"Are you kidding me?" Raine said as he plopped down on Levi's bed. "If anyone is fit to be a rancher, it's you."

"What makes you think so?"

"Now you're just fishing for compliments," his brother teased as he leaned forward, folding his hands together and resting his elbows on his legs. "I have never seen anyone take to horses the way you do. You have an uncanny way with them. They respond to you...almost like you speak the same language."

"Good skills for a wrangler."

"I don't think you appreciate just how exceptional you are. You have abilities I've never seen in anyone before."

"For a wrangler," he said again. "That is not the same as running an entire ranch."

"You're missing a few things, little brother."

"Like what?"

"Like the fact that you and Levi have coordinated thousands of original practical jokes throughout the years."

"Really?" he asked sarcastically. While he had to admit they'd been pretty creative growing up, it wasn't the same as having real grown-up responsibility.

Raine laughed.

"You also held many positions of command during the war. I know you hate to think about that time, but I understand, more than most, the challenges that came with that responsibility. A lot of men let their experiences break them, but you learned from them. I have seen the type of leader you can be and know you have the capacity to do whatever you put your mind to."

Raine lay back on the bed and crossed his arms behind his head.

Tag contemplated everything his brother had said for a good while before responding.

"You do remember that the Oak Meadow Ranch is in Texas, right?"

"Yep."

"I'd be a good month's ride away from home at any time."

"Yep."

"I'm not like you, or Rafe, or Levi. The need to explore is not in my blood."

"Isn't it?"

"I mean, I guess I do enjoy seeing new places and meeting new people. But, I get to do that enough on our drives. I don't need to move away from my friends, my family, and everything I know and love."

"Right."

"I keep asking myself if that's really where I want to be. I…don't know what to do." He let out an exasperated sigh.

"Mmmhmmm."

"I mean, Texas is a big place. I guess I do want more for my life than working myself into the ground from sunup to sundown every day. I guess I do want a wife…" he held up a hand, "someday," he clarified to his smiling brother, "and a place to call my own."

"Yep."

"Is that all you can say?"

"Yep." Raine laughed, then sat up. "Listen to yourself, little brother. To your gut. And if it's Flor Hipple you're worried about—"

"What is it with everyone and Flor Hipple? It was one friendly afternoon."

"I know," Raine said, obviously unable or unwilling to keep the amusement from his voice.

Tag picked up his pillow and threw it at his brother's head in the hopes of wiping that mischievous grin from his face.

Raine caught it, tucking it into his belly and hunching over. "Seriously, Tag, you'll know what to do when the time comes."

"Yeah, well, the time is here," Tag said as he lay back against his own mattress, his arms behind his head. "Marriage is the last thing on my mind…"

"That's okay. You still have a few months yet."

"What are you talking about?"

Raine stared at him, his eyebrows raised as if waiting for Tag to have some epiphany.

Ding.

Epiphany hit.

Inheritance.

Granddad Deardon had believed that any man over the age of twenty-five was a nuisance to society. He stipulated in his will that all grandchildren had to be married before twenty-six or forgo their inheritance. And, from what he understood, it was no mere chickenfeed.

"Marriage, with *all* its benefits can wait, and if I miss the deadline for the inheritance, so what? But Dad is expecting an answer soon."

"So, give him one." Raine threw the pillow back at him. "I only wish I could come along. I love a good adventure as much as the next fella."

"Then, come!" Tag sat up straight on the edge of his bed. "We could do this together."

"How would you ever find a wife then?" Raine asked, a single brow raised as he brushed at his vest with the backs of his fingertips, visibly working to keep the smile from cracking onto his face.

"Ha. Ha. Very funny." He cocked his arm back to throw the pillow again, but instead, shook his head and returned it to the bed.

Raine laughed out loud. Again.

"Seriously, I do want a wife. Eventually."

"But you think that Janie Walters is the one for you?"

Tag shot a surprised look at his brother. "What? How did you...?"

Raine laughed again. "Everyone knows you've been a little sweet on her since you and Levi tied her hair in a knot around Old Wickham's Maple sapling."

"That was more than ten years ago," Tag protested, though one look at Raine's expression and he knew he was found out. "She *is* quite becoming," he admitted, "but if she were the one, don't you think I would have had the courage to ask permission to court her before now? I imagine when I find the right one I will know because everything will just fall into place with no complications."

Raine guffawed. "Keep telling yourself that, little brother."

"I am not going to let Granddad's will determine when I decide to get married."

Tag had never had trouble garnering a woman's affections, but he'd never seemed to have that special connection with any of them either that he expected or even hoped for. That feeling in his gut that told him she was the one. It wasn't until Levi had gotten hitched that he'd started to consider that maybe it was time to start actually looking for a wife. Now, with the opportunity at the Texas ranch, he would have to rethink that idea.

"There are women in Texas, Tag," Raine said as if reading his thoughts. "In fact, I hear that the town where the Oak Meadow is located, is crawling with unattached women. Word has it that the ratio of women to men is six for every one."

"That's not true." *It couldn't be.* Weren't there tons of men seeking mail-order-brides all over the West? Why would they need to do that if there were already six women to every man? Maybe the women there were all too…unpleasant to behold—in appearance or demeanor. Whatever the reason, it didn't seem right.

"That's what I heard."

Tag raised a brow, but as he watched his brother, he could see the sadness behind his joviality.

"Do you miss her?" he asked quietly. "Sarah, I mean?"

Raine reached over and snatched Tag's pillow from beside him and lay back against the headboard of the bed, tucking the cushion beneath his head and folding his arms across his chest. "Every day, little brother. Every single day."

Tag took a deep breath and exhaled.

"Marriage is wonderful," Raine said honestly. "It becomes a part of you and I would highly recommend it."

"Even after what you've lost?"

"What is that saying? It is better to have loved and lost…"

"Tennyson, I think. Do you believe it's true?"

"Without a doubt. And the inheritance isn't so bad either." Raine sat up and threw Tag's pillow back at him as he stood. "You'll never gain anything worthwhile without taking a risk.

Remember that. Complications and all. Now, come on," he said, extending his hand, "or we'll be late for supper."

Risk. Hmmm.

Oak Meadow Ranch, Texas, April

Brenna Scott never imagined she would have to start over again after less than a month of marriage, but here she was, widowed nearly a year now, far from home, and still quite unsure of what the future would hold for her. The large homestead provided more space than one woman could possibly ever need for herself, but having a place to meet mattered to the children.

"He's been gone over a year, Bren. When are you going to stop this nonsense and come home?" Her brother grabbed a handful of the freshly coated candied pecans from a ceramic dish on the kitchen counter and tossed a few into his mouth.

"What I'm doing here is important, Jeb. There is nothing for me back in Hillsboro."

"Eddie's there."

"Eddie?" Her brows scrunched together as her mind churned until she realized to whom he referred. "Edward Landerson?" she said with disdain. "The same boy who threw rocks at me on my way home from school most every day? The same boy who put a different frog in my lunch pail once a week for months? That Edward Landerson?"

"Ah, he ain't so bad anymore."

"*Isn't* so bad," she corrected.

"Now, why you gotta go correctin' me all the time?"

She ignored his pouting expression. "If you're trying to marry me off again just so you don't have to take care of your poor unmarried sister, don't bother. I'd rather take my chances here than return home to be courted by that oaf or any of those boys." She pulled back the blue gingham curtains to allow the morning sun to enter the room and reveled for a moment at the warmth it spread across her face.

"They're not boys anymore, Bren. They're men. *We're* men. Or haven't you noticed we've all grown up?"

Truth was, Peter had only been gone for one winter and she had no desire to find another man. It seemed as if everyone wanted to decide what was best for her. She'd tried the married path and it hadn't worked out for her. Now, it was time they all realized she had a mind of her own and could take care of herself—homestead, ranch, and all. Husband or not.

If she had any misgivings about her situation, she surely wasn't going to tell anyone about them—she barely could admit them to herself. What did she know about ranching? Nothing, but still…

"I'm not moving home, Jeb, and I am not marrying Edward Landerson or anybody else for that matter." She placed her hands on her hips for emphasis.

"But—" her brother tried to protest.

Brenna put up her hand, palm out.

Her daddy hadn't approved of Peter from the beginning. She imagined that any father would be protective of his only daughter, but Peter's letters had touched her and after months of getting to know him through his posts, she'd been willing to leave the comfortable life with her father because she believed that she and Peter would be able to build a good life together.

Ezekiel Mallory had believed differently. According to him, any man who had to find a wife through the mail had something to hide. But her mind had already been made up, so, while he hadn't tried to stop her, he had insisted on driving her down to Serenity Hollow himself to meet the man she'd intended to marry.

"We miss you, Bren," Jeb said with resignation, pulling her thoughts back to the present. "Pa may not have liked Peter much—it was only because he didn't seem to care for you as much as he cared for…for…well, you know."

His money.

It was true that her father hadn't been any more taken with Peter after they'd met than before, so now that her husband was gone, Brenna imagined Daddy would see it as a second chance to find her the perfect match.

His idea of perfect, not hers.

"I've made my decision," she said matter-of-factly.

Jeb opened his mouth to say something, then closed it again.

Brenna glanced up at the clock hanging above the sink and reached behind her back to untie her apron strings. "The children will be here soon," she said, hanging the pinafore from the hook on the back of the door. "Go get yourself washed up. You'll need to be presentable if you are going to help me today with the children."

Jeb grabbed another handful of pecans and darted from the room before she could swat him. She laughed, grateful she had a family who loved and cared about her—even if it felt a little constricting at times. Many of the women in this little town weren't as lucky.

As Brenna made her way to the makeshift classroom at the back of the house, she couldn't help but think of the irony in her presence here. The war had taken its toll in Serenity Hollow. Several of the women had lost husbands, but most everyone had lost someone…family and friends. Very few of the widows had any extended relations close by who could take them in or help in any way, financial or otherwise. Little did she know, that when she'd accepted Peter's proposal, she would become a part of a healing town only to then experience an unspeakable tragedy of her own. They'd been married less than a month when Peter died.

Brenna shook her head, brushed the material at the front of her dress with her hands, and rolled her shoulders back. Now was not the time to consider what she'd lost, but instead, all the things she'd been able to accomplish as she learned to cope with her own loss.

As she walked into the small classroom at the back of the homestead, she smiled. The children had given her something to work toward. It had been nearly eight months since their original schoolmaster had died in a fire that had burned Serenity Hollow's one-roomed school to the ground.

The town had been left without a teacher or a place for the children to gather, but Brenna's education at Texas University and her willingness to help had made her the most suited candidate to take his place and she had welcomed the opportunity. She guessed it hadn't hurt that she'd volunteered for the position and had offered to open her home to the children.

She strode over to the portable chalkboard that now blocked her desk from view and picked up the eraser. She gave the already cleaned board a once over before writing the words, *Observing the world around us*, in thin white lettering. Once satisfied with its appearance, she wheeled the monstrosity to the side of the room, opposite the window.

"Nice to see you again, Mrs. Scott."

Brenna jumped at the sound of a man's voice.

Tobias Pane removed his mud-covered boots from her desk, sat up in her chair, and removed the hat from atop his scraggly-haired head as he stood to greet her.

"Mr. Pane, what are you doing in my classroom?" she asked, more than a little flustered to find the ale-soaked ruffian in her home like he owned the place. "Didn't anyone ever teach you that it's not polite to put your feet up on the furniture? One ought not to go sneaking about or enter a person's home without invitation." She took a deep breath to help compose herself.

There were several things about the man that made her skin crawl, but she forced herself to be civil.

"I thought it was about time," he said, casually leaning back against her desk, "we had that conversation." He picked something from his yellowed teeth with his tongue.

Brenna cringed. She'd run into him at the luncheon last Sunday after church services in the parson's meadow. He'd said something about having matters to discuss, but she hadn't paid much attention at the time, as she'd just been volunteered to help run the town's Founder's Festival and had been too focused on trying to keep herself upright to think about much else.

"You've had your time to grieve, Mrs. Scott. I allowed you that much. But now, I've come to collect what's mine."

"Mr. Pane, I assure you that there will be time to discuss…whatever it is you'd like to discuss," she waved her hand dismissively in the air, "but, now is not that time. School is about to begin, so I must ask you to take your leave."

The door at the back of the room creaked open and one of the oldest of her students poked his head inside. "Water is still only coming out in a trickle from the pump, Mrs. Scott," the boy said. When he saw Mr. Pane, he stood up to his considerable full height for fourteen, and stepped all the way through the door, and into the classroom. "Is everything all right, Mrs. Scott?" His eyes flitted between her and the scroungy-looking man.

"Yes, Jayson. Thank you. Mr. Pane was just leaving."

The man bowed his head, a frustrated snarl rolling deep in his throat, then he mustered what she could only guess was a smile. "Ma'am," he said quietly as he twisted his hat in his hands. "I'll be by to call on ya later, then?"

"Later, Mr. Pane," she confirmed, anxious to be rid of the man.

Without another word, he exited her classroom, shoving his hat back on his greasy head, and Brenna leaned back against the front of her desk with a relieved breath. Something about the brute gave her the creeps.

"Mrs. Scott?" Jayson still stood in the doorway.

"Oh, yes, the pump." She worried the well could be drying

up and wondered how she'd be able to provide refreshment for her students throughout the upcoming days and weeks if it did.

Having the children carry buckets from the stream would take a significant amount of time away from their classwork and their play. She would have to meet with some of the surrounding ranchers and farmers to get their opinions on the matter. She certainly had no idea how to fix it.

"Thank you for letting me know, Jayson. I'll have Mr. Mallory take a look at it." Not that there was much she thought Jeb could do about a dying well, but it was worth asking.

Jayson nodded and closed the door behind him.

Brenna glanced around the space at the back of her home that, with the addition of a partitioned wall and a new door, had been transformed into a workable classroom. The good reverend had been kind enough to donate the few school supplies he'd still had in storage and Mr. Reeves, one of her student's father and a carpenter, had built several tables and chairs for their use. With only thirteen students in the class, it hadn't been too hard to accommodate them.

She'd considered offering the room as a permanent place for the church to assemble, but realized it would be too small even for their modest congregation. Besides, she rather enjoyed gathering outside in the parson's meadow, or at the stables in town when the weather was uncooperative.

"Mrs. Scott?"

Brenna was startled by the slight tug on her skirt and the wee voice that called to her. She had not heard the door open and was surprised to see young Gemma Hamblin, whose bright red pigtails framed her small face and her green eyes shown with excitement.

"You're early," Brenna said, crouching down to eye level with the young girl.

The child nodded eagerly. "It is today, Mrs. Scott, isn't it?"

"Yes, Gemma. We *are* taking our nature excursion today. We get to collect different types of rocks to study."

The young girl bobbed her head in acknowledgement, her smile brightening her already angelic face.

"Head on back outside. I'll be right there."

As the weather warmed, the children had become more anxious to stay outdoors during the day instead of cooped up inside the classroom. Brenna was more than happy to provide a day of sunshine and adventure for them. The small creek running through the forested land on the north side of her property would give them ample opportunity to collect rocks and study some of the different types of land formations.

With one brief glance into the looking glass hung next to the door, Brenna pinched her cheeks, grabbed her jacket from the hook, and put on her most welcoming smile as she walked out the door.

Children ranging in age from six to fourteen dotted the yard. Brenna couldn't help but smile as she watched them play.

"You done a good thing here, sis." Jeb stepped out onto the back porch alongside her.

"You've done," Brenna corrected as she playfully nudged her brother.

"*You've* done a good thing here," he indulged as he placed an arm over her shoulders.

"Thank you."

Her head snapped to the left at the sound of one shrill scream, only to find Marilee, Gemma's older sister, running across the field followed by the two oldest boys in the class chasing her with critters in their hands.

"Jayson Cromwell and Ernest Stevens!" she called loudly.

They stopped in their tracks and looked over at her, shoving their hands behind their backs, and smiling innocently.

"Yes, ma'am?" they asked in unison.

She raised a brow at them and slowly, they released one fat looking toad and a little garden variety snake. She nodded, then motioned for all the children to join her in front of the steps.

The sound of crunching gravel pulled everyone's attention

to the worn black buggy headed for the house. It looked like Mr. Cummings, the postmaster. The man rarely left his shop, so it seemed odd that he would be making a house call.

"Stay here, children. I will be right back." She slipped down the steps and walked out to the edge of the fence to meet the man.

"What can I do for you this morning, Mr. Cummings?" she asked as he adjusted his spectacles, shifted his slight form, grabbed onto a metal bracket, and swung himself down out of his buggy.

"I have a letter for you from Mr. Scott."

Brenna's heart constricted and her jaw tightened as all heat left her face. How could her dead husband have sent her a letter?

"Oh, no. No, no," Mr. Cummings said as he leapt forward, his eyes wide with embarrassment. "I apologize, ma'am, for the confusion." He stretched over the fence as if to help steady her. "Not *that* Mr. Scott. It's from Peter's father. Josiah Scott."

Brenna breathed in deeply several times before she trusted herself to hold her balance.

Of course, it was. Heat rushed back into her cheeks as she sheepishly reached out for the letter. *Dead husbands don't write letters.*

"What does it say?" she asked, feeling like a dolt as she looked down at the sealed envelope.

The postmaster shrugged. "I just know it's marked urgent, and has already been delayed several weeks from a stage raid just outside of Austin." He shook his head. "I guess the bandits upended the mail sacks and the mail folks spent days trying to collect and sort all the post that had been scattered." He tipped his hat and climbed back into his buggy. "You're lucky it came at all."

"Austin?" she repeated. Her in-laws just lived in the next town over in Round Rock. Why would a letter from them be routed through Austin? Better yet, why hadn't they just made the short trip to come see her in person?

Without another word, Mr. Cummings climbed back into his buggy, turned it around, and headed back toward town.

She held the letter, walking back over to where her brother and students awaited her.

"Well," Jeb prodded after a few moments, "what does it say?"

Brenna looked down at the crisp yellow envelope with the intricate penmanship. She caressed the letters of her name and took another deep breath before turning it over to break the large, green wax seal with a fancy S embossed in the center.

"Is it bad news, Mrs. Scott?" Gemma asked, concern lining her sweet little voice.

Brenna scanned the contents of the letter, cleared her throat, then folded the paper and placed it in the pocket of her dress.

She managed a smile she didn't feel, as she crouched down to place a hand on the young girl's shoulder. "Everything is going to be just fine, Gemma. Thank you for asking."

The child nodded her acknowledgement.

Brenna stood up straight and called out to the rest of the children. "We need everyone to pair up with one or two other partners. I don't want anyone to be left alone. Do you all have your bags?"

Most of the children held up little knapsacks that she guessed held their lunches. She supposed the knotted cloths would serve a double purpose today—to hold their food now and after lunch to carry the rocks they found to take back to class for analysis.

One small boy in worn overalls and a dark green shirt stood by himself against the house in the morning's shadow at the bottom of the stairs, his head dropped. Brenna's heart sank. The youngster was new to Serenity Hollow, but from what she could gather, his family didn't have much money and she'd noticed that he'd skipped lunch more than once in the short time he'd been coming to school.

To her satisfaction, she'd had the foresight to have prepared three additional sacks with butter and jelly sandwiches in them for the off chance that some of the children would not have them. She pulled one of the bags from the box on the porch and stepped down to where the youth stood, slipping it slyly beneath his chin.

He looked up, then down at the sack. Then, with wide eyes, wet with gratitude, and a single tear trailing down his reddened cheeks, he rushed into her skirt and hugged her legs.

"Oh, thank you, ma'am." His words were muffled by her dress, but she understood.

She dropped down to meet him at eye level. "You are most welcome, Everett."

The boy smiled.

In the entire week he'd been in her class, he hadn't seemed interested in getting to know any of the other children or playing with them.

"Now," she said, patting him lightly on the back, "who have you decided to partner up with for our excursion today?"

He shrugged.

"Don't know no one," he replied.

"I don't know *anyone*," she corrected, stealing a glance at her brother who still stood on the back porch.

"How come *you* don't know anyone?" he asked with wonder. "You're the teacher. Don't you know everyone?"

"No, Everett," she shook her head lightly with a laugh. "I mean…Nevermind," she said as she stood up and called out to the others. "Who will include Everett into their group?"

"We will, Mrs. Scott," Gemma raised her hand high in the air, practically jumping in place.

"The kid can come with us," Jayson Cromwell, the older boy, said casually as he leaned against the fence and motioned to Ernie and his little brother, Charlie.

Brenna looked down at the boy, proud of the children in her class for making an effort to include him. "It looks like you've got a choice to make, Everett."

The boy glanced from Gemma to Jayson and back again, then up at her.

She smiled. "It's all right," she told him.

Without any hesitation, he ran past Gemma and the two young girls with her to where Jayson and Ernie stood. Once he reached them, he spun around, beaming.

While many of the children here were spirited all right, she could speak to each of their hearts. They were good kids and she enjoyed teaching them.

She patted the pocket where the letter from her father-in-law sat and her smile faltered.

Jeb stepped down the stairs and leaned close to her, speaking quietly. "You don't look so good, sis."

Brenna turned squinted eyes on her brother, pinched her cheeks once again, and stood up as tall as her five-foot five-inch frame would allow.

"Never you mind," she whispered back. "We'll discuss it later," she said as she clapped her hands, watching to make sure each child had buddied up with at least one friend. As much as she tried to ignore the sinking feeling in her gut, it weighed on her.

How could they do this to her? To this town?

They only had days, maybe a week. She had to think of something.

Fast.

CHAPTER FOUR

Tag spotted a small cove protruding from the stream amidst a large copse of trees. After nearly a month on the road, the beautiful inlet, with its trickling cascades and dense foliage, was a welcome discovery. They'd arrived in town as expected and the temptation for a bath was too great to pass up.

"Why are we stopping?" Cole asked.

"I thought I'd clean up a bit to be presentable when we meet with Scott's widow."

"We can't be more than a mile or two from the place. Aren't you anxious to see it in person?"

"I have years to explore, remember?" Tag slid down from his horse to stretch his legs.

He had to admit that when his father had first presented the opportunity to purchase Oak Meadow, he'd not been sure about moving half way across the country, but now, the realization of having a place of his own was starting to sink in and he relished the sense of satisfaction it provided.

Maybe the place'll grow on me, he thought as he looked around.

He couldn't wait to start training and breeding unique top-quality horses. It had been a long-standing dream, one he didn't want to squander. He just wanted to ease himself into it.

"I'm not in any rush."

"Even so," Cole said, leaning down onto his saddle horn, "you want to bathe now? Won't your new place have an indoor bathtub?" Cole rode up to the edge of the stream and leaned over. "That water has got to be freezing."

"Do Mama and Dad know just how over-indulged you are?" Tag laughed as he pulled his water pouch from the side of his horse. "Besides, it's Texas. How cold can it be?" He leaned over the banks edge and glanced down at the water with a shrug. "You know," he said as he dropped down onto his haunches and reached into the stream with his pouch, "I've seen about as much of the place as you have. None of it—though, from the map I'm pretty sure we've been on the Scott property for the last couple of miles or so."

The water was cool and refreshing. Just what he needed.

Cole whistled as he glanced around. "Maybe *I* should have taken Dad's offer."

"Like you'd ever leave home, your precious friends, or all those girls." Tag snorted.

"I'm here, aren't I?"

They laughed.

"That you are." Tag had to give it to his brother. Young as he was, he never shirked responsibility.

The land in Texas was varied, not unlike their home at Redbourne Ranch in Stone Creek, Kansas. There were trees and hills, streams and wide, open spaces that stretched for miles. He had to admit, winters and Christmas without snow would be bittersweet, but when he signed that contract, he would be committing to a lifetime, no matter what his father said.

"Why don't you head into town with the fellas and I'll meet you there around noon?" he said as he took off his hat and reached for the top button of his shirt.

Cole nodded, then pulled his mount around and headed back toward the others. They'd brought along a team of their most trusted drovers—ten in total, including the cook and his chuck wagon.

Tag didn't waste any time and jumped in.

The water was chillier than he'd expected, but it felt good

on his tired muscles. He was grateful that his mother had insisted on sending him with an ample supply of her soaps and poultices.

Once he'd washed up, he dove beneath the water to rinse his hair and body of the fresh-scented lather. When he raised his head up out of the crisp cool stream, the sound of muffled laughter raised the hair on the back of his neck. He wiped his eyes and ran his fingers through his too-long hair, pushing it away from his face and glanced from one side of the hidden alcove to the other.

No one.

He shook his head and tapped at his ear. Lack of sleep and decent conversation had obviously played with his mind and he was hearing things.

Giggle.

There it was again. He flicked his head toward the bushes where he'd lain his clothing. Two very young boys, wearing mischievous grins, met his eyes—one held his trousers, chaps, and boots, and the other his shirt, vest, and drawers. Something in their eyes reflected an image of him and his twin brother, Levi, at their age, all full of trouble.

He shook his head and motioned forward, but the youths disappeared behind some shrubbery before he could reach them, leaving a very naked Tag with nothing but his sopping bright blue handkerchief and a bar of his mother's soap to save his pride.

He shot a look at the tree where he'd left his Stetson and breathed a sigh of relief as the worn rust-colored, leather hat lay untouched. At least they'd been kind enough to leave it alone— along with the holster and side piece it covered.

Tag treaded through the water toward the bank, but stopped just short of emerging from the river at the sound of a woman's voice.

"Everett Hanson and Gandy Stevens, where did you get those things?"

The boys muttered something he could not hear.

"What do you mean there's a man swimming in my alcove?"

My alcove? It couldn't be. He'd been told that the Scott's hadn't had any children.

Tag flicked his head from one side of the inlet to the other, searching for a place to take cover, but short of leaving the water and hiding in the trees, he was out of luck.

"It's not funny, Charlie," the woman continued. "What have I taught you boys about taking things that don't belong to you?"

A splash of purple filled in the slits at the bottom of the trees and moments later, a woman, much younger than he'd anticipated, stepped through the bushes and into view as she continued to chastise the boys, his clothes in her arms.

"Stay put and I'll handle this," she told the children.

There was nowhere for Tag to go to protect the woman's sensibilities. With one hand, he made small ripples around him. At least the movement of the water would serve as some sort of covering and he still had the handkerchief in his hand he could use for cover.

"Where did you get th..." her words faded as she searched the alcove until she met his eyes.

She obviously hadn't expected him—especially in this state of undress, although she did hold the evidence of his obvious vulnerability in her hands. Her face filled with color as she cleared her throat and spun away, facing the brush from which she'd appeared.

"Who are you?" she asked, shifting his boots in her arms. "What are you doing on my property? Bathing in my alcove?"

"I would be happy to answer all of your questions, ma'am, if you would just...hand me my things."

"Oh, sorry." She set his boots on the ground next to her and jutted her arm outward, clothing draped over it.

Tag slipped from the water, acutely aware of his

surroundings, and climbed up onto the bank, retrieving his clothing. He quickly donned his trousers.

"Thank you. It's all right to turn around now," he said as he shoved his arms into the sleeves of his shirt.

The woman slowly spun around. Her eyes widened and her gaze darted from his open shirt to his face without blinking. She swallowed hard, then looked upward.

"Is…is it common…for you to…uh,…

Tag smiled to himself as color burned into her cheeks.

"…bathe," she finally managed, "on someone else's land, Mr…" Her eyes squinted as if trying to recall a name.

Tag loved the way the light glinted off her silky brown hair, causing a few lighter streaks to breathe through.

"Redbourne," he furnished, extending his hand. "My name is Taggert Redbourne, ma'am. I believe you are expecting me."

"Redbourne?" She met his gaze, her eyes lit with recognition. "Already?" She dropped her hands to her sides as he snatched the last piece of garment from her arms. "You weren't supposed to be here for another week." She raised her head high.

"Granddad always said I had a knack for punctuality." He smiled, hoping to gain a little good will with humor.

"Well, Mr. Redbourne, I think there has been a misunderstanding," she said as she turned away from him and tromped back into the brush and behind the trees.

He tried to follow her, but the rocks and sticks beneath his bare feet made it difficult.

"You can turn right around and go back to where you came from," she called back. "The ranch is *not* for sale."

He tiptoed as quickly as he could back to the tree where he'd deposited the remainder of his things and sat down, yanking on his socks and boots, then retrieving his hat and gun. He collected the horse's leads and went after her on foot.

"Ma'am," he called as he glimpsed a flash of color ahead of him. The forest was not densely populated, but the trunks were thick and she seemed to know her way around them.

No response.

"Ma'am," he tried again when he was a little farther along, grateful when she finally came into view.

"Hmhmmm," a little voice said, trying to get his attention and Tag looked down to see the young boy who'd stolen his boots. "Sorry about taking your things, Mister," he said with a half-smile.

Giggles erupted.

Startled, Tag glanced past the woman to see several young faces staring back at him.

Where did they all come from?

Heaven help him.

Maybe a bath hadn't been such a great idea without knowing the area or the tenants.

"They said it would be funny," the boy continued. "I didn't mean no harm. Really I didn't."

"Any harm," the woman corrected the child as she appeared out of nowhere. "And that was a very nice apology, Everett."

"I didn't mean *any* harm," the child repeated.

Tag dropped down on his haunches. "I got them back. See?" He pointed to his booted feet. "No harm done," he said, messing up the boy's hair as he stood.

The kid smiled, apparently satisfied.

Tag smiled back, then redirected his attention to the woman.

"Pardon my confusion, ma'am, but would you clarify what kind of a misunderstanding you think we may have had? We are just here for a final inspection before we finalized our deal with Mr. Josiah Scott to purchase the Oak Meadow Ranch."

The lady whipped around to face him, her eyes flecked with gold fire dust. "Oak Meadow is not for sale."

Tag itched to taunt the woman further—he liked the way she bit her lip when she was flustered, but constrained himself against it, choosing instead to be direct.

"I'm afraid, ma'am," he rotated the rim of his hat in his hand, then looked her directly in the eyes, "our signed contract says otherwise."

Why doesn't he button up his shirt?

Brenna bit her lip at the sight of Taggert Redbourne, standing there, challenging her. The feelings that unwittingly bubbled to the surface were unexpected. Generally, she was not an admirer of facial hair, but she had to admit, he wore it well. She had never been so attracted to any man in all her life, but it didn't matter. He would be leaving shortly.

Stop it! She chastised herself for the direction her thoughts were taking her.

Handsome as he was, he stood to take everything away from her and she couldn't allow that. Wouldn't. Oak Meadow was not for sale.

"Look at the rocks I found, Mrs. Scott," Gemma said brightly, holding out her hand with several small stones.

Brenna could not take her eyes off the stranger standing in front of her. He was proving to be quite a distraction and she needed to get rid of him. Now.

"Mrs. Scott?" There was a light quiver in Gemma's voice. "Are you all right?"

Brenna shook her head, prying her gaze away from the rugged trespasser, and turned her attention to her students.

"I am fine, children, but I think it's time we headed back now, don't you? Say goodbye to Mr. Redbourne."

"Goodbye, Mr. Redbourne," they cooed in unison as they fell in step behind her as she started back toward the house.

For as long as she could, Brenna fought the urge to turn

around for one more look, but alas, she couldn't help herself. She smiled as the man stood his ground and didn't follow—though, admittedly, she was a little disappointed.

As they passed the small arched bridge that provided a path over the creek, Jeb and the two older boys looked up from the collection of rocks they'd been digging. Her brother's eyes narrowed. He rubbed his dirty hands on his trousers.

"Headed back already?"

"We've been out here for hours, Jeb. I thought we'd stop and eat our lunch in the east meadow on our way back," she said. Then, pointing to Jayson and Ernie added, "I'd like to have a word with the two of you after lunch. Pick out a handful of those rocks for your assignment and come along."

"Yes, ma'am."

"Yes, ma'am."

They exchanged wary smiles.

By the time everyone had found a place to sit and eat their lunches, the sun had masterfully found its way to the top of the sky with no cloud in sight. Jeb flattened a nice piece of grass for them to sit and enjoy their meal beneath a large, shady umbrella-like tree.

As Brenna opened her mouth to take a bite of her sandwich, she glanced up to see Mr. Redbourne jaunting across the field toward them with something she couldn't distinguish in tow over his shoulder. She set the food down without tasting it and stared as he approached with a grin protruding from behind his beard and mustache.

"You look surprised," Mr. Redbourne said as he strode up to where they were seated. "You're not going to get rid of me that easily. Do you mind if I join you?"

"As a matter of fact," she said off-handedly, then reconsidered as he took a blanket from his shoulder, shook it out, and placed it on the grass next to her. She relented. "As you wish."

"Who's this?" her brother asked, obviously amused.

"Tag Redbourne," the stranger said as he reached out to shake a reluctant Jeb's hand.

"He thinks he owns the place," Brenna told him begrudgingly.

She imagined that Jeb's look of confusion mirrored her own.

"I've been informed by this lovely lady that there is some type of misunderstanding and I thought we could take a moment to clear it up." Tag pulled some foodstuffs from a small satchel and took a bite from a chunk of what looked and smelled like peach fruit jerky.

Jeb turned to her in a whisper. "Does this have something to do with that letter you got today?"

Brenna nodded.

"Today?" Tag nearly choked on his food.

"Mr. Redbourne," Brenna said with a calmness she did not feel, "this is neither the time nor the place to be discussing such things." She glanced around at the children. "If you'd like to meet me in town after school is out, I would be happy to ride into Round Rock with you to meet with my father-in-law. I'm sure we'll be able to clear up any misunderstandings then."

"School children," he said, nodding his head in sudden understanding. "That explains it."

"Explains what?" Heat grew in Brenna's cheeks again. "Surely, you didn't think these were all *my* children?"

Tag cleared his throat. "Of course not. I just didn't take you for a schoolmarm is all. You certainly don't look like any of my school teachers."

"What is that supposed to mean?"

Tag shook his head as he got to his feet. "What time would you like to meet in town?"

Brenna narrowed her eyes at the man, whose enormous frame blocked the sun from her eyes. "Would three-thirty be sufficient? At the mercantile."

"Three-thirty it is. I have to meet my brother and the rest

of my men in town this morning anyway. I imagine we're going to need to replenish some supplies and that should give me ample time to get a few things together and make some arrangements. I will see you then." He tipped his hat and took a step toward the house. "Oh," he said, twisting back to see her, and glancing down at the blanket he'd deposited next to her, "I'll collect the quilt later." He winked, then nodded at her brother. "Jeb."

"Tag." Jeb returned the nod.

Brenna watched him as he made his way back to where his horse grazed, then smacked her brother on the arm. "Traitor."

"What? He seems nice. Now, are you going to tell me what's going on or do I have to keep guessing?"

"I will. I promise."

CHAPTER FIVE

Fearful shouts could be heard above the buildings as Tag rode into Serenity Hollow. Men scrambled for cover. Women ushered their small children into buildings.

"Look out!" someone yelled in his direction.

Before Tag could react, something whizzed past his feet and his horse pranced nervously, rearing his head with a nervous whinny.

"Whoa, boy," he said, patting the gelding's side as he lay low and glanced around.

Small wisps of smoke strung through the street.

BOOM!

An explosion sounded behind him and he quickly slid down from his mount, entwining his hand in the lead and reaching for his pistol.

What in the...

BOOM!

His first instinct was to duck, but he forced his vision upward as a slim projectile flew into the air and burst open in brilliant red flashes above the town. Several streaks of feather-like plumes sprawled against the bright blue of the sky and trickled downward until they disappeared.

Fireworks.

Tag shook his head and forced himself to take a few deep breaths as he slipped his gun back into his holster.

A large wooden crate with a scorched rim sat in front of the mercantile. Two men cowered behind the store's steps and peered above the railing. After a few moments, all was quiet and the townsfolk slowly emerged from their hiding places. It had appeared that some idiot had not learned how to care for the celebratory explosives properly.

"Sorry, folks," a man with brown suspenders and a crushed felt hat waved at people as he hurried toward the box. "It's over now." He and a companion each took one side of the crate and gingerly carried it toward the back of the mercantile.

They were lucky no one had been hurt.

Tag figured the town was getting a jump on some type of celebration. He'd find out soon enough as this was to be his home.

It didn't take him too long to locate the others. Their horses had all been strapped to the hitching post outside of the town's only restaurant and hotel, and a small crowd of women had gathered around the front bay window.

Six to one. Raine's words slid into his mind.

Tag breathed a defeated laugh.

"It appears you were right, big brother," he said under his breath as he made his way to the restaurant.

"Ladies," he said, tipping his hat in their direction as he passed by them on the boardwalk.

Excited giggles put a smile on his face and he swung open the door to find Cole and the rest of the men sitting around several small tables, deep in discussion.

Cole cleared his throat. "And here he is now," he said, pulling out the chair next to him.

"Ma'am," Tag said to the woman who seemed to cling to every word Cole spoke. He removed his hat and held it in his hand, then turned to his brother. "Have you all eaten?"

"We ate a couple of hours ago, boss," Kade, the man who'd be staying on as foreman, said. "And we discovered something very interesting. There aren't a lot of men in this town."

"Something I noticed when I arrived." Tag nodded toward the window where the group of ladies still gawked at them. It would be hard to find new hired hands if the only people here were women.

"I think I'd like it here," Cole said with a raised brow. "Too bad we have to head back so soon."

The rest of the men laughed.

If Mrs. Scott hadn't known they were coming, he imagined that Oak Meadow would not have the foodstuffs or other necessities that they would need, even to last him and his team through the weekend.

"I'm going to head over to the general store to purchase a few supplies. Then, I've got to go into Round Rock this afternoon with Mrs. Scott to settle some business."

Cole nodded.

"Why don't you fellas get yourselves cleaned up a bit," he turned his attention to the rest of his team. "I noticed a bathhouse at the edge of town. Then, I'll meet you all back here in an hour and we'll have some supper."

Chairs scratched against the wooden floors as each of the men stood to follow his directions. He'd picked a good team and he wished he could keep them all on at the ranch, but only two would be staying with him at Oak Meadow.

"You too," he said to Cole. "We'll talk at supper."

They'd been on the road a long while and he imagined that a hot bath would be welcomed by most of them. He laughed inwardly. Getting dirty was a very real part of being a ranch hand, but he had to admit, after a month on the trail, the smell had even gotten to him. Besides, for some inexplicable reason, he wanted them to be presentable when he introduced them to the local school teacher—one Mrs. Brenna Scott.

When his father had told him that the current occupant of the ranch was the previous owner's widow, Tag had not expected the likes of the woman he'd encountered. Beautiful, spirited, and a devoted teacher to boot—a combination that could prove to be quite a distraction. The kind he would be happy to entertain *after* the completion of the Oak Meadow purchase.

Without doing an inventory at the ranch, he wasn't sure what supplies or how much of them would be needed, but he settled on purchasing enough foodstuffs to feed him and his crew over the next few days and then enough supplies to get Cook and the others ready for their upcoming drive back to Kansas.

After a few days of familiarizing himself with the ranch and seeing to what extent repairs were needed, he would be better equipped to make adjustments and see to any additional purchases that may be required.

For now, the basics would have to do.

When Tag returned to the restaurant, the rest of them had already been seated and their food delivered.

"Tag. Sit. You have got to try some of this pecan pie," Cole said as he shoveled another fork-full of the pastry into his mouth. "With cream," he added between bites.

Tag hung his brown-leather Stetson on the hook behind the table and took a seat next to his brother.

While Cook had made satisfactory meals along the route to Texas, it had been too long since they'd all eaten a nice, complete home-cooked meal that didn't consist of dried meats, runny oatmeal, and flapjacks. Tag's mouth watered at the combined savory and sweet smells that wove through the air of the quaint little eatery.

"I'll have the Chicken Fried Steak and mashed potatoes, please," he told the woman who'd come to take his order.

"Nice choice. One of O'Malley's specialties." The tall, slender woman nodded, shoving her pencil back behind her ear as she collected his menu. "Can I grab you some coffee while you wait?" she asked.

"I'll take a lemonade, if you've got it."

"Lemonade?" she asked with a hint of surprise. "Sure thing, love. Anything else?"

"I'm telling you, big brother, you'll want some pie." Cole winked at the waitress.

"You better bring me some of that pie." Tag smiled, shaking his head. "From what I hear, it's quite good." He chuckled as he watched his brother devour the pastry.

"You won't regret it," Cole told him.

"Another slice of pie, coming up."

"So," Cole said, licking the last of the crumbs from his plate like a man who'd gone without food for weeks, "if you're going into Round Rock, when are we headed out to meet the widow?"

"Already met her."

"You what? Where? When?"

Tag held up his hand. "Hold on, now. I...sort of...ran into her back at the...uh, stream." He cleared his throat—something that was happening way too often lately.

"At the..." Cole looked at Tag and narrowed his eyes, one brow lifted, then his eyes grew wide, lit with sudden understanding. "You don't mean to tell me..."

Tag nodded slowly.

"Whoa," Cole laughed heartily. "This I've got to hear."

"There's nothing to tell." Tag smacked Cole in the arm. "And keep your voice down." He glanced around, but the others were embedded in their own conversations.

"Ow," Cole whined, rubbing his arm. "What'd you go and do that for?"

"Sorry." The image of Mrs. Scott standing there, color staining her cheeks as she stared at him with those honey-colored eyes had burned into his memory.

"It must have been some meeting. What happened?"

It was no use trying to deny it, so he spent the next ten minutes recounting his misadventures with the beautiful widow and her mischievous class. It felt good to laugh at himself again. It had been too long.

"So, she didn't know anything about us coming out here until today?" Cole shook his head. "Who would do that to a person? Sell their home right out from underneath them?"

"I'm escorting her into Round Rock this afternoon, but who knows how long it will be before we can get some answers."

"She's going to Round Rock with you? Alone?" Cole smiled knowingly.

"It's not like that," Tag protested.

"Isn't it? Besides, what kind of answers do you need? Isn't the sale a done deal?"

"I think this trip will be more for her benefit. She's claiming the property isn't for sale. As long as the ranch is what Scott claimed it would be, I will hand over the signed contract and that will be that, but I don't want to finalize the deal until we've had a chance to look over the land, the homestead, and the outbuildings."

"Didn't you do that this morning?"

"Let's just say, there wasn't enough time to do a thorough inspection, but I intend to correct that as soon as I return. In the meantime, we're going to have some work to do. I only got a glimpse of the homestead as I passed it on the way into town, but from what I could tell, it looks as if it hasn't been used as a working ranch in quite some time. The bunkhouse looks like it hasn't even been opened in months. I saw two horses in the stable, a few chickens in the yard, a milk cow, and a pig, but I didn't see any other livestock."

"And wait, don't tell me, the fences need mending."

Tag laughed. Mending fences was Cole's least favorite chore.

"The main fences around the homestead and the corrals look to be in pretty good condition, but I didn't take the time to roam the property. You should take Kade and Felix while I'm gone and take a look. Mrs. Scott's brother, Jeb, seems like a nice enough fella. I'm sure he'd be willing to show you around the place."

"Here you are, love," the waitress said as she placed his steaming food in front of him.

It smelled heavenly.

"Thank you kindly, ma'am."

"The pleasure is mine, Mr….?"

"Redbourne, ma'am. Tag Redbourne."

She tapped Cole on the shoulder and lifted her chin. "This must be the brother I've heard so much about."

Tag glanced at a sheepish Cole.

"Yes, ma'am. I'm new to these parts, but it's a pleasure to meet your acquaintance, Miss…?" He wiped his fingers on the napkin in his lap and extended a hand to the woman.

"Sophronia Miles," she answered. "Welcome. Where about are y'all livin'?"

"We'll be out at Oak Meadow."

"Does Mrs. Scott know that?" Sophronia asked.

Tag was unsure how to answer the question. His conversations with Mrs. Scott hadn't exactly gotten that far.

"Thought not. Well, good luck with that, handsome. She don't take kindly to many menfolk. Not since Peter. Her husband." She leaned over and whispered. "Poor man was found floating face down in the river and his horse at the top of the ravine." She tsked. "Brenna went and stayed with Mrs. Wheatley for a few days after they found him."

"Accident?" Cole asked, clearly interested in the woman's tale.

"Some say it was an accident. Others say he was murdered for his money. I say he was no saint and got in with the wrong crowd, if you know what I mean. No one knows for sure. But it took nearly four days for the sheriff to figure out whose body it was they found. Say he was hardly recognizable. Shame. Poor dear. I can't imagine…"

Well, there was no guesswork needed in figuring out who the town busybody was. Every town had one and Miss Sophronia Miles was most definitely Serenity Hollow's. When she engaged the others in conversation, Tag turned his attention elsewhere.

He couldn't help but watch the people in this town as they bustled about while he ate. They were, after all, going to be his neighbors and he wanted to see what they were like. As much as he hated to admit it, Raine had been right. Dress shops, confectionaries, and other small women-run shops lined the streets. There was a smithy and stable in the town, but it was void of many of the typical male-run businesses. No gun shop, tanner, or even barber to be seen.

Tag stroked his beard. He imagined it was time for a shave, but had grown accustomed to having facial hair. His mother would tell him just to make sure that if he was going to wear a beard to keep it trimmed and well kempt. Maybe the mercantile would have some clipping shears he could purchase.

"Here's your slice of pie, love," Sophronia said, placing the warm treat down in front of him. "Are you finished with that?" she asked, referring to his near empty plate.

He nodded.

Palpable steam rose from the nutty pastry and he took in a deep breath. The small scoop of ice-cream to the side had already started to melt. He took his fork and sectioned off a bite, making sure to lap up some of the liquefied cream.

Anticipation grew as he placed the pie onto his tongue. He closed his eyes at the delectably buttery concoction. This pie alone was worth stopping by Serenity Hollow. Mr. or Mrs. O'Malley had certainly outdone themselves.

Tag had made a stop or two in Hillsboro and Round Rock while running cattle and horses over the last few years, but had never even considered the towns that fell in between or round about. He'd had no idea Serenity Hollow had even existed until his father had sat him down with the details of this little adventure of theirs. By comparison to the other places he'd visited, this place probably would only merit a tiny dot on one of Levi's railroad planning maps. Too bad. At least the town had a restaurant, a mercantile, and a post office—even if it didn't come equipped with a telegraph, which he thought odd.

"So, I couldn't help but overhear that you're purchasing the Scott place." An older man with a large white hat and grey whiskers pulled a chair up next to Tag's. "I hadn't realized it was for sale." He held out his hand. "Name's Grimace and I own the property to the northwest of Oak Meadow. We're neighbors, for all intents and purposes."

Tag was glad to meet another rancher, though, by the looks of the man's hands, he wasn't one to do the work himself. He reluctantly set down his fork and turned to face the man. "Do you mind my asking, how big is your spread?"

"Eh," Grimace dismissed, "it's about four-hundred acres I suppose. Never did much with it. The missus passed a few years ago and I'm an old man. Too old to be running around in a young man's business."

Tag got the feeling this wasn't just a friendly welcome.

"Funny you should show up when you did, Mr. Redbourne, was it?"

Tag nodded.

"My daughter sent word just last week that she'd like me to come and live with her family in Dallas. I figure maybe it's time." He took a drink of the beverage he'd brought with him to the table. "There's not much left for me here. My wife is gone, all four of my children have moved away."

"Is there something I can do for you, Mr. Grimace?"

"Oh, it's not Mr. Grimace," he said, wiping his moustache with the back of his hand. "Just Grimace."

"Well, now, I think there may be something we can do for each other." He turned over his shoulder. "Another drink, Sophronia," he called, then returned his attention to Tag. "See, I used to be…well, a drunk," he said bluntly, "but I haven't had a drop of liquor in eight years." He held up his glass. "Sarsaparilla," he announced with a satisfied nod.

"Congratulations," Tag said, glancing over to see if Cole was listening to any of this exchange. He wasn't. "But what does that have to do with me?"

"Well, all I've ever wanted was for my children to be proud of their daddy. I wanted to be worth something to them, to be able to do something for them, other than embarrass them, that is." He took another sip of his drink. "You see, I won that land fair and square a few years back from the doc. I have the deed and all, but I have no interest in trying to break up the parcel and sell it off a little at a time. I'd like to sell it as a whole, but the only one around here who wants to buy it is Tobias Pane," he tipped his head toward the corner of the restaurant where four men sat, huddled together in the corner, playing cards.

At that moment, one of them looked up and caught his glance. The man's eye twitched before he pulled his dingy hat lower on his head and returned to his game.

"And you don't want to sell to this Mr. Pane."

"Not for what he's done offering me. It's robbery I tell ya. It wouldn't even be enough to get a stage ticket to Dallas, but folks around here is afraid of him and there ain't nobody who'll stand up against him."

"And you thought that I would?"

"Well, you being a stranger in town and all. And being so...well, so big," his arms raised in the air to demonstrate Tag's apparent stature. "I figured you wouldn't be so afraid. Besides, my land nestles up nice and close to yours. These fellas," he motioned to Cole and the others, "said that you was going to get Oak Meadow back up and running as a working ranch. I would think that a man of your business savvy could use all the land you could get your hands on, no?"

The man had a point.

"How much you want for it?" he asked.

"Anything's better than what Pane's offerin'. Ain't got no

house or nothing on it, mind you, but you seem like decent folks, what do you think is fair?"

Tag considered the situation a moment.

"Kade," he called.

"Yes, sir?" The only blond man at the table leaned forward to look past Cole, who nudged him in the arm. "Sorry."

"I'm looking at buying a parcel of land from Mr. Grimace here. Think you could head out with him when you're finished eating and look it over? Make sure his paperwork is authentic and assess the value?"

Redbournes weren't anything if not fair. If it was a solid offer, he'd compensate the man equitably.

"Yep. You want me to head out now?" Kade asked, reaching for his hat.

Sophronia placed a fresh mug in front of the older man.

"I think we'll let Grimace finish his drink first," Tag said with an amused smile as the former drunk eagerly picked up the glass and took a long swig.

"Yes, si…rrrr…boss."

"It's all right, Kade."

He and the man had been friends a long time, but all of them—including his little brother—had insisted on calling him sir. It was time to get over it and leave the bad memories associated with the title where they belonged. In the past. The war had been over a long time.

Grimace sloshed his cup down onto the table top. "And, you may want to talk to Mr. Cranston. I hear he may be looking to sell his parcel too," the man informed him. "He owns the property to the east."

Tag had only been in town the better half of a day and already people were wanting to sell their land. Something was going on in this place and he needed to find out what it was— sooner rather than later.

"I have a feeling that you may just give Mae Taylor a run for her money."

"Mae Taylor?"

"She runs the ranch to the south of yours. The largest in the area. She's a real goer, but she's not someone I would cross."

Tag made a mental note to take a ride out to the Taylor's and introduce himself. It was always best to meet potential rivals or conflicts head on.

"Why not sell your property to her?"

"If you decide you don't want it, I'll speak with her. But there's something about you that says you is a man that can be trusted. Best watch your back when it comes to them Taylors."

The sight of a wagon coming into town from the north caught his attention and he smacked Cole in the chest with the back of his hand.

"She's here."

Cole shifted his weight in his chair to peer out the window and catch a glimpse of the approaching buckboard. Grimace also followed his line of sight and nodded.

As the wagon approached, Tag recognized the two horses from her stable.

Mrs. Scott pulled up in front of the restaurant. She wrapped the reins around the hitch and placed her hands in her lap, glancing around the town, presumably looking for him.

"*That* is the widow?" Cole asked with wonder.

"That's her all right."

"I thought you were exaggerating, but she's downright lovely."

"Lovely?" Tag laughed. "You've been hanging around Hannah too much," he said as he dabbed at his mouth with a napkin, then dropped it onto his empty plate as he pushed out his chair and stood.

"Grimace, it's been a pleasure." He shook the man's hand. "I'll be in touch."

"Be careful with that one," the old man warned. "Her last husband wound up…" he dragged a finger across his throat.

"I'll keep that in mind."

CHAPTER SIX

After settling the bill for the whole table of men, including Grimace's sarsaparilla, he headed out into the street to join Mrs. Scott, who was already down on the boardwalk in conversation with another young woman.

"Thanks, Agatha," Brenna said as she made her way back over to her buckboard. "I know this year's Founder's Festival will be wonderful with you in charge."

By the quick upturn of her cheeks and the new twinkle in her eye, the dark-haired woman in a feather-brimmed hat and blue-bustled dress was obviously pleased with Brenna's comment.

"Don't forget our meeting at the end of the week," she said, one finger raised in the air. "You are quite a welcome addition to the committee this year."

The young woman looked like she'd fit right in with big city social circles with some of the newest fashions available in Chicago. When she turned around, she glanced up at Tag, her eyes darting from his toe to his head before settling on his eyes, and another, more appraising smile captured her lips.

She jutted out her gloved hand in greeting. "Agatha Taylor."

"Taggert Redbourne," he said with a shake. It was highly unusual for a woman to be so forthcoming and bold, but he found it refreshing.

Taylor? While she looked more the part of a debutante, he guessed she belonged to the rancher woman he'd heard about.

"Welcome to Serenity Hollow, Mr. Redbourne. I'm sure the town will be able to count on your help for this year's Founder's Festival."

She didn't waste a moment.

"I'm sure you will," he said with a tip of his hat.

"Good." Miss Taylor gave a quick nod of finality.

"Until Monday then, Mrs. Scott." She dragged her eyes away from Tag, bobbed her head up at Brenna, who now sat on the seat of the buckboard, then hustled toward the mercantile.

"I see you and your brothers have gained a few admirers," Brenna said, nodding at the crowd of women still gathered around the bay window.

"I'm afraid only one of my brothers is with me on this trip. The rest of them are my ranch hands."

"How many did you bring with you?"

"Including my brother, Cole, there are ten of us," he said, collecting the reins for his horse.

"I hope they're not planning on staying long." She put her hand up to block the sun from her face as she looked at him.

Tag liked how the light added a glow through the edges of her hair.

"Just two of us, ma'am. Me and Kade are the only ones who'll call Oak Meadow home." He winked and smiled with a tip of his hat.

"Well," she said, "I'm sure there are plenty of folks around here who will be sad to see you *all* go. As you may have noticed, Serenity Hollow is shy a few men. The war wasn't easy on this town."

"The war wasn't easy on any of us."

Brenna's eyes widened and she bowed her head, shaking it back and forth, then she looked back at him. "I'm sorry. I didn't think…"

"I'm actually surprised that Jeb hasn't found himself a good woman here." Tag held up a hand to help her down from the buckboard.

"Oh, Jeb's not from Serenity Hollow," she said, ignoring his hand. "He's only been here a few days. And, he has." She did not elaborate. "Are we not headed to Round Rock?" She stared down at him expectantly.

"Yes, ma'am," he said with a nod, extending his hand again. "Can I help you down?"

"Whatever for?"

"So, we can go. To Round Rock." Hadn't they just established that?

She reached down to unlash the reins from the hitch, but he covered her hand with his.

"We can leave the wagon here. A ride will be faster." There was a lot to be done and spending the extra time navigating every crevice and rut in the road was unnecessary.

"On horseback?"

"Yyyyes."

"I'd rather take the wagon, but if you'd like to ride behind me, you are most welcome."

"Do you have a chaperone?"

Mrs. Scott snorted. "Do I need one?" she asked, cocking her head as she looked at him, one brow raised, then she shook her head. "If you're worried about my reputation, Mr. Redbourne, don't."

"Ma'am?" She may not be worried about her reputation, but he was. Hers and his own. It would be improper for an unmarried man and an unmarried woman to travel such a distance in a wagon together without a chaperone. He was new to the area and preferred to keep the Redbourne name respectable. But that wasn't the only issue here. If she didn't have a chaperone, there was no need to take a wagon. They were picking up information, not supplies.

"Look," she said, pointing to the man who'd just finished loading his wagon at the mercantile. "See Mr. Jensen over there?" She waved when the man looked up and he returned the gesture. "He's making a delivery to Round Rock this afternoon and will be heading out just behind us. My reputation will be safe. And...so will yours," she added as if sensing his apprehension.

"Exactly how far away is Round Rock from here anyway?" he asked.

"About four miles south."

Four miles would take them roughly an hour or so at a leisurely pace if they travelled by horseback, but a wagon would likely more than double that time.

"The ride will be faster on horseback."

"Not if I have to unhitch this thing and find a saddle. The wagon is fine."

Without responding, he held up a finger, then jaunted back into the restaurant.

"I'm going to need to borrow Mav," he told Cole. "Take Mrs. Scott's wagon back to Oak Meadow and I'll see you later tonight."

He turned around and left before his brother had time to protest. He collected both his and Cole's mounts, walked over to the wagon, and held up the reins. Hopefully, he would be able to break through some of her cool exterior before they reached their destination. It would be easier on all of them if they could find an amiable solution to the unexpected dilemma that had presented itself.

"All set," he said with a self-satisfied smile.

She didn't move.

"Would you like some help down?" he said, taking the reins of both horses in one hand and extending the other toward her.

"No, thank you! I am perfectly capable of doing it on my own."

"Of that, I have no doubt," he said a little louder than he'd thought. Though, Cole's black Arabian was a spirited stallion and he had no idea the extent of the woman's horse-riding capabilities. After all, she'd come to town in a wagon. All he needed was for her to get herself killed the first day he'd come to town. His current mount, on the other hand, was fast, but as gentle as any Sunday ride pony.

Mrs. Scott glared at him a moment before stepping up to his horse.

"Mrs. Scott, meet Gentry. He'll be your ride this afternoon."

She looked down at her dress, then back at the saddle. Suddenly, Tag's smugness diminished as he realized riding in a dress like hers might prove difficult and uncomfortable for the hour-long ride ahead of them.

Idiot.

At least the skirt of the dress was fuller than some of those he'd seen a few of the women wear back home.

Just as he started toward her, she surprised him by lifting her skirt nearly to her knees and heat flooded the back of Tag's neck just beneath the collar.

Brenna placed a foot in the stirrup, and reached up for the saddle horn, pulling herself up into a seated position. Then, she repositioned her skirt and feigned a smile.

"Are you always this exasperating?" she asked him.

He laughed, impressed at her gumption. "Yep. Just ask my mama." With another satisfied grin, he climbed up onto his own mount. "Ready?"

Brenna shifted in the saddle, her posture exaggeratedly tall.

"Well, what are we waiting for?"

Brenna had kept a few paces ahead of Tag the entire trip into Round Rock.

He'd tried to start a conversation once or twice, but she'd not wanted to like him any more than she already did.

Why does he have to be so charming?

He said all the right words, was a gentleman to a fault, and had expressed real interest in her and her work at the school this afternoon. But the fact of the matter was, if he was somehow able to purchase Oak Meadow out from under her, she'd have no choice but to return home to Hillsboro. And, as much as she loved her family, that was the last thing she wanted to do.

What would become of the children? The school?

As she pulled up to her in-laws' home, she took a deep breath and said a silent prayer that everything would work out the way it was supposed to, then dismounted.

"Mrs. Scott. I didn't know we were expecting you today?" Nigel, the Scott's long-time ranch hand, pulled a handkerchief from his back pocket and wiped his hands.

"I must speak with Mr. Scott. Is he home?" She handed the reins to the man.

"Yes, ma'am. He's inside with the doctor. Mrs. Scott has had one of her fainting spells again."

Brenna rolled her eyes. "Of course, she has."

Nigel chuckled.

Peter's mom had been in seemingly poor health ever since Brenna had met the woman. If she'd believed for even one moment that the woman was truly ill, she would be the first to offer a sympathetic ear, but there was something about the dramatic way she exploited her condition that made Brenna believe she was faking.

"Friend of yours?" Nigel asked as Tag rode up behind her.

"Not exactly, but he *is* here…with me."

"Oh. Kay."

Tag slid off his horse, wrapped the reins around the fence post, and pushed his hat up higher on his head.

"Tag Redbourne, is that you?" Recognition lit the ranch hand's face.

"Nigel? I didn't expect to see you here."

Both men gripped hands and embraced each other in a man-like hug, clapping each other on the back, grins spread wide across their faces.

"It's been a long time, my friend. Are you on a run?"

"Not today. I'm actually moving out here—purchasing the Oak Meadow Ranch."

Nigel shot a look at Brenna, a look of understanding crossing his face.

"Ah, so you're the buyer who's taking his precious time signing the paperwork."

"Guilty."

Brenna turned away from them and knocked at the door, but as much as she wanted to block their conversation, she could still hear them.

"I thought you were heading up to Montana," Tag said. "Last I heard, you were taking that job with my uncle."

It irked Brenna that Tag and Nigel knew each other well enough that Tag would remember the details of their encounters.

"Got hitched instead." Nigel beamed.

The door opened and Josiah Scott's eyes opened in surprise.

"Brenna, dear. We weren't expecting you." He stood back and swept his hand across the open doorway. "Please, come inside."

"I'm afraid I have a matter of some importance to discuss with you," she said as she motioned to enter the house, but before she could, Josiah glanced beyond her, a relieved expression crossing his face.

"Taggert Redbourne!" he called, pushing past Brenna as she stepped over the threshold into the house.

She turned to find him sauntering out the door toward the exasperatingly charming man. He extended a hand and shook Tag's vigorously.

"Seriously?" she said aloud.

The odds were not weighing in her favor. They knew each other—Josiah and Tag. That couldn't be good for her. Brenna rounded her cheeks as she filled them with air and blew out a slow breath, her mind racing for some course of action that could turn the tables.

"It's good to see you, Mr. Scott!" Tag said with enthusiasm.

"I guess your father sent you with our…" he half-turned back to look at her and nodded his head as if understanding the reason for her visit, "…signed contract."

"I'm actually looking to purchase the property myself."

"What a wonderful turn of events. Always said your father had good sense. Can't think of anyone better. Come on inside. Let's have a chat, shall we?"

"It's good to see you, Nigel," Tag said with a wave as he headed toward the house.

"You too. Good luck," Nigel added with a chuckle.

"Wait until Maxine sees you. She will be delighted. You were always her favorite, you know?"

Brenna rolled her eyes.

Of course, he was.

"Come in. Come in," Josiah said robustly as he guided them both to his office.

"Are you all right?" Tag leaned down to whisper in her ear as they headed in. "You've lost a little color in your cheeks."

She snapped her head to look at him, unsure whether or not he mocked her, but the look on his face showed true concern and a little ice melted from around her heart.

Blast it all!

Josiah motioned for both Brenna and Tag to sit in the two overstuffed, green, velvet-backed arm chairs across from his desk. Once everyone was seated, the man rested his elbows on his desk, his hands folded beneath his chin.

"I think I can guess what this is about," he said knowingly.

Brenna held up the letter with the broken Scott seal.

"Forgive me, but you couldn't make the hour-long trip into Serenity Hollow to talk to me about this in person?" she asked, tossing the letter on his desk, trying to keep the bitter accusation from her voice.

She couldn't apologize for getting right to the point as she wanted answers, and beating around the bush would only serve to elongate the difficult conversation.

"Yes, well," he twisted his neck as if his collar were a tad too tight, "I wasn't sure when everything would be final."

"Final?" her voice raised a little. "Why wasn't I consulted from the beginning? Oak Meadow is my home. All Peter left me. I should have a say in what is done with it." She was afraid that he might not believe she could manage a property of that size on her own, but women owned and worked their land all the time now, especially in Serenity Hollow. A vision of Mae Taylor rounding up a herd flashed through her mind. But, she feared that her father-in-law would not see it that way.

"Oh, dear," Josiah said, blinking several times before reaching down to retrieve something from a drawer in his desk. "I see the problem." He thumbed through a folder of paperwork and stopped when he reached a document that he pulled from the file and placed on the desk, facing Brenna.

She scooted forward on her seat to examine the paper closely.

"Oak Meadow may have been your home for a time, my dear, but I'm afraid it does not belong to you. It belongs to Scott Holdings. And that's…well, me."

Brenna glanced from the document deed up to her father-in-law and back down again.

"What do you mean Oak Meadow doesn't belong to me?" Brenna's heart sank. She couldn't believe what she was hearing or reading. "It was my husband's place." So, how did Josiah have the deed?

"I can see that you are upset."

"Upset?" She shot out of her chair. "What makes you think that I am upset?" Her voice grew louder with each word. "That I find out, in a letter no less, THE VERY MORNING a man," she flippantly tossed a hand toward Tag, "arrives to usurp me from my home? Or, the fact that my own father-in-law is trying to swindle me out of what is rightly mine? My home. My land. My livelihood?" She sat back down, the wind rapidly deflating from her sails as the truth of her words started to sink in. "I expected more from you."

"Wait just a moment, young lady," Josiah said sternly as he stood from behind his desk and marched around to stand in front of her. "I have come to care for you a great deal over the last year, Brenna. That is why I waited so long before deciding to sell, but alas, it no longer made sense to hold onto the property. Without a working ranch to keep it thriving, I knew the property would fall into disrepair and I couldn't allow that to happen." He leaned back against his desk. "What with you only having lived there a short time, I truly believed that you would return to Hillsboro. Most women in your situation would."

"I am not most women. I don't want to leave Serenity Hollow. I have created a life there." She moved to sit on the edge of her chair. "I opened a school for the town's children, and..." What more could she say?

"I'm glad that you were able to be productive in your grief. I'm sorry, my dear, I had no idea."

"You should have talked to me." She knew it was a bold idea and he certainly did not need her approval—especially, if the home indeed belonged to Scott Holdings.

"I appreciate your candor, Brenna, but it wouldn't have changed anything. My mind is made up. What's done is done."

"What's done is done? How can you say that to me? I was married to your son. Your only son."

"And he died shortly thereafter."

Brenna sat slowly back down into her chair. "You blame me?" she asked quietly.

"What? No, of course not." Josiah stood and began pacing behind his desk. "But we hardly know you."

"I don't...know what to say." Her eyes trailed the patterns

of the floor, then traced the contours of the brick walls.

"I'm sorry we didn't come out to Oak Meadow and talk to you in person. My lawyer asked me to write a formal letter to you for legality purposes, informing you of the sale. I had it written months ago. He took it back with him to Austin and assured me that it would be delivered with plenty of notice. You should have received it long before now."

"Does it matter?" her voice was steady, calm, and quiet. "Why didn't you? Come, I mean, to talk to me?"

He opened and closed his mouth several times, as if trying to find the right words to say. After a few moments, he dropped his shoulders and looked out the window.

"I wanted to. I tried, but I didn't know what to say." His eyes were wet and his face strained with emotion and Brenna realized that Peter's loss was not her pain alone to bear. This man had lost a son. A son he'd watched grow from an infant to manhood, a boy he'd loved his whole life. Her attachment to the younger Scott had been far less than that and suddenly her heart ached for the man in front of her.

"I thought," Josiah said quietly, "that since I hadn't heard from you, that…that…"

She searched his face and found sincerity in his eyes. She stood up and wrapped her arms around him. As hard as it was to admit, she understood his reasonings.

"He's gone, Josiah. I have to live with that and so do you, but we'll figure it out."

At first, Josiah didn't move, he kept his arms to his sides, but Brenna didn't care. He needed to be consoled as much as she did. More even. After a few moments, he placed a quick kiss on the top of her head, cleared his throat, and turned away— breaking her embrace around him. He strode over to the library of books shelved on the walls that he'd collected throughout the years, then pushed open the window at the far side of the room and looked out.

"Ranching is an ever-changing business, my dear. I'm afraid

ours has changed enough that we are sizing down our holdings enough to be able to live out our days in comfort."

Brenna was feeling more collected and in control of herself, but she still needed some answers.

"Josiah," she began, "Peter told me that Oak Meadow was his outright and that it would someday belong to our children." She stole an awkward glance at Tag. "Now, you're showing me the deed and telling me that, as his widow, I do not have rights to the property. Our property. Why?"

"The land surrounding the Oak Meadow homestead has always belonged to Scott Holdings, but there was a time that the house and the land in its immediate vicinity did belong to Peter." Josiah came around to sit back on the corner of his desk in front of her.

"There was *a time* it belonged to him?"

"A few days before he died, Peter came to us and told me that he was in trouble. Financial trouble. And he needed my help. I offered to lend him the money he needed, but he wouldn't hear of it. He offered to sell me back the Oak Meadow homestead and property for a considerable sum—much higher than the property would have ever sold for, but…he was desperate, and he was…my son. So, I gave it to him."

My pearls, Brenna thought, her hand inadvertently sliding to her neck where the jewelry resided. They'd been an early gift for their one-month anniversary. She'd complained they were too expensive, but Peter had just smiled and said that one day he would be able to shower her in pearls. That was also just a few days before the accident.

"I'm sure he intended to buy back the property, but…never had the chance." Josiah looked her straight in the eye. "Peter was our only child and with him gone, there was no one to whom we could leave our legacy." He cleared his throat. "No one, that is, who could or would want to run the ranch." He winked at her. "We have already made arrangements for a sizeable stipend to be given you until you are remarried, along with enough for an ample dowry."

"Married? I don't want to get married again. Not now, maybe not ever." Heat crept into her cheeks as she considered the man sitting next to her. "Did you ever think that maybe *I* would want to run the ranch?" she asked. "Technically, I don't have to have a husband to do that anymore."

Josiah laughed, but his joviality quickly diminished as he evaluated the look on her face. "Oh, you are serious," he said, clearing his throat again.

"Very. I am as capable a woman as any."

"I see. And, do you? Want to run the ranch?" the man asked in clarification. "What do you know about the ranching business?"

"Well, I want to run a school out of the ranch. It is my home after all and the students need a place to meet for class."

"Oak Meadow is meant for more than just being a school, my dear," Josiah told her kindly. "It was once the largest ranch in all of Serenity Hollow and the surrounding areas. People, like Mr. Redbourne here, used to come from hundreds of miles away just to purchase some of our livestock—though most were routed through our facility here in Round Rock. Now, as you know, my dear, that title belongs to that swell-headed female cowpuncher, Mae Taylor. She's ruthless, I tell you."

"Now, don't you believe a word he says." Maxine Scott leaned weakly against the doorframe of the office. "My husband, bless his heart, was quite taken with Mae once."

"Maxine, dear," Mr. Scott said, his face red as he flexed his jaw.

The woman ignored her husband, her eyes brightening as she settled her focus on Tag. "Do my eyes deceive me or is that Taggert Redbourne?" She waved for him to come closer.

Tag arose and strode over to her, offering his arm. "Why, Mrs. Scott…"

Brenna cringed that she shared a name with the dramatic woman.

"…you look as lovely as ever, but I hear that you've been feeling ill." He guided her to his now vacant chair in front of Josiah's desk.

"It's my heart, you know," she said, fanning her face. "But seeing you here in our home is good for me. You do make things seem a little brighter, doesn't he, Josiah?"

Josiah rolled his eyes and Brenna had to stifle a giggle.

"Well, Josiah," a short, slender, white-haired man with a flat-topped hat and a black medical bag said as he stepped into the room writing something into a small notebook, "there's not much else I can do for her right now. I suggest that she get plenty of rest and recommend she avoid any excitement." He wasn't looking where he was headed and nearly ran into Tag's chest. He looked up, his eyes growing big. "Oh, I'm sorry," he said nervously, then turned to Mr. Scott. "I didn't realize you had company."

"It's all right, Dr. Mullins. They're family." Josiah winked at her.

"Very well. I'll be back at the end of the week to check on Mrs. Scott." The doctor handed her father-in-law a small piece of paper, then nodded at her as he exited the room.

Josiah glanced at the note, then tucked it into his pocket with a slight shake of his head. "Now, as I was saying before my darling wife decided to interrupt," he cleared his throat, still seeming a little distracted, "yes, um…oh, yes. With the Redbournes taking over, I believe Oak Meadow can once again give the woman a run for her money and be great again."

"So, you just up and sold it?" Brenna stood up and walked over toward the library wall. She could not remain seated in what felt like a confined space with Josiah looming over her and her mother-in-law looking down her nose at her.

"Well, I haven't yet received the signed paperwork, but, yes, the Redbournes," he nodded at Tag, "have been offered a contract deal for all of Scott Holdings in Serenity Hollow. I believe they have the know-how and abilities that will return

Oak Meadow to its former glory. Better even."

Brenna looked over at the man now leaning against the edge of a tall bookcase, his arms folded and his legs crossed at the ankle. He'd been very quiet during the exchange and she swallowed.

"Can I use my stipend to buy the ranch?" She knew she was grasping at straws, but couldn't pass up one last chance. "Or even just the homestead?"

Maxine scoffed.

Josiah chuckled. "You are a persistent little thing, aren't you? No wonder my son wanted you in his life. Your courtship letters showed a lot of spunk, but I am afraid they did not do you justice." He shook his head. "I'm sorry, dear. Our offer to Mr. Redbourne stands. I'm still waiting on the signed contract, so the decision is his."

They both looked at Tag, who cleared his throat and nodded curtly.

"Yes, sir. I just rode into town this morning and haven't had much of an opportunity to inspect the property, but from what I've seen," he pushed away from the wall and came to stand directly behind her. "I think we are still on track to complete the purchase by the end of the week."

Brenna turned to look up at him, but he avoided her eyes.

"And, my school?" she pleaded with Josiah.

"While it is a noble thing you've done for the children there, my hands are tied. That'll be something you'll have to take up with *him*." Her father-in-law nodded at Tag, then made his way back behind his desk. "I'm sorry, darlin', that things didn't work out the way you had hoped. Maybe you can use some of your monthly stipend to have another building erected."

What could she say?

A part of her wanted to tell him that she didn't want his money, but another part of her was grateful it would buy her some time to think of another way.

When Brenna had woken up that morning, she would never

have guessed how one little thing like having her home ripped out from under her could have changed her life so completely within a matter of hours.

The idea of returning home to Hillsboro sat in her belly like a lump of her grandmother's Christmas cake. She didn't want to think about it until she could talk to Jeb.

"Should I tell Dinah to set out a place for the both of you for supper?"

"That won't be necessary," Tag said, extending a hand to help Brenna to her feet. "We best be getting back."

She ignored his hand and stood. It wasn't his fault. He was just caught in the middle of it all, and she knew it was childish, but couldn't help herself. Her students would be the first to remind her that she should be gracious and she immediately regretted her act of indifference, but it was too late.

"Thank you, Josiah." While it had not turned out as she had hoped, the man had offered her substantial financial compensation—though that was not what she had been looking for. "I am truly grateful for your generosity and appreciate you taking the time to speak with me." She walked past Tag, careful to avoid touching him, and made her way to the door at the back of the study.

"Mrs. Scott," Tag said.

"Yes?" both Brenna and Maxine said in unison, though in very different tones.

Tag nodded with a smile at her husband's mother, then closed the distance between Brenna and himself. "Mrs. Scott," he said again. "I am sure we will be able to find a reasonable solution for your school. Just give me some time to consider the situation."

"Now, that sounds like a sensible idea," Josiah piped in. "I've never known a Redbourne to be anything, but fair." The man glanced between them, obviously eager to end the topic of conversation. "Well, now," he said, clapping his hands together, "are you sure you won't stay for dinner?" he asked them.

"Of course, they're staying," Maxine said with finality. "Aren't you, dear?" She looked up at Tag with a look that reminded Brenna of a begging pup.

Brenna's stomach grumbled loudly. Heat rose in her face and she brought her hands to her cursed belly.

Tag's mouth twitched.

"I…"

Josiah snorted and raised his hand to his face, his crooked forefinger resting directly beneath his nose, the corners of his mouth spreading into a poorly hidden smile.

Her jaw tightened and her teeth clenched, but one look at Tag's reddening face and all three of them burst out into laughter.

"I guess we're staying," Tag said with a wink in her direction.

"I'll tell Dinah," Josiah said with a pat on her shoulder as he left the study.

"This doesn't mean I'm not mad at you," she whispered to the man who she'd just met, but who'd completely upended her life.

"I wouldn't expect anything different."

"And why didn't you tell me that you knew my father-in-law?"

"You had your mind set and I figured that nothing I said would have changed that."

She considered his response. "You're probably right."

"We have a lot to discuss. I'm guessing that now you'll be ready to listen."

"Maybe after I get something to eat." She smiled, despite of herself.

"I look forward to it."

CHAPTER SEVEN

"I can't help but feel we got started out on the wrong foot." Tag pulled up alongside Brenna as they began the short journey back to Serenity Hollow. "I don't want to be your enemy."

"I know," she said without looking at him. "It was just such a shock to learn that my home belonged, or would belong, to someone else, a stranger no less, and there is not a thing I can do about it."

"I'm sorry," he said sincerely.

Brenna nodded, but didn't say anything more.

He truly felt bad for the woman's predicament. While he'd sat in Mr. Scott's study and listened to the conversation between the young widow and her father-in-law, he'd tried to come up with a solution that would work for everyone.

He'd had one idea, but his gut told him she wouldn't like it. And he wasn't so sure he was prepared to take such a drastic step himself—no matter how much he liked the color that stained her cheeks every time she looked at him—but surely it wouldn't be difficult to find someone. Mr. Scott had told her that he'd set her up with a considerable dowry. It was possible, that if she married, the funds would be enough to cover the cost of the materials needed to build at least a one-room school

house. All that would be left to handle would be the land to put
it on and the labor for construction. He reasoned that he could
probably provide both of those things.

Kade was out surveying the land Grimace had offered to
sell. If the parcel was as good as he suspected it would be, Tag
figured he could donate a portion of the property closest to the
town. As for labor, he could work something out. Not that he
was culpable for the situation, but he imagined that helping her
with a new schoolhouse would assuage any guilt that would
prick at him.

As much as he hated to admit it, the idea of finding her a
husband sparked a thread of jealousy inside of him and he
racked his brain searching for an alternative. One way or
another, they would find the answer, but for now, it eluded
him—unless…

Nope.

Maybe.

Nope.

Maybe.

STOP!

Tag didn't appreciate the directions his thoughts had
turned.

"It's not happening," he murmured under his breath.

The sun rode very low in the sky. Tag didn't like traveling
at night—especially in unfamiliar territory, and with a woman.
He found himself, more than once, checking his side piece and
scanning the area ahead for any potential dangers that could be
lurking along the road home.

Home.

It was a funny word.

Stone Creek had been his home for as long as he could
remember and the thought of building a life anywhere but there
felt…odd. The idea of sleeping in an actual bed after nearly a
month of being on the road, however, greatly appealed to him
and he prodded his mount a little faster. It had been one long

day.

While Tag made sure their horses kept pace with one another, they rode in silence the rest of the way to Serenity Hollow. The homestead sat just another mile or so outside of town, but he appreciated the sight of something so newly familiar. Lights still decorated the rooms above the restaurant as well as the lone saloon in town, but the rest of the place was dark, quiet.

Stars emerged one by one, sparkling against the darkening sky. It wouldn't be long now.

"Maybe I'll just stay in town tonight," Brenna said, breaking their silence.

Tag hadn't even considered the possibility that Peter Scott's widow would not have made previous arrangements prior to their arrival, but now, after learning she'd just found out about the sale, it made sense. As much as he didn't want to displace her, even for one night, sleeping arrangements would prove to be a dilemma.

If he wasn't worried about her reputation before, he certainly was now. What would people think to learn that nine men had bombarded the Oak Meadow Ranch, with one very attractive and unattached female inside?

"I'm afraid my mama would have my hide if I allowed you to do that, ma'am," he finally said in response. Then it hit him. "The boys and I will sleep in the bunkhouse tonight and we can discuss the rest tomorrow when we've all had a good night's sleep."

"Mr. Redbourne…"

"Don't *Mr. Redbourne* me. If I've learned one thing about you today, it's that you are a resourceful, smart, and caring woman. It doesn't make any sense for you to pay for an overnight room with none of your essentials when you have a perfectly good room at the homestead and a brother who can serve as chaperone, if needed."

She opened her mouth.

"No."

She opened it again.

"No."

"If you would just let me get a word in, *Mr. Redbourne*…"

He opened his mouth, then closed his lips tight and nodded.

"I wanted to say…" she adjusted herself in her seat and rolled her shoulders backward, "thank you."

Tag laughed to himself. Brave and gracious could be added to that ever-growing list of qualities.

"You're welcome."

As they neared the homestead, the musty scent of burning wood filled his nostrils. He glanced toward the ranch. Smoke ascended from the back of the house and a lively tune rose above it and carried on the breeze.

He loved that sound. It marked the end of a journey.

"I haven't heard music like that in a very long time," Brenna said, appreciation lining her voice. "It's lovely."

Without much forethought, the words rolled off his tongue in song. "Cowboys, take my advice, setting out for to roam," he sang. "But you better stay at home with your kind and loving little wife."

"Why do you have to go and do that?" Brenna asked him.

"Do what?"

"Make me like you even more," she said with an exasperated sigh.

"You…like me?" he asked, unable to keep the amusement from his voice or the smile from his face.

She turned her horse about face and clicked her heels into his flanks just enough to spur him to a light canter.

"She likes me," he said under his breath as he motioned Maverick to catch up with her. Truth was, he liked her too.

As he rode through the gate, he thought of his family. They'd always been very musical and he couldn't be more grateful than at this moment. Listening to the boys sing now, reminded him of home. He loved music. He loved to sing.

As they approached the stables, Cole and the others sat around a campfire, with Jeb, singing their harmonic tales. Cole was the first to see them. He jumped up to greet them.

"I'm sorry, ma'am," Tag's youngest brother said as he rushed forward to help Brenna down from his horse. "I apologize for all this," he motioned to the circle of men surrounding a makeshift pit, "but Jeb said it would be all right if we started a fire tonight. It's kind of tradition."

Brenna turned back to Tag. "I'd bet the ranch *he's* related to you," she said with a playful smirk.

"You'd win that bet. He's my baby brother, Cole. Cole, this is Mrs. Brenna Scott."

Cole took off his hat and tipped it toward her. "It's a pleasure to meet you, ma'am. Uh, *Jeb's* already told us a lot about you, but I'm afraid he didn't do you justice. You might just be the prettiest thing I have ever seen."

Tag cleared his throat and raised a brow.

Incorrigible.

"Was that inappropriate of me to say? My mama always taught us to tell the truth…"

It was hard to gage Brenna's reaction in the dim light, though he couldn't disagree with Cole's assessment.

"I think that's just about enough 'honesty' for now, little brother."

Cole nodded at Mrs. Scott, then turned to Tag. "We set up in the bunkhouse. I hope that's all right. I figured it would be more appropriate with Mrs. Scott in the house and all."

He should have known. Cole also had that Redbourne gut.

"That's exactly what I was thinking."

Tag took a moment to introduce Brenna to all the others he'd brought along with him—though he didn't expect her to remember their names as most of them would only be staying long enough to complete the purchase of several hundred longhorns and a good five-dozen horses at auction and then they'd be leaving on the drive back to Stone Creek. He figured while he had the manpower, they could make a few repairs to the place. He'd need to get some additional help soon, but he'd worry about that later.

"It's very nice to meet you, gentlemen, but if you'll excuse me." She collected the cloth of her skirt and raised the hem from the ground. "It's been a long day and I'm a little tired." She turned back to the horse she'd been riding and ran a hand down his neck, then grasped the reins in her hands.

"The boys'll take care of him," Tag said, reaching down to collect the reins from her, but the moment his hand connected with hers, an unnerving sensation shot through his body and he lingered a moment, reveling in her touch.

Brenna drew her hand back, tucked her hair behind her ear, and bit her lip.

He handed the reins to Cole.

"Thank you," she said when Cole took the horse from his brother. She looked up at Tag. "Look, Mr. Redbourne, I appreciate the situation we've put you in and since Oak Meadow now belongs to you, I think it best that—"

"Let's discuss it in the morning. I'll walk you up to the house."

"That's not necessary."

"Maybe not, but I'll do it all the same." He was a little ashamed that he hadn't tried harder to get to know the woman on their long ride and determined that amidst all the work there was to do, he would do better tomorrow.

When they reached the porch, he ascended the few stairs in front of her and pulled open the screen door, resting his hand at the top to hold it while Brenna opened the interior. She turned back to look at him, her eyes, alight with a reflection from the fire's flames, burned into him and he resisted the urge to bend down and kiss her smack on the mouth. The impulse surprised him. He hadn't wanted it and surely hadn't expected it, but now, the thought of it filled his belly with fireflies.

Tag didn't trust himself to speak in anything but low tones. "Good evening, Mrs. Scott."

She held his gaze for a moment, nodded, then stepped inside the house.

"And, don't worry," he added as she paused on the other side of the threshold, "things have an uncanny way of working out."

"It's good to know you think so too," she said with a wearisome smile. "Goodnight, Mr. Redbourne."

"Goodnight," he whispered, leaning his head against the wood.

She slipped inside the house and slowly closed the door behind her.

What was happening to him? He didn't have time to be fussing over a woman—especially not a woman with no interest in men or marriage. There was work to be done. Livestock to buy. He would do what he could to help her, but he could not become invested. There was too much at stake. Tag hit the top of the door lightly with the palm of his hand and turned back to the yard where the men had gathered.

The music had died to a low hum as each of them stared into the fire, dreaming, thinking, and longing for home—a luxury he could no longer afford.

"The cock's crow comes early, boys," he reminded them. "Let's get a move on."

Immediately, the tired cowpokes jumped to their feet, most heading for the bunkhouse.

Tag headed to the stables.

Lowly nickers sounded from the corral that stemmed from the rundown building. Cole and the others had been busy while he'd been away. The horses had already been fed and there was fresh water in the trough. He only hoped he would be able to hire as good a crew as the men who were headed back to Stone Creek with the new herd. He knew nothing about the folks around Serenity Hollow, but understood all too well the importance of hiring men that would work hard, had a good temperament, and played well with others.

As he entered the stable, the smell of fresh hay greeted him. Mrs. Scott's horses, along with the two he and the teacher had taken on their little excursion into Round Rock, had been housed inside. The two latter horses would have to be brushed down and settled for the night—something that would help him ponder and evaluate the curious predicament in which he found himself.

Each of the occupied stalls had already been fitted with makeshift water troughs and clean bedding—another tribute to the caliber of men he'd chosen for this trip.

A warm glow came from the far side of the stable and as Tag made his way toward it, he stepped into a veiled sheet of cobwebs that had sprawled across the corner of the main beam and an unused stall. He peeled the sticky strands from his face, and cursed himself for entering the old, recently vacant building without a lantern.

By the time he reached the lit stall, he'd been able to eliminate the last of the fiber-like remnants from the assault on his scraggly beard.

"Hey, boss," Kade said as he leaned onto the gate with his forearms. The light emanating from the lantern sitting on the floor cast a halo on the tips of the foreman's hair, but shadowed his face as he worked on Gentry.

"Mind if I take over?" Tag asked, unlatching the stall's gate.

"No, s…boss." Kade stood and handed the pick to him. "Cole has already taken care of Maverick, but this fella here hasn't been brushed yet."

"Why don't you go and get ready for bed. I'll finish up in here."

Kade pulled off his gloves and clapped them against his trousers. "Mrs. Scott's horses both need to be reshod," he said. "The shoes they've got have to be at least a few months old, if not more." He shook his head. "I'm not sure how they've made it this long. It's a surprise neither of them has gone lame."

Tag's jaw flexed, his teeth clenched. If the woman didn't know how to take care of her livestock, she really had no business keeping horses.

"See they get treated first thing," he said with a curt nod.

"Will do." Kade affirmed before leaving the stable.

From what he'd been able to gather, no one had been here to take care of the ranch for a very long time—even though Mrs. Scott had been running the school out of the homestead. She'd told him that Jeb had only arrived a few days ago and it appeared he hadn't been able to do much on his own in that time. It would definitely take some work to get Oak Meadow back into working condition, but he had every confidence it could be done. He had several dilemmas facing him and there was a lot to consider, but he had a feeling everything would be much clearer in the morning after a good night's sleep.

Once Tag finished brushing down his mount, he grabbed his pack and bedroll, then headed into the bunkhouse.

When he opened door, he was surprised to see that there was only one set of bunks in the whole place and even that had only a single mattress situated on the top bunk. Several bedrolls had been laid out on the floor, most with men already lying down in them, and he guessed they'd left the bed for him. He shook his head. If the boys couldn't sleep on a bed tonight, he wouldn't either.

He set his pack on the ground next to the bedframe as quietly as he could, and rolled his blanket out onto the floor next to a snoring Cole. He chuckled when his little brother snorted and rolled over. They'd had a long day. A long month. He imagined that the hardwood floor wouldn't be much better than the ground, but when they worked as hard as they had, a man could sleep just about anywhere.

Tag lay down on top of the blanket, his arms folded behind his head, and he mulled over everything that had happened throughout the day. There had been many unexpected twists to how he thought this day would play out, not the least of which was the spirited woman who slept just a hop, skip, and a jump away. She'd intrigued him and he hoped that tomorrow would bring some answers that would keep her close—though he'd learned a long time ago that tomorrows often held empty promises.

Maybe not this time. Just maybe.

CHAPTER EIGHT

Brenna didn't know when she'd finally fallen asleep. Unwelcomed visions of the handsome stranger had invaded her thoughts for a good portion of the night and she'd cursed herself for her foolish imaginings. Morning brought with it hope. The sun's rays spilt into her room and onto her face, but she longed to stay in her bed just five more minutes.

The children!

She shot upright, grabbing the clock on her nightstand and staring at the hands through one open eye.

Seven-thirty.

"No. No. No!" Her voice grew louder with each protest as she slammed the clock back in its place, threw the heavy quilt off from on top of her, and ran to the old wardrobe. She tore open the doors and quickly combed through the few dress selections until she found something she felt would be the most appropriate for the day.

"Blue, I think," she said aloud as she held it up against her and glanced at her reflection in the mirror.

Just because the Oak Meadow Ranch would no longer belong to her, was no reason not to provide the children of Serenity Hollow lessons—at least for today or for as long as she could convince Mr. Redbourne to keep the school open. She pinned her hair up into a simple quaff, pinched her cheeks, and started for the stairs, but with a second thought, darted back to the vanity and opened her tin of colored gloss and quickly applied it to her lips with the tip of her middle finger. She folded them together and smiled. Satisfied, she headed down to the schoolroom.

As Brenna passed the kitchen, she noticed a basket full of eggs sitting on the counter along with a fresh pail of milk and a bowl of blackberries. She hadn't checked on the berries in a few weeks, but obviously, some had ripened on the vine and someone had taken the initiative to collect a few. Jeb had never been so ambitious as to have his chores done before noon, so that left only one possibility.

Tag.

She rolled her glossed lips together again, ignoring the smile of anticipation that twitched there. Slipping one of the blackberries from the bowl, Brenna popped it in her mouth, and had to stop herself from bouncing the rest of the way to the back of the house. The inexplicably light feelings that swelled inside of her contrasted greatly with the heavy weight she'd been carrying for months.

There had to be a way. She believed Mr. Redbourne to be a reasonable man and she was sure that if she could think of something, he would at least listen to what she had to say.

She picked up one of the slates with yesterday's assignment written on it and sat down behind her desk skimming over it, but her focus was elsewhere and after re-reading the same sentence several times, she tossed the assignment back down on top of the others and exhaled heavily.

The creak of the door pulled her attention upward and a little girl pushed her way into the classroom. "Good morning, Mrs. Scott." Gemma's bright, cheerful voice brought the light in with her.

"Good morning, Gemma," Brenna answered as she stood up to greet the child. The warm, cheeriness of her own voice came as a surprise. She still wanted to be mad. Should have been worried at the least for what the immediate future would hold.

But, something inside of her just wouldn't listen and she felt different than she had in a very long time.

Happy.

She felt happy.

The little girl smiled broadly with an energetic wave, then set her lunch pail on the shelf near the door and ran outside to play with the other children who already dotted the yard.

Brenna wiped down the chalkboard, then pulled out the Geology book they were studying and sat down again behind her desk. After a few moments, she glanced up and looked out through the front windows where she could see the children playing gleefully with one another. Even Ernie and Jayson were involved, tossing a ball to the younger boys holding sticks. It felt good to know that she had provided something worthwhile for them to do. A way for them to congregate with others around their ages and get an education.

A moment of doubt worked its way into her otherwise hopeful morning and she shook her head, hoping to clear all pessimism from her mind.

"What am I going to do?" she said under her breath.

"Now, are you going to tell me what's going on?"

Brenna jumped at the sound of Jeb's voice behind her.

"After my conversation with Cole and the fellas last night, I gathered that his brother bought the place. What I can't figure out is why you sold it."

"*I* didn't."

With another glance at the children, then at the clock, she quickly provided her brother a rundown of what had happened in the last twenty-four hours.

"So, what are you going to do?" Jeb asked when she'd finished.

"I don't know, but we have a few days to figure it out." She picked up the bell Peter had purchased for her and walked outside.

Clankety. Ring. Clankety. Ring.

The children stopped what they were doing and ran to line up at the bottom of the stairs, the older boys bringing up the back.

"Are we doing something special today, Mrs. Scott?" Gemma asked brightly, twisting her head up to look at her teacher.

"Are they coming to school too?" Charlie, Ernie's little brother, pointed at the men who bustled about the yard working on various tasks.

Brenna breathed a laugh. "Those men have work to do, but you will be seeing them around the ranch all the rest of the week."

The lesson she had prepared for the day hardly seemed appropriate now and she thought she needed to do something to help the children prepare for the change that would imminently come. She dropped her hands to her sides and looked down at the fire pit the cowboys had created last night. Then, an idea popped into her head. If there was ever a time to change the lesson plan, now was it.

"And, yes, Gemma, we are going to do something *very* special today." She stood back, away from the door, and allowed the children to enter.

"Yeah!" A male voice rang out through the yard.

Brenna shot a look to where the scream had come from to see a full burst of water splash into the bucket the man held beneath the pump. He set it down and threw both of his hands into the air.

"I got it working!" he yelled to the others, who soon joined him with several tin cups and canteens.

She smiled to herself. Maybe the well hadn't dried up after all. It had just taken someone with the right knowledge to get it to work.

It might be good to have them around, she thought, then remembered it was only a matter of time before it would be her leaving Oak Meadow. It took a moment for the fact to sink in, but she quickly pushed the inevitable aside to focus on her class.

The children sat at their desks, murmuring excitedly with one another, as she closed the door.

"Everyone take out your slates. I'd like you to write a short essay about something you learned yesterday on our little excursion outdoors."

A few giggles erupted from the students and Brenna's brows scrunched together.

"But, Mrs. Scott," Emaline said with a broad smile, "you've got our slates with yesterday's assignment on them."

Silly, you just looked at them. Something had her overly distracted and his name was Taggert Redbourne. She placed a hand on top of the stack of slates and laughed breathily, but a thought came to mind.

"You are absolutely right, Emaline." Brenna stood up and brushed at the light wrinkles that had formed on the front of her dress. "Why don't you come up and lead everyone in practice for our song for the festival?"

The young girl nodded enthusiastically as she jumped out of her seat and hustled to the front of the room as the rest of the children murmured excitedly—likely at the prospect of less writing exercises.

"I'll just be in the next room for a few minutes. Ernie," she said, looking at the older boy, "will you keep an eye on things?"

"Yes, ma'am!" he said with a puffed chest, pride beaming from his grinning face.

Brenna closed the door behind her as she stepped into the kitchen to scan the shelves for the tin can containing today's spontaneous treasure. There it was, sitting inconspicuously at the center of the tallest ledge next to the stove.

Of course.

She quickly found the small, round stepping stool beneath the middle working cabinet and dragged it out by the straight wooden handle that protruded from the seat. It couldn't have been more than a foot tall and she hoped it would give her the height needed to reach the tin. She stepped up. The legs wobbled unevenly, but she managed to balance as she raised her hand upward.

Not quite.

She reached a little farther. The stool slid just enough across the newly polished wood floor that it threw her askew and her arms shot out in an attempt to regain control, to no avail. She squealed as her foot came off the stool and she fell backward, bracing for a painful impact. Instead, she found herself scooped up into a pair of warm, muscular arms and she quickly grasped a hold of her rescuer.

"I was hoping you'd fall for me," Tag said, his voice deep and throaty, "but this is more than I could have hoped for."

Brenna's heart thumped wildly in her chest—partially from the exhilaration of her near fall and partially from Tag's proximity. She glanced up, her eyes meeting his and little butterflies fluttered in her belly at the appearance of the small dimple now accompanying his playful smile. Slowly, he lowered her down to the floor.

She breathed a relieved sigh as her feet touched the ground, her solid footing regained. "Thank you," was all she could think to say. Her eyes still locked with his, she took a quick step backward.

"It looks like you could use a little assistance, ma'am?" Tag reached up and easily retrieved the tin she'd been attempting to collect. "Is this what you were after?"

Brenna nodded as she took it from him. "Yes. Thank you." She groaned inwardly.

Don't you have something more interesting to say to the man? she chided herself. It took her a moment, but she finally blurted, "I trust you slept well?"

"As good as any night over the last month," he said with a barely suppressed grin. "We picked up a few things in town yesterday—some foodstuffs and such." He pointed to the counter where a large box sat, filled with jerky, nuts, flour, and a few other items.

None of those things in and of themselves would make for very delicious meals, but she nodded anyway. She guessed they'd probably lived on worse.

"But before we purchase anything else, food or otherwise, I'd like to ride out over the property borders today and look at all of the ranch holdings to determine what additional supplies or tools may be needed. I told Mr. Scott that I would finalize our purchase by the end of the week and I intend to keep that promise."

A man who took his commitments seriously. She liked that. Even if it was to her detriment.

Tag cleared his throat. "It would be nice to have some company." He rolled his hat in his hands. "Maybe someone who knows the area," he added. "Would you care to join me?"

Brenna gripped the can in her hands even tighter. She'd lived at Oak Meadow for over a year, but she didn't know as much about the property as Mr. Redbourne likely expected. Part of her really wanted to say yes, if only to be close to the man, but she was a teacher first and foremost and needed to be there for the children. Especially now in such a time of change.

"I'm sorry," she said, shaking her head a little, "that just won't be possible."

Her heart skipped a beat at the fleeting look of disappointment that crossed the man's face.

"I mean," she started again, "I would love to…I mean… I just can't." Her shoulders deflated some. "I'm sorry." She held up the tin, shook it a little, and ducked around him. Her mind reeled as she tried to think of something she could do.

You don't teach all day, her inner voice whispered.

As Brenna reached the classroom door, she turned to look back at him. "But," she said, "if you wouldn't mind waiting until three…"

"Three it is." Tag winked, grabbed a handful of blackberries and a few candied pecans out of their respective bowls on the counter, and strode back outside without giving her a chance to change her mind. He tossed one of the treats into his mouth and headed for the stables.

Brenna shook her head, a smile grazing her lips as she pulled an oven mitt from the counter drawer before heading back into the classroom.

The popper.

She quickly backed up a few steps and unhooked the unique utensil from the nail in the wall, excited to finally use the wedding gift her favorite uncle had given her. She scooped up a large bowl for the finished treat and with her arms overly full, she waddled into class, careful not to trip.

This is going to be so much fun.

Once she'd joined the children again in the school room, several of her students jumped up to relieve her of the items in her arms.

"What are these?" Gemma asked with awed wonder.

"Tools for this afternoon's lesson. But we have some essays to listen to first."

"Awww," the children groaned in unison.

Brenna set the tin on the edge of her desk and sat down, blowing a stray hair away from her face. Movement on the other side of the window caught her eye and she looked up just as Tag passed by on his way to the stable. Brenna sucked her bottom lip between her teeth with a smile.

Focus, Brenna.

"All right," she said to the children, "who is going to go first?"

Most of her students looked down at their desks, but the newest young addition to the group shot his hand into the air.

She nodded with a knowing smile and he made his way to the front of the class.

"I learned that…" Everett started his reading, though she guessed by the look on his face and his wide eyes, that he was about to tell the story rather than read it from his slate. He stole a look at her, "…you shouldn't steal clothes from a man bathing in the woods." He grinned wide.

The children laughed.

Everett's ears turned bright pink, and even Brenna had to cover her mouth to stifle a giggle. Poor Mr. Redbourne. Her face heated at the thought of him in the stream with nothing more than a bright blue handkerchief to cover himself. Never before had she seen the likes of such a man.

"Thank you, Everett. I'm glad you learned something."

The boy sat down and several of the other children patted him on the back or shoulder. He beamed under their approval and she smiled, grateful he'd already made friends.

Many of the other student's short essays were much along the same lines. After some time evaluating the grammar and spelling on their written essays and working on their arithmetic, the lunch hour was upon them.

"All right, students, put your slates away for the day. After lunch, we will be having a special activity."

"Are we going on another excursion into the woods?" Charlie asked with hopeful eyes.

"No. But I think you'll like what we are going to do."

"What is it?" Gemma piped up from her desk.

"You'll just have to wait and see."

Light commotion ensued as the children quickly cleared their desks and hustled to collect their lunches from the shelf.

"The suspense is killing me," Everett said dramatically as he tucked his slate up under his arm.

Brenna giggled.

"Get along, now," she said to the two young boys still lingering. "You don't want to miss out on a game of stickball, do you?" She nodded at the two older boys who'd already cleaned up their things and were headed out the door.

Charlie and Everett perked up, smiles on their faces, and darted over to the shelf where they deposited their supplies and grabbed their lunches before running out the door to catch up with the older boys.

While the children ate their lunches and played in the yard, Brenna walked down the front path, intent on starting a fire in the pit. She'd never started a fire outside before, but didn't imagine it would be much different than starting the fire in her cooktop stove.

A nice woodpile sat at the backside of the bunkhouse, so she enlisted the help of a few of the children that had finished their meals to gather some dried grasses and a few logs from the pile. Then, she sent Jayson into the house to grab the tinderbox from the heat stove in the classroom.

"Are we making fire? Outside?" Gemma's brother asked, his eyes wide with wonder.

"We are. Have any of you had a fire outside before?" She was surprised how many of the children raised their hands.

"We cooked outside for a whole year when our stove cracked and our crops didn't provide enough to have it repaired," James, the obvious son of a farmer, said as if he were an expert.

Brenna placed a hand on her chest, more acutely aware of the struggles and challenges her students had already faced in their young lives.

"Would you like to help?" she asked.

The boy nodded energetically, his brows raised. "Yes, please."

Brenna laughed. "I'll let you know as soon as I need you," she told him and he walked away with a light spring in his step. She pulled her father's old pocket watch from the folds of her skirt and clicked it open. "Five more minutes, children," she called out to those playing in the yard.

Those who'd been standing around her ran off to get in their last few moments of playtime, while she sat in the shade of the umbrella of leaves that extended from the large pecan tree and watched them.

CRASH!

Brenna's attention quickly diverted to the man standing on the roof of the bunkhouse with a board and nails.

Tag disappeared.

The children froze and gaped.

Brenna's heart sunk, but she shot to her feet, her heart racing with fear, and ran toward the building as did several of the men.

The wooden roof had caved in under his weight.

As she reached the bunkhouse door, Cole flung it open and, to her relief, there sat Tag on the top bed of the old bunk, brushing dust and splinters from the shoulders of his shirt.

Gratitude welled up inside of her.

Tag looked up to see the lot of them.

"I guess the bed wasn't so useless after all."

The men laughed, but Brenna turned away, afraid he might see the unwanted tear escaping down her cheek. She quickly brushed it away and marched toward the school to grab her bell.

Lunch recess was over.

Why did the thought of losing him affect her so?

"Mrs. Scott," Tag called from some distance behind her.

She focused forward, intent on avoiding him.

"Mrs. Scott," he tried again.

She didn't turn around. Couldn't.

"Brenna, wait!"

Something in his familiarity tugged at her conscience and she stopped, afraid to look at him. How had she grown to care about a man she'd only known the better half of a day?

He placed a hand on her shoulder.

"I'm all right," he said quietly.

She didn't trust herself to speak.

"Look at me," he coaxed.

She took a deep breath, wiped her cheeks just below her eyes, and turned to face him.

He took her shoulders in his hands and bent down to look at her.

"I'm all right," he assured her again. "And we'll replace the roof on the bunkhouse. Everything is all right."

She wished she felt the same.

"I…," she swallowed hard.

Everything was not all right.

"Ooooo," one of the boys called loudly. "Mrs. Scott has a new beau."

Brenna dropped her head with an uneasy chuckle, then took a deep breath, feeling emotionally exposed, and she cursed the tears that lined her lids.

"Thank you," she said, managing a close-lipped smile. "The children are waiting. I have to go."

Tag dropped his hold on her and shoved his hands into his pockets.

She didn't move, but continued to stare at him.

"Go," he prodded.

She turned toward her students, took a few steps, then turned back to him. "I'm very glad you weren't hurt, Mr. Redbourne."

He smiled with a nod of acknowledgement.

As she walked back up the school steps, she smiled at the sound of him whistling an unfamiliar, but happy tune.

"Are you going to marry him, Mrs. Scott?" Gemma asked sweetly. "My mama says it's about time you find yourself a new man."

Brenna laughed out loud. "No, Gemma, Mr. Redbourne and I are…"

What were they? Friends? Acquaintances?

"…well, we just met. We are most certainly *not* getting married."

"Me thinks the lady doth protest too much," Jayson said, quoting back last week's literature lesson on Hamlet.

"Me thinks the lady wants to build a fire," she responded.

"Yea," several of the children yelled at once.

Marriage? Where would they have gotten that idea?

CHAPTER NINE

Brenna stole another quick glance at Mr. Redbourne. Not that she would mind getting to know the man better.

When she returned her focus to the students, Jayson caught her eye, a knowing smile on his face. At least he'd been paying attention in literature class, she reasoned. She narrowed her eyes and shook her head playfully.

After the kindling and logs were appropriately set in the pit, Brenna opened the tinderbox, but to her chagrin, the flint was missing. Her eyes flitted from side to side as she thought about what could have possibly happened to it. She looked over the awaiting faces of all the children, unable to accept the possibility that she would disappoint them.

Two of Tag's cowboys passed by the outer fence, laughing. They'd had a fire last night, so surely, they had a flint stone.

"Bren?" Jeb cleared his throat as he pulled her thoughts from the men. "Mrs. Scott," he corrected when he received several strange looks from her students. "I'm headed into town. The hitch on the wagon snapped and we'll have to replace it before we can pick up any more supplies on Saturday. If the wainwright in town doesn't have it, we may have to place an order to have one sent from Austin."

She had noticed that the metal piece had been covered in rust, but never imagined it would break. Weren't those things supposed to last forever? She shrugged and nodded.

Her brother turned for the stable.

"Hey, Jeb," she called after him. "The flint stone is missing out of the tinderbox. Have you seen it?"

"It was there last night when we started the fire."

"Well," she said matter-of-factly as she placed her hands on her hips, "it's not here now." She opened the padded wooden box, removed the steel, and turned it upside down for effect.

"It's not here," she mouthed at him. She figured they could probably go into the classroom and get her magnifying glass. It was daytime and the sun shone high in the sky. The refraction of the light should allow them to burn the dead grasses and hopefully start the fire.

"Maybe this will help." Mr. Redbourne held out a single red-topped match.

Brenna's arms cascaded in gooseflesh at the sound of his voice.

"Children, this is Mr. Redbourne. He is…new to Serenity Hollow. Can you all welcome him to town?"

Calls of greeting and welcome sounded all at once.

"Hey, aren't you the one—"

"Yes, well, thank you, Mr. Redbourne, for helping us with the fire," she said, glaring at Eddie and raising a brow.

The boy shrugged with a mischievous smirk.

Tag tipped his hat, then pulled out a small box. She looked up at him and he winked at her, then bent down to drag the stick across its black striking surface near the wood.

"Wait," she said, placing her hand on his shoulder and looked up for one of her students. "James," she called.

The young boy moved himself to the front. "Yes, ma'am?"

"We're ready for you." She glanced over at Tag and nodded toward the youngster.

Tag demonstrated what to do with the match by striking it against the textured black paper. "Got it?"

James nodded.

Tag pulled another match from a small wallet-like fold in his pocket and handed it to the boy who beamed up at the handsome man.

The youth struck the match against the texture as directed and his eyes widened when the flame leapt to life. He held one hand around it as he lowered it to the kindling. A sharp burst of wind snuffed out the flicker and a small stream of smoke rose from the stick. James looked at Tag in horror, but the man simply winked at him and handed him another match.

With an obviously relieved sigh, the boy then crouched down right next to the grasses in the pit and tried again. This time, the kindling caught fire and before long, the flames had moved to the larger pieces and eventually to the logs.

The children clapped, excited about the seemingly mundane task of starting a fire.

"Thank you," she mouthed to Tag.

He nodded with a soft smile and strode back toward the bunkhouse to continue picking up the mess from the damaged roof.

Brenna watched him long enough that Jayson cleared his throat. She narrowed her eyes at his smirk, then shook her tin can. "Can anyone guess what's inside?"

They all listened for a moment.

"Rice!" one child yelled.

"Beans," called another.

"Buttons."

"Pebbles."

Brenna shook her head and leaned in toward the children. "What would you say if I told you it was a most delicious treat."

"Lemon drops!" Gemma shouted enthusiastically.

"Gum drops."

Brenna loved the gusto the children displayed. She flipped the latch on the tin.

A chorus of children sucking in excited breaths, warmed her heart.

She opened the lid and carefully poured a small amount into her hands to show them, laughing as they all gathered in for a closer look, quizzical expressions crossing their faces.

"That doesn't look like a delicious treat to me," Ernie said with a grimace.

"Does anyone know what these are?"

Each child looked at another, then to another, their heads shaking.

"Seeds of some sort?" James asked cautiously.

"Very good, James. They can be used as seeds, but we're going to be able to eat the treat today," she said, satisfied at several awed gasps.

Jayson reached in, took one, and popped it in his mouth.

"Careful not to bite down too…"

"Ow," he said, pulling the kernel from his mouth and tossing it into the bushes next to the house.

"…hard," she finished, a bit deflated.

"That doesn't seem like a very good treat to me," the young man said, rubbing his mouth and jaw.

Brenna laughed along with the other children, though she felt bad he'd hurt his teeth.

"That is because they are not yet ready to eat."

"Are we going to grind them up like wheat?" Gemma asked.

Brenna had sampled some of the girl's mother's sweet rolls and knew Mrs. Hamblin to be a talented baker.

"Nope."

"Do you boil them like beans or rice?" Charlie piped up.

"No, but you're getting warmer."

The children glanced from one to another, but no one had another guess.

Brenna smiled. "They are corn," she told them.

"That doesn't look like the corn my papa grows," Gemma's best friend said.

"Well, Emaline, you are right. It is not the type of corn we typically grow around here, but it's a special kind of maize, grown by the Indians, that make these seed-like, hard-shelled nuggets."

"So, we're going to eat vegetables as a treat?" Ernie asked with a scrunched nose.

"No," Brenna said, laughing breathily as she spoke, "we are going to pop them."

"Pop them? What does that mean, Mrs. Scott?" Gemma asked.

"It means we are going to heat them up until they burst open."

"On the fire?" James asked. "Won't they get ashes all over them?"

"That is why we have a special pan to cook them in." She picked up the mesh wire contraption with the long metal and wooden handles.

"How does it work?" Jayson asked, reaching out to touch the fine metal.

"Well, inside each one of these little nuggets is a big, fluffy white, treat. In order to get to the edible part, the nugget needs to be heated enough so that the moisture inside of it turns to steam. Does anyone know what happens when steam doesn't have anywhere to go?"

"It pops the top," Ernie shouted, then his eyes opened wide. "Pops," he said again appreciatively with a satisfied nod.

"That's right. The shell is going to pop open to reveal the fluffy white inside."

"Let's do it," James said eagerly, rubbing his hands together.

Once there were some good embers below the fire, Brenna demonstrated how to open the popper pan, then had Emaline help her pour about a half cup full of the kernels inside. She latched the tool shut and allowed the children to take turns holding and shaking it over the fire, instructing them to be careful not to allow the pan to sit directly in the flames, but over the cinders.

When the first kernel popped, the children clapped and

laughed excitedly. Even the older ones.

Pop. Pop. Pop.

"May I have a turn?" Gemma asked Jayson, who'd been holding it a little longer than the others.

He looked reluctant, but one glance at Brenna who winked at him, and he handed it happily over to the young girl.

It only took a couple of minutes before all the kernels had burst open and were ready to be poured into the bowl. Brenna grabbed the oven mitt and unlatched the hook on the hot metal pan, then carefully dumped the popped corn into the large bowl.

They repeated the process several times until the bowl was near full.

"May I help?" Tag's deep, rich voice sent gooseflesh down her arms, again, and she turned to see him holding up her butter dish and salt cellar.

He has to stop doing that. She rubbed her arms.

"You're familiar with popcorn?"

"In many varieties," he said with a grin.

"Please," she invited.

"Well," he said, turning his attention to the children. "Popcorn can be covered with all sorts of fun things…a caramel coating and flavored sugar among them, but sometimes it's just plain delicious with a little butter and salt." He scooped some of the butter into a small, cast iron frying pan he'd brought over with him and proceeded to melt it over the fire.

Brenna was amazed at how comfortable he was around her students. When he glanced up and caught her stare, heat flooded her face. Her belly turned over from the inside when he smiled at her as he continued to instruct the children.

Once the butter was in liquid form, Tag gently poured it over the popped corn, then scooped out a small amount of salt and sprinkled it over the top. He picked up the bowl and gently shook it until it seemed that each kernel had been exposed.

"Now, it is ready for consumption, wouldn't you say, Mrs. Scott?"

She reached into the bowl and pulled out one especially fluffy piece and popped it into her mouth, closing her eyes.

"Mmmmmmm," she groaned loudly, exaggerating her response—though, in all honesty, it wasn't much of an exaggeration. The popcorn tasted delightful and she couldn't wait for the children to try it.

"Do you all have your tin cups?" she asked.

The students scrambled to collect their wares.

"You are just full of surprises, aren't you, Mr. Redbourne?" she said quietly, lightly leaning into him.

"Yep," he said, grabbing a small handful of the treat and popping a few of the kernels into his mouth. "Now, if you'll excuse me." He tipped his hat and headed back toward the entrance gate where some of the other men were working to repair the broken planks.

Brenna laughed to herself.

"See you at three," he called back to her, turning around with a light wave. His eyes held a hint of mischief and Brenna found herself anticipating the end of the school day.

The children enjoyed the popcorn as much as she did.

"Where can we get some of this type of corn?" Jayson asked.

Brenna hadn't really thought about that. "I'll talk to Mrs. Wheatley to see if it's something she might be able to order. If not, I'll find out and will get back to you."

After everyone had enjoyed their fair share, she pulled them all into a semi-circle around the fire. Now, it was time to apply the metaphorical lesson to the practical experience. She reached into the tin can and pulled out a small handful of kernels, opening her fingers to display them.

"Who can tell me what these are?" she asked for a second time.

Hands shot up all around her.

"James," she said, calling on the young boy with his hand raised the highest—his derrière nearly off the ground he stretched so tall.

"Popcorn seeds!" he bellowed.

"Yes. Now, I want you to think back to just over an hour ago about how you felt when I first introduced you to these odd little nuggets. Tell me what you were thinking or feeling."

"I thought you wanted us to break our teeth," Jayson said, rubbing his mouth again.

The children laughed.

"I was scared that you weren't going to be our teacher anymore."

"Oh, James, why would you say that?"

"Because I thought people might think you'd gone mad."

Brenna guffawed, then threw a hand over her mouth to hide her embarrassment. The children all laughed again.

"And what do you think now?" she asked as she returned the new kernels to her tin.

"That you are the smartest teacher in the whole world," little Gemma said proudly.

"Popcorn is tasty," Ernie said, patting and rubbing his stomach.

Murmurs of agreement rumbled through the small crowd.

"Well, sometimes we have things happen in our lives that seem like dreary, drab, little, hard-shelled nuggets, and we can't see what is inside of them. Problems come…loss of a parent," she looked at Ernie, then at Charlie, "a new home or community," she looked at Everett. "Or, other things that bring change to our lives. These things are the heat we experience." She picked up the bowl, where the popped corn used to be and turned it upside down, spilling the remaining kernels into her palm.

"Why didn't those ones pop?" Emaline asked.

"That's a very good question." Brenna thought for a moment. "These kernels are like people who are so afraid of change that they do not allow themselves to grow or become what they are meant to be. They are held back by their fears, preferring to simply always be a kernel."

"What are you trying to tell us, Mrs. Scott?" Jayson asked wisely.

Some of these kids were smart beyond their years.

"We've all experienced change in our lives. Change is the one thing that never changes. It is inevitable. We experienced change when we came together after the schoolhouse burned down to become a class here at Oak Meadow. We experienced change when Everett's family moved to Serenity Hollow and he joined us. And we even experienced a change today, when we learned something new."

"About popcorn," Charlie yelled.

"Yes, about popcorn."

"And your new beau," Gemma said dreamily.

Mr. Redbourne certainly was bringing a hefty amount of change to her life, but being her new beau was not one of them. She dared a glance at him.

"I don't have a new beau, Miss Hamblin, but there are more changes coming. We may not know what or when, but there will always be changes coming."

"Should we be scared?" Merilee asked, her eyes wide.

"Are you going to get burned up too, like the old schoolmaster?" Emaline asked, tears brimming in her eyes.

"Oh, no, children, it's nothing like that," she assured them. "Change is not something to be feared. We just need to be prepared and to remember that if we can learn to embrace the changes that come into our lives instead of fighting them, beautiful and delicious things will happen for us just like the popped corn."

"What's changing, Mrs. Scott?"

"Are you gettin' hitched?" Charlie asked.

Again, with the getting married. She took a deep breath and smiled. *Just be honest with them.*

"Well, the truth is, children, that starting next week, we may not be able to meet here at the ranch for school."

"Why not? Are you leaving?"

"There are a few things that are still unsettled, but Oak Meadow doesn't belong to me anymore."

"Who does it belong to?"

Brenna glanced up and locked eyes with Tag.

"Him?" Jayson asked, pointing with his chin.

"He likes you," Gemma said dreamily. "That much is obvious. So, why don't you just marry him and we'll all have lots of popcorn?" The little girl's hands clasped together in front of her and she batted her eyelashes as she looked upward.

"Mr. Redbourne and I are *not* getting married." The words came out stronger than she'd intended and she cleared her throat, then took another deep breath. Once she felt a little more composed, she looked down at the surprised children and smiled. "What would you say if I let school out a little early today?"

"Yea!"

Brenna laughed. "Well, you're dismissed. I will see you in the morning."

Most of the children did not wait for her to change her mind, but Jayson stayed back just a moment.

"I'd say someone wants to remain a kernel," he said knowingly. "In my opinion, Mrs. Scott, you would make a man some mighty fine popped corn." He tipped an imaginary hat and then ran to join Ernie and the others as they collected their things and left for home.

Brenna breathed a pleasantly surprised laugh. She had the best students.

Boys.

She shook her head.

One look at the fire still burning in the pit and she regretted having let them all go so early. She separated the wood with a large stick and immediately the flames started to dwindle, but the fire was large enough that it would take some water to put it out completely and she was grateful that Tag's men had figured out the problem with the pump.

The butter dish, salt cellar, and her popcorn tin all fit into the large bowl as she gathered the items up into her arms. She picked up the popper, now cooled enough to hold, and draped the leather strap from the handle over her fingers, then headed into the house to retrieve a water bucket to extinguish the rest of the fire. Why she hadn't thought to have one on hand escaped her. It would have been the responsible thing to do, but luckily, nothing had gotten out of hand.

"Married?" she snorted at the notion. The idea was absurd. She'd tried it once already and look what it had done to her. While she couldn't deny that she was attracted to Tag Redbourne, she didn't know if her heart could take another loss. She feared this time, it would be much worse—especially because she already felt more connected to him than she ever had with Peter.

When her husband died, it had taken every ounce of strength to get out of bed in the morning. He'd been her hope at a new kind of life, an introduction to what love could have been, and with him gone, she'd dreaded having to return to her father's home…alone and a widow.

If it hadn't been for the opportunity to teach the children and make a school for them, she didn't know what would have happened. And, she never wanted to feel like that again. While she had no desire to return to Hillsboro, she did need a plan. It had to be something that would allow her to stay in Serenity Hollow, but far, far away from Mr. Taggert Redbourne. At least for now.

CHAPTER TEN

Tag pried another board loose from the roof of the bunkhouse as he watched Mrs. Scott dismiss the children early. She cleaned up the area around the pit, then headed into the house—flames still licking portions of the wood.

He pulled the watch from his vest pocket.

One-thirty.

That was too early for school to be getting out and he wondered what the school teacher was up to. The woman intrigued him—more than he cared to admit.

He stuffed the watch back into his vest, then reached down to pull off another plank, shaking his head as it came off a little easier than anticipated and he nearly lost his balance.

"So, what do you think?" Cole stared up at him from the ground.

Tag had been so lost in thought that he'd missed most of what his brother was saying, but he tuned in to the last few words as he continued to stare at the unguarded fire.

Cole whistled this time to get his attention. "Tag!"

"What?"

"Where did you go?"

He ignored the question as he climbed down from the roof, swept up Harvey's bucket, and strode to the spigot where he pumped a few large sprays.

"I'll be right back."

Did the woman not know she needed to put out a fire before leaving it unattended?

This female had gotten under his skin and he couldn't stop thinking about her. He'd found himself more than once today neglecting his responsibilities to be near her. To talk to her. Well, enough was enough. He'd considered allowing her to stay on at the ranch and teach her precious school, but at this rate, he'd lose the ranch due to neglect.

Or fire, he mused.

No, it was probably best for everyone if she found a place in town. At least for the first few months while he was getting acclimated to Texas living and running a ranch.

As he made his way over to the fire, he kicked something hard in the ground and reached down to retrieve the missing flint stone. He tossed it into the air and caught it again, closing his fingers tightly around the cool rock.

"It's not a sign, Mother," he said aloud, knowing just what she'd say if she were here.

He glanced around for the tinderbox. Brenna must have taken it into the house with the rest of her things. Maybe he could just leave it out here on one of the log seats and she would find it later.

"Tag," Cole called as he caught up to him. "There's not much else we can do until we pick up supplies in town. We're out of nails, rope, and have used the last of the boards we bought yesterday."

"We're going to need a lot more than I originally expected." He set the bucket down on the ground next to him as he spoke with his brother. "We won't be able to maintain a large herd until we get fences constructed around the northwest property." He motioned toward the new parcel of land.

"You decided to purchase Grimace's land?" Cole removed his gloves and tucked them in his back pocket.

"Kade rode out there yesterday and was impressed with the quality of the earth. He said it would be a great addition to the ranch and I trust him, so, yes, I'm buying it. Made an offer just this morning. I am concerned about one of the locals, though. Apparently, he's been trying to bully some of the ranchers around here to sell him their land. I can't imagine he'll be too happy to learn he's got some competition."

"Is he going to be a problem?"

"Let's hope not. For his sake."

The man had looked like he belonged on the face of a wanted poster and from the scowl he'd worn at O'Malley's, Tag knew he'd need to be on alert.

"What about the Cranston place?" Cole asked.

"I haven't had a chance to speak with Mr. Cranston, but if the price is right, then I guess we'll be expanding to the east as well." His savings more than covered the cost of Oak Meadow and then most of Grimace's, but to purchase the additional spread, he'd have to tap into the money from his father's investment. While he didn't love the idea, his father had wanted to be a partner.

He still didn't understand why this Mae Taylor woman wasn't offering bids on any of these ranches or why she hadn't shown any interest in him or the land. If she ran as big an operation as he'd been led to believe, something was definitely off. Before long, he'd have to pay her a visit.

"This suits you," Cole said with a slight nod.

"What's that?" Tag glanced over at the pit where the once lively flames had died down to occasional flickers, though the newly whitened wood still glowed with red hot embers.

"Being in charge."

Tag laughed. "I'll place an order with the miller in Austin for the wood first thing tomorrow." He picked up the bucket, strode over to the remains of Mrs. Scott's popcorn object lesson and poured water over the dying coals.

It sizzled and smoked more than he would have thought.

Tag brushed his hands together and sat down on one of the logs.

Cole placed a foot next to him on the felled trunk and leaned over with an elbow on his knee.

"We all know the ranch is more than worth the asking price, so why didn't you just hand over the papers yesterday when you went out to see Josiah?" He upturned his hands. "I mean, I understand that you want to inspect every square inch of this place. There's plenty of time to do that. We may be heading back next week, but you're going to be here a while. Take your time to do it right."

"When did you become so wise?"

"It's just a fluke." Cole dropped his foot and sat down next to him. "What are you waiting for? If I know anything about you, which I do, your mind was made up as soon as you saw that stream."

His brother knew him too well.

"I know."

Cole stared at him, one brow raised.

"No, you're right. I'm just…"

"A little scared?"

Tag looked over at his little brother. "Of course not. I've done this kind of thing my whole life. What's there to be scared of?"

"Oh, I don't know. Disappointing Dad."

"Thanks for that."

Cole sat up straight. "Hey, big brother. I know you can do this. And, so does Dad. Otherwise, he would have never sent you here."

"Well, I plan on getting everything finalized on our way to Austin tomorrow. Mrs. Scott said that she would ride out with me around the property lines this afternoon."

"Of course, she will," Cole said with a knowing grin. "She is quite pretty, isn't she?"

"Who?"

"Who?" his brother scoffed. "Don't pretend like you haven't noticed. I've seen the way you've been acting around her all day. Don't think I haven't seen you go out of your way to talk to the woman."

Tag wasn't sure what to say. He hadn't realized that his interest had been noticed by anyone else and he shook his head. "What is it about her?" he relented in an exasperated breath.

"What do you mean?"

"She's definitely something to look at, sure," Tag acknowledged with a nod. "Her eyes are hazel, but quite unlike anything I've ever seen before. Her lips are full and she's healthy and spry, so full of life, but it's more than that. There is just something about her that makes me want to be near her, to learn everything about her. I can't explain it."

"You are besotted, my brother."

"Besotted? What does that even mean?" he looked at Cole, not really expecting an answer. "Sure, I'm taken with her," he admitted, "but she's too much of a distraction right now. Any woman would be. There is a lot of work to do around the ranch if we are going to get it up to Redbourne standards. We have livestock to purchase, fences to mend," he smiled at Cole's grimace, "and roofs to patch. I don't have time for any woman."

"You keep telling yourself that, Tag. If I've learned anything from watching Levi, Ethan, and Will, you can try to fight it, but you won't win." Cole smiled mischievously.

Tag grabbed his little brother, pulling his head into the clutch of his arms, and roughed up his hair. "You don't know what you're talking about."

Cole pushed away from him. "You've really got it bad," he said with an incredulous chuckle, combing his fingers through his now straggly hair, dodging a swipe in his direction.

Tag raised a brow at his brother.

"Okay. Okay. I'll leave it alone…" He put his hands up in front of him as if preparing for an attack. "…for now. But I wouldn't let Mama or Hannah hear you say that a woman is too much of a distraction as an excuse for getting your work done. You know as well as I do that women can be a huge help around the ranch."

He was right, but it was a little more complicated than that.

"Better be careful, little brother," Tag said, leaning forward and picking up a piece of wood from the ground. "Mama has had her eye on several of the girls back home for you to marry. You may have to put off your Oxford plans if she has things her way. You may just find yourself married to one of the Dawson twins."

This seemed to sober Cole immediately. The kid had already made arrangements with their brother, Will, to stay with him and his new wife in England in order to attend school there. He wasn't ready to settle down.

"So, what do you want us to do?" Cole asked with a shrug.

"Why don't you take Harvey and Ben into town. We're going to need a couple of wagons. The wainwright's stable is next to the mercantile. Now, before you go getting all riled, I know you're more fond of horses than buckboards, but we'll need two wagons to start, good and sturdy like Mr. Filson's back home. I trust you'll take your time. I'll join you in town after I'm able to ride out and assess the rest of the property."

Cole's jaw flexed as he held back the grin that still cracked the corners of his mouth.

Tag ignored it. "We'll pick up a few extra working mounts while we're in Austin. But, with you and the boys headed out soon, we'll need to hire a few hands who'll stay on here at Oak Meadow. Why don't you check around town and put out the word that we're looking?"

"Do you think you're going to find any here? From what I could tell, there aren't many men to choose from."

"We'll never know until we try. Reach out to some of our contacts in the surrounding areas."

"No telegraph, remember?"

What is it with this town?

"Maybe I should take after Granddad Deardon and have a telegraph wired directly to the house."

Both of them laughed.

"I don't know if you could deal with the amount of people you'd have to entertain."

Tag hadn't thought about that. He'd only been partially joking, but if he did that, he might as well get one for the town too. Cole was right, Tag wasn't exactly the social type, and besides, it wasn't like there were a lot of men to spare. He'd have to see what he could do about contacting Levi. The railroad always put in a telegraph line on their routes. He would know who to contact.

"Maybe just sign the deed, first," Cole said, bumping into Tag's shoulder with his own.

"I will. Now, go!" Tag pushed his little brother off the log. "I'll catch up with you this evening."

"Yes, sir," Cole said, jumping to his feet with a salute.

Tag didn't appreciate the gesture. It was too reminiscent of his command in the war and most of his memories of that time were ones he didn't care to remember. So much loss, regret, and destruction.

"Sorry," Cole said, understanding crossing his face.

He didn't want to think about it. There were plenty of other things that took precedent over the past, the ranch being at the forefront of those things.

All the cowpokes he'd come to know over the last couple of years were already working for respectable ranches. He just hoped they'd be able to find a few able-bodied men with a strong work ethic and a willingness to learn—even if they had to go as far as San Antonio or Houston to get them. Ranching wasn't an easy business and certainly not for the faint-hearted.

"We can use as many hands as you can find. I figure it won't take long to weed out any freeloaders with all the work there is to do." Tag exhaled loudly. "Getting started is going to take more work than Kade and I can do alone. Especially, if we're able to pick up any decent horses to work with. It's going to be a long couple of days. Weeks."

"Months?"

"Ha! Maybe."

"All right, we'll get going." Cole turned toward the bunkhouse, then paused and looked back. "By the way, Sophronia told me that there is a large herd of wild horses that have been sighted quite a few times over the last few weeks. Some of the ranchers aren't very happy about it and some are even threatening to put them down."

"They want to kill the horses?" he squeezed the block of wood in his fist until it hurt.

"The mustangs are infringing on their grazing lands and, well, they don't have the talent that you have in connecting with them."

Tag had heard of the mustangs that ran through Texas and looked forward to an opportunity to see them up close and to work with them. If they had even half the qualities he'd been told about, they would be ideal for breeding with some of their Quarter horses for new stock. He just wished other ranchers could appreciate their beauty and not just see them as a menace.

"We'll deal with that when the time comes. Why don't you take the fellas back to O'Malley's?" Tag told Cole. "We'll give Cook a few days break before you head out again. They all deserve it."

"You'll get no argument from me. Did you taste that pecan pie?" Cole raised his brows and nodded his head in obvious approval.

"And, if you hear of anyone in town who'd be interested in taking on the position of cook at the ranch, send them my way as well. I might be able to make a delectable chicken pot pie, but my culinary skills are lacking much beyond that."

"Again, no argument from me." Cole laughed. "So, what about you? Oh, wait, you're going to play suitor to a very pretty, young school teacher."

"Ah, get out of here," Tag said, swatting at his little brother. Cole laughed again as he jumped out of reach and ran toward the others.

"It's just a business arrangement!" Tag called after him.

A splash of color caught his eye and he looked up at the house to see Brenna coming out of the front door with a bucket in her hands, swinging it as she walked toward the water pump. Maybe she hadn't forgotten the fire after all—though he may need to discuss with her alternative ways of extinguishing the flames and not leaving it.

He leaned forward on the log seat and picked up a chunk of wood to examine, occasionally glancing up to watch the woman he couldn't get out of his mind.

Brenna hummed as she made her way down the walkway and Tag couldn't help but stare. He liked the way her skirt swished from side to side as she moved and how her brown curls bounced with each step.

Besotted, he thought as he exhaled slowly, disgusted with himself for being so vulnerable to her obvious charms.

He glanced back down at the piece of wood, holding it up, mentally assessing its weight, and examining it for flaws—though sometimes the flaws were the foundation of making a piece most unique and beautiful. It had been a long time since he'd whittled at a nice block of wood. With everything they had to get done, he figured he would need something to provide a little relief from all the hard work cut out for them. He missed it—working to create something with his hands. He gathered a few more of the scraps that littered the area around him, figuring that they must have been dropped from branches and logs as they had been hauled to the pile.

Several pecan and oak trees dotted the property, but the wood Tag held in his hands was too soft to be from those trees. He guessed it to be Acacia, but he hadn't seen any of those trees in his immediate surroundings. It was funny that these blocks of lumber seemed to call to him, inspire him.

Maybe it's not just the wood.

He sat up tall at the thought. He glanced over again at

Brenna and watched as she leaned forward, set her bucket down
on the ground beneath the spout, then pulled up firmly on the
large iron force rod handle. The woman obviously knew what
she was doing. But, he made a mental note that it was time to
pipe the pump into the main house. Before they knew it, winter
would be upon them.

He shook his head. Not that it mattered.

Texas.

It would be strange not to wake up to a few feet of snow in
the middle of January.

As Brenna pushed down hard onto the handle and the
water obediently rushed from the spigot, her face lit up with a
smile that surreptitiously spread across her face, evoking an
unexpected groan from Tag's lips. She was the most beautiful
woman he'd ever laid eyes on. Warmth spread through his torso,
deep into the pit of his belly.

Brenna picked up the now full bucket, struggling with the
load as she made her way toward him.

Why are you still sitting here? he asked himself.

His mama would be none too proud that he just sat there
and observed instead of jumping up to help her, but he lingered
a few moments longer, appreciating the strength he saw in her,
the determination.

Go!

He glanced at the pit. The water was no longer necessary,
but he didn't want to be the one to point it out. Maybe next time
he'd have a little faith that she was responsible and smart enough
to put out a fire. Still, he'd have to discuss with her the
repercussions of leaving even the smaller of blazes
unattended—especially with the Texas heat.

Tag grabbed a handful of kindling and a couple twigs, then
pulled the matches from his pocket and quickly lit a new fire. It
didn't need to be big, just needed to appear that it was still
burning. The damp foundation created more smoke than fire,
but he figured that would be enough.

When he glanced back up at Brenna, she'd only taken a few steps and he couldn't hold back from helping her any longer. He tossed the potential wood carving pieces still in his hand onto the stacked pile behind one of the log benches. A low rumble sounded as the whole pile shifted and a few of the thicker cut branches tumbled to the ground.

I'll get back to it, he thought as he headed toward Brenna, but he stopped short as his little brother swooped in to help, reaching her before he could.

"Can I help you with that, ma'am?" Cole said with his boyish charm that had endeared him to so many of the womenfolk back home. Young, old, plump, skinny, didn't matter, women loved the scamp.

Tag cursed himself for having waited even one moment.

It wouldn't happen again.

"Why, thank you, Mr. Red—" Brenna started with an appreciative smile.

The ache in Tag's gut burned. That smile should have been for him.

Never again.

He took in a deep breath and smiled, prepared to greet her.

He leapt forward before she could finish her sentence.

"I've got it, Cole," Tag said, effectively cutting her off. He nodded at his brother, his hand extended expectantly. "Get a move on. I'd like to have those wagons before nightfall."

Cole raised a brow, a knowing smile touching his face, but he did not object as he handed Tag the semi-full bucket.

"Yes, sir," he said as he turned back toward the men who waited for him, then stopped and looked back over his shoulder. "I mean, you'll have them."

Tag managed a half-smile as he nodded.

"It's been a long time since I've had anyone fussing over me. I must admit, it's nice. Thank you."

The ache in Tag's belly was quickly replaced with a light flutter.

"What about your brother?" he asked.

"I grew up with three of them," she told him. "I can't say they've ever 'denied me the opportunity to grow,'" she said with a giggle. "I was raised on a farm and there was no shortage of chores. I did my fair share, just like the boys," she said proudly.

Tag understood perfectly. He and his brothers loved their little sister, but they'd never 'denied *her* any opportunities' either. She may have been the only girl, but she'd been raised to work hard alongside the rest of them.

When they reached the fire pit, Tag froze.

Buzzzzz. Zzzzzzz. Bzzzzz.

A bee.

He glanced around for any visual clues as to where the insect lurked, inadvertently swatting behind his ears, the water in Brenna's bucket sloshing slightly. While he had an appreciation for the creatures and the sweet goods they could provide, he'd been on the wrong end of a stinger one too many times and did not care to repeat the experience.

Bzzzzzz.

There it was again, but now, it had grown into a low, buzzing hum.

Tag's heart sped up a beat or two as visions of youthful shenanigans gone awry pierced his memory.

"Are you all right?" Brenna asked, stepping in front of him.

Words would not formulate.

Get hold of yourself, Taggert Redbourne. *You are bigger than them.*

He'd been through a war for heaven's sake. What damage could a little old bee do that a bullet or sword couldn't? He inhaled deeply, closing his eyes for a moment to focus on calming his breath.

Bzzzzzz.

Nope.

He handed her the bucket.

"I just remembered that I…uh…" he started as he backed

away from the pit. His shoulders and arms suddenly tingled as if the bees were crawling on him and he shuddered them off in a little dance.

Brenna laughed as she repeated her question. "Are you all right, Mr. Redbourne?"

He couldn't blame her for giggling. He was sure his antics were more than amusing, so he stomped a foot on the ground, forcing himself to stand upright.

"I'm fine," he said with a light squeak to his normally baritone voice, twisting his head to rid his neck of the tickling sensation there.

Seemingly satisfied, Brenna swung the bucket backward to toss the water onto the fire and Tag's eyes opened wide as a single bee flew next to her beautiful face. With only a moment to react and no time to debate, he jumped toward her, his arm swishing through the air in an attempt to deter the creature from harming the lady.

Swoosh.

Cold water slapped Tag in the face, streaming down his cheeks and neck.

Brenna gasped, her hand covering her mouth as she squeaked out a mortified chuckle.

"I. Am. So. Sorry," she breathed.

Tag wiped the length of his face and beard, flicking the excess water onto the ground, staring at her, one eye open. His fear momentarily forgotten, he laughed.

"I needed that."

In a fraction of a second, several bees swarmed lazily around the log pile behind one of the benches and Tag stopped all movement. He must have stirred them when he tossed the Acacia scraps on top of it and the excess water had been the tip of the scales. These bees, however, acted differently than he'd ever seen the insects act before. Slower. Almost like they were inebriated.

"It's the smoke," Brenna said as she moved closer to the

lazy swarm, waving her arms in a slow circle from the newly doused fire to the bees. She must have seen the dread on his face, despite all attempts to conceal it.

"What are you doing?"

"We need to find out which log the hive is in."

"Are you mad? Just how are we supposed to do that?"

"The smoke calms the bees enough that we can be around them without fear of being stung."

"Easier said than done. But, what do you mean, the smoke calms them and how, exactly, do you know that?"

"The smoke makes them think that their home is on fire," she said as she gently picked through the large logs of wood. "Therefore, instead of defending the hive against intruders, they start eating the honey they make in preparation of moving to a new place to live. Just like most of the men I know," she smiled back at him, causing a little flutter in his chest, "they become calm and a little lethargic after such a big meal and therefore, they slow down."

He was impressed.

"My family farm is one of the main sources of honey production to local markets in several surrounding areas of my home. I grew up around bees."

"I grew up around bees too, but never found them to be the friendly type."

Brenna laughed. "Most likely you've not encountered bees, but the nastier hornets or wasps. They are ornery little creatures."

Tag shivered as he remembered the day he and Levi had encountered a black bear swatting at a beehive.

"No. I'm pretty sure they were bees, but that is a conversation for another day."

He and his brother had been quite the adventurers back then and had found themselves stuck indoors slathered in their mother's salve for days until the swelling and redness had gone down on what had seemed like hundreds of stings. It was sad, really, that he was now more scared of the bees than the bears. Not that he would openly admit it.

Brenna glanced at the ends of several logs until she found the one she'd been looking for. She carefully pulled the branch closer to the fire and waved smoke toward the end of it.

Tag was grateful that his new little fire had produced more smoke than flames.

Serendipitous, he thought with a self-satisfied smile.

After a few moments, Brenna picked up the branch with little effort and carried it over to the cluster of beautifully blooming Redbuds at the edge of the yard where a large, felled tree sat away from all the others. The bees followed as if she had bewitched them.

She'd certainly bewitched him.

Brenna set the branch log down near the base of one of the larger trees and walked away, not an ounce of fear, only a grin of satisfaction.

Tag didn't know what to say.

"If you're going to live at Oak Meadow, Mr. Redbourne," she said airily, "you'll have to learn how to coexist with the wildlife."

"Ha. Ha. Very funny." His heart had finally slowed to a respectable rhythm, only to have it skip a beat as she challenged him. For the first time in several minutes, he could think straight. "We should get a move on." He picked up his own empty bucket. "I'd like to see the property while it's still light outside."

"Of course," she said, her brows scrunched together as she glanced down at the object in his hand. "I, uh, just need to run in and change first." Brenna dusted her hands off on her apron and marched past him toward the house.

I wouldn't change a thing.

Stop it, he warred with himself.

Maybe her last name.

It was almost as if he had two voices in his head, warring

with each other. Smart. Fearless. Beautiful. He couldn't deny
that she intrigued him. He raised a brow as he watched her walk
away from him, a slight sway to her hips.

Arggg.

Why was he so preoccupied with her name? It was no secret
that he desired what some of his brothers had found—purpose,
meaning, love—but he barely knew the woman. How could he
possibly even be entertaining the idea of…marrying her? He
knew nothing about her—other than she was a widow who'd
grown up with three brothers and she and her family were
beekeepers. That was hardly enough for him to base a life on.
Though, he argued, he'd known several men who'd married
women they'd never even laid eyes on before—the mail-order
kind—and it had seemed to work out for them.

Well, most of the time.

He brushed a piece of shredded bark from his still wet
shoulder and contemplated whether or not he should change as
well.

"It'll dry," he said aloud, opting to wait.

There would be plenty of time to figure things out later. He
was now living in Serenity Hollow after all. He didn't imagine it
would hurt anything if he got to know the school teacher better
while he worked. What harm could there be?

He took in another deep breath.

He was in trouble.

CHAPTER ELEVEN

Brenna closed the front door and leaned against it, biting her bottom lip with a smile. Tag Redbourne was every inch a man, but somehow, his fear of bees endeared him to her. She pushed off the door and headed for her room. This time, she had no intention of riding uncomfortably in the saddle. She had just the skirt for the occasion. Peter had bought it for her the first week they were married—had said it would make getting around the place easier.

She hadn't had a chance to wear it before he'd been killed, but now seemed like the perfect opportunity and she grabbed a tie from her wardrobe. Even though he'd unwittingly bought the skirt two sizes too big for her at the time, it would be easy to cinch up the waist.

She slipped on the garment and glanced in the mirrored vanity, frowning at her waistline. While she'd expected there to be a significant gap, it now snuggled up against her waistline as if it had been made specifically for her at the size she'd been a few years back. Since Peter's death, she'd put back on a little weight, but until that moment, she hadn't realized just how much.

Mrs. Hamblin, Gemma's mother, kept telling her she was still too skinny and needed to put a little more meat on her bones if she was going to attract another man with any taste. Of course, this came from a woman with ample curves to spare. She had to admit though, she liked the healthy glow in her cheeks and she threw the tie down on the bed, then placed her hands on her hips, and twisted back and forth in the mirror, admiring her reflection.

Brenna's light chuckle quickly turned into a disappointed whimper. While she didn't need, or want another man in her life right now, she couldn't deny how nice it was to have her clothes actually fit her again, instead of draping off her slight form.

How had she not noticed before now?

She squared her shoulders and shook her head. There was no time for vanity right now as Mr. Redbourne was waiting for her.

As Brenna passed by the kitchen, her stomach made an unseemly noise and she realized that she had neglected to eat with the children. Surely, Mr. Redbourne wouldn't mind waiting a few more minutes if she brought food with her. She made quick work of collecting some food stuffs on the counter—a fresh loaf of bread, some currant jelly, a small block of cheese, a short tin of honey-butter, and a knapsack full of candied pecans. As she passed by the blackberries, she had to stop herself from licking her lips. How could she transport them without smashing them? She glanced around the kitchen shelves and spotted a small spice box on the bottom that would do just the trick.

The box had been empty for quite some time, but if she'd thrown away all her containers, the kitchen would have looked quite bare, so she'd been reluctant to get rid of it and had simply put it up for display instead. A couple dozen berries fit nicely inside. She looked at the food on her counter, smiling as she slipped the basket from the hook in the entry and filled it.

By the time Brenna joined him in the stables, Tag already had two horses saddled and ready to ride.

"I hope you don't mind," she said, holding out the basket to him. "I didn't have much supper myself and I thought you might also be hungry, so I packed a few things to eat along the way."

Tag chuckled. "That's mighty kind of you, ma'am," he said, taking the basket and strapping it by the handle to the side of his mount. "I'm not complaining."

She knew he wanted to see the property as soon and as quickly as possible. They'd have to stop somewhere along the way to eat, but from what she'd learned about the man already, she doubted he would protest.

"Fact is, I am a little hungry myself," he said, patting his belly. "I sent the others into town to eat without me at O'Malley's and I'm rightly grateful that fruit jerky won't have to suffice as supper."

Brenna giggled, pleased, then stopped herself. What did it matter if Mr. Redbourne liked her cooking? Just because there weren't many men who would. She had not inherited her mother's talents in the kitchen, but there were a couple of specialty items that she did well.

As much as she hated to admit it, especially in light of their situation, she enjoyed spending time with this man, this stranger who had popped into her life so unexpectedly.

Sadness suddenly filled her heart at the thought of leaving Oak Meadow behind and the new man who owned it.

"Shall we?" Tag asked, holding out the reins to her horse.

"Thank you." She shook the gloomy thoughts from her mind and climbed up onto the mare.

"That's a mighty fine skirt you've got yourself there."

Brenna felt the blush creep into her cheeks at his appraisal. "It's practical."

Tag laughed. "That it is," he said, pulling himself up into his own saddle. "That it is, but I've never seen something so practical look so lovely." He caught her eyes.

She liked the way he looked at her.

"You lead the way, ma'am. I am in your hands."

Brenna clicked her tongue and pulled around toward the creek and the heat in her face deepened at the memory of their first meeting.

Why did he affect her so? Sure, he was handsome and wealthy, but there was something more about him. Something...special.

She breathed in the afternoon air, lifted her face to feel the warmth of the sun beating down on her, and exhaled. She wasn't sure whether she should show him the best parts of the property or the worst, but, somehow, she doubted even the worst parts of Oak Meadow would scare him away from buying the place. She would show him everything.

If they started at the creek, they could work their way leisurely around the rest of the property with plenty of time to stop, eat, and return before nightfall.

Squawk.

Brenna's eyes darted toward the sound.

It appeared that one of the chickens had wandered into the copse of her beautifully blooming redbud trees and had gotten her foot caught between two small branches of a felled log.

"You always let your chickens run loose around here?" Tag asked as he stopped and slipped down off his horse. "Aren't you afraid of attracting coyotes?" He strode over to the distressed hen.

"We don't see too many coyotes around here," she said, pulling her mount around to watch Tag. "But, we do have to watch out for foxes. Usually, they come around after sundown. Jeb gathers the chickens," she glanced up toward the sun, "about now actually, to put them up in the coop for the night. He has put them on a regular feeding schedule that makes it easier for him to collect them."

Tag reached down and gently grasped a hold of the hen's foot. Her wings flapped wildly. Little white and brown-red puffs of feathers flew in every direction. Tag tilted his head to avoid the onslaught of plumages, and before long, he was able to free the chick from the fallen branch. The bird squawked again before quickly strutting back toward the others that had now gathered around the coop.

"Foxes, huh?" Tag asked as he strode back to his mount and stuck a foot in his stirrup. "What other types of wildlife do I need to be aware of?"

A small, particularly fluffy-looking white feather had stuck in his beard, a stark contrast against his dark hair.

"Besides bees, I mean."

Brenna hardly heard the question as she worked to keep the smile from her face. "I'm sorry," she said with a light shake of her head. "Wildlife?" she asked rhetorically. "Uh, we've seen a few black bears and bobcats. There is a family of otters living just upstream from the cove."

Tag pulled his horse around so he was facing her and she found herself staring at the feather trapped in his beard. She could not stop the giggle from bubbling up from her throat.

"You've got," she brushed at the side of her face, "a feather, right here." She again motioned to the section right below her cheek.

Tag scrubbed at his chin and jawline with the back of his fingers, but the down feather remained. He questioned her with a glance, raising his face.

She shook her head.

He opened his palm and ran his hand from his cheeks down the length of his beard and neck, but the fluffy plume had still not budged.

Brenna laughed again, easing her horse closer to his and raising her arm. She reached over to pull the wispy puff from his beard, surprised at the difference in texture there, and hesitated from pulling away.

After lingering a few seconds too long, she held the feather out to show him, but when she mustered the courage to glance up at him, he met her eyes firmly, not looking at the object in her hand, but directly at her. She sucked in a breath, the pit of her stomach becoming like a wind tunnel, almost hollow, but she refused to look away.

"I got it," she said proudly, raising the feather higher into his line of sight.

Tag placed his hand over hers, his warm touch sending gooseflesh up her arms as he pushed down softly until it no longer blocked her view of his face. His gaze locked again on her eyes and he leaned forward. For one inexplicable moment, she thought he might kiss her.

He turned his head and blew the feather from her hand. "Thank you," he whispered with a smile that touched his eyes. His face was so close to hers. She bit her lip, her eyes sweeping shut as she breathed a laugh, relieved, and surprisingly...disappointed.

"You ready?" he said, pulling on his reins and turning his horse about.

"Let's go," she affirmed, her bottom lip curling up between her teeth.

Tag inspected every last inch of the property—the cove, hills, vales, fences, and the small one-room cabin in the woods near the lake, but when they reached the orchard, they stopped.

Brenna gasped as the beauty of it took her breath away. She inhaled deeply the sweet aroma of the magnificent array of delicate pink blossoms. Last spring she'd barely had the energy to leave the house and had not been to the orchard since the blooms had all appeared and she was surprised to see so many of the peach trees still with flowers this late in the season, but the view was awe inspiring.

Tag slid down off his mount and unhooked the basket with their foodstuffs.

"I don't know about you, but I am famished." He held out his hand to help her down from her horse, but the heel of her boot caught in the stirrup and she fell into him.

Hard.

Tag lost his footing and they tumbled backward onto the ground. He shifted enough that he would take the brunt of the fall. She landed face first on top of him.

"Mrs. Scott, if you wanted to get a little closer to me, all you had to do was ask."

She didn't know whether to be amused or offended.

When he chuckled in jest, she decided it would be better to laugh at the situation than curse it. After all, he was very attractive and it had been an innocent mishap.

Tag unexpectedly wrapped his arm around her, rolled her onto her back so that he was to the side of her—their faces once again mere inches apart. Her chest heaved and fell, her heart racing. His eyes moved to her lips, then they closed, his jaw flexing, and he maneuvered himself into a sitting position.

"Seriously, ma'am, are you all right?" he asked, turning onto his knees and looking down at her. "No broken bones?" His brows scrunched together as he moved back enough that she could move.

"I'm fine. My ego may be a little bruised," she said, grateful she'd had the foresight to wear the split skirt, "but I think I'll manage."

He stood up, basket still in hand, and reached down to help her to her feet.

Brenna liked the way her hand felt in his. She took a step toward him and winced a little at the tenderness in her knee.

You're fine, Brenna Scott. Just smile.

Tag nodded at her, seemingly satisfied she would live, then removed the saddle blanket from the back of his horse and spread it on the ground beneath one of the only peach trees in the orchard without any blossoms. It was set apart from the others, but its leaves still provided ample shade against the waning sun. She guessed he'd had enough bees for one day and chuckled softly to herself.

He looked very comfortable in his own skin as he lay back against the blanket, his elbows resting behind him and his ankles crossed as he looked up into the sky.

Brenna glanced upward. They could not have asked for a more beautiful day. Her knee throbbed, but she wasn't about to tell him.

It doesn't hurt. It doesn't hurt, she tried to convince herself as she tested her pain level by attempting to put some weight on that foot.

"Ow," she gasped slightly. "It hurts. It hurts," she breathed quietly.

"What was that?" Tag asked, glancing in her direction.

"What? Oh, nothing. I, um…" She couldn't think what to say, so she just smiled instead. "Nothing," she reaffirmed.

His eyes narrowed at her for a moment before he turned back to look out over the orchard.

She needed to be, or at least appear to be strong—especially under the circumstances. A little thing like a bump on the knee wouldn't deter her. Brenna was glad that Tag no longer watched her. She could walk, limp at least, she just moved a little slower than she would have liked. When she reached the blanket, she gingerly sat down next to him on the blanket and smoothed her skirt around her.

After a few moments, he sat up and folded his arms around his knees, his eyes narrowing at her.

She ground her teeth together, bent on keeping any discomfort from showing on her face.

"Hurts, doesn't it?" he asked casually as he rested his arm on one bent knee.

She looked up at him, searching his eyes. "How?" She shook her head. "How did you know?"

"I've had my fair share of injuries to recognize when someone is trying to hide one. But, you can walk. That's a good sign. Did you twist it when we fell?"

She shook her head. "My knee…hit the ground."

"I'm sure it's just bruised, but I can take a look, if you like."

For some inexplicable reason, Brenna already trusted the man. All sense of propriety aside, she would feel better if she knew that there wasn't a worse problem. The last thing she needed was to be crippled for the next few weeks. Or longer.

"All right," she said softly.

Tag motioned for her to come closer.

She swiveled her legs toward him and planted her feet on the ground, her knees bent, then carefully lifted the wide hemmed section of her split skirt until the result of her injury was exposed. Heat flooded her face.

A large red splotch appeared just beneath the place where her knee bended and it was already starting to swell.

Tag reached up and carefully squeezed the sides of her leg, watching for her reaction. Brenna refrained from flinching as gooseflesh sprung up on her arms and legs at his touch. She buckled her lips together to conceal a cross between a wince and a smile.

The corners of his mouth upturned, but he said nothing.

When his fingers grazed the reddened area, she unwittingly sucked in a little breath and held it. It had been a long time since she'd been physically hurt.

"Good news, professor," he said, "you're going to be fine. It will smart a little for a few days, but it's only bruised. Nothing broken or torn. You should be able to walk on it as much as the pain allows. So, when you're ready..."

Professor?

She smiled, despite herself. "A little pain never hurt anyone, right?"

They both laughed at the contradiction in her words.

"We'll rest for a bit." Tag opened the basket. His eyes widened and a smile graced his beautiful lips. "Well, I'm sorry to say that the jelly didn't make it." He pulled out a broken jar with currant jelly dripping from the edges.

"Is the glass everywhere?" she asked, concerned for the other food.

"Looks like it was a clean break, though there may be a shard or two in the basket." He looked around as if searching for somewhere he could place the jar.

Brenna reached into the basket and pulled out her pecan-filled knapsack. There was a small clump of jelly on one side, but not enough that her plan wouldn't work.

"Untuck your shirt," she instructed.

"Excuse me?" he asked incredulously.

Her face heated again as she unfolded the cloth sack to reveal its contents.

"Ah," he said, obviously better understanding her request. He used his unoccupied hand to pull his shirt from the waistline of his trousers, exposing momentarily his taut midriff.

Brenna's throat went dry. Why hadn't she thought to bring them something to drink?

Tag lifted the corner of his shirt and held it out, creating a dip big enough to hold the candy and Brenna dumped the pecans into the makeshift bowl.

Once empty, she held out her hand for the broken jar. Tag handed it to her and she carefully wrapped it inside of the knapsack. Then, she reached into the basket and pulled out the remaining pieces of jelly encased glass, adding them to the knapsack. Once she was finished, she cleaned her fingers on the edge of the cloth.

"I'd be happy to eat all these pecans, but I'd rather not have the belly ache that would certainly come with it," he said, glancing down at the pecans she'd entrusted in his care.

She laughed, acutely aware of how comfortable she felt around him.

"I have an idea," he said as he stood, careful not to dump the contents of his shirt.

Brenna held up her hands, palms out, unsure whether or not they'd be big enough to hold the delicacy. "Would you like me to take those?" She reasoned that she could always make more if they all fell to the ground. It wasn't like pecans were a commodity of short supply, it just took some work to shell them and add the coating.

Tag laughed warmly. "I appreciate the gesture, but…" he said holding up one of his large hands to hers and tilting to size up the difference, then shaking his head.

Her giggle turned to a light whimper as she smoothed the material of her skirt to hide the split, the movement sending another wave of pain up her entire leg. She breathed in deeply and a smile returned to her face.

"I think my lap will be big enough, don't you?"

Tag watched her for a moment before emptying the contents of his shirt-bowl onto her lap, then he stood and strode over to his mount, digging something from his saddle bag.

"Sometimes it pays to have a father who is interested in every new invention that passes by his desk," he said with amusement, pulling out a few large pieces of folded, thick white paper.

"Your idea is to, what? Write about them?"

"O ye of little faith," he said, quickly turning the paper over one way, then another with creases, tucks, and folds.

Did he just quote the bible? The more she learned about the man, the more she liked him and the more she realized she wanted to know him.

In just moments he had transformed one sheet of paper into a small paperboard box with flaps that folded together to close. Then, he repeated the process with the second sheet. Together, they were large enough to hold all the candied pecans. He held one out to her and she quickly scooped up some of the nuts into her hands and held them over the top. She opened her palms at the bottom until the hole was big enough to allow the treats to fall into the box like a funnel.

"Now, where in the world did you learn to do that?" she asked, astounded at what she had just seen. The box looked like something she could order out of the catalog at Wheatley's Mercantile.

"A traveling salesman sold something like it to my dad, then my mama and sister spent a few weeks figuring out all different alternatives for different looks. I had to help fold a few hundred of these for the Stone Creek Fall Harvest Festival last year and," he shrugged, "well, I guess it stuck."

"And you just happen to carry the paper around with you in your saddle bag?"

"You can use any type of paper, really. I just happened to see some of these in town at the mercantile yesterday. They had been packed in the boxes with some of the produce and Mrs. Wheatley sold them to me. I put them in my saddle bag, but forgot about them until just now. Lucky for us, I guess."

Brenna had a feeling that the man was full of surprises. "Maybe I'll have you make some up so I can sell my pecans at our Founder's Festival in September." Luckily, she had harvested several large crates worth last fall—enough to last well into the winter months.

"I could probably manage." Tag grinned wide as he leaned over to the picnic basket and peeked down inside. "What else you got in there?" he asked, pulling out a tin with some currant jelly residue on the rim.

Brenna reached into the basket for the bread. It had taken her months to perfect her recipe, but now, hers could compete with some of the best in town. She inspected it for any glass. Satisfied it was clean, she ripped off two chunks and handed one to Tag.

"We make a good team. Too bad about the red currant jelly, though," he said, sucking the residue from his fingers. "That's good. Did you make it?" he asked, taking the bread from her.

She wasn't about to tell him that she was generally a disaster in the kitchen, even though there were a few things she did well. Jelly just wasn't one of them.

"Nope," she said truthfully, though she couldn't wait to hear how he felt about the bread. Or the honey-butter for that matter. She'd made both. "The ladies of Serenity Hollow saw to it that I had plenty of preserves and other foodstuffs after…Peter…died."

For the first time in a very long time it didn't hurt to talk about Peter. Truth was, they'd only courted by mail a few months before getting married. She'd up and left her family and everything she'd known for the promise of a brighter future, outside of the honey-making business.

"It must have been hard."

"I'd only been in Serenity Hollow a short while and it took me…time to get back on my feet."

Why was she telling all of this to a perfect stranger? Why did he have to make her feel so at ease?

"But, honestly," she continued, "I barely knew him. After his death, I discovered that I was tougher than I'd ever believed possible. It was hard, but I've been able to make it work. With some help."

"I'm sorry about everything you've lost," he said quietly, slipping his hand along her jawline up until he cradled her face in his palm, his fingers resting gently behind her ear. He lifted her face upward, staring down into her eyes. "You are *so* beautiful. Strong and brave and…"

How could he know what she needed to hear?

"…I am going to do everything I can to make sure you don't lose any more."

She did not waver her eyes from his. Could not peel them away from him as she willed away the tears that threatened.

"Don't say that." Brenna swallowed hard and he dropped his hand from her face. "There is always something to lose. In the last twenty-four hours, I found out that I've lost my home, my school, my life as I know it here in Serenity Hollow." She sat up a little taller, careful not to jostle her knee. "I understand business, Mr. Redbourne. I don't own this place," she motioned to the trees and surrounding land, "nor do I have the means to buy it myself, but…but—"

"You want to stay," Tag finished for her as if knowing her thoughts.

"Yes," she breathed. "Not just for me, but—"

"For the children," he said knowingly.

Did he know how irritating it was that he seemed to know

what she was going to say? She raised a brow and stared at him, her eyes narrowing slightly.

"I've been thinking about our little situation," Tag said, scrubbing his face with the back of his hand, "and I'd like you to stay as well. At least for a while, until I can figure out something of a more permanent nature."

What was he suggesting? She'd thought him a man of integrity, but maybe she'd misjudged him.

"Oh, I couldn't. I…"

"No," he shook his head as if understanding her concern. He cleared his throat and sat up straight, glancing out into the orchard. "I will stay in the bunkhouse with the fellas for now. There will be no impropriety on my part, ma'am, I assure you. My mama taught me better." He broke off a smaller chunk of bread and put it in his mouth.

She stared at him for a good long moment as if being alone together right now at the far edge of the property did not scream impropriety.

"Why would you do that?" she asked quietly, almost as if to herself. "For me?" She shook her head. "I'm sorry, Mr. Redbourne, but you don't know me. You don't know anything about me, so why? Why would you…?"

He swallowed. "I don't know," he answered matter-of-factly, shoving his hand through his too-long hair. "I can't explain it, even to myself—though, believe me," he looked at her meaningfully with a shrug, "I've tried. But, from the moment I met you…" He paused as if searching for the right words. "It's as if I am supposed to…I don't know, protect you somehow. To make sure you're all right."

"I don't need protecting." She returned her bread to the basket, no longer hungry. The last thing she needed was another big brother. She already had three. "You said it yourself, I am a strong woman. I didn't know just how strong until I lost my husband and didn't have my daddy close to fall back on, but I made it through. I'll do it again and not because of your pity or anyone else's. I don't need your charity, Mr. Redbourne."

She considered marching right over to her horse and leaving him here in the orchard to find his own way back, but recognized immediately how childish and impertinent it would be. Besides, with her knee in sorts, she'd probably just end up making a fool of herself anyway.

"You are just as stubborn as I'd expected you to be," he said. Then, taking a deep breath, he offered another solution. "What if I offered you a job in exchange for room and board at Oak Meadow?"

"What kind of job?" she asked, her eyes narrowing in speculation.

"The kind where you *cook* for me and the boys. At least the morning and evening meals."

Cook? She swallowed hard.

"Let me understand you correctly," she said, looking everywhere, but at him. "You're going to let me live at Oak Meadow in exchange for *me*, cooking your food?"

He had to be speaking in jest. Of course, what woman living in the West didn't know how to cook?

This woman, she thought sadly.

"Oh, I'll buy all the supplies, you'll just have to cook them."

Cook them? Panic seeped into her heart.

"Me? Cook? Wouldn't you rather I help train horses or herd cattle?" she asked half-jokingly.

"Can you train horses or herd cattle?" he asked with interest, his brows raised.

"Well, no, but…"

Tag laughed, a deep, rich sound that warmed her insides. "Let's just stick to cooking for now."

"How many men?"

How was she actually considering this? She couldn't cook. Maybe if they wanted a steady diet of candied pecans, fresh bread, and honey-butter.

"Cole and all but one of the others are headed back to Stone

Creek next week with the new herd. There are nine of us right now, but Kade and I will be the only ones staying on, so I figure we'll need to hire another good five or six men to start."

"Eight then, or so," she mused. "And the school?"

"I don't know about that," he said with an edge of humor in his voice. "Apparently, an education around here involves learning how to steal a bathing man's clothes."

She pushed against him.

He laughed loudly.

A moment later, she joined in, despite the heat creeping into her cheeks.

"The classroom is yours until we find a better solution," he said with another chuckle.

"Done," she said, holding out her hand to seal their agreement.

He looked down at her hand, amused, then took it with a firm grip.

"Morning and evening meals every day for you and your men," she said with a raised brow, "in exchange for my room and board, and the school staying open."

Stop! What are you doing?

"Done."

CHAPTER TWELVE

Besotted. The word would not leave Tag's mind.

Brenna's hand fit perfectly in his and he liked the feel of it there.

What had he done?

Though it would be nice to have two home-cooked meals every day, Oak Meadow was going to take a lot more work than a mere six or eight men could handle. Tag figured he'd only have Cole long enough to drive the herd to Serenity Hollow from Austin and maybe a day or two before they headed out, back to Kansas.

The problem was, he knew the team he'd brought along with him from home—their strengths, their weaknesses—and he had no doubts about their abilities. They would be able to get a lot accomplished in the short period of time before they left, but fixing what ailed Oak Meadow would take a lot longer than a few days. Unless his little brother had been able to miraculously find a few hired hands in this small town who needed the work, repairs would take weeks, if not months to handle.

"Bzzzzz."

Tag froze at the sound, his jaw flexed.

Brenna giggled as she made another buzzing sound.

"Very funny," he said, realizing her hand was still encased in his. He released his grip on her. "Sorry."

He looked out over the landscape, appreciating the beauty around him. The orchard was stunning to behold, but on the practical side, just to harvest the fruit from the trees alone would take several workers. Maybe he could hire some day laborers to handle some of the more tedious tasks while the soon-to-be new hired hands managed to finish repairs, build fences, and get the rest of the property back into shape.

The ranch had good bones, and the land was ripe with room for expansion. He had a feeling that a horse ranch like the Redbourne's could prosper in Serenity Hollow, especially considering he'd decided to purchase the land from Grimace. He had plans to speak with Mr. Cranston when they returned from Austin. With the addition of that spread, they would easily be one of, if not the, largest ranch in the area. Cranston's place supposedly had a single structure on site, but he figured they could always build what they needed as they went along. Expansion wasn't about the immediacy of it, but the potential.

At least Serenity Hollow had a blacksmith shop, though he worried about having to have wood transported in from Round Rock and the wheels in his head started to turn. It was time to bring men back to Serenity Hollow and opening a mill would do just the trick.

He had just the man in mind, but it would be a long shot. Eli Whittaker liked his cool Oregon weather. Convincing him to move to Texas would be quite the task.

Brenna held out her hand, palm up. "Please pass me the honey-butter," she said, pulling him from his thoughts of expansion.

"Honey-butter?" he perked up at the idea. "Where?" Visions of Lottie's last batch drizzled over her fried bread had been etched into his memory. His mouth watered as those thoughts rushed to the forefront of his mind.

"The tin," Brenna encouraged with a small jut of her chin.

He picked up the round container he'd pulled from the basket earlier. "This?" he asked, holding it up and inspecting the label. "And here I thought it was molasses candy. That *is* what it says."

She grabbed it before he could pull it out of her reach and she smiled—the best reward he could have hoped for.

"The candy is gone, Mr. Redbourne, but if you'd prefer some horehound over this," she opened the lid and passed it beneath his nose, "then I'm sure I could get you a whole tin of your own."

The container swirled with a combination of light scents. A mixture of something floral and woody at the same time, but the light, creamy purple color was different than any other honey-butter he'd ever seen or tasted.

"Is it made with some of your family's honey?"

"Yes. I brought several jars with me when I left home." She pulled a butter knife from the side of the basket and dipped it into the tin, pulling out a large clump of the delicious-looking concoction and spreading it across the chunk of bread in her hand.

Twigs snapped a distance behind them, sending the birds to the skies, and at an instant Tag was on alert.

A rock dropped in his gut and he immediately reached for his gun, but it wasn't on his belt. He'd left his pistol back at the homestead and his rifle was tucked neatly in the side holster of his mount several feet away. He whipped around to see a small group of men now approaching on horseback and he immediately jumped to his feet, all joviality gone.

"What's wrong?" Brenna asked as her eyes darted from her bread to him, her brows scrunched together.

"Who is that?" he asked, his eyes unwavering from the men.

Brenna groaned as she followed his gaze.

"Tobias Pane," she said, her expression deflated. "He showed up in my classroom yesterday morning before you arrived and said that he had something he needed to talk to me about. I think it had something to do with Peter's death. I don't know how he found us out here."

As the men got closer, Tag recognized them as the ruffians from O'Malley's who'd sat in the corner playing cards. He took a sideways step, casually closing the distance between him and his horse, not taking his eyes off the approaching group.

"What can I do for you, gentlemen?" he asked once they were within ear shot. He ran a hand down his horse's neck while covertly unlatching his gun from the holster.

"I've got business with the lady," the man at the front said before spitting at the ground.

Brenna gingerly got to her feet. "What do you want, Mr. Pane?" she asked, her face pinching against the waning sun.

"Who's your friend there, Brenna?" Pane asked, jutting his chin toward Tag.

"My name is Taggert Redbourne, sir," he said, meeting the man's look of disdain with one of his own. "If you've got business to discuss with Mrs. Scott, I am sure we can meet you in town."

"We?" Pane snorted, then turned his attention back to Brenna. "He speakin' for you now, *Mrs. Scott?*" He and the others chuckled.

As far as Tag could tell, there were only four of them, but even then, he couldn't risk the chance of Brenna getting hurt. He needed to get them away from here, to a place that wasn't quite so secluded.

"A smart man knows everything that happens on his ranch," he told the brute. "I am a smart man, Mr. Pane, and since you are on my land…"

Anger flashed across the man's face and he slowly turned to look at Tag, his eyes squinted, his lip curled in a snarl.

"…I'll ask again," Tag said, his voice strong and bold. "Is there something I can do for you?"

"It sounds like we've got ourselves a little dispute here, boys," Mr. Pane called back to the other three men behind him. "He thinks this is *his* ranch," he said, slapping the chest of the man next to him with the back of his hand.

The gang all laughed raucously as if on cue.

Tag had seen this kind of behavior before and he narrowed his focus. They were definitely trouble.

The lead brute reached into the inner pocket of his jacket and pulled out an old, worn piece of paper with writing too small for Tag to see from a distance. "But, you see," he said with a self-satisfied grin, "Oak Meadow belongs to *me*, Tobias Pane. See for yourself." He extended his arm completely, the paper crinkling beneath his grimy fingers.

"And just what is that supposed to be?" Tag asked with a raised brow. "'Cause I know it's not the deed."

Mr. Pane's eyes fell to slits, his lip curling with disdain. "It's an I.O.U. signed right here," he slammed his finger into the paper, drool from his tobacco slipping from the corner of his mouth, "by Mr. Peter Scott himself."

"That's impossible," Brenna stated emphatically as she took one rushed leap forward, then stopped. "Peter's gone."

Tag took a protective step in front her, his rifle resting easily now in his hand.

"That's the beauty of it, darlin'." Pane spat into the ground. "This note was signed a week before your precious husband done and got himself killed, leaving me the rightful owner of this ranch."

"Peter would never have signed over anything to the likes of you, Mr. Pane, especially this ranch. Why would he? He didn't like you and would have never trusted you to...to..."

"She doesn't even know, does she, boys?" Pane laughed, then looked at Brenna with a gaze as cold as steel.

"Know what?" Brenna's voice held a light tremble.

Tag could hear the indignation, the hurt in her voice.

"Your late husband was a gambler, *Mrs. Scott*," he spat her name with emphasis. "The worst kind. He didn't know when to give up and just kept going. He lost a lot more than just the deed to this ranch." Tobias leaned forward in his saddle, his elbow resting on the horn. "In fact, a few nights before he was killed, he offered *you* as collateral to a certain Mr. Haines on a game of chance. Lucky for you, that was one of the only times he actually won somethin' asides a strong drink and a box of cigareets...a pretty string of pearls, if I remember correctly."

Tag remembered the pearls that had so graciously adorned Brenna's neck on their little jaunt to the Scott home in Round Rock.

"You're lying," Brenna called out, then her voice quieted eerily. "You're lying," she said again in a tone barely above a whisper, the catch in her voice betraying her attempt to convince herself it was a lie.

"If Mr. Scott signed over his ranch to you over a year ago," Tag started, "where is the deed and why have you waited so long to claim it?"

"Out of respect for the dead, uh course. I wasn't in no hurry, but now there's been plenty of time for the Mrs. to grieve and I've come to take over what's rightfully mine. I don't need no deed, I've got this I.O.U."

Tag had to bite back the maddening laughter that threatened to burst from his gut.

"I'm afraid you're going to be disappointed, Mr. Pane. I have a signed contract. Mr. Scott will be turning the genuine deed over to me in a day's time."

"Ain't you heard? Or are you just plum slow? Mr. Scott is dead."

"No," Tag said, willing every last ounce of patience he had to the surface. "Peter Scott is dead. Josiah Scott, the man who actually owns the Oak Meadow, is not."

Pane's face fell.

"You see, Mr. Pane, Peter Scott did not own Oak Meadow. There was no way for him to have lost it to you in a game as you cannot wager something that is not yours. Josiah Scott has signed the full property over to me," Tag stated with a light shrug, "and I'm not looking to sell."

The brute's nostrils flared.

"Oh, and you'd probably like to know that I made Grimace a lucrative offer on his property this morning. I'll be expanding."

Mr. Pane's hand shot to his hip.

Tag's rifle raised and aimed in a blink. "I wouldn't, if I were you. I'm a great shot," he said. "Don't make me show you."

Brenna came up directly behind him, her body pressed closely into him, her hands resting at his hips.

"You're making a huge mistake making an enemy out of me, friend." Tobias Pane raised his hands as if to show he wasn't going for his gun. The man behind him wasn't so smart and pulled his weapon to shoot.

Tag was faster.

The would-be-shooter's shoulder jerked backward as Tag's shot slammed into him. The man managed to remain upright, but his gun dropped from his hand as he slumped forward in his saddle.

"Maybe you're not as good as you think you are, friend. You missed," Pane taunted.

"I'm not looking to kill anyone today," Tag assured him, "but I will defend myself and Mrs. Scott. And, I'm not your friend."

"Dewitt," Pane said, flipping his hand forward as if calling another of the men to arms.

"I wouldn't," Tag cautioned, diverting his aim to the second horseman.

The man looked from Pane to Tag, then dropped his weapon on the ground and raised his hands. "I ain't takin' a bullet for you, Tobias."

"The law is on our side, Pane," Tag tried to reason with the man. "Sounds like you made a fool's bet, sir. Peter Scott did not own this land when he signed over that note to you, so that I.O.U is not even worth the paper it's written on. Let's just call it a day, all right? Your associate there doesn't look so good. I bet he could use a doctor."

Tobias stared him down long and hard, his eyes squinting

and lip twitching several times before he broke away and turned his horse around. "This isn't over, Redbourne," he called back coolly.

"Yes, it is," Tag said under his breath.

He waited until the men were completely out of sight before lowering his weapon. He turned to face Brenna, who jumped backward a step. She looked into his face, then rushed into him, her arms cuddled up in front of her, and she buried her face in his shoulder.

"It's all right, professor," he said, wrapping his arms around her shivering frame. "He's gone now." Tag stroked her hair. "Shhhh," he whispered and placed a light kiss on the top of her head. "He's gone."

Brenna didn't know how long she'd been wrapped in Tag's arms, but she wasn't ready to leave. He was just a stranger to her, but somehow, she felt safe with him.

Trusted him. They fit.

She'd dealt with Tobias Pane before, but had never felt so helpless, so scared of him as she had been today. And the things he'd said about Peter, she just didn't know what to believe. Not that any of it mattered now. Her husband was gone. Oak Meadow belonged to Tag. And she faced the very real possibility that at some point she would have to return to her father's home in Hillsboro. Once Tag had a taste of her cooking, it could be sooner, rather than later.

The folks in Serenity Hollow just did not have the funds to build a new schoolhouse right now and still have enough left over to pay a teacher to run it. What else could she do?

"I need to ride into town to see the sheriff," Tag said as he pulled away from her enough that she could look up into his concerned face. "But, I'll escort you home first. Are you going to be all right?"

She nodded.

Then, the events of the past few minutes washed over her like rain. She did not like how vulnerable and scared she'd felt and she straightened her back and raised her chin as she took a step backward, out of Tag's arms, and brushed off the imagined dirt from the front of her dress.

"I think I'm going to have to learn how to shoot," she said with uncanny clarity in her voice, her words surprising even her.

"One step at a time, professor," Tag said with an appreciative chuckle. He shifted the rifle into his other hand and stepped over to his horse.

He looked back at Brenna, whose hands now rested on her hips.

"I have a feeling you are going to be just fine, Mrs. Brenna Scott. Just fine." He smiled, tipped his hat, and replaced the rifle into his mounted holster. "I'll take you back to the homestead and have Jeb run you a nice, hot bath."

That's laughable, she thought as an unbecoming snort escaped her. She threw a hand up to cover her mouth, her eyes wide.

Jeb wouldn't be caught dead playing maidservant to his sister, heating water over the stove, carrying it to another room, and filling a bath. And besides, the biggest tub they had was a tin washtub they used for laundry. Though, a hot bath did sound wonderful.

"There is a ladies' steam bath house in town," she provided hopefully. "Maybe I could accompany you into Serenity Hollow and stop in there while you speak with the sheriff."

"I'd prefer to know you were safe at home with Jeb and the others."

"A hot soak sounds heavenly, but there's nowhere to get that at home."

"There's not an indoor bathing basin at Oak Meadow?" he asked, obviously surprised at the revelation.

"No."

She'd never even imagined having an indoor bathtub at the homestead, though she'd heard of some of the houses back east having them.

"Do you?" she asked with wonder. "Have an indoor bathtub? Back at your home, I mean…I mean…oh, never mind," she said, feeling a little flustered at their topic of conversation. She rubbed her arms. "I'm not sure how Miss Liza at the bathhouse will feel about my stopping by at this time of night anyway, but it's worth a try if you're willing to take me along."

Tag eyed her a moment as if trying to determine the right course of action.

"We'll still need to stop by the homestead first. There's something I need to collect—just in case Mr. Pane decides to cause trouble."

She imagined he was referring to another weapon.

Tag picked up the cloth with the broken jar and set it carefully inside the basket.

Brenna rushed over to help, noticing that, while her knee still throbbed, the pain no longer stopped her from moving around as she pleased, and she bent down to gather the tin of honey-butter and half-loaf of bread, returning them to the basket. Then, she picked up the two chunks of uneaten bread that had been abandoned when Mr. Pane had so rudely interrupted their repose and she handed one of them to Tag with a shrug. It would probably be dry by now, but it was something to fill their hungry bellies.

"I'm sorry we didn't get to eat much," Tag said, taking the portion of bread from her with a gracious nod and stuffing it into his mouth as he carried the basket and blanket over to the horses.

"There'll be more," she said, hoping to remind him of their agreement.

"I'm counting on it."

Brenna's thoughts turned to the man who'd been shot and

her heart thumped in her chest. What if he died? She stole a glance at Tag as he finished strapping the basket to his horse.

Thank you for keeping him alive, she prayed, realizing just how close he'd come to dying right in front of her.

She'd known him for a whole of two days, but didn't want to imagine a world without him in it. The thought surprised her. Even after months of corresponding and near a month living together under the same roof as husband and wife, she and Peter had still been like strangers, awkward and…polite. So, how could she already feel so close to Tag?

While Pane's brute may have gotten what he deserved, she hoped he wouldn't die. There had been too much death in this town already. She didn't even know the man's name and wondered if he had any family close by.

A light nicker from her horse pulled her from her thoughts.

"I know, girl. Let's get home." The mare had done surprisingly well amidst the ruckus. Most of the horse's she'd been around would have bolted at the sound of a gunshot, but while this horse had pawed at the ground and whinnied uneasily, she'd stayed put.

Gratitude filled Brenna as she reached up to grab the saddle horn. They were lucky that they wouldn't have to walk back to the ranch in the waning hours of sunlight. She situated her foot in the stirrup and attempted to pull herself up into her seat.

Heave.

Nope. Her injured leg was just too weak.

She dropped back onto her supporting leg. Pain throbbed in her knee, but she was determined. She clenched her teeth and tried again.

Heave. Nothing, and her weight returned to her back leg once again. The knee just would not cooperate.

"Here, let me help," Tag said, and without further warning, lifted her from behind and settled her securely in the saddle.

She tried to think of something witty to say, but nothing came. Heat filled her cheeks and her heart raced.

"Thank you," finally spilled from her lips. And that was enough to earn her another glimpse at the dimple that formed whenever he smiled. She couldn't help but wonder what it would look like without the beard.

The quiet ride back to the homestead gave Brenna time to reflect on the last couple of days. Change was inevitable and like she'd taught her students, she needed to embrace it.

The sun had started its descent and she wondered if their trip into town might be better served in the morning. Smoke rose above the house from the back, its pungent pine aroma filling the air, and Brenna guessed that Tag's men had started another fire in the pit.

As she pulled through the gate, she noticed that several of the fences, as well as the large entrance arch, had been repaired. The roof on the bunkhouse no longer had a gaping hole where Tag had fallen through it, and the stable doors were back on their hinges. It amazed her how much work could be done in such a short time with more than one or two sets of hands and a little knowhow.

She followed Tag to the barn where two brand new wagons sat along the side.

"'Bout time you got back," Cole said, jumping to his feet.

"Whoa, little brother," Tag said as he dismounted. "What happened to you?" He stepped forward, reaching up to touch Cole's face.

Brenna couldn't see him very well from her position in the diminishing light. She slid down off her own horse and approached the brothers, the throbbing in her knee increasing with each step. It would probably be best if she could just sit down for a bit.

"It's nothing." Cole pushed Tag's hands away from him. "We had a little trouble in town and the sheriff, here, helped us out." He moved aside and Brenna was surprised to see Sheriff Hunt, his new badge catching an orange glint from the setting sun.

The lawman had just moved to Serenity Hollow a couple of weeks ago and, as Mrs. Wheatley had put it, there were already dozens of women who had flocked to him like he was water in the desert. Looking at him now, she could appreciate the analogy.

"Ma'am," the sheriff said in greeting, tipping his hat in her direction.

"It's nice to see you again, Sheriff." They'd only met briefly, once before, when he'd first moved to town, but she hadn't had much of a chance to get to know him. "I'm glad you're here. We were just stopping home to collect something before coming into town to find you. You've saved us the trip." She turned to Tag. "And me a visit to Miss Liza's." The heat of her blush creeped up her neck. Her mother would have had a heyday with her newly brazen speech. While she regretted not being able to soak in a hot bath, she was grateful to be spared the trip into town.

Tag handed his reins to the new foreman who'd appeared from nowhere.

"Kade will take care of your mount," he motioned for her to follow suit. "We have much to discuss with the sheriff."

Brenna handed the leather straps to the man who then led both horses toward the stable.

We? It felt good to be included—especially under the circumstances. Peter had always wanted to handle everything to do with the ranch's affairs himself. And, as she was learning, he'd left her out of a whole lot more than that.

"Sheriff," Tag said as he reached out to shake the lawman's hand, "I'm Taggert Redbourne, the new owner here at Oak Meadow. While I'm very interested in what happened in town," he shot a meaningful glance at his brother, "I'd like to discuss Tobias Pane and an incident out at my orchard."

Brenna breathed in deeply.

His orchard.

She exhaled, blowing a strand of hair out of her face. Her knee throbbed and aside from feeling a little overwrought at having watched a man shot in front of her, she'd felt like she was handling the situation better than she ever would have expected.

"You coming?" Tag asked as he held out a hand to her.

She took a step. Pain shot up her leg and a very unpretty noise escaped her lips. She froze.

Tag's brows scrunched together and he was at her side in a moment.

"Why don't you just sit by the fire and rest for a few minutes," he placed a finger under her chin, raising her face to look at him. "I'll be back in a minute."

Brenna nodded.

"Everything all right, Mrs. Scott?" the sheriff asked.

She peeled her eyes from Tag's.

"Just a little bruise, Sheriff. Nothing to worry about." She mustered a smile.

Before she could protest, Tag swept her up into his arms, carried her over to the fire, and set her down on the log next to her brother.

Heat again flooded her neck and face. She could feel her brother's stare boring into the side of her head.

Tag and the others walked toward the barn and stopped just out of earshot.

It wasn't like Oak Meadow was her place any longer and she tried to convince herself that she didn't really need to be there to listen when they talked about Tobias Pane or anything else to do with the ranch.

Her brother leaned into her. "You'll never guess what happened," Jeb said in an excited whisper.

The low rumble of voices coming from the barn drew her attention back to the men speaking there, and she watched as the foreman slipped back out of the stable to join them. She wished she could hear what they were saying. Why hadn't she told Tag she wanted to join them, tired or not? In pain or not.

It didn't matter that she didn't own the place, whatever they decided did concern her, but for now, she had to be content just to sit.

"Brenna? Bren?"

"What, Jeb?" she asked, a slight edge in her voice that she regretted immediately. With some effort, she pulled her gaze from the men to focus on her brother. "What? What happened?" she asked, resigned…for the moment.

"You should have seen him in action. While we were at the wainwright's place looking to purchase a couple of wagons, one of that Pane fella's cronies came in and threatened Mr. Bledell."

Brenna's ears perked at the mention of Tobias Pane.

"After we'd looked over all the wagons he had for sale, the brute barged into the barn and told Mr. Bledell that all of the wagons in his shop were already spoken for and that he'd better not sell them to anyone else. And, he said it all right in front of Cole."

She glanced over at the wagons near the barn.

"I know," Jeb said, following her gaze. "Those Redbournes are a tough breed. They aren't intimidated easily."

So she'd learned.

Her eyes trailed from the wagons to rest on Tag. His muscular frame was outlined by the vivid streaks of orange and purple that now traced the horizon and she exhaled strongly.

"When Cole told him which of the wagons he wanted, Pane's brute stepped up behind Mr. Bledell, held a gun at his side, and said that maybe he didn't hear so good. Then he challenged him outright to a gunfight. Right there in the shop."

"Challenged who? Mr. Bledell?" Brenna's full attention focused on her brother.

"No. Cole," Jeb said with vigor, shifting in his seat and clenching his fists. "Aren't you listening? And then guess what he did. Cole. Guess what Cole did. Just guess."

"Shot the man," Brenna said, half-jokingly, but all of a

sudden, she didn't feel very good.

"No," Jeb said, shaking his head with a confused expression on his face. "Of course not." His brows raised. "In fact, he took off his gun belt and handed it to Kade, the new foreman, and told the man they'd settle it with their fists and that if the man was good enough to beat him fair and square, he would give him a thousand dollars and would walk away without buying any of the wagons."

A thousand dollars? She'd known the Redbournes had money, but...a thousand dollars? Over a brawl? Who did that?

"So, what happened?" she asked with growing interest.

"They went outside into the middle of the street. A crowd quickly gathered around them—mostly women and these fellas," he gestured toward the men Tag had brought with him from Kansas, "and we all watched as the both of them engaged in the fiercest of battles." He threw his arms out wide and spread his hand across the air as if recounting a grand tale.

Brenna rolled her eyes at her brother's description.

"The brute got in a couple of good punches. Have you seen Cole's eye?" Jeb winced and touched his own face. "Anyway, after only a minute or two, Cole had the man pinned to the ground beneath him, one arm twisted behind his back. It was about that time the sheriff broke through the crowd, gun drawn. He shot the ground next to the thug's unpinned hand." Jeb faced the fire, but continued to speak. "Cole raised his hands," he said, imitating the actions, "and rose to his feet. When the sheriff pulled the brute from the ground, he relieved the man of a little six-shooter that had been hiding in his sleeve, unbeknownst to Cole or the rest of us. The cheating b—," he looked at her, cleared his throat, and cut it short when she raised a brow at him. "*He*," he corrected, "would have killed Cole, right there in the middle of town."

"Lucky the sheriff was there."

"I'll say. That's why Cole bought two whole pies from O'Malley's and invited the sheriff back to the house for a slice."

Jeb turned back to look at her. "Though, a thousand dollars, Bren. Can you believe it? A thousand for a fight. Too bad we're heading back to Hillsboro soon. I would imagine life at Oak Meadow isn't going to be at all dull now. Not with them around." He pulled a chunk of dried meat from his pocket and took a large bite.

"And it's dull now, with me?"

Jeb shrugged. "How was your tour?"

"Let's just say, there's no question Mr. Redbourne is buying the ranch."

How was she going to tell Jeb that he'd come all this way for nothing? Best just to say it. Outright.

"And...I'm not going back to Hillsboro with you." She spat out the last as quickly as possible, then held her breath, waiting for his response.

"What do you mean, you're not coming back?" Jeb asked incredulously. "Where are you going? I mean, it's not like you can stay here. How will you provide for yourself? From the sounds of it, you don't have a school to teach in—not that they pay you much of anything to teach in this little town." He turned a narrowed eye on her. "You're not fixing to be one of them mail-order-brides now or nothing, are ya?"

"One of *those* mail-order-brides," she corrected. "And, no. I have no intention of getting married again anytime soon. Maybe never. Mr. Redbourne has offered me a position to stay on at the ranch...as his cook."

Jeb burst forward with a loud guffaw, slapped his knee, and settled back onto the log with another hearty chuckle as he looked at her, then sobered almost immediately. "Oh," he said, the smile dripping off his face, "you're serious."

She nodded.

"He know you can't cook?"

"Well, I..."

"You ain't done told him." Jeb laughed again.

"Jebbediah Mallory, you are speaking like a scroungy

backwoodsman who hasn't had the privilege of any amount of education. You sound like a buffoon." Her already hot cheeks flared both from the accuracy of his words and the irritation at her brother's lazy vocabulary.

"I guess if he is going to live on bread alone…" he annunciated every word.

She hit him in the arm.

"Seriously, sis, your bread is," he glanced at her, "quite enjoyable, especially with some of that blackberry honey-butter, and I'd eat your candied pecans all day long. I'm sure you would do fine with a little learning—*if* you were staying."

"I *am* staying."

Gravel crunched behind them. Brenna whipped around into a standing position to meet Tag, the sheriff, Cole, and Kade face to face as they approached.

"Thank you, Sheriff," Tag said, patting the lawman on the back. "Seems we've all got our work cut out for us."

"I'm glad I can count on you folks to stand up to Mr. Pane. I was sent here to clean up the riffraff, and maybe with you around too, he'll decide this little town isn't worth the effort and move along on his own."

"Don't count on it," Brenna whispered under her breath. She'd known Tobias Pane too long to believe he would give up without a fight.

Tag shot her an inquiring look, but she glanced away.

"I'm heading out to Austin on Saturday," he said. "I've got livestock to purchase and collect, so I'll be gone the better half of the weekend, but I should return first thing Monday morning. In the meantime, let me know if there is anything you need me to do," he said, extending his hand to the sheriff.

"I appreciate you letting me know about your run-in with Pane and his associates, and for giving me your side of the story. Who knows what cockamamie tale he'll come up with. From what I've already learned about Tobias Pane, he does not take kindly to anyone who goes against him. So, be careful." Sheriff

Hunt turned to look at Brenna. "Sounds like you had quite a scare today, ma'am. I'm glad to see it hasn't sent you running for the hills. We need women like you in this town, Mrs. Scott. And, from what I hear, you'll be staying on a while as teacher."

Brenna nodded, pleased that someone recognized the importance of having a school in Serenity Hollow.

"Redbourne, I'll let you know when Pane and his men come back into town."

"I appreciate that, Sheriff. With a direct hit in the shoulder like that, I can't imagine they'll stay away very long. He'll need to see the doc sooner rather than later, though I imagine it'll be a long while before he shoots another gun. I still can't shake the feeling that something is going to happen. There is something off about that set."

"I'm just glad that Mrs. Scott, here, wasn't out there alone. I hate to think of what could have happened."

Brenna shivered at the thought.

"It'll sure be nice to have the likes of you around town. Ever considered a job change?' the sheriff asked with a grin.

"Afraid not. I've got two brothers who've chosen that path—a bounty hunter and a deputy sheriff—but working with horses is where I'm meant to be."

"Well, all right then, best be going before it's too dark to find my way home." Sheriff Hunt turned to Brenna and winked. "Ma'am, it's been a real pleasure," he said with a warm smile.

Her heart did a little flutter. He would certainly not have any problem finding a wife here.

"Cole, thanks for the pie. Tag, we'll be seeing you around. And, like I said, I've had my fair share of experience working with horses, so if you need any help..." He shook their respective hands and headed for the stable where Brenna guessed he'd left his mount.

They all stood there a moment, the silence deafening.

"I'm heading back in to see to those horses," Kade said, excusing himself with a tip of his hat.

"And, I have some pie to finish," Cole said with a semi-apologetic smile.

"Mrs. Scott, I—"

"It's been a long day," she cut Tag off, worried he might take back his offer after what had happened. "I think I'm going to turn in for the night." She stood, fighting back the whimper that threatened as pain sliced up her leg.

He closed his mouth and nodded. "Goodnight," he said, rocking back and forth on his heels.

"Goodnight." She wrapped her arms around herself and took a step toward the house.

Tag started forward, opening his mouth to speak, but closed it again when Jeb took ahold of her arm and draped it over his shoulders as he helped her to the stairs.

"Things will look better after a good night's sleep," she whispered to herself.

When they reached the top step of the porch, she turned back just as the men started to sing again around the fire.

"Thanks, Jeb," she said quietly.

"You gonna be all right?" he asked, concern lacing his brows. "What happened exactly?"

"I fell. That's all. I should be fine by morning." She managed a meager smile.

"Night, sis," he said as he turned back around to join the others by the fire.

Brenna wrapped an arm around the rail post and leaned forward, her eyes drawn to the man who'd been her protector in every sense of the word today. Tag settled back against the fence rail, his arms and ankles folded in front of him. He exuded strength, but she'd been one of a lucky few she guessed who'd witnessed first-hand his vulnerability, his tenderness.

Maybe 'never' had been too strong of a word before.

Someday.

That was better.

CHAPTER THIRTEEN

Three a.m. and sleep still eluded him. Tag turned over in his bedroll, determined to order some beds for the bunkhouse before he left for Austin on Saturday morning.

It had been a long time since he'd shot a man. The sickening sound of bullets piercing flesh and the acrid stench of blood still haunted him after all these years, but when the man had drawn his weapon this afternoon, all he could think was to protect the woman whose hazel eyes, strong demeanor, and easy smile had bewitched him.

He could still hear the man's grunt of pain ringing in his ears, could still see him collapsing forward with groans of agony. Tag scrunched his eyes tighter, willing the images and sounds to leave him in peace.

The hoot of an owl brought calm to the chaos of his mind and he sat up. The early morning hours held a chill, but he needed some fresh air. He tugged on his boots, reached for the quilt his mother had given him before he'd left home, and wrapped it snugly around his shoulders before stepping outside, careful not to let the edges touch the ground.

He breathed in deeply, the images from his dreams dissipating with the breeze. The crisp morning air was just what he needed. As he glanced across the landscape, he smiled. This land was his. It took a moment for the thought to truly sink in.

The breathtaking view filled him with awe. The moon

looked bigger than he'd remembered it on previous runs through Texas. Crickets chirped, frogs croaked, and Cole's snores could still be heard even outside the bunkhouse. He chuckled quietly to himself.

The gentle creak of the porch swing drew his attention to the house.

It took a moment for his eyes to adjust to the darkness of the early morning, but as he got closer, he saw Brenna sitting with one knee clutched in her arms, the other resting on the swing, and a blanket wrapped around her slight form.

He made his way to the porch.

"You couldn't sleep either?" he asked quietly from the bottom step.

She sucked in a quick breath and sat up taller in the swing. "Taggert Redbourne, you startled me," she said, her hand clutched around the blanket at her heart as she took another breath. Her legs dropped in front of her, the wince of pain obvious, even though she'd tried to hide it.

"Sorry," he said sincerely, climbing the front steps. "May I?" he asked, motioning to the empty space now next to her on the swing.

"Please."

The pins had been pulled from her hair and it cascaded down one shoulder. He wondered if it was as soft as it looked, but restrained himself from finding out. The moon's light glinted off her darkened honey colored locks and illuminated her creamy skin.

Brenna Scott was simply beautiful.

Tag pulled the quilt from his shoulders and sat down next to her. The chains protested under his weight, but once he was sure they would hold, he laid his mother's quilt over his lap and rested an arm behind Brenna on the seat.

"Are you doing all right?" he asked quietly.

Brenna took a deep breath in and released it, then nodded. "Life was pretty simple before I met you." She spoke, face-forward, a light catch in her voice. "I had a home of my own, a schoolhouse to teach in, a sense of safety, and just about all the pecans a girl could ever want." She laughed softly.

Tag looked out at the several pecan trees that dotted the front yard of the house in the shadows.

"Now, my life has been turned completely upside down and, yet, I feel strangely calm about it." She turned to look at him. "Would you believe that I'm actually worried about the man who was shot today?"

Tag's appreciation for the woman grew exponentially with her admission.

"Me too."

"Really?" she asked, searching his face.

"Really."

Brenna smiled softly. "I mean, I know he was trying to hurt…us, but I think God loves all his children. Even creatures like Tobias Pane and his associates."

Tag breathed an amused laugh at her choice of words and he pondered them for a moment. "I didn't *want* to shoot him, you know."

"I know. You did what you had to. I'm mighty grateful. If you hadn't been there, I don't know what would have happened, but it scares me to even think about." She shivered. "I'd like to say I would have done the same, but I'm afraid I wasn't kidding about those lessons. I never did learn how to use a gun. My daddy said that was for the menfolk."

"Not in my family." He leaned closer to her for a moment. "I would never admit it to her face, but I think my sister, Hannah, is a better shot than most of us boys."

"No," she said, disbelievingly.

"Yep. My dad made sure she could take care of herself—especially with seven older brothers to pick on her." He laughed. "He made her work as hard around the ranch as the rest of us too. Well, almost. She's not only daddy's little girl, but our baby sister, and there is nothing any of us wouldn't do to protect her."

"Wait, did you say seven? Boys?" she asked followed by the long whew.

"Yep."

"You must have an incredible mother. Patient at least."

"The best."

A comfortable silence passed between them for a time.

"After we lost Billy in the war," Brenna said, her voice soft, "our family wasn't quite ever the same. Daddy became extra protective of me. He didn't like Peter much and certainly didn't approve of us getting married, but I thought I knew what was going to be best for me. He didn't understand why I didn't want to spend my life raising bees and selling honey. Don't get me wrong," she said with a light smile, "it's an honorable profession, it just wasn't what I wanted to do. I was lucky, though, that he allowed me to attend university. Most of the girls in our little town didn't get that chance and ended up tending children or doing somebody else's wash." She pushed against the floorboard with her feet to move the swing in an easy sway.

"Ow," she said, almost apologetically. After a moment, she continued. "It hurt him when I moved to Serenity Hollow. My father, I mean."

Tag wasn't sure what to say. He hadn't expected her to open up to him so freely.

"I'm sorry about your brother."

"It was hard…" she opened her mouth as if to say more, but the words never came and she closed it again.

The Redbourne family had been luckier than most. William, Ethan, and Cole had been too young to fight, but even though Raine, Rafe, Levi, and himself had been of age, they'd been fortunate to walk away with only a few scars and the damage done to their souls. None of them talked much about that time.

"Your pa sounds like a good man. Trying to look out for the best interests of his little girl."

"Oh, he is. But, Daddy doesn't think it proper for me to

stay here, away from family, without a husband. That's why Jeb's here—to take me home."

"Then why do you want to stay?" Tag liked listening to her talk about herself and hearing stories about her family. "Besides the children, of course" he added, knowing that was a big draw for her to remain in Serenity Hollow.

She thought for a moment. "Most of all, I think it's the independence. I like living my life the way that I see fit and not the way anybody else wants me to live it."

"I can see that about you."

She glanced up at him. "I know it's optimistic for a woman to believe she can make her own choices in life, but here, I can. At least I could." She shook her head. "I'm sorry. Listen to me go on about nothing. Sleeping on the ground out in the bunkhouse can't be comfortable for you." She eluded to the reason she probably thought he was awake in the middle of the night.

"At least there are straight floor boards in there. It's better than sleeping on a bed full of rocks of various shapes and sizes and mounds and valleys of uneven dirt along the trail. I will say, though, I'm riding into town first thing Saturday to order a bunkhouse full of proper beds. I need hands whose backs aren't so sore from sleeping that they can't get any work done."

He smiled when Brenna giggled.

"I have to admit, I kind of miss my room back home at Redbourne Ranch. It wasn't anything if not cozy. And my bed…" Heat crept up the back of Tag's neck as he realized their topic of conversation had moved beyond what was proper. "Excuse me," he said, clearing his throat.

"I wish things could be different," she said apologetically.

"Do you?" He couldn't help himself.

"I mean, if you were my *brother*, you wouldn't have to sleep out there."

"Do you think of me like your brother?" He really wanted to know.

She turned to look at him, her eyes glittering with moonlight.

"No," she said, shaking her head. "Not at all." Her bottom lip folded beneath her teeth, her eyes not wavering from his.

"That's good," he said in a low voice, a smile dancing on his lips. He winked at her with an approving nod.

"Why, Taggert Redbourne, are you flirting with me?"

"Yes, ma'am."

She smiled broadly, but turned to face forward. "Good."

Tag's insides felt like caged butterflies trying not to get stuck in pools of red currant jelly. It had been a long time since he'd felt something real for a woman.

Too long.

Of course, the last time was over Miss Henderson who taught him in the fifth grade at the Stone Creek school. Maybe he just had a thing for school teachers.

A light breeze blew through the trees and up onto the porch, catching Brenna's hair. She pulled her little blanket closer around her, but her hunched shoulders and shivering lips told Tag that she was still cold.

"There's still time to get a little shut-eye if you'd like to turn in," he said.

"Just a little while longer?" she asked in a light plea, glancing up and catching his eyes with hers. "It is getting a little chillier, though. Maybe I'll just run in and grab another blanket."

Tag held open his quilt, inviting her to share. To the devil with propriety. There was no one out here to judge them for sharing a swing and, by dang it, he was a gentleman.

She still held his gaze for another moment before sliding closer, snuggling up against him, and resting her head in the nook between his chest and shoulder. It was as if she'd been made to fit perfectly into that spot. He dropped his hand onto the top of her arm and rubbed briskly for a moment, trying to warm her. Then, with a light squeeze he returned his hand to the back of the swing.

This had to be what heaven was like.

Brenna awoke to the sound of hammers pounding against wood. She opened one eye, then the other.

"Did you sleep out here all night?"

She looked up to see Jeb standing over her with a steaming mug of what she hoped was hot apple cider and a slice of bread, smothered in blackberry honey-butter. Tag was nowhere to be seen, but he'd left his quilt behind. She squelched the trickle of disappointment that wove through her chest.

"Jeb, I think you're picking up a thing or two from these Redbournes." She took a sip of the warm liquid. She smiled softly. "You know me well, my dear brother. Thank you."

After tossing and turning in her bed last night, she'd taken sanctuary on the porch. It had been a happy coincidence that Tag had struggled with the same inability to sleep and had joined her on the swing.

She smiled, remembering how her sense of impropriety had been thrown out the window with the warmth and comfort he'd provided as she'd snuggled into him. It was no wonder that she'd fallen asleep on the swing in his arms. She felt safe there. She pulled Tag's quilt up to nestle around her waist and took another sip of her cider.

"We need to talk about this cooking thing," Jeb said, all amusement gone.

This was the first time in a long time that her brother had sounded so serious.

"It's hard to keep a straight face, isn't it?" she asked when she noticed his lips twitch as he tried to conceal his amusement. "Well, a girl can learn to cook, Jebbediah, and I don't want to go home. I realized that I've come to appreciate the independence that I have here. We'll find a way to build a new schoolhouse and once the townsfolk are able to start paying another teacher, I'll eventually have enough that I can get a small place of my own. Cooking is just a way to make do for now."

"You're not foolin' anybody, sis. I can see the way you and Tag look at each other."

"What do you mean?"

"I know you said you ain't ready to get married again."

"Aren't ready," she corrected with a smile, eliciting pursed lips, a clenched jaw, and a narrowed stare from Jeb.

"But, well," he continued, "maybe you should."

"Should what?" Tag asked as he hopped up the porch steps.

Brenna sat up straight, her fingers self-consciously combing through her hair, her lip catching between her teeth.

OUCH! She squealed inside her head.

She'd moved without thinking and pain shot up again through her leg. Hopefully, it wouldn't be long before she could walk, or even move, without the discomfort.

Jeb threw a wide-eyed glance in her direction. "Should, uh…"

She could see the wheels turning in her brother's head.

"He was just saying that he thinks I should…sell some of my candied pecans in town."

"Good thinking, Jeb," Tag agreed. "I'd have to second that. I don't know that I've ever had some quite as tasty."

Suddenly, she was afraid to look at him, afraid of what she might see in his face. Maybe she'd imagined their connection last night. Maybe he'd believed her to be too brazen. Too familiar. Would she see disappointment? A loss of respect?

"Mrs. Scott," Tag said in a voice that would melt butter, "I'm heading into town to buy," he cleared his throat, "furniture for the bunkhouse, and wondered if you might like to accompany me."

Her eyes flitted upward, but unlike anything she had expected, what she saw there mirrored her own feelings…inexplicable, undeniable hope. She folded her lips together and gingerly stood up.

"What time is it?" she asked, her eyes widening. "The children will be here any moment. I'm sorry, Mr. Redbourne, I wish I could, but…"

"The children need a teacher," he finished for her with a nod of understanding.

Jeb cleared his own throat and stood next to her. "Yes, well, I've got chickens to attend to," he said before hopping down from the porch.

Breakfast. Oh, no!

She shoved the blackberry buttered bread toward Tag. "Have you eaten?"

"Nothing that smells or looks as good as this," he said, raising the food to his mouth.

Brenna found herself holding her breath as he took a bite.

"Delicious," he said through a mouthful. "Sorry." He wiped the back of his hand across his face. "I think I made the right choice hiring you." He winked.

Guilt edged its way into her heart. She was sure she could get some of the ladies from town to teach her a few things, but doubted she'd ever be as good of a cook as any of them.

"Mr. Redbourne, you probably should know tha—"

"Tag," Kade yelled as he rode up next to the house astride a brown and white paint mount. "Wild herd. Just over the ridge. Figured you'd want to come along."

"I'll be back," Tag said, bending down and placing a light kiss on her cheek before jumping from the porch at a run toward the stables.

Brenna reached up to her cheek, shocked at the unexpected display of affection. She watched Tag disappear into the stable only to emerge moments later astride one of the taller quarter horses, galloping a few yards behind the new foreman.

She breathed a happy chuckle as she folded up the quilt and headed into the house to change her clothes, quaff her hair, and prepare to meet the children.

CHAPTER FOURTEEN

He'd kissed her.

On the cheek.

But Tag could not get the thought of her beautiful mouth out of his mind.

What had he been thinking?

Wild horses, that's what. He'd been so caught up in the excitement that he'd actually kissed the unsuspecting beautiful young widow. It had seemed so natural. It amazed him how comfortable he felt around the woman and he could appreciate a small glimmer of what some of his brothers had experienced.

I'd like to call on her, he thought to himself as they rode out to the last area where the wild horses had been spotted. Once he realized the truth of that thought, he decided that as soon as he returned, he would ask Jeb permission to court his sister. Maybe he should write a letter to her father in Hillsboro. Maybe he should ride up there and ask him in person. Maybe—

"There they go," Cole yelled, pointing at a distant copse of trees at the edge of the flat, rolling hillside.

All thoughts of courtship fell back.

Tag loved mustangs. He was thrilled that the wild horses were venturing onto his land. He grabbed onto his reins, hunched low, and broke his stride into the direction Cole had indicated. His heart sped. His anticipation grew as he glided over the countryside.

The chase lasted hours before Tag finally relented to the fact it wasn't going to happen today. The animals were just too far ahead of them and more familiar with the area for his crew to gain any advantage.

He pulled his mount to a stop and sat back in his saddle. The river of horses flowed across the landscape in a methodic dance of rhythm and motion. The morning mist, still hovering lightly over the ground, added an air of enchantment. Tag breathed in deeply, both awed and inspired.

Their strength, power, unity—it was a sight to behold—one not many had the opportunity to appreciate and he reveled in the moment.

"Next time," Cole said in consolation as he pulled up alongside Tag. "But, aren't they beautiful? I can hardly believe we've been here less than a week and here they are." He looked out over the valley, watching the mustangs. "You just don't see herds like that in Kansas anymore."

"Looks like one of your paintings," Tag said, remembering one of Cole's art pieces hanging on the living room wall at Redbourne Ranch.

"Sure wish I had some paints, but I'll sketch it out before we leave. You remember Sophronia, the waitress from O'Malley's?"

How could he forget?

"She said that there are only a few wild herds left around Serenity Hollow and some ranchers prefer it that way. Most folks went months before they even laid eyes on them, let alone run practically alongside them like we've been doing all morning."

"Sorry, boss," Kade said as he approached from the south, a thick layer of dust covering his face and clothes. "It just took us too long to get out there this morning. They were too far ahead to begin with."

"I doubt that's the last we've seen of them." Tag clicked his tongue and pulled on his reins. "It's probably for the best anyway. There is still quite a bit of work to do before we take on a whole unexpected herd. We'll barely have room for those we're picking up tomorrow. Until we can get a new stable built and a few more corrals, we'll just have to be patient."

Patience was not something Tag came by naturally.

Kade whistled and motioned for the others to join them.

Tag hadn't realized how far they'd gone and wondered if they were still on his property. He determined that he would need to take the time to figure out the boundaries, but if he could purchase the surrounding properties, it would make it much easier and he made a mental note to speak with the neighbors.

Unlike other wranglers, Tag took a different approach to taming horses. His brother, Rafe, had lived among the Pawnee. He'd learned and refined an old Indian method from them based on common respect, trust, and mutual understanding instead of the more common methods that used fear and dominance to break the horse's spirit. That was the last thing he wanted to do. He loved horses and appreciated their different personalities.

With the purchase of a new herd, he would have his work cut out for him. It was not uncommon for Tag to have a mustang or bucking pony ready for the saddle within a day or two instead of the weeks or months it often took others. His less aggressive style worked well for him and over the years he'd gained a reputation for gentling the wildest of horses.

CRACK!

A shot rang through the air and at close range.

Tag reached for his gun, which after yesterday's incident, sat reliably at his hip. His heart sank when one of the mustangs fell hard against the ground, causing several others to stumble around him. And within a few minutes, the horses disappeared completely behind the tree line.

"Who fired that shot?" Tag demanded, pulling his horse in circles as he scanned his surroundings for the offender. It had not come from one of his men, so who?

The land was mostly flat with a few easy rolling hills, but this part of the land had an abundance of trees along the river and whoever had fired that shot was cleverly hidden out of sight.

"Be on alert, boys. Stay low. Harvey, Ben, you take the north ridge," he directed, two fingers together, pointing at the rock formation to his right.

They both nodded.

"Hector, take Cook and the others and head to the south side of that tree line. Work inward and converge in the middle. We'll truss 'em out."

Hector whooped, raising a hand above his head in a circular motion while turning his mount toward the trees. The rest of the men, including Cook, followed, and within moments they'd all gone their separate directions, leaving only Cole and the foreman with Tag.

"Kade," he said, turning to the only man who'd be staying on with him in Texas, "ride on back to Oak Meadow. If there is going to be trouble, I don't want Mrs. Scott or the ranch left unprotected."

Jeb should still be there, but he wouldn't be prepared for an assault. Tag felt better having someone he knew and trusted, who could handle himself in a situation, even if it was only a precaution.

The foreman tipped his hat and started for the ranch.

"Cole, you and I are going to check on that horse."

As they began riding toward the downed mustang, a horse unlike Tag had ever seen before appeared through the thicket, its head low and swaying. It gingerly made its way toward the fallen wild roan, which started twisting and turning in an attempt to get up.

It's alive!

Tag's heart skipped a beat, but until he could get a better look at the horse, he didn't know whether or not it would survive for long. It was cast on its back, legs in the air. It had fallen into a small depressed area of unlevel ground and was up against a ridge tall enough that it was unable to stand. The mustang wouldn't last long in that position, injured or not.

"Hold up," Tag whispered loud enough that Cole could hear, but not so much as to startle the wild horses.

Their well-trained mounts remained at ease while they waited and watched the beautiful uninjured mustang as it snorted and sniffed its friend, shaking its head with an occasional whinny.

Tag slid down from his horse slowly. He needed to get to the injured animal and get it righted or it would not survive long. He retrieved the canteen from his saddle bag and strapped it over his shoulder, then pulled out a small tin full of his mother's white healing poultice and slipped it into his pocket.

"Get your rope ready," he told Cole.

"What are you doing?" his brother asked quietly out of the corner of his mouth.

"I'm going to need your help. I can't get the horse turned over by myself." Tag handed Cole his reins. "Give me a minute." He held up his hands and slowly walked through the tall grasses toward the mustangs. Once he was within a few yards, he stopped and waited, his hands raised in the air, palms out. He met the horse's eyes and held them as he lowered himself to the ground and sat cross-legged, still watching.

After some time, it seemed that the horse recognized that he was trying to help and it backed away enough to let Tag know it was watching him, but not too far.

Common sense and a little visual inspection confirmed that both horses were female. From the protective nature of the uninjured animal, he guessed she was this one's dam—though he had seen some strong bonding relationships between other unrelated horses he'd worked with in the past. If she were the dam, it would explain why she had strayed from the herd to come back for the younger one. Even still, it was a little odd for a mustang to be so loyal with a filly nearing the age of maturity.

Tag rose to his feet and turned very slowly, motioning for Cole to join him—pushing down the air in front of him to show his brother to proceed gingerly. Then, slow step by slow step he made his way over to the injured animal, coaxing her softly with his words. Her ears were cocked backward, the tension and apprehension obvious in the young mustang's demeanor.

With both hands raised, Tag gently lay his hands on the horse's side and ran them the length of her, allowing the creature time to adjust to his scent and acclimate to his presence while visually examining the obvious wound sitting beneath the shoulder. His hands grazed over the pool of sticky liquid that slowly oozed from the wound. The horse's head twisted, her eyes wide, and she snorted.

"I know, girl," he said in a low, calm voice. "Let's see what we can do to get you patched up." He shifted his position to avoid the extended hooves. The last thing he needed was a kick in the head.

The bullet had missed her chest by mere inches. The hole was low enough that he could feel around the width of her forearm. If he wanted to gain the trust of any of the mustangs, he could not put this horse down. However, if the slug had shattered the bone, there would be no choice in the matter. If it had missed the bone, it would need to be removed and the wound would need to be cleaned and bound for their slow journey back to the homestead. He'd have more time, space, and tools to better take care of her injury there.

Please, Lord, let it have missed the bone.

As he moved around the horse, he was careful not to break his physical contact with her. He needed the mustang to trust him, and trust did not usually come easy from horses raised in the wild.

As he reached over her, he wrapped his hands around her

forearm and felt both sides of the hole. He breathed a sigh of relief as he realized the bullet had indeed missed the bone and had gone clean through her flesh. He once again closed his eyes.

Thank you, he said silently. The arduous task of removing a bullet was not a pretty one and he was grateful for the pass. Most people would call him crazy for even attempting to save the horse, but something inside of him bid him try.

With the encouraging news, he quickly removed the canteen from around his neck and arm, followed by his shirt. The bullet hole would be easier to dress if the filly was on her feet, but these horses were unpredictable around people. He had no way of knowing how she would respond to him once she was up.

Trust your gut.

There was no time to waste.

With the same soothing voice he'd used to talk to the horse, he called to his brother. "Cole." It was taking longer than expected for him to bring the supplies and Tag didn't want to risk leaving the young filly.

Where is he?

Several moments later, Tag looked up to see Cole still a fair distance away from him, taking a single tiptoed step, then stopping to breathe, another step, then a stop and Tag resisted the urge to laugh. His little brother was one who typically threw caution to the wind, but was pleased by his respect for the animal. And, for him.

"She'll be an old grey mare before you make it over here, little brother. Just take it nice and easy…be quiet, but quick about it. We need to get this horse over and onto her feet."

Cole heaved the rope up more securely over his shoulders and with another deep breath, crept the rest of the way to him. "What do you need me to do?"

"The grassy underbrush should serve as traction for her, but we need to get some leverage in order to get her onto her side. Mustangs are nothing if not stubborn. We just need enough advantage to get her to roll over her withers, then, hopefully, she'll have enough strength and determination to do the rest on her own."

"So, how do we do that?"

"That's where this," Tag slipped the rope from Cole's shoulder, "comes in." He glanced over at the dam. She stood like a sentinel, observing every movement, every action, with interest and warning. He nodded at her, trusting that they had an understanding. At least for the moment.

"We need to wrap each end around the fetlocks on the opposite side we are going to roll her, then we'll gently pull her legs down over her trunk." He handed his brother the open end of the rope. "Remember not to tie it. She'll probably try to run as soon as she's up and I don't want to hurt her any more than she already is. Or one of us."

Cole nodded.

In order to wrap the foot farthest away from them, he had to move around to the front of the cast mustang. As he rounded the filly, the injured horse's dam reared back a foot or so with an alarmed whinny. She shook her head and pawed at the ground. Cole froze and glanced over at Tag, who immediately stepped in front of him.

Tag rotated his head slowly, focusing on the horse until he gained eye contact. Then, he proceeded to breathe in, then out in slow rhythmic motions, allowing all tension to melt away. As the dam focused on him, he was able to elicit the same reaction from her.

A blow, followed by a snort, then, a conceding whinny. The beautiful animal held contact for a few more moments before galloping away from them, then circling back around and standing again in her original distant position.

Tag loved the moments when something otherworldly seemed to pass between man and animal, something akin to a kindred connection, and he felt it now with the older mare—though she couldn't be much older than three or four.

Connected.

She was majestic to say the least and he hoped for the chance to work more closely with her.

Once the dam had been calmed, it only took a moment for them to wrap the rope around the cast mustang's feet. Then, Tag and Cole, together in one fluid motion, gently eased her legs to the ground. Then, they backed away enough to give the filly room as she struggled. They watched with a sense of accomplishment as she finally made it to her feet.

The newly uncast mustang tried to run, but stumbled, falling to her front knees, unable to support her weight on her injured leg. She pushed herself back up and limped over to where her dam still waited. The older of the two sniffed at her companion, then twisted her head, swaying it back and forth before she ran in a small circle as if trying to entice the other horse to join her, to no avail.

Tag looked over at Cole. "You okay riding bareback?" he asked, knowing his brother had been practicing with his black Arabian.

"I think Mav can handle it," he replied proudly, glancing over at his horse as if he himself didn't need any practice.

Tag shook his head at the boy's arrogance, but in all fairness, he probably didn't.

If they could get the tack from Cole's horse—at least the lead rope—they should be able to get the young mustang back to the ranch. The only question would be the dam. They could sure use some more help about now.

As Tag watched the interaction between the two horses, an approaching figure caught his eye just above them and he looked up to focus on the incoming riders. Harvey and Ben, along with a couple of the men from Hector's group, approached from the north, without their lead. They must have seen the horses and looped around so as not to scare the wild mustangs between them.

"Sorry, boss," Harvey said once they were close enough to

converse. "If anyone was in that thicket, they're long gone. Is that...?"

"Bullet went straight through. I think we can save her. I'm glad you're here. We need to get these two back to the ranch and it will be a lot easier if we have a couple of drovers to help." Tag glanced around. "Where are Hector and Felix?" he asked.

"Felix's horse lost a shoe and Hector didn't want to leave him behind. They said they'll meet us back at the ranch."

Tag nodded. They'd been on the trail for several weeks and he imagined it was time to re-shoe all their mounts. "All right, then, let's do it," he said and the riders all took their positions behind the two mustangs.

Tag climbed up onto his horse.

"I never thought I'd see a time," Cole said as he rode up next to him with a saddle, but no leads, his brow raised.

"What?"

"Six men, two horses." Cole laughed.

Tag joined. "Hopefully, it'll be the last." He clicked his tongue. "Let's go."

Brenna released the children for lunch, laughing as they set up the yard for stickball. When she glanced up and saw the group of men, with Tag at the front, leading a couple of horses through the gate, her heart lurched in her chest and she raised a hand to cover it, an excited smile touching her lips.

She'd never felt this way about a man before—not even with Peter. Of course, it had been expected that she would fall in love with her husband over time, but they hadn't been given enough time together to learn much of anything about the other, let alone how to love each other.

"Mrs. Scott," Everett said, tugging on her skirt.

She glanced down at the worried expression crossing the young boy's face. "Yes, Everett?"

"Mrs. Scott," he repeated, "I think something is wrong with Jeb."

Brenna glanced around the yard, but didn't see her brother anywhere.

Strange.

He'd collected all the eggs, milked the cow, and had been working with some of Tag's men on one of the downed fences before the Kansans had ridden out this morning. Jeb normally didn't return to the homestead until noon—in time to grab some supper—so, she hadn't thought much of the fact she hadn't seen him in a while.

"What makes you say that?" Brenna pulled her pocket watch from the waistband pocket in her skirt.

Half past.

An unwelcome trepidation suddenly washed over her and she fought inwardly to calm her breathing. After the incident with Tobias Pane, she was a little more on edge than usual and was careful not to overreact in front of her young student.

"Where *is* Jeb, Everett?" she asked as she crouched down to look the boy at eye level, placing her hands gently on his shoulders. "Have you seen him?"

He nodded.

"He stumbled for a minute from behind there," the youngster pointed over to a particularly tall section of grass next to the barn, "then he dropped down onto his knees and then he fell onto his belly. Face first. I thought he was playin', but now, he's not movin' or nothin'."

"Or anything," she corrected, unable to stop herself as she rushed down off the steps, her knee screaming in protest, and toward the nearly dilapidated structure at the far edge of the yard.

Jeb. Her mind raced with all the potential hazards her brother could have encountered, including brutes like Tobias.

When she reached the barn, she saw his hat lying in the grass before she saw him. His large body was all but concealed in the brush. She hurried to his side, kneeling down in the grass next to him, touching his face. It was cool to the touch.

"Jeb," she called, quietly at first.

No response.

"Jeb," she tried again, a little louder as she tried to shake him awake. Fear loomed over her like a starless night and she grabbed him by the shoulders. "Jebbediah Francis Mallory, you answer me when I'm talking to you!" Her brother had two and a half years on her, but she figured if she could imitate their mama well enough, he'd listen.

His eyes flitted open, then closed again, but a soft moan escaped his lips.

He's alive!

Her gratitude squeezed her heart and she took his hand and brought it up to her mouth with a kiss, then sat back on her heels and looked heavenward.

"Thank you," she said aloud, her voice choked, as grateful tears trailed down her cheeks.

Whispers alerted her to the several children who had gathered around to see what had happened.

"Is he all right, Mrs. Scott?" Everett asked. His voice hadn't been that timid since his first day in class.

"I don't know," she answered honestly. "Run and get Mr. Redbourne. Tell him we need him right away."

"No need. I'm right here."

Brenna breathed a relieved sigh. Hope washed over her as he bent down and scooped Jeb up into his arms.

She gasped, bringing her hand up to cover her mouth, as several pieces of grass stuck to the blood on the back of her brother's head.

Get control, Brenna Scott. Don't scare the children.

"Where's his room?" Tag's deep, throaty voice brought a level of comfort that she hadn't expected.

She cleared her throat and nodded. "I'll show you."

Not wasting any time, she got to her feet as quickly as her

pained leg would allow and turned toward the house, but when she started forward, she was met with the concerned glances of her students.

"I'm sure Mr. Mallory will be just fine."

She hoped God was listening and would hear the plea in her words.

"Class is dismissed for the day, children," she told them with the most comforting smile she could muster as she continued limping as quickly as possible toward the steps. "I will see you all bright and early on Monday morning," she called over her shoulder before opening the door and leading Tag inside, through the kitchen, and into her bedroom that sat just off the dining area.

Jeb's room was on the second floor, but under the circumstances, she felt he would be better served if he could rest comfortably downstairs where she could keep a close eye on him.

Tag waited patiently as she grabbed a towel from the closet in the hall, pulled back the covers, and spread the cloth over the pillow at the head of her bed.

He laid Jeb down effortlessly on top of the mattress.

"I need some water and clean rags," he instructed. His voice held authority, but there was a kindness that endeared him to her even more and she was quick to do his bidding.

Her brother was going to be all right. He just had to be.

Brenna pulled a large washbasin from the shelf in the kitchen and hobbled outside to the pump.

"Let me help you with that, Mrs. Scott." Kade stepped up to the spigot and took the basin from her grasp.

When she released the ceramic bowl, her hands shook and she wrung them together to stop the quiver. "Thank you," she said quickly before turning back to the house. "Will you bring it inside when it's full?"

"Of course."

Before long she had an armful of towels and wash rags, the

bottle of whiskey Jeb thought he'd hidden from her, and a needle and thread. If the amount of blood had been any indication, the wound on Jeb's head would need to be stitched.

When she walked into her room, Tag sat on the edge of the mattress talking to an unresponsive Jeb. He looked up as she dropped her load on top of the quilt at the foot of the bed.

"How long has he been like this?" he asked.

Brenna shrugged. "I…I don't know. One of the boys found him. Everett. It's been about ten minutes or so—just after you returned."

"He's a lucky man to still be breathing. This was no accident."

Her heart started racing again.

Who would want to hurt Jeb? He wasn't a threat to anyone and he didn't have any stake in the ranch…unless…no, she didn't want to think about any 'unlesses'.

"Did you hear me?" Tag asked, meeting her eyes with furrowed brows. "This was intentional, Brenna."

Her face heated—whether from the man's intimate use of her given name or the insinuation in his voice, she was unsure.

"You mean someone really did this to him? On purpose?"

"Yes, ma'am." He shifted around on the bed to face her.

"Why?" she echoed her question aloud. "Why would someone want to hurt my brother?"

"That's what we're going to find out," he promised, holding out his hand.

She slipped her hand inside of his, the warmth of it immediately offering comfort.

"Not that I'm complaining," he said with a squeeze and a smile that turned her insides to jelly, "but, I need one of those rags if I'm going to be able to clean up this wound." His eyes indicated the towels she'd brought in earlier.

Her cheeks grew hotter and she snapped her hand back, realizing he hadn't held out his hand for her, but for a clean towel.

"Brenna," he cooed, his head tilted slightly to one side.

She spun around and grabbed one of the rags, but as she turned back to give it to him, Kade stepped inside the room with a full basin of water and she knocked it hard enough that much of the contents doused Tag's face and shirt.

She gasped.

Not again.

"If I didn't know any better," he said, wiping the excess from his eyes, "I would think you didn't like me much." He chuckled as he took the rag from her and dipped it in the bowl still clutched in Kade's hands.

"Sorry, boss," the foreman said sheepishly as Tag took the basin from him and set it on the end table next to the bed. "I'll go get more."

Tag ignored them both as he turned Jeb gently onto his side, assumedly so he could get a better look at the back his head.

Brenna wasn't sure she wanted to see, but curiosity overtook her and she stepped up behind Tag and glanced over his shoulder at her brother's injury. Even in the dim light of the room, she could see that blood covered a good portion of his scalp, making the wound impossible to see. She quickly strode over to the windows and pulled back the curtains enough to allow the sunlight in more fully.

"Better?" she asked.

"Better," he confirmed as he wrung out the cloth from the basin and applied it to the back of Jeb's head.

As Tag worked to clean the wound, Jeb didn't make a sound. Several times Brenna stared at her brother for any sign that he was still alive, and each time, she relaxed a little when she saw his chest rise and fall.

Kade returned with a clean metal bucket full of water and placed it on the table next to the basin, then turned back for the door. He paused with his hand gripping the frame. "Cole rode into town to fetch a doctor," he said. "I thought you'd also want to know that the young mustang filly is becoming quite agitated. I'm afraid she might hurt herself."

Tag nodded. "There's not much more I can do here for the time being." He took one of the oversized bread cloths Brenna had brought in and with a quick slit of his knife, began tearing it into strips. "It looks like the bleeding has stopped, at least for now, and he isn't feverish, so I think it would be best if we just let him sleep."

"Is that what he's doing?" she asked hopefully. "Sleeping?"

He looked at her, reached up and placed a hand to the side of her neck, and rubbed her jawline with his thumb. "That's what I hope, professor, but we won't know the extent of the injury until the doctor arrives."

"Thank you," she said, unable to pull her gaze away from his lips. "I don't know what I would have done without you here."

The angular part of his jaw flexed as he looked down at her. She held her breath, unable to steal her eyes away from him as he leaned down toward her.

Not now, she said, a plea in her thought. *Not now. Not now!* As much as she'd dreamt about Tag's lips pressed against hers, Jeb was at the forefront of her mind right now. She slipped off the bed and out of Tag's trajectory, only to find that he'd been reaching for a fallen piece of cloth from the bed.

Silly girl, she chided. *He's not going to kiss you when your brother lies here unconscious.*

She was glad he was not looking at her as she was sure that her cheeks were the color of poppies.

As Tag continued to wrap Jeb's head with the torn rags, the foreman's words finally registered.

"Mr…um," she paused, realizing that she'd never learned Kade's surname, "Kade, is there something wrong with the horses you brought back to the ranch today?" she asked, intent on forgetting her embarrassment.

"Someone took a shot at the mustang herd we were

following. A filly was hit. We think the other horse may be her mama."

"Mae Taylor, no doubt, and her hired hands. She doesn't tolerate the wild horses grazing on her land."

Tag looked up at her. "So, she just kills them?"

"She's not the only one. I've heard much discussion from the ranchers in town on how they will deal with the problem, but few of them are willing to listen to anything other than extermination."

"Well, I can assure you that now that I am here, there will be an alternative."

She'd upset him.

"I…" she didn't know exactly what to say. Then, a thought came to her.

"Was Jeb," she swallowed, "shot?" She knew it was a stupid question the moment it left her lips. If her brother had been shot in the back of the head, he wouldn't be breathing.

"I've seen my fair share of gunshot wounds and this looks more like someone hit him from behind rather than grazed him with a bullet."

Brenna was grateful Tag hadn't mocked her, but had been diplomatic in his response.

He met her eyes and held them for a moment before speaking.

"I'd better head out to the stable." He wiped his hands on one of the towels as he stepped toward the door, then paused and turned around. "We'll find whoever did this, Brenna," Tag said with a nod. He held her gaze for another moment before turning on his heel and heading outside.

"How do you like that?" Brenna said, moving over to the bed and plopping down next to Jeb, trying to lighten the dread that filled her heart as she glanced over the still form of her favorite brother. "I'm stuck on a man, who kissed me…" she qualified the kiss on her cheek in her mind, "and you're not even awake enough to tease me about it."

Her smile faded as a tear slipped down the side of her face and rested at the top of her lips.

"I want to tell you all about it," she said quietly, reaching up to wipe a dirt smudge from his cheek. "Wake up, Jeb." Her voice faded into a whisper. "Wake up."

CHAPTER FIFTEEN

Saturday Morning

A sharp jab in Tag's ribs woke him from sleep. He ran his hand down the length of the pistol he'd kept beneath his pillow last night and he wrapped his fingers around the grip and slipped his finger into the trigger guard.

"I wouldn't," a familiar, low voice whispered.

Tag released his hold on the gun and spun around to see his younger brother, Rafe, perched on the edge of his bedroll, leaning against the wall, his feet extended and crossed in front of him.

"You almost got yourself shot, doc," he said, shoving the blanket off him and scrambling to his feet.

He held out a hand to help his brother to his feet.

"Of all the places I thought I'd run into that mug, this little Texas town didn't make the list," Tag said quietly, careful not to wake the others.

He pulled Rafe into a fierce hug.

It had been a long time since he'd seen his brother.

Too long.

"How'd you find me?"

Rafe raised a brow.

"All right. All right. No need to be a braggart."

"It's not bragging if it's true, right?" Rafe smiled wide.

His brother was not only a bounty hunter, but his time living among the Pawnee had taught him many things, becoming an excellent tracker was one of them.

Tag shook his head. "Come on, now you've got me up before the old rooster's crow, we might as well cook us up some breakfast." He'd let Brenna sleep a little longer. Besides, nobody made flapjacks quite like Rafe. He smiled to himself as he shrugged into his trousers and boots, then buttoned up his shirt.

"Hey," Rafe said quietly as they stepped outside the bunkhouse. "I thought you owned the place."

"I do, or rather, I will. I'm heading into Austin this morning, but I'll stop in Round Rock to hand over the signed papers," he replied, his chest swelling at the thought.

"Then, why in the world, big brother, are you sleeping in the bunkhouse?"

Tag didn't get a chance to respond as it didn't take more than a moment before Rafe answered his own question.

"A woman," he guessed, turning to look at Tag for confirmation.

What could he say? Rafe was right. Again. He shrugged.

"I knew it. My big brother has been ensnared by the trappings of some young woman. What's her name?"

"Who said there was a woman involved?" he asked, struggling to keep the corners of his mouth from lifting. He kept his head down as he made his way to the kitchen door.

"You like her," Rafe accused, his amusement growing with each passing second.

Tag knew his brother would not relent until he got what he was looking for.

"Brenna," he whispered as he stepped inside the house, a single finger raised to his lips. "Her name is Brenna."

Rafe shook his head. "Distractions, I'm telling you. The

whole lot of 'em."

The morning sun's rays had barely broken through the window above the stove, but it was enough for Tag to make his way around the kitchen.

"I guess you don't meet a lot of 'distractions' in your line of work." Tag raised a brow as he reached up to grab one of the pans hanging from the ceiling above the counter. "How's bounty hunting treating you anyway?" he asked casually.

"It's doing its job," Rafe responded with a shrug.

His brother had been less than a year away from graduating from Harvard's medical school when an unfortunate incident with a woman and an altar had driven him to take up a profession that allowed for a little more aggression than medicine.

"What brings you out my way?" Tag asked, knowing it wasn't just to catch up, and certainly wasn't coincidence.

One of the pans clanked against the stove. Worried he would wake up Jeb or Brenna, he shrunk down, his eyes open wide, as he gently laid it down on the cook stove.

He waited.

Silence greeted him and he relaxed. No one had been disturbed.

"I'm looking for someone," Rafe said casually.

"What?" Tag asked, distracted by his own thoughts. "Oh, right, of course you are," he said as he stood upright and began collecting the ingredients. He made another mental note to pick up another slab of bacon from the butcher along with several other luxury foodstuffs.

They'd barely had time to make a list of supplies to get in town, let alone go and pick them up. Even though they were headed down to Austin this morning, he figured he could stop in town on their way out with a list for the mercantile owner. Most of the items were the basics and he didn't think there would be too much of a problem filling it. He guessed that if he paid a little extra, they wouldn't mind having someone deliver the order out to the ranch.

"So, you tracked one of your bounties here?"

"I think he's actually headed farther south, but I had to stop in and see my big brother."

"South? Like Austin?"

"I'm not sure yet. I figured I'd stop in town later today and talk with the sheriff before I head out."

"Maybe you can ride with us. The big auction is today in Austin. We'll be leaving in a few hours."

A flicker of movement caught Tag's eye and he looked up to see a disheveled Brenna rushing into the kitchen, her face flushed.

"Well, good morning," he said with a low voice.

She gasped in surprise as she brought her hand up to her chest. "You startled me."

"We were just tal—"

"I'm glad you're here," she said quickly, effectively stopping his comment short, her voice urgent as she reached out and grabbed his hand, pulling him out the door and toward her bedroom.

Tag looked back at Rafe, whose brow raised, but he didn't say a word as he followed them, his curiosity obviously piqued.

When they got into the room, Jeb sat up against the wall on the bed, pulling at the bandages on his head.

"He won't listen to me," she said, releasing his hand to raise her own in the air. "And, he insists the wrappings be removed."

Jeb looked up at them, his eyes flitting between them, his confusion apparent.

"Since when did you start inviting strange men into your bedroom, Bren?"

Brenna's eyes widened in horror, color flooded her cheeks, then she placed her hands on her hips.

"Jebbediah Mallory, you take that back this instant. You know very well that Mr. Redbourne is the new owner here and the only reason he is in this room right now is to set you straight.

He's the one who bandaged you up last night and I'm hoping he'll be able to talk some sense into that thick skull of yours."

Rafe stepped into the room and dutifully up to the bed, then hunched down enough to look at Jeb's face and at his eyes.

"What do you mean?" Jeb leaned to one side, trying to see Brenna. "New owner? Does this mean you've decided to come home with me? Did you sell Oak Meadow?"

Brenna threw her hands up in the air. "Don't you remember? He's been here for days."

Jeb pulled back and looked up at Rafe. "If that's the case, how come I don't remember him?" he asked, squinting his eyes at the large man blocking his sister's view of him.

Rafe chuckled. "Not me, friend." He motioned toward Tag. "Him."

Jeb glanced over at Tag, but there was no hint of recognition.

Tag mused at his brother's timing and praised that Redbourne gut he and his other siblings had learned to trust. It was serendipitous that Rafe had shown up when he had. Cole had returned from town yesterday with the news that the doctor had headed up to a small town about twenty-five miles north to attend to one of his patients and wouldn't be returning for a few days' time.

"What happened here?" Rafe asked, his medical curiosity getting the better of him.

"Some of the school children found him yesterday afternoon, lying down in the grass. It looks like he was struck in the back of the head. Didn't know if he was going to make it there for a while. I cleaned the wound as best I could, but…" Tag breathed out a relieved sigh. "I'm just glad you're here." He turned to look at the woman next to him. "Brenna, this is my little brother, Rafe."

Rafe turned to look at Brenna and nodded in greeting. "Ma'am," he said in that low voice that always seemed to make the women swoon.

Tag rolled his eyes.

Brenna gulped.

"Your little brother?" she nearly choked on the words. "If he's your *little* brother, I can't imagine the size of your *big* brother."

Tag laughed. It was a common reaction to the Redbourne brothers, who all stood well over six feet tall.

"You'd like my oldest brother, Raine. Everybody does," he replied simply. "Rafe, here, is one of the most talented 'near-physicians' I've ever met."

His brother looked over at him with squinted eyes, a raised brow, and a clenched jaw—a look that said a sardonic, 'very funny.'

Tag chuckled.

"What is a near-physician?" Brenna asked, one brow arched inquisitively.

"Long story," both Tag and Rafe responded at the same time.

"While he's obviously experiencing some memory loss, ma'am, he recognizes you, and that is a very good sign. I'm sure the local doctor will want to keep an eye on him." The bounty hunter in the man moved to leave the room.

"Rafe," Tag asked, a light plea in his voice.

"I'm a bounty hunter now. I don't do that anymore," Rafe said simply.

"Of course, you do. You always will. Even if you don't want to admit it, you miss working in medicine. You miss helping people that way." Tag tilted his head and placed a hand on his brother's arm. "The only doc for miles has gone upstate and isn't expected to return for another week." He knew as much as his brother tried to protest, he would never leave someone who needed his help. "Please?" he asked with raised brows.

After a moment of no response, he shrugged.

"There's no one else. No one better than you."

Rafe stood up tall, took in a deep breath, and exhaled

loudly. "Where can I wash up?" the doctor in him relented, holding up his weathered hands, dry from months on the road.

"This way," Tag said, directing him outside. He didn't want to give Rafe any time to change his mind, not that he would, but he didn't want to take any chances. He turned to Brenna. "I'll explain everything in a minute," he said, holding her briefly by the shoulders, then he joined Rafe at the door. "There's a pump out front. I'll grab some soap." He shot Brenna a meaningful look before striding out of the room and into the kitchen where a chunk of soap dangled from a hook next to the door.

Rafe took it from him without a word and headed out the back door.

Tag grabbed a small towel from the kitchen shelf and followed.

"She's real beautiful," Rafe said as he raised the handle on the pump. "I can see why you're taken with her."

"She *is* pretty, but it's not just that. She's smart—a teacher, and—"

"Ah, like Miss Henderson," Rafe teased.

"Hey, for an old-maid schoolmarm, Miss Henderson was quite a catch."

"Yes, she was. Too bad Mr. Graves came along and swept her off her feet before you were old enough to shave. Though," he said, rubbing his own stubbled chin, "it looks like now you've forgotten how. To shave I mean."

"You're sooooo funny."

"I think so."

They both laughed.

"I don't know. It's just that Brenna is also kind, and spirited, and well, I don't know…I just feel a connection with her." What else could he say? "She makes me feel…" he said, a smile stretching his face at the thought of her.

"What?"

"That's it. She makes me *feel*."

"I'll bet she does," Rafe said with a snicker.

"You are a funny man, Rafe Redbourne," he said as he punched his brother in the arm. "Very funny." He shook his head. "Seriously though, I wasn't even sure it was possible for me to care about someone again…not like this."

The war had taken its toll on him and he'd doubted for a long time that he would ever be able to open his heart. He'd seen so much loss, had experienced first-hand the wrenching pain that had come as his comrades fell, or when a friend or neighbor had died. He couldn't even imagine the agony that would come if he'd ever lost someone really special—especially someone he loved.

Losing someone like that would be unbearable, but his oldest brother, Raine, always told him that without risk there would be no reward and he had a feeling that Brenna Scott was a reward worth risking everything.

"I know you saw a lot of death and suffering during the war, big brother. We all did. And if you think that this Brenna woman is going to fix what ails you, then who am I to stop you?" Rafe eyed his lathered hands and then the handle. "Would you mind?"

Tag pumped the water over Rafe's newly cleaned hands and handed him the dry towel he'd flung over his shoulder.

"I know Tessa hurt you—" Tag started.

"I don't want to talk about her." Rafe tossed him back the dampened towel and strode purposefully back to the house. His demeanor had grown cold. He was obviously still bitter about being left at the altar, but Tag couldn't blame him. It had been a real black moment for him. And the family.

"Lexa's in the barn. I'll need my bag."

It only took a few minutes for Tag to locate Rafe's horse and the black bag he always carried with him, full of medical instruments and supplies. Being a doctor was a part of him, of who he was, no matter how hard he tried to deny it. He ran his hands along Rafe's large strawberry roan mare and patted her on the back.

"He's a good man, my brother," he said with a smile. "Thank you for watching out for him."

Lexa whinnied.

"Good girl."

When Tag reached the bedroom door, the ebb and flow of natural conversation came to a halt. The tension in the room was apparent, but when he looked at Rafe for an explanation, his brother's eyes opened a little wider, his head tilted to one side, and he shrugged.

Whatever it was had not been caused by Rafe.

"Thank you, Mr. Redbourne, for your help," Brenna said as she looked up at Rafe with her beautiful brown eyes.

A twinge of unwarranted jealousy twisted in Tag's belly.

"I'm sorry if he's a difficult patient," she continued. "He will allow you to help." She shot a look of warning her brother's direction.

Rafe made his way toward Jeb and sat down on the bed next to the man.

"Well, let's have a look." He leaned toward Jeb. "Let's finish getting these bandages off…"

"That's what I said," Jeb responded, eager to relieve himself of the stripped cloths. "See, Brenna." He sounded like a gloating child.

"…so I can see the damage," Rafe finished.

Jeb seemed in good spirits, though a little frightened as Rafe leaned forward to help remove the makeshift bandages.

After a few winces and pained grunts from Jeb, Rafe pulled the man's head down to where he could see the wound. He whistled.

"You've got yourself a mighty deep cut there, Mr. Mallory. It's a wonder you have any wits about you at all." He turned to Tag. "I have to say, big brother, I'm impressed. You very well may have saved this man's life."

"So, he's going to be all right?" Brenna asked, stepping forward, hope exuding from her.

"These types of wounds are easily infected and he's not out of the woods yet, but because my brother did such a good job cleaning and bandaging it, there's a good chance he won't experience any complications."

Tag's chest swelled a little at Rafe's praise.

Brenna breathed a sigh of relief. "And his memory?"

"The brain is a finicky thing. With a hit like that, it's a wonder he's alive, let alone up and talking. He may remember the incident within a couple of hours, or the memories may never return. It's hard to say." Rafe held out his hand.

Tag gave him the black bag he'd retrieved from the barn.

Rafe proceeded to clean the wound again.

"It'll need a few stitches and then it won't be long before you're as good as new," he told Jeb. "I'm afraid we'll have to apply some new bandages to keep it as clean as possible, but I imagine another day or two and they'll no longer be necessary."

Jeb's disapproval was obvious, but he sat still while Rafe sewed up the cut, his face often contorting with pain.

"You'll need to take it easy for a few days, Mr. Mallory," Rafe said as he rebandaged the wound with some materials from his bag. "I wouldn't advise any travel in the near future. I'm guessing your sister, here, will be gracious enough, Mr. Mallory, to allow you to stay here for the time being." He glanced at Brenna expectantly.

She shot a look at Tag. "Well, I don't believe it's really up to me anymore. Once Mr. Redbourne visits my father-in-law this afternoon, he'll be the new owner. So, I guess it's up to him, now, isn't it?"

A strange expression flickered across Rafe's face, then it was gone. He turned to look at Tag. "Mr. Redbourne?" he inquired with a knowing look.

What was he going to do? Kick the man out of his house? He resented the idea that there was even a question.

"Of course, he can stay."

Rafe stood up and Brenna took his place on the bed next

to Jeb, taking her brother's hand in hers.

"Seems like you didn't really need me after all," Rafe whispered as he looked back at the siblings. "Can I talk to you a minute?" he asked, nodding toward the kitchen.

Tag followed him into the other room.

"I need to know where you found him."

"Why?" Tag studied his brother's face a moment. "What aren't you telling me?"

"That woman in there is Brenna *Scott*."

"I know."

"Peter Scott!" Rafe said firmly, but in low tones as to not draw attention to them.

"Brenna's husband?"

"Yes, husband," Rafe repeated the word as if there were some scandalous meaning behind it.

"She's widowed, Rafe. I'm not carrying on with a married woman, if that's what you think."

"That's just it, big brother. You are."

Tag's brows scrunched together. "What do you mean?"

"I mean that woman in there is Peter Scott's wife."

"Was, Rafe. *Was* Peter Scott's wife. The man is dead. Are you so angry and bitter that you would deny me a chance for the kind of happiness that Ethan and Levi have just because Tessa walked out on you? Not all women are like her."

Rafe shook his head. "Don't be a dolt."

"What is it then? You're not happy, so no one else should be happy either."

"Arggg," Rafe grunted in frustration. "You're not understanding me."

"Explain it to me then. Without all the babble."

"So much for me trying to break it to you easy." Rafe reached into his vest pocket and pulled out a piece of parchment with a scribbled drawing of a man and the words '*Wanted: Dead or Alive, Peter Scott, known aliases Abe Chapman, Cuthbert O'Brien, and Frances Brady*' adorned the bottom in a bold black print.

Tag snatched the paper from him, studying it. "You're trying to collect a bounty on a dead man?" Even as he spoke the words, he knew what Rafe was going to say and dread washed over him.

"That's what I'm trying to tell you, Tag. Peter Scott is alive."

CHAPTER SIXTEEN

Brenna slipped out of the house for a much-needed reprieve. She'd spent the majority of the night sitting in the chair next to the bed and hadn't gotten much sleep, but, now that Jeb was resting peacefully, she hoped a nice walk in the fresh morning air would do her some good.

The yard bustled with cowhands as they prepared for their trip to auction. She had to admit, it was nice to have a little commotion around the ranch again. It had been quiet too long. She missed the hustle of everyday life on the ranch. After Peter passed away, all ranching operations had simply come to a halt. Josiah had paid the men their wages and they'd left to seek work elsewhere.

As she limped past the chicken coop, she spotted Cole sitting on an upturned bucket trying to milk Gertrude. She'd taken for granted all the things that Jeb had been doing since he'd arrived. It appeared as though the chickens had already been fed and her two horses had been turned out to pasture.

"Thank you for stepping in and doing Jeb's chores. I don't know what I would have done without all of you."

Cole pulled the bucket out from beneath the cow, poured it into the near full milk tin, and pounded the metal lid on tight.

"Thank you for making us breakfast. Can hardly concentrate on my chores with all the delicious smells coming from the house."

Brenna dropped her head with more than an ounce of guilt. Two days had passed since she'd agreed to cook for the men in exchange for her room and board at Oak Meadow, but for the second day in a row, she'd failed to do just that and yet the men hadn't complained.

Today, she'd gotten off easy. Once Rafe had finished with Jeb, he and Tag had gone straight to the kitchen and had started making flapjacks, eggs, and bacon—though she hadn't had very much of the meat on hand.

"I'm afraid I can't take the credit. There are two Mr. Redbournes in the kitchen."

Cole's head perked up. "Did you say two? Besides me? Another of my brothers is here? Which one?"

"The bounty hunter doctor."

"Rafe?"

Brenna nodded, a smile touching her lips at his obvious excitement. "You didn't know?"

"No, ma'am, I started on these chores as soon as there was light. You say he's making flapjacks?" Cole licked his lips and rolled his eyes heavenward. "It's my lucky day. Well, if you'll excuse me, ma'am," he said with a tip of his hat, "I'll just get your cow turned out to the pasture so I can go see my brother." He took a hold of Gertie's lead, then turned back to her a moment. "And his flapjacks," he said with a wink.

Brenna giggled, but it quickly turned to an exaggerated whimper.

These men worked hard and they deserved a good home-cooked meal every day. Maybe she could ride into town this morning and talk with Mrs. Wheatley about learning how to make a few simple meals that would get her through the next few weeks, though she realized that she needed to start thinking more about her future. She couldn't very well stay at Oak Meadow forever. People would talk. As if they didn't already have enough to talk about.

She wondered if everyone in town had known about Peter's

gambling problem. Had they looked on her with pity? Or, had they been just as naïve as she'd been?

"No matter now, Brenna," she told herself quietly as she reached the corral gate.

"Mrs. Scott?"

Brenna whipped around to see Sheriff Hunt dismount from his horse. She'd been too lost in her thoughts to hear him approach.

"Mornin', ma'am," he said as he tipped his hat. "Redbourne still around?" he asked, flipping his reins over one of the corral slats.

"Which one?"

"Excuse me?"

It had been a valid question as there were now three of them at the ranch, but she knew to whom he referred. "Never mind. He's up at the house." She raised her hand to block the sun as she looked up at him. "What brings you out here again this early in the morning? Did someone come and get you about my brother?"

"You're brother? Did something happen to Jeb?"

"He was attacked early yesterday afternoon."

"Attacked by whom?"

Brenna shrugged. "I was hoping you might have some answers."

"I'm afraid not, ma'am." He removed his hat and looked at her, his eyes scrunched slightly, his brows furrowed with concern.

"What is it then? Why have you come?" she asked when he hesitated. "Have you found Tobias Pane?"

"No, ma'am, but I am afraid I have some bad news. A man's body was left in front of the doctor's office late last night. No one saw who left it there. And with the doc out of town and all, I thought Redbourne would want to know."

Brenna's heart jumped to a start.

A man?

A sudden memory flash of the last sheriff showing up at her doorstep had her reliving the heart-crushing moments when she'd been told of Peter's accident. Everything had changed in that moment. A delivery notice of death was the last thing she ever wanted to experience again.

"Who?" she asked. "Was it the man Tag shot?"

"Not unless he left out a few details. My understanding was that Redbourne shot him in the shoulder. This man…well, this man wasn't shot in the shoulder." He looked away, seemingly hesitant to share more.

"Sheriff?" she persisted. "What is it?"

"Well, ma'am, he was shot in the head."

Brenna couldn't formulate any more words. She simply stared at the sheriff, each breath growing increasingly harder to catch.

"Now, look, I'd seen him around before, but don't know his name as I'm still getting to know the folks around here. He was one of those who liked to play cards at O'Malley's. I hate to speculate, but my best guess is that he is the other man who was with Pane in the orchard yesterday."

The man who defied Tobias. A sickening feeling washed over her.

"Are you all right, ma'am. You look like you need to sit a spell."

Brenna cleared her throat as she worked to focus on the sheriff. "Yes, I am…fine," she said as she brushed at the front of her dress. "Mr. Pane?"

"It looks that way, ma'am. Forgive me for being so blunt."

"I'd rather know the facts, Sheriff, so I can face them head on. Thank you."

The sheriff stood up a little straighter and bobbed his head. "Mrs. Wheatley was right about you. You are something else. I imagine that most women in your situation would be running home to daddy, but you're a brave little thing. I like that."

Brenna's face heated. Before she could respond, she caught

a glimpse of Tag and Rafe headed toward them and her heart lifted inside at the sight.

"Everything all right, Sheriff?" Tag asked, reaching out to shake the man's hand.

The sight of him filled her with gratitude. Had he not been a skilled marksman, the tables could have easily been turned. But he was alive and she was glad he was here. The idea startled her and she was taken aback by her pleasantly unexpected connection to the man.

"A body showed up last night." Sheriff Hunt got right to the point. "Showed up in town this morning with a bullet to the head. From your description, it looks like Pane's goon is dead."

Tag's jaw clenched, his head twisting. "The shoulder?"

The sheriff shook his head.

"And Pane?"

"No one's seen hide nor hair of him since yesterday afternoon."

Tag slapped his gloves on the leg of his denims and turned to Kade, mumbling something she couldn't hear. After a short discussion, the foreman nodded and headed toward the barn.

"I don't have the manpower," the sheriff explained, "to send out a formal search, so I've been riding out to all of the farms and ranches surrounding the town and warning them to be on the lookout."

"Thanks, Sheriff, but Pane may not be our only problem."

"I heard. Mrs. Scott was just telling me about Jeb. Why didn't anyone come and get me?"

"We would have called on you today, but, once again, you've saved us the trouble."

"So, you don't think it was Pane?" the sheriff asked, scanning the small group.

Brenna turned to Tag. This was the first she had heard that there may be another danger. "Who else would it be?"

Tag wasn't ready to tell her about Peter, he'd barely been able to swallow the information himself, so he ignored the question as he directed his attention to the lawman. "Sheriff, this is my brother, Rafe. He's come a long way with some information that might interest you."

Rafe handed the sheriff the old and slightly crumpled wanted poster he'd shown Tag earlier with Peter's face front and center and several aliases listed.

When the sheriff unfolded it, he glanced over its contents, his brows knitting more tightly together. He looked up at Brenna, then at Rafe. "You a bounty hunter?"

"Yes, sir."

"One of the best," Tag added.

The sheriff nodded his understanding. "Is this who I think it is?" he asked, glancing back and forth between Rafe and Tag.

Tag nodded, one brow raised.

"Who?" Brenna asked, irked that they seemed to be having some sort of coded conversation to which she was not privy. "And what possible reason could this person have to hurt Jeb?" Her brother had only been in Serenity Hollow for a few weeks and had still not met very many people in the area. It was hard to fathom anyone who knew him capable of trying or wanting to murder him.

"I hate to ask how," the sheriff ignored her question and posed one of his own to Tag, "but…*how* is this possible? I thought he d—"

"We don't know," Tag cut him off, holding out his hand for the parchment, "but until we find out, we need you to understand how dangerous it is here for Mrs. Scott."

Sheriff Hunt folded the poster and gave it to Tag, who shoved it into his back pocket.

"Gentlemen," Brenna piped up, "I'm not sure what's going on here, but Jeb is my brother. I deserve to know who is trying to hurt him?" she tried to reason with them.

Tag turned to her, looking her straight in the eyes for the first time since joining the conversation. "Rafe tracked a very dangerous man here to Serenity Hollow," he said solemnly. "A criminal, Brenna, with ties to this place. It is more than likely he is the one behind the attack on Jeb. We believe your brother was just in the wrong place at the wrong time. When I think about…" he looked away, shaking his head. "Damn it, professor, if it had been you instead of your brother—"

"It wasn't me." She placed a hand on his forearm and managed a smile. She appreciated his concern.

Tag cleared his throat. "The bottom line is that you are not safe here, Mrs. Scott," he said matter-of-factly, now avoiding her eyes. "At least, not for the time being."

When had he reverted to calling her Mrs. Scott? She pulled her hand back and used it to brush down the front folds of her skirt—keenly aware of how the others watched them. Heat crept into her face.

"Are you trying to tell me that with you, the sheriff, Cole, Kade, Hector, Ben…and…" she paused a moment trying to remember all the names of the men he'd brought with him to no avail, "and the others," she conceded, "that Pane or anyone else is going to get close enough to hurt me?"

"That's just it, ma'am," Tag said, "someone got to Jeb while we were out just for a few hours yesterday morning. What would stop anyone from getting to you when we're gone for any real length of time?"

She tried to think of a witty retort, but how could she argue with that? He was right, but it seemed there wouldn't be much of a choice. She had her brother to consider. Rafe had told her he couldn't be moved.

"We're leaving in an hour for Austin," Tag said, "and we will be gone the entire weekend. There won't be anyone else around. You would essentially be alone out here with who knows who lurking in the shadows."

"So, stay," she said simply, knowing she asked the impossible.

"I wish I could, but this is the last big auction of the season. My father is depending on me."

"Then, I don't see that there's much of a choice. I'm sure the sheriff would be willing to check in on us while you're gone, won't you sheriff?"

"Yes, ma'am," he said with a light tug on the rim of his hat.

"You see. Everything will be fine."

"I don't like it."

"Well, until you sign your papers, *Mr. Redbourne,* this is still my home. I can't think of anywhere safer. There is a roof over my head," she pointed upward with both her hand and her eyes, "locks on the doors—"

"That is not the point," he ground out at her.

"Then, what *is* the point?"

"The fact that there won't be anyone here to protect you when he comes. And, mark my words, he will come."

"Who, Tag? Who will come?" she asked, her hands balling into fists in front of her. "Pane? What's he going to do? After today, Oak Meadow won't belong to me, so hurting me or threatening me won't do him any good."

"It's not Pane I'm worried about."

"Then, who?"

Tag could not bring himself to say the man's name aloud. Peter Scott had walked away from everything. How could he tell Brenna that her husband had willingly walked away from her? Left her to grieve? Left her alone?

He refused to do the same.

"Kade is hitching the wagon as we speak," he told her, motioning toward the house. "I think maybe it's best if you come with us. You should pack. It's a fair jaunt to Austin and the auction begins at five, so we best be getting a move on." They would need some time to look over the cattle and horses that were being offered before the actual bidding began.

"Rafe!" Cole called as he ran up the yard to join them, a

huge grin plastered across his face. He and his brother clutched each other in a bear hug. "Let me look at ya. It's been too long, big brother." He glanced around and his excitement quelled into dreadful curiosity. "What's going on?"

Rafe draped an arm over his shoulders. "Come on, baby brother. I'll tell you all about it, but first I want to hear about you." He pulled Cole aside along with the sheriff.

Tag knew Brenna wanted answers. Hell, she even deserved them, but there just wasn't time to break the news of Peter being alive easily. He'd have plenty of time to talk to her about it on the way to Austin, but, for now, it would be better, he decided, if she didn't know of her husband's betrayal.

Husband. A wave of fierce anger mixed with a splash of jealousy at having been so close to finding that special someone he could see himself growing old with, then having it ripped away from him within a few mere moments, pounded down on top of him with tremendous force.

What was he going to do?

Once Rafe, Cole, and the sheriff were out of ear shot, Brenna took a step closer to him and instinctively, he took a step back.

Married.

Brenna's brows scrunched together and a fleeting look of hurt and disappointment crossed her face before being quickly replaced with indignation. She raised her chin and firmed her jaw, her lips pursed together, unsmiling.

He knew she didn't understand.

"You can't really expect me to travel with you all the way to Austin? Don't you think you are being a little unreasonable? What about Jeb? School? I can't just up and leave. I won't."

It was unfair to ask this of her, but he didn't see a viable alternative. He couldn't protect her if he was in Austin and she was at Oak Meadow, and if Peter Scott was in fact the one who attacked Jeb, it was just a matter of time before he came for Brenna.

"The children will be fine with one day off from school," he said as he strode toward the stable. "It's probably safer for them to stay at home anyway, at least until this outlaw is caught and Pane is behind bars. Besides, I'll have you back by Monday."

She followed him.

"And Jeb? He's in no condition to be left here alone. Someone has to look after him."

He spun around to face her and she nearly ran into him.

"And who'll look after you if Pane comes back while we're gone? If the fugitive knocks down your door looking for trouble?"

"Then, he'll find it."

"And what exactly are you going to do to defend yourself or your brother?"

It may not have been so bad if the woman actually knew how to shoot a gun, but, by her own admission, she'd never learned.

Brenna opened her mouth, but without saying anything, she closed it again.

"It's settled then," he confirmed.

"Not by a long shot." Brenna turned away from him and started toward the house, the limp in her stride still apparent.

A twinge of guilt wrenched his belly as he recalled the fall that had resulted in her injury. He'd tried to protect her from the ground, but had failed. He wasn't about to fail again. Especially, not with something of this magnitude.

Felix passed him the reins to his already saddled horse.

Jeb had been sitting up, talking to them. He seemed all right. He may not be able to make it all the way to Austin, but maybe he could stay down at the jail with the sheriff.

That is a terrible idea. But what other options were there? He'd think of something.

Each man on his team had a job to do. If anything, they were short one man. It would be difficult to leave one behind.

"You're coming with us."

"I'll take my chances here."

Stubborn woman.

"Not good enough," he called as he hustled to catch up to her, his horse in tow. "You can't just walk away from this. The threat is real. I cannot, in good conscience, leave you here unprotected."

Brenna stopped and spun to face him.

"Pardon my saying so, *Mr. Redbourne*, but you are purchasing this ranch," her voice grew louder with each passing word, "not me or the right to tell me what to do. I don't know who you think you are, but until you've turned over those signed papers you've been holding onto, you have no say in what I do, or where I do or do not go. Jeb needs me. I'm staying."

"No, you're not."

"Tag," she said in a voice barely above a whisper, "he's my brother."

Why did she have to look at him like that? Of course, she would choose to protect her brother. He would have done the same and he admired her for it, but he was low on options, and the only one that made sense was the last thing he wanted to do.

If Rafe had believed that Peter Scott was still in Serenity Hollow, why would he be headed south? Maybe asking the sheriff to step in would be for the best. Tag was interested in a married woman and he couldn't let that happen. He would find a way to protect her, but now, anything more was out of the question.

CHAPTER SEVENTEEN

"What would you have me do?" Brenna asked as she took a step toward Tag, reaching out to touch his hand, but he pulled back as if he'd been burned.

Brenna cleared her throat and folded her hands together, humiliated at his overt rejection.

What was she doing? Why did she want to stay?

It was more than independence. It was more than the children. Serenity Hollow had become her home. The people there like family. She was building a new life for herself and no one was going to take that away from her.

"You about ready, Tag?" Cole called, looking at the watch he'd pulled from his pocket.

Brenna knew they needed to be going soon or they wouldn't make it to Austin in time for their auction, so they had to settle this quickly.

"Maybe it's time you return to your father's house in Hillsboro. At least you'd be safe there."

Brenna stood there a moment, staring at him, her mouth gaping open, speechless at his words. Maybe everything she'd felt over the last few days, that she'd believed he'd felt too, had been in her overly active imagination. They'd talked about her childhood home. He knew she didn't want to go back there, and he knew the reasons why.

What had happened to make him change so swiftly?

Suddenly, any fear that had rooted inside of her was replaced with indignation. "Make no mistake, *Mr. Redbourne*, if you want me away from Oak Meadow so badly, I'll be gone by the time you return from Austin, but I am not abandoning Jeb or those children. I will find a way with or without your help."

Tag's jaw flexed, his teeth clenched.

She turned to walk away.

"Come on. I didn't mean to—"

"You can stay with me," Sheriff Hunt interjected as he and Rafe joined back into the conversation.

Brenna had almost forgotten he was there. She'd nearly forgotten about all of them and she glanced around. Their fiery display had garnered the attention of everyone at the ranch, but at her acknowledgement of their presence, the hands quickly returned to their work.

She turned back to the sheriff. "Don't you live in the jail?" she asked apprehensively, trying to envision herself and her brother trying to get some rest in one of the jail's cells.

The sheriff laughed. "While I do sleep there sometimes, I just bought the old Carter place on the far west side of town, next to the Taylor's. It needs some work, but there's plenty of room for Jeb and you. And there's a bedroom in the loft above the barn where I can sleep."

A look akin to jealousy crossed Tag's face and suddenly it seemed like the perfect idea.

"You can't complain about that," she said, turning to Tag. "He is a lawman. Is there anyone better suited to protect me than him?" She taunted the man and she knew it.

Tag was hiding something from her, she could feel it. For him to have changed so completely in just the last little while, there had to be something she was missing and she refused to believe otherwise. If she had to goad him into telling her what was going on, so be it.

Tag's hands balled into fists.

The sheriff leaned down toward her. "I don't know that

there is room for a classroom inside exactly, but there are currently no animals in the barn. You are welcome to hold school there for a day or two. Or longer, if needed."

"Sheriff, that is a most generous offer," she said a little more boisterously than she'd intended. "Thank you!"

"No!" Tag stated his objection loudly.

"Why ever not?" Brenna asked innocently, then turned to the sheriff. "It won't take me too long to pack a small overnight bag. I can come back later to get the rest. How can I ever repay your kindness?" she asked.

"How about allowing me to escort you to dinner at O'Malley's."

Brenna's heart skipped a beat. While the sheriff was certainly handsome, she couldn't help but think what it would have been like had Tag asked her the same question and she dared a quick glance at the man.

"Mrs. Scott," Tag said through a tightened jaw and clenched teeth, "may I speak with you a moment?"

"Whatever for? You've made yourself perfectly clear, Mr. Redbourne."

His rejection still stung.

"Sheriff," she said sweetly, "would you mind helping me collect a few things from my classroom?"

The very handsome lawman jutted out his arm and she slipped her hand in the crook of it.

Tag groaned.

"Rafe," he said in a plea-like voice, as if warranting additional support.

"Don't look at me," he said. "It's like you've told me my whole life, big brother. You got yourself into this mess. You need to get yourself out of it."

Tag moved in front of them. "Mrs. Scott," he said, his voice still hard and rigid. "I apologize if I gave you the impression you were no longer welcome at Oak Meadow. I don't know why, but for some reason, I feel responsible for you. If anything happened while you were living under my roof…" his voice softened as it trailed.

"Mrs. Scott, if I may," Rafe said, catching her attention. "I understand that my brother is an idiot, but he really does mean well."

"Thanks," Tag said quietly. "Not helping!"

Brenna bit back a smile.

Rafe ignored him.

"Despite what all y'all figure out, I meant what I said before, ma'am. Jeb should not be traveling in his condition—not even a few miles. Maybe in a couple of days or a week he could travel that short a distance, but he really needs his rest. Brain injuries are often deceiving, making you believe things are all right for a while and then everything takes a turn for the worse. I've seen it too many times with irreparable damage and would strongly advise you to stay put. However," he shot a look of warning at Tag, "until then, I am sure my brother would not object to the fine sheriff staying here in the bunkhouse while he's gone." Rafe nudged him hard in the ribs.

Brenna placed her fingers above her mouth to help contain the laugh that threatened.

Tag stood up to his full height—just an inch or so taller than the man on her arm. He glanced between the two of them as if conflicted on what he should do.

"Sheriff," he finally said, "I would be," he rubbed his neck, "much obliged if you would, uh, stick around Oak Meadow tonight and look after Mrs. Scott and her brother while we're gone."

The sheriff looked down at her.

Brenna nodded. She didn't know what she would do if Jeb's health took 'a turn for the worse' because of her stubborn pride. Besides, having Sheriff Hunt around could prove to be useful.

"I accept," he said with a smile that lit his bright blue eyes.

If she were any other woman or if it were another time or place, she probably would have melted right into the man's arms, but as it were, the only arms she wanted to be in belonged to one Mr. Taggert Redbourne.

Sunday Evening

Tag stared up into the night sky, his arms folded behind his head. Stars glittered across the heavens and small wafts of smoke wove around each other as they climbed from the dying embers of the fire. Clouds beckoned from the north and the smell of rain was in the air. After everything that had happened yesterday, all he could think about was Brenna and that blasted sheriff.

The lowing of cattle and the soft nicker of horses did little tonight to calm his mind. He'd acted like an idiot and the sheriff had been right there to swoop in and save the day.

"She'll forgive you," Rafe said as he held out a tin of steaming cocoa.

Tag sat up. "Who?"

Rafe raised a brow.

"All right, fine. How did you know?"

"It doesn't take a genius to see that you are smitten. I'm sorry about the husband."

"You and me both." Tag took a sip of his drink and wrapped his arms around his knees.

"I don't know the last time I saw you so…"

"Brooding? Irrational?"

"I was going to say passionate, but those work too."

Most of the men had already settled in for the night. They would all rotate in shifts as they watched over the new herd. He and Rafe were the last two by the fire and he was glad for the company.

"Why do I feel so protective of her?" he asked. "It's as if she's been left in my care and I am responsible for her. I guess it didn't help that when we showed up, she'd had no idea we were coming or even that the ranch was being sold." He took a sip of his drink.

"I still can't believe that Josiah didn't show the courtesy of telling her you were buying the place."

"He said he'd believed she'd received the letter. I imagine it would be a hard situation to face—the widow of your only son. He seemed sincerely apologetic, but it doesn't change the predicament he put me in. Seriously, I've only known the woman the better half of a week, but I can't get her out of my mind. I don't know what it is between us, or what was between us, but I've likely made it so that she never wants to talk to me again."

"Well," Rafe tossed something into the fire, "there's no denying that you acted like an idiot with her yesterday."

"Yeah, it wasn't my finest moment."

A flash of light cracked the sky through the clouds that had now settled overhead. He snorted breathily.

Rafe looked up at the sky with a smile, then pulled his hat a little lower on his head. "I'm telling you, big brother, love has a way of doing funny things to a man."

"Love? Who said anything about love?" Tag took another sip of his drink. "It's true we have a connection. I feel comfortable with her, like we've known each other a long time. I was even prepared to ask her brother his permission to court her, but now…" He shook his head considering what Rafe had said.

Love? Was it even possible?

"We just met. How could I possibly be in love with her?"

"You can deny it all you want, but you're as besotted as they come." Rafe clicked his tongue and nodded, then took a sip of his drink.

"You been talking to Cole?"

"No, why?"

"It's just something he said."

A few moments of quiet passed between them interspersed with a few rounds of rolling thunder. At least it was still just a sprinkle. Tag had no desire to sleep in a wet bedroll.

"It's not that I'm against love, by the way." Rafe said, leaning into Tag. "You said something earlier about me being too angry and bitter to allow anyone else to find happiness in love. Truth is, I'm just as hopeful as anyone, but I'm wary. Tessa had me fooled."

Rafe normally kept his thoughts and feelings about Tessa to himself. It was nice to hear him talk so openly about his once-betrothed.

"I can now see all the warning signs—and trust me—they were there. I am angry and still a little bitter, but I'm working on it." Rafe downed the last of the liquid in his cup.

"You think you'll ever get married?"

Rafe snorted. "Don't push it."

Tag laughed.

"You said there were signs."

"Yeah."

"Do you see any of those things with Brenna? Things I should be aware of?" Tag was almost afraid to ask, but he trusted his brother's insight. It was always better to learn from others' mistakes than to have to make them all on one's own.

"Not from what I've seen—which isn't much, mind you," he said, raising a finger. "But, she's a strong woman. After everything she went through in losing a spouse—or what she believed was losing him, she still arose from her grief to offer an education to the children around her home. To do something productive with her life."

"She's something special, all right."

"And I have to give it to her. Mrs. Scott was willing to stand up and go head to head with the likes of you to protect her brother. She knows there's a bad man out there who wants the ranch, and yet she was willing to put herself in harm's way for those she loves. Yes, I would say she's pretty special. And not too bad to look at either." He grinned as he stared into the dying fire.

"You'll get no argument from me."

"You know, for all that Tessa was beautiful, she never had that kind of selflessness. Brenna looks at you the way Ma still looks at Pa—with wonder and amusement. With the exception of this morning, that is." He turned to look at Tag, shaking his head. "I still can't believe you tried to demand she do your bidding. Have you learned nothing about women after living with Hannah and Mother or even Lottie all these years?"

"I know," Tag said with a half-hearted and embarrassed laugh. "I know!" He screamed, frustrated with his actions.

"Will you two get some sleep?" Harvey said as he turned over in his bedroll.

"Sorry," they said in unison as the fire sizzled beneath the light drizzle.

They sat in silence for a moment.

"You know, I think I was just so angry that Peter Scott is alive. And being hunted—by my brother, no less. I felt like I'd finally found the woman with whom I could…"

"Spend the rest of your life," Rafe provided.

Tag shrugged. "Maybe. But now, everything is so much more complicated. No matter what he's done, he's still her husband. He's already caused her so much grief. I don't know what this will do to her," he stared deep into the red coals glowing in the fire. "She said it's taken her a long time to cope with his death. I can't imagine how she will react to learn he faked it and she's still married—to a criminal."

"If *your* reaction was any indication, well…"

"You're a funny man.," he slugged his brother in the shoulder. "Seriously, what would you have done?"

"I would have known better than to try to control her or command her to do my bidding."

"I don't know what I was thinking." Tag pinched the bridge of his nose and he shook his head. "But, now there is this Tobias

Pane character coming after her." He looked up, took off his hat, and ran his fingers through his hair. "I was scared, am scared," he corrected, even as he swallowed his pride, "that something might happen to her. That I won't be there to protect her. And if her husband is back in the picture, I have no idea what kind of trouble he'll bring with him." He relaxed his posture. "I guess being angry and scared is not really the best combination. It brought out something in me I haven't seen in a long time. I don't know. I guess I could just feel the possibility of being with her slipping away."

He hung his head and exhaled heavily, ignoring the nagging feeling in his gut.

What was he going to do?

His brother remained quiet.

"She's married, Rafe. What am I supposed to do with that?"

"You know…the great state of Texas allows a woman a divorce from a felon."

Tag scoffed.

"Peter Scott definitely qualifies, so don't give up so easily."

"Really?"

"Really."

For the first time all day, hope overtook the gloom. He knew he should feel a shred of remorse, but marriage was special, sacred even, and the idea of Brenna being with such a scoundrel negated any guilt. She deserved better than Peter Scott. If he were honest with himself, she deserved better than him.

"Seriously, what kind of man fakes his own death and leaves behind his new bride?" He still couldn't believe the lengths the man had gone to and the maddening consequences of his selfishness.

"He's dangerous, Tag. Don't be fooled by his good taste in women. He's killed, likely more than once, and he's back in Serenity Hollow for a reason. Which reminds me…" Rafe didn't finish his sentence.

"What?"

"I'm not sure I should have come. Here, I mean. On the drive."

Tag stared at his brother, his brows scrunched together.

"There's something wrong."

"You feel it too?"

"I've just got this feeling that Scott was waiting for us to leave to make his move. We haven't seen hide nor hair of him and neither have any of my contacts in Austin. He may have doubled back."

As much as Tag resented the sheriff for being with Brenna tonight, he was grateful she had someone there to protect her while he was away. He'd tried to tell himself that the likelihood of Peter Scott showing up on this particular weekend was slim, but he'd had that nagging feeling in his gut all night—an unease he was sure would not abate until he was back at the ranch. With Brenna.

After all, someone attacked Jeb and if it was Peter, he may not have travelled south like Rafe had first thought, or, it would have been easy enough for him to double-back.

"I'm glad you're here. It's been a long time since we've had a chance to talk—though I may have felt better if it were you staying at the ranch instead of that dandy sheriff." As if he didn't have a not-so-dead husband to deal with, he preferred not to add competition to the mix.

Rafe laughed. The kind that spread to his eyes. It was good to see him in lighter spirits. It had been a long time. Maybe it was good Rafe wasn't at Oak Meadow. The last thing he needed was for the woman he cared for, falling for his brother.

"Maybe not," he echoed his thoughts aloud. "I wouldn't want you stealing my girl with those dimples of yours."

"Trust me," Rafe said with a light chuckle, "from the way that woman looks at you and *your* dimples, I wouldn't have a chance. Nobody would."

Tag smiled, despite himself. He hoped that was true.

It had been a long couple of days. He'd purchased Oak Meadow for himself and a good fifteen hundred head of cattle and eighty horses for Redbourne Ranch. They'd made it more than half way home before darkness had fallen. So, he figured, it would only be a couple hours ride home in the morning. If they left first thing, they'd possibly make it there by noon.

Home. He liked the sound of that.

"But, maybe we should get an even earlier start than usual. I'll just feel better when I'm there."

"Done." Rafe stretched and stood up. "Well," he said, rinsing his cup with water from his canteen and throwing the remainder into the fire, "you are officially the owner of the Oak Meadow Ranch in Serenity Hollow, Texas. Congratulations, big brother."

They'd stopped off in Round Rock to speak with Josiah Scott. Before handing over the signed contract, they had informed him about Peter. Mr. Scott's obvious shock hadn't deterred his decision to sell the ranch and Tag had closed the deal with a clean conscience.

Yet, as he thought more about his new responsibilities, he thought about the young mustang that he'd left back at the ranch and was grateful that the sheriff had at least had some experience working with wild horses before he'd come to Serenity Hollow. The lawman had agreed to look after the filly for the two days he'd be gone and Tag hoped to find all well when he returned, though he couldn't shake the unsettling feeling stirring in his gut.

"I still am not sure if congratulations are warranted or if condolences would be better suited," Tag said with a sigh.

Rafe laughed as he rolled out his bed for the night. "Get some sleep, Tag. It'll do you a world of good."

'Snort! Zzzzzz.'

Tag and Rafe both glanced over to where Cole slept, his bear-like snore more prominent against the quiet of the night.

They both chuckled.

"It'll be a miracle if any of us get some sleep." Tag set his empty tin down next to him and lay back with his arms resting above his head as he watched the ever-darkening clouds crawl across the sky until they loomed overhead. "And with that storm coming in, it's going to make for a long night."

The memory of his last stormy exchange with Brenna haunted his thoughts and visions of the sheriff waltzing in and snatching her away from him—with all his eye-rollingly dashing charms—would not leave him alone. After the way he'd acted, he wouldn't blame Brenna if she chose to be with the sheriff over him, after all, he'd been the one to step up and provide her a suitable option. He'd been the hero. Blast it all if he didn't like the man himself.

Stop wallowing, he told himself. *It won't do you any good.* And he determined that he would do everything he could to make it up to her when he returned.

Tag blinked a few times to rid his eyes of the falling droplets of rain that sprinkled from the sky.

"Go to sleep," Rafe said, his hat now covering his face. "I can hear you thinking from here."

"How…? Never mind. Goodnight."

"Uhmhmmm. 'Night."

CHAPTER EIGHTEEN

Brenna pulled her shawl tighter around her shoulders as a cool evening breeze caressed her cheek and brushed her hair. She would miss the view from this porch when she was gone. The colors of the setting sun were nothing but slim splashes of orange and pink across the horizon. It was breathtaking. She leaned against the railing pillars and took a deep breath. It smelled like rain.

A twig snapped to her left.

She shot up straight, her heart skipping a beat.

"Thought we could use some firewood."

Brenna exhaled at the sound of the sheriff's voice.

"Looks like a storm's headed in." He started up the stairs, but when his eyes met hers, he set down his load and was at her side in a moment. "What's wrong?" he asked. "You're shaking." He ran his hands up and down her arms.

"You startled me is all. And it's getting colder out here."

"Well," he said as he bent down to pick up the small bundle of logs he'd collected, "let's get you into the house and start a fire."

"I'll be right in," she said with a smile, grateful to have someone looking out for her tonight.

The sheriff nodded and headed into the house without her.

Brenna looked out over the yard and all that had been accomplished over the last few days. She hadn't realized how much the place had fallen into disrepair without having someone, other than her brother, around to help take care of it. She glanced over at the bunkhouse roof and stifled a giggle at the memory of Tag sitting all disheveled on the top bunk of the only bed in the room after falling through the worn roof. It had scared her half to death, but now, it would be a fond memory. It was odd how quickly he'd become a part of the ranch. And her life.

She wrapped her arms around herself and took a deep breath.

She missed him. Even the ornery him.

One more night, she told herself, finding it increasingly difficult to wait until Monday to see his handsome face. The sheriff had stayed faithfully by her side, helping her with any little task she'd needed. While she appreciated him and all that he'd neglected in his life to be there with her, she wished it had been Tag collecting wood for their fire.

One drop. Two. She held her hand out and she smiled at the beads of water that landed in a splash. It had been a while since it last rained and she was sure the peaches and other fruits in the orchard would benefit greatly from the moisture.

The door squeaked open.

The sheriff leaned against the frame, his hands in his pockets and his feet crossed.

"Jeb's asleep," he said in a low, raspy voice.

"Really? He must have been more tired than I thought. I expected him to be much more protective with you here." She smiled.

To think that a few days ago, she had no potential suitors, nor any desire for one, now she had two men seeking her attentions.

"Thank you for checking in on him. I know this must be inconvenient for you, being away from town." She wasn't sure what to do with her hands and she turned back to face the yard.

"Eh, I like my job," he said simply.

The sound of his voice so closely behind her gave her a start.

"But, I like it even more," Sheriff Hunt continued, "when it means I get to spend time with the most beautiful woman in Serenity Hollow."

The pressure of his palms on her hips brought heat to Brenna's cheeks and she turned to face him.

"Now, you're just sweet-talking me," she said with a knowing smile.

He was a little too close for comfort.

"Is it working?" he asked as he reached up to brush a stray hair from her face.

Visions of Tag's smile popped into her mind and she bit her lip.

"I don't think so," she said with a smile.

When his grin faltered, she placed a hand on his forearm. "You have been so kind to stay here at Oak Meadow to watch over me, but…I'm afraid my heart belongs to another."

The thought sobered her. She pulled back from his semblance of an embrace, her eyes narrowing at the window sill behind him as she pondered what she'd just said.

Her voice softened in wonder. "My heart belongs to another," she repeated. She knew even as she said it, that the words were true.

"You don't mean Redbourne?" Sheriff Hunt asked with a scoffing-like chuckle. "What am I saying? Of course, it's Redbourne. As much as I hate to admit it, I think if I were a gal, I'd probably want him too." He cleared his throat. "I just mean…never mind."

Brenna giggled. "I know exactly what you mean."

"Does he know?" The sheriff dropped his hands and took a step backward.

She shook her head, her eyes widening at the idea of it.

"You should tell him," he said, shoving his hands into his pockets.

Brenna looked up to meet the lawman's eyes. "But, we just met. How can I possibly…"

"If it were me," he stopped her from saying more, "I'd want to know." He pushed open the door, inviting her inside. "No matter how much time had or had not passed. Come on," he encouraged. "I've already got a fire going. Let's get you inside and warmed up and I'll make us some coffee."

She bit her lip and scrunched her shoulders apologetically. "I'm afraid we don't have any coffee."

"How is that even possible?" he asked with a high, incredulous pitch to his voice. "Is this not a ranch? I don't know that I've ever known a rancher who didn't have coffee in his stores."

"It ran out a long time ago," she said apologetically, "and it was just not a priority to replace."

"Where are your priorities?" he joked, hanging his hat on the hook just inside the door.

"We could make some hot chocolate to drink instead," she offered as she crossed the threshold and headed toward the kitchen.

"You mean you drink melted chocolate?" he asked with awe as he fell in step behind her. "That's a little thick, ain't it?"

"Isn't it," she corrected him over her shoulder before she could stop herself. She paused and looked back at him. "Sorry. I guess I just can't turn off the school teacher inside of me." She shrugged. "Habit."

"I have a feeling there is a lot I could learn from you, Mrs. Scott."

She ignored him, but couldn't keep the pleased smile from her face. "Hot chocolate is not simply melted chocolate. It's a…a…oh, come on," she said turning back for the kitchen, "I'll show you."

If this was going to be the sheriff's first time having hot chocolate, she wanted to make his experience a good one. Her aunt had sent her a special blend just after she'd gotten married.

They'd only used it once before Peter had passed, but she still remembered the creamy, delicious concoction as if it were yesterday.

Brenna strung her shawl over the back of one of the chairs and rolled up her sleeves as she pushed the stool with her foot until it was directly below her shelf of tins. Though after her latest experience and having sized up the height of the ledge, she smiled sheepishly and turned back to the sheriff.

"Would you mind?" she asked, pointing to the top shelf at the tin next to the popcorn.

"One of the many benefits of being tall," he said, chuckling as he slid the stool out of the way and reached up to collect the tin. "It's heavy," he said with surprise. "What do you have in there? Solid gold chocolate bars?" he asked as he pulled out a chair and sat down at the table.

Brenna's brows scrunched together as she took the tin from him, the weight surprising her. It was heavy. Too heavy. Cocoa powder was generally very light. Maybe she'd mislabeled the tin, but that was unlikely. She placed it on the counter and with some effort removed the lid. She stared down at the contents, shocked.

"What's wrong?" he asked, then sat back against the chair with his arms folded. "Bugs?" he said knowingly.

She looked over at him, her eyes wide. "Not exactly," she said as she shook her head.

Where did it all come from?

"Why do you look like you just saw a ghost?" Sheriff Hunt asked, coming to his feet, concern lacing his brow. "Mrs. Scott? What is it?"

What could she say? She reached inside and pulled out a fistful of bills.

"You keep your money in with your hot chocolate?"

"No." She shook the container, coins of all sizes jingling clunkily amongst the paper notes. There had to be several hundred dollars inside. "That's just it. This," she shook the money in front of her, "doesn't belong to me. I…" she looked up at him, and took a step toward him. "I don't know where it came from."

"Shhh…" the sheriff said, his hand sliding to his hip as he stared hard at the wall in front of the store cupboard.

Brenna followed the man's line of sight, her brows now scrunching together.

"I really wish you hadn't found that," a hauntingly familiar voice came from the pantry.

Brenna gasped. She dropped the can, money scattering all over the kitchen floor as time seemed to slow around her and she raised a hand to her mouth.

NO! Impossible.

The sheriff drew his weapon.

She swallowed, her heart thumping intensely within her chest. She blinked hard, her breath steadily getting harder to catch as she turned to face her past.

"Peter?" she asked, almost in a whisper.

It can't be. How…? Surely, she was hearing things.

"It's me, buttercup'," the man said as he stepped out into the dim lamplight of the kitchen.

When she met his eyes, he opened his arms as if inviting her to run to him, but she didn't miss the pistol adorning his hand or the warning bells suddenly sounding in her head. She didn't move.

The man's usually kempt hair had grown to his shoulders, his face unshaven, and his clothes old and ragged, but the man standing before her was most definitely Peter Scott. Her husband.

Her momentary relief gave way to apprehension. Something inside of her warned her to be wary. People didn't just come back from the dead.

"Peter?" She took a step toward him, one hand extended toward his face. "What…?" She wasn't sure what to say. "How…? What…happened to you? Where have you been?"

"Drop it, Scott," the sheriff warned.

Peter ignored him and continued to focus on her.

She took a step toward the dead man.

"Mrs. Scott, I wouldn't advise—"

She barely heard the sheriff as she took another step toward Peter. "How are you not…"

"Dead?" her husband snorted a laugh.

She nodded. "I saw your…body. I…" She raised her fingers to her mouth, desperately trying to recall the day she'd been called upon to identify him.

"Well, buttercup…"

"Please don't call me that," she said, remembering the day he'd first called her by the name of the poisonous blooms.

"Well, *my dear*, that's a long story, one I will be happy to tell you after I get what I came for."

"Where have you been?" she asked, a slight plea for answers in her voice.

He stared at her, but did not answer.

"I buried you, Peter. Mourned your death. And," she glanced up at him and waved her hand flippantly, "here you are. Alive and well." Anger now welled up inside of her as the realization of what he had done washed over her. She balled her hands into fists. "How am I supposed to react to that? How am I supposed to feel?"

"I thought you'd be happy to see me." He rounded the corner, so that he stood before her unapologetically. He leaned forward.

Brenna bent backward.

He reached past her and picked up a handful of berries from the counter and popped one into his mouth. "I was a good husband, after all, wasn't I?" He smiled, and admittedly, it was one of the things she'd missed most about him. But, when he took another step, reducing the space between them to no more than the bible, she took a step back, running into the counter with nowhere else to go and put her hand up to stop him from coming any closer.

He halted, a slight curl to his lip.

The stench of his breath reached her and she cringed.

Brenna dropped her head and sidestepped away from him, closer to the edge of the counter. "I thought we were going to build a life together. I know you didn't marry me for love, but I thought we would grow into that. I believed I could trust you." She shook her head. "But now…" She looked up and met his eyes. "It's been a year, Peter. Where have you been?" she asked again, this time meeting his eyes straight on.

"Mrs. Scott," the sheriff said again, the warning stronger in his voice this time. "I know you need answers, but listen to me. Peter Scott is—"

"Who *are* you?" Peter cut him off, his voice laced with disdain, and for the first time he turned his attention to the lawman. "And what are you doing in my house? With my wife?" He waved his gun haphazardly as he spoke.

The sheriff carefully pulled back his vest to reveal his shiny star-shaped badge, then cocked his gun, still pointed at the man. "This isn't your house and dead men don't have wives."

"Well, as you can see deputy…"

"Sheriff," Hunt corrected.

"Right. Well, as you can see, *Sheriff*, I ain't dead."

"I'm not dead," Brenna corrected before thinking better of it.

"And there she is," Peter said appreciatively as he clapped his hands together, then waved his gun in her general direction, "that bride of mine, all smart with her university education." He tapped the barrel of his pistol to his temple. "I *am not* dead," he reiterated as he nodded his acknowledgement of his error as if waiting for her approval.

The sheriff's jaw flexed, a smug smile touching his lips. "A fact I think many people would like to know—including a very gifted bounty hunter who's in town looking for you, along with Tobias Pane, and a few of the fellas down at O'Malley's to whom you seemed to have owed a lot of money when you…died."

"Now, what did you have to go and bring them up for? I thought we were going to handle this all civilized like."

"Drop the gun, Scott, and turn yourself in. It'll be a lot better for you if you come with me willingly."

"Turn himself in? For what?" She slid out from between the counter and her husband then turned to look at Peter.

His pinched face and flared nostrils spoke volumes.

"What exactly did you do?" she asked.

"Are you going to tell her, or am I?" Sheriff Hunt asked.

"Tell me what?"

"Exactly!" Peter spat. "There's nothin' to tell. I'm sure this is all just one big misunderstanding."

The sheriff pulled a folded parchment from his pocket, not taking his eyes off Peter, and handed it to her. "There's no misunderstanding."

"What is this?" Brenna unfolded the paper and saw a sketched version of Peter's face staring back at her, then held it up for the straggly man to see.

She didn't know what to say.

"It's a pretty good likeness, wouldn't you say?" Peter's misguided boast contorted his features with a self-satisfied grin.

"This says there is a five-hundred-dollar reward," she read, "for the capture of the man who killed Deputy Justin Flannigan." Brenna stared at the man who'd just turned her world upside down. Again. "Murder, Peter? You killed a man? A deputy?"

"You can't go believing everything you read." He took a step toward her, coins clinking together beneath his booted feet. "Brenna, please. Just let me collect what I come for."

"And then, what? You'll disappear again? You'll go back to playing dead?"

"If that's what you want." He reached out, grabbing her around the waist, and pulled her into him hard, staring down at her with a raised brow and a lusty leer.

She heard the sheriff's boots scuff against the floor and she waved at him to stop.

"Let. Me. Go," she said, pushing against Peter. "This isn't you." She struggled against him, not allowing her fear to make her succumb.

"Isn't it?" His fingers twisted in her hair and he pulled her head to him, his lips greedily smashing against hers.

She opened her mouth and bit him.

"Ouch," he spat, shoving her away from him and tapping the side of his lips with his finger, then looking at it.

No blood.

His rough demeanor changed in an instant. "Yes," he said, the sickeningly sweet and sudden change in the tone of his voice leaving an eerie sensation in her belly, "I get what I came for and you'll never see me again."

Brenna took a sideways step, then one back toward Sheriff Hunt. The lawman's gun was still pointed at Peter, but her husband hadn't seemed to notice. Or care.

"What did you come back for, Peter? You've been gone a long time. Why now?"

"Mrs. Scott, I'm sorry, but I've got to take him in. You can ask all the questions you want down at the jail." The sheriff moved toward her husband, one hand holding his gun, the other at his hip retrieving his cuffs.

"That's not going to happen," Peter said, aiming his gun purposefully for the first time.

Sheriff Hunt stopped.

"See, you can't arrest me," he touched his chest with his gun-laden hand. "I was never here. I'm dead. Invisible." He shrugged mockingly. "But, I heard all y'all have been having some trouble with Tobias Pane. The way I see it, ol' Toby came around to claim his stake in the ranch—yes, I know he told you about my little promissory note and gambling…hobby," he said with a distorted smile. "—and this time, when you refused to turn it over to him, he done killed anyone who stood in his way, getting himself shot in the process."

Brenna couldn't believe what she was hearing.

"Peter?" she jutted forward.

He pulled another gun from his belt and pointed it at her. "Not this time, *buttercup!*"

Brenna's heart sank. How had she been so wrong? "You wouldn't."

"Wouldn't I?"

Her married life had been a total sham. One big gamble. And she'd obviously been on the losing end. Peter Scott wasn't at all the man she'd believed him to be. She reviewed his previous words, '*I get what I came for and you'll never see me again*'. The sickening realization hit her as she understood that he aimed to kill her. And the sheriff. All of them, including Tobias Pane.

"It was you," she said aloud, horrified. "How could I have missed it? How?" she shook her head, trying to review all the events surrounding the time of his death, but there was nothing.

"I'm afraid I don't have a lot of time, darlin', so I'll just collect what I come for and be on my way."

There. He said it again. What had he come for?

"Peter, tell me you aren't the one who attacked my brother." She needed more time to think.

"Oh, that. Well, the kid saw me lurking around the barn and I couldn't very well have him tell anybody, now could I? I am a walking dead man after all."

"But, he's family. Doesn't that mean anything to you? You could have killed him."

"That may have mattered to me in the beginning, but being dead has taught me a few things about survival. And I must admit, I was quite surprised…no, disappointed to see he's still alive when I came into the house earlier." He picked something from his teeth and threw it on the ground. "Something that will soon be rectified."

Brenna shot a look at the bedroom where Jeb slept, but all she could see was the lump of blankets covering him.

Please let him be all right. Please let him be all right.

Peter bent down and picked up a wad of bills she'd dropped onto the floor.

"Shame you found this before I'd had a chance to take it," he said, holding up the bills. "Just makes what I have to do that much more complicated."

"You're going to kill us for a few hundred dollars?"

"Oh, it's not just the money," he said, crouching down to retrieve a few of the spilled coins.

She could not take her eyes off the gun he waved about so casually.

"Why then, Peter? Why are you doing this?"

"This was never my place. Not really. Sure, I held the deed for a while, but ranching is hard work and it didn't take me long to realize I wanted a different kind of life."

"The kind that stops you from bathing or wearing clean, kempt clothing?" she asked. She knew it was bold.

He chortled. "This," he pulled at the front of his tattered shirt, "is just temporary. I didn't have time to stop by the tailor and have my new suit fitted." His eyes darted wildly between her and the sheriff as he spoke.

"If you weren't happy here, then, why marry me at all?" She scanned the room for something she could use to protect herself.

"I thought I could have the best of both worlds. When I made enough money at the tables, I could hire men to do the work at the ranch, but it was only a matter of time before I couldn't fool myself anymore. I was never going to be the rancher my pa wanted me to be. So, when the opportunity presented itself, I jumped on it and I am not going to let you or anyone else take it away from me."

"How could you be so...so...calculating? Heartless?"

She stared at him, shocked at his callous nonchalance. At

that moment, she knew the man meant what he'd said. He planned to kill them and blame it on Tobias. But, it had been a year since he'd lost that game of poker. How could he have possibly known about the brute coming by to claim the ranch? Come to think of it, how did he know his father was even selling the ranch? Unless…someone local was helping him.

Brenna noticed movement. As Peter was focused on her, the sheriff, one slow step at a time, made his way closer to the man. She needed to keep her no-good husband talking.

"What happened to you, Peter?" she asked as she sat down on one of the kitchen chairs. She wasn't sure how much longer her legs would continue to support her. "How can you do this?" Although it seemed like she'd asked the same question over again, she needed to keep him talking long enough to figure out how they were going to get away from him.

It took a significant amount of effort to refrain from looking at the sheriff. Surely, she or the lawman would come up with some way out of their predicament before it ended badly for all of them.

"Did you ever care for me at all?" she asked, unable to think of something else to say.

"Awww, darlin', of course, I did," he said as he joined her at the table.

He brushed a finger over her cheek. A sickening feeling swept down the length of her and she turned away from him.

"You were the perfect wife—beautiful, charming, smart, if not a bit quirky."

If those words had been from any other man, she would have been very pleased, but as it were, she had to keep the bile from rising in her throat.

"Let her go, Scott," Sheriff Hunt called.

"Because of you, my father gave me the ranch," Peter said, ignoring the sheriff, "which I sold, bartered, and lost in one poker game or another too many times to count. I guess the sale that really counted was when I sold it back to my father because he insisted on me handing over the deed. Ultimately, you and I wanted different things. I wanted out of this life, and you...well..."

Anger swelled inside her belly. Brenna's hands clenched again into fists and she moved to stand, but Peter forcibly pushed her by the shoulder back into her seat.

"I know you think you're being sly there, Sheriff, but I can see you. And unless you want my pretty little wife here to get hurt..." he gathered a fistful of her hair and tugged enough that it brought her to her feet and in front of him, a small squeal escaping her lips, "then, I suggest you come back over here where I can keep an eye on you."

"Peter, you're hurting me," she said, gripping his wrist to take off some of the pressure. He'd gone absolutely mad. However, whether it was from sheer arrogance or plain stupidity, he'd allowed the sheriff to keep his gun. That gave her some semblance of hope.

"Why don't you just take what you came for, Scott, and leave the lady alone?"

Peter guffawed loudly.

"And have you and every bounty hunter between here and New York City looking for me? I don't think so." He gestured at the sheriff's pistol as if having read her thoughts. "Now, drop it," he said quietly.

The sheriff didn't move.

"Now!" Peter yelled at the hesitation.

The lawman set his gun down on the table and took a step backward, his hands raised to his shoulders, palms out.

"Besides," Peter continued, "last I checked, she was my wife." He nuzzled the back of her neck with his grizzly face and ran a hand around her belly, pulling her tight against him.

Brenna crinkled her nose. He smelled as if he hadn't bathed in a year.

"No!" she screamed, digging her fingers beneath his palm, trying desperately to pull his hand away from her body. "Let go of me!"

He laughed, but her struggles only encouraged him to pull her even closer.

"I'm warning you, Scott. Get away from her."

Peter aimed his gun at the sheriff. "And just what are you going to do about it?" Peter asked.

"No!" she screamed as she rushed to deter his aim.

He grabbed her, whipping her around in his arms, and smashed his lips onto hers with bruising effect.

She pushed against his chest, twisting and turning to pull free from his grasp. Once his grip loosened enough that she could push away from him, she slapped him as hard as she could.

What did I just do?

He twisted his face back up to meet hers, this time his eyes were dark, soulless, and he rubbed his face with his fingers, an evil leer splaying across his face.

"You ought not to have done that, my dear," he said, his voice empty.

She took a step backward, but the counter blocked her retreat. She refused to look away from him or to apologize for her actions.

"A man by the name of Redbourne came by yesterday looking for you." The sheriff attempted to change his line of thought.

The color seemed to drain from Peter's face.

"He's a bounty hunter. It seems there are already plenty of folks who know you're alive. I imagine by now, your father knows too."

"Leave my father out of this," he spat.

Despite what he said, she knew that Peter had always striven to gain his father's approval.

He ground his teeth together and paced the floor as if trying to decide how to proceed, the gun waving haphazardly with his movements.

The sheriff slowly leaned down and grabbed ahold of one pant leg and inched it up on his leg until the butt of another gun shown just above his boot.

RUMBLE! Thunder rolled across the sky, shaking the ranch house with its power and startling Brenna.

"Peter Scott," Sheriff Hunt said, pulling his weapon as he rose to a stand in one smooth forward movement, "you are under arrest for—"

CRACK!

CRACK!

"NO!" Brenna screamed as the sheriff dropped to one knee, blood streaming from his thigh. Without a thought, she grabbed a towel from the top of the counter and hurried to his side, glancing up for Peter's whereabouts, but she couldn't see him from her position.

"Jeb!" she screamed for her brother, unknowing whether or not he lived. "I need your help!"

CHAPTER NINETEEN

The moon sat low in the sky, providing adequate light for Tag's travels between several assemblages of ominous clouds. Rain had fallen in spurts through the night and both he and his horse were soaked to the bone. He couldn't wait to get back to the house and change into some warm clothes.

Once the outline of the homestead came into view, all seemed quiet—the house still stood, no flames licked the timbers, and Tag briefly second-guessed his decision to leave the drive in the middle of the night. He reminded himself that both Rafe and Cole were highly capable, as were the men on his crew, and he slowed his horse to a leisurely walk, welcoming the now soft pitter-patter of raindrops as they tapped against the ground.

He would have to face Brenna soon enough, why hadn't he just waited to leave camp until morning?

As he'd lain on his bedroll last night waiting for sleep to overtake him, visions of the beautiful school teacher had not allowed him any peace. His unsettled gut, combined with the incessant splashes on his face, had driven him to get up and go on ahead of his team to make the rest of the two-hour trek home in the dark by himself.

What was I thinking?

The booming rumble of thunder seemed to answer back.

Maybe he could sleep in the bunkhouse and she would never know the difference.

CRACK!
CRACK!
What in the…

Tag urged his steed to a run, his heart matching the horse's pace. The gunshots had come from inside the house.

"Brenna!" he yelled as he slid down from his horse, pulling his pistol from his belt, and ran for the house. "Brenna, where are you?" When he reached the porch, he took the stairs two at a time and threw open the door, his gun in hand. He darted a look inside, but didn't see an immediate threat. "Hunt? Jeb?" he called as he entered the kitchen.

The sheriff sat on the floor, leaning up against the wall next to the table, his leg covered with a bloody towel.

"Where's Brenna?" he demanded.

"I can't wake him," she said, rushing into the kitchen.

Relief washed over Tag at the sight of her. He holstered his weapon and within moments had closed the distance between them.

"You're back!" she said, rushing into him and wrapping her arms around his trunk.

He pulled her close, holding her tight, one hand nestling her head into his shoulder. After a moment, he pulled away enough that he could look down into her face. He found a tear trailing down her cheek and he reached up to wipe it away.

"I'm so sorry I wasn't here."

"You're here now."

His eyes fell to her beautiful mouth and he flexed his jaw.

She was a beautiful sight.

And she was alive.

She's married.

"Hmhmmm," the sheriff said, clearing his throat to get their attention. He'd dragged himself up against the wall and had cut the leg of his trousers enough to expose the wound.

Tag let go of Brenna and stepped away, afraid that if he stayed even a moment longer he would kiss her straight on the mouth.

Cole was right. He was besotted.

Blast it all. He tore his gaze away from her.

"I heard a gunshot." He turned to the sheriff, realizing for the first time he'd never learned the man's given name. "What happened here, Hunt?" he asked, turning his focus to the bleeding sheriff.

He knelt down next to the man. It appeared that the bullet had gone straight through the muscled exterior of his leg. Tag would have expected there to be more blood, but guessed it was a good sign.

"It's just a graze," the sheriff dismissed with a wave of his hand. "I've had a whole lot worse. I'll be fine, but, Tag…*he's* here."

"Who?" Tag's concern quickly escalated to apprehension. "Pane?" He pulled his gun back out of the holster.

The sheriff shook his head slowly, glancing briefly at Brenna.

Peter Scott.

Tag's jaw clenched and his hands balled into fists as he took a deep breath. "He did this?"

The sheriff nodded.

"Where is he?" Tag finally managed. The man had already put Brenna through so much and now, he was back. There was no telling what the man was capable of.

Unacceptable.

"I hit him," the sheriff pointed toward several droplets of blood. "But, you can't go after him on your own. We'll wait until it's light and we'll get a few men together to go after him."

"Jeb," Brenna breathed. She hurried forward, taking Tag by the hand, and dragged him into the bedroom where Jeb seemed to have slept through the ordeal.

"I need to secure the house."

"But, there's something wrong." She bent down and shook her brother. "He's breathing, but he won't wake up. Please tell me he's not…" Her hands shot to her mouth.

Tag went to his side and felt his head. There was no fever and his skin felt normal to the touch. His chest heaved and fell in normal rhythm.

"It just appears like he is sleeping," he said, then patted her brother on the cheek. "Jeb?"

No response.

Tag shook his shoulders. "Jeb!" he called again, louder this time.

Still nothing.

"He's unconscious, but it's really not my area of expertise." He'd seen many wounds in the war, and several people who'd been knocked unconscious, but then he had a thought. He glanced around the room and found a small rag that had been crumpled up and discarded on the floor next to the bed. He reached down and picked it up, carefully bringing it up to his face. He took a light whiff and quickly pulled it away from his nose.

Chloroform.

He nodded with relief as he moved to the other side of the bed where Brenna sat, holding her brother's hand.

"He's going to be fine, Brenna," he said, leaning down and placing a light kiss on her head before thinking. "It looks like Peter just knocked him out with a form of anesthesia."

She turned to look at him, the dim light from the lantern she'd lit on the nightstand casting a warm glow around her hair.

"Why?"

"I'm sorry?"

"Why, when he tried to kill him before, did he only knock him out this time? He could have killed him, even said he would do it soon enough, so why not now?"

It was a good question, one for which Tag did not have an answer…yet.

"I don't know, professor, but he's alive. Thank the Lord for that."

"Of course," she said as she lay down across Jeb's chest and reached her arm around her brother in an awkward hug. Then, she sat up straight, turned, and stood. "Wait," she said, her forehead scrunched.

She faced him, searching his eyes for something.

Peter. Tag had mentioned his name. It seemed he'd avoided one fire by starting another.

"Look, Brenna," he said, taking ahold of her shoulders. He needed to explain.

"How did you know?" she asked without letting him finish. "How...? Excuse me," she said, then wove around him, grabbing a sheet from the closet in the hall. She strode back out into the kitchen with purpose, mumbling something to herself.

He followed closely behind her. He hadn't meant for her to find out like this.

She marched over to the counter and pulled a knife from the drawer and with purpose, she stabbed the sheet. It had already been pieced and Tag guessed it was the same sheet they'd used the other night when they were preparing bandages for Jeb's head. She started ripping the sheet into strips.

"Here, let me help," he said, reaching out to take the sheet.

Brenna slammed the knife down on the counter and ran the back of her hand across her face.

She was crying.

"Brenna, I..."

She looked up at him, her eyes darting back and forth between his. "You...knew?" she asked.

He'd thought he'd been protecting her, but as she searched his face for answers, he wondered if he'd really just wanted to put off the inevitable as long as possible.

"You knew Peter was alive?" she asked again. "And you didn't say anything to me?"

"Don't be too hard on him, Mrs. Scott. He had no way of knowing your husband would come back here."

Husband. The word stabbed a sharp pain in his gut. And, of course, he knew that Peter Scott would show up at Oak Meadow sometime. He just hadn't expected it to be so soon.

"Shhh…" she held up her open hand and snapped her fingers shut together. "I haven't even started with you yet." She put her hands on her hips. "I cannot believe that both of you knew that *my husband* was alive and neither of you cared to say anything to me about it."

"Brenna, I…" He sounded like an ignoramus, repeating himself and stumbling over his words.

She was obviously upset. He reached out to touch her hand, to offer comfort.

She's married, he reminded himself, and snatched his hand back, thrusting it into his pocket.

How could he explain why he hadn't told her about her husband when he was unsure of his reasons himself? He should have let her know, plain and simple. His mama had taught him to always own up to his mistakes. So, he took a deep breath.

"You're right. I should have told you." He resisted the urge to reach out to her.

What is wrong with me?

It was as if moving to Texas had made him lose his mind. He'd been acting out of character ever since he'd arrived— though, he'd felt more like himself than he had in years.

Brenna's brows raised and she opened her mouth, obviously surprised that he'd conceded her point.

"How long?"

"I'm sorry?"

"How long have you known?"

"Since Friday morning, when Rafe showed up." He didn't want to keep anything else from her.

She nodded, staring at him, pools of unshed tears still brimming on her lashes. Instead of saying anything, she took the few strips she'd cut, and walked over to where the sheriff still sat on the floor applying pressure to his injury. She grabbed the same bottle of spirits that they'd used on Jeb's head wound, then hunched down over the injured man and proceeded to bind his leg.

"I'm guessing your brothers will be here in the morning," she said matter-of-factly.

"Yes, ma'am."

"Good." She looked at the sheriff. "I think we've done all we can for now, but when Mr. Redbourne…" She cleared her throat. "…when the…when Rafe gets here," she finally settled on the right words, "I'm sure he will be able to do a much better job of this than I have done. I'm afraid I don't have any experience caring for a gunshot."

If he'd only been here a few minutes earlier, maybe he could have stopped Scott. Maybe he should never have left. Guilt stabbed at his gut, but it warred with the sense of duty he had to his family, to the ranch. It had been his responsibility to purchase cattle and horses at the last big auction of the season. How could he have done things differently?

Brenna shifted on the floor, wrapping bandages around the sheriff's thigh and, for a brief moment, as he watched the way she touched him, Tag wished it had been him who'd taken the bullet.

He had to change the direction his thoughts were taking him.

"Well, Peter Scott is not going to get back in here tonight," he said, striding the few steps it took to get to the back door. "I'll see to that." He noted the blood trail that led outside and battled his impulse to follow it. Curiosity and darkness were not compatible companions—not when the hunted had a gun and the advantage of a familiarity with the terrain.

"Mr. Redbourne?" Brenna called, looking up from her task.

Mr. Redbourne? She was angry. And with reason. He should have listened to Rafe from the beginning and kept his distance. He'd read once that 'it was better to have loved and lost'…well, he wasn't quite sure it was love, yet, but the thought of losing Brenna twisted in his gut like gnarled wood and there was nothing he could do about it.

"Come dry yourself by the fire," she said. "You won't be of any use to me if you take ill. I'll be expecting that shooting lesson tomorrow."

The woman was definitely full of surprises.

"Yes, ma'am."

Early Monday Morning

Brenna lay on the chaise in her bedroom until the storm finally let up in the early hours of the morning. She normally found comfort in the sound of the rain tapping against the roof, but her mind wrestled with her dilemma. Sleep eluded her, something that happened more often now that Tag had come to Oak Meadow Ranch than it ever had. She gathered the quilt around her and headed for the door. The fresh air would do her some good.

As she headed out, she nearly tripped over the large, overstuffed chair that had been moved just outside of the bedroom door.

Her eyes had already adjusted to the dark and she made out Tag's large form sprawled across the seat at an awkward angle as he slept, his long legs extending across the width of the hall, and his hand clutched around his gun across his chest.

"Going somewhere?" he asked, his eyes still closed.

Her heart skipped a beat and she raised a hand to her chest. She hit him on the shoulder.

"You startled me," she whispered, careful not to wake the two injured men in the house.

"We have to stop making a habit of this." Tag raised his arms and stretched, then jumped to his feet, standing mere inches in front of her.

She could hardly breathe, but she refused to let it show, and smiled through her discomfort. "I'm still mad at you," she said, folding her arms across her chest, inadvertently brushing against him. Heat rose immediately in her cheeks. She was grateful that it would be too dark for Tag to see the color she was sure emblazoned her face.

"I know." His voice was low and gravelly, and sent gooseflesh cascading down her arms.

"How's Jeb this morning?" she asked, her voice still a little gravelly from lack of use.

"Still sleeping, last I checked."

Brenna hugged herself as she stepped around him and headed toward the front door, determined to get some air. She would feel a lot better once she knew that Jeb was going to be all right.

"I'm afraid I can't let you leave," he said.

She stopped short as he stepped in front of her, effectively blocking her retreat.

"Without an escort anyway," he added with a boyish grin. "Scott may still be lurking outside."

It was all still so unreal. Just when she'd met Tag and he'd awakened feelings in her she hadn't even known existed, her late husband showed up, alive and wanting her dead.

How had this happened? When had her life become so…messy?

She was reluctant to look up at Tag, afraid she wouldn't be able to look away.

"All right," she relented. "If you think it's necessary," she said as she stepped around him again. "You may accompany me." When she got to the door, a large chest blocked her exit. She got on one side and attempted to push it out of the way, but it was just too heavy.

"Would you like some help?" Tag asked.

She could hear the laughter in his voice.

"Please," she invited with a chuckle of her own.

Once the doorway was clear, she stepped out onto the large

covered porch. The air held a surprising chill for the time of year and Brenna pulled her quilt tighter around her shoulders. She slipped over to the porch swing.

"Wait, before you sit down," Tag said as he threw the door back open and bent down to grab a towel from just inside. He darted over to the swing and laid the towel down in front of her, sopping up the puddles of rainwater that had accumulated there.

"You don't make it very easy for me to stay angry with you."

"Good," he said as he draped the newly damp towel over the railing by the stairs. Instead of sitting down next to her, he leaned against the pillar and glanced out into the yard, his arms folded.

Brenna pulled the blanket up around her, finding it increasingly difficult to stop ogling the very handsome cowboy who'd ridden into her life so unexpectedly.

"I was going to wait to tell you," he said without turning to look at her, "but under the circumstances, I think it's better if I just tell you things upfront and right away. I'm, uh," he scratched the back of his head, "buying the Cranston place and Grimace's spread. I think they will make a nice addition to Oak Meadow."

"Congratulations."

He nodded. "There's a little cabin at the edge of the Cranston property that borders Oak Meadow. I've been thinking that maybe I'd stay out there for a while. Once we catch Peter and resolve this issue with Pane."

Her heart deflated a little at his words.

"At least until we can get the new school built for you and the children," he continued, glancing back for a moment, then forward again without making eye contact, "with a small room for a teacher's living quarters on the back."

She sat there, quiet, unsure of what to react to first.

"You're leaving?" she asked, finally able to find her voice.

He turned around to face her, still inclined against the railing, his ankles and arms crossed. The moon sat low in the sky, directly behind him, creating a silhouette that didn't allow her to see the details of his face.

"I don't want to, but, under the circumstances, I think it will be for the best if I distance myself from the ranch."

"From the ranch or from me?" It was a bold question, but they'd been candid with each other since the day they'd met and she wanted to know.

"Listen, Brenna, I know our coming here was…unexpected, but—"

"I can't argue with that, but…I'm glad that you're here. I can't explain it, but, I don't want you to leave. This is your home now. You have a place here. And it's time you start building your life at Oak Meadow."

"You have got to stop doing that." He looked out at the early morning sky as he leaned on the porch rail.

"Doing what?" She stood up, strung her quilt over the edge of the swing, and joined him at the railing.

He shook his head, hit the top of the rail, then finally turned to look at her, standing at his full height.

"Making me fall in love with you." He reached down to brush a hair from her face, then tucked it behind her ear.

Warmth spread through her body and a light, airy feeling bubbled up in her chest.

"You love me?" she asked, hope swelling in her heart.

"From the moment you told me I could 'go back to wherever I came from' that first day at the alcove," he breathed an incredulous laugh, "though I doubt I would have admitted it then."

Brenna stood close enough to him that she could see his smile. She giggled. "I did say that, didn't I?"

He nodded, his gaze falling to her mouth and she bit her lip.

She didn't realize just how much she wanted him to kiss her until that moment.

"You are so beautiful." Tag smiled, his thumb caressing her

cheek. He exhaled sharply, then dropped his hand from her face and turned back to look out at the yard. "I'm sorry I wasn't here."

"What more could you have done?" she asked, aching to reach out and reassure him with her touch, but she refrained.

"I guess we'll never know."

Silence passed between them for a few moments, before Tag stood up, still looking forward, avoiding her gaze.

"I can't do this," he said. "I can't be here knowing you belong to another man. I just think it's best if I stay as far away as I can."

She wanted to tell him not to go, but she knew that would be unfair and selfish. As long as she was married, whether it was to a miscreant criminal or not, she knew he was right to stay away.

"For how long?"

"Until I can be around you without wanting to hold you, to kiss you." He cleared his throat and stood up straight. "I'm going to do a quick check around the perimeter of the house. Peter was bleeding pretty good. I imagine he's crawled back into a hole to patch himself up by now, but…" he hopped down the first couple of steps before turning back to look at her, "…I have to be sure. You should get back inside and get some sleep. My brothers will be back tomorrow with the herd and it will be a busy day around the ranch." He nodded. "Goodnight, Mrs. Scott." He tipped an imaginary hat, then ran down the rest of the stairs.

She watched with squinted eyes until he disappeared into the darkness.

"He loves me." What should have been a moment of hope for a bright future with the man who'd captured her heart in every way, hung over her with regret of what seemed impossible. She was a married woman and Tag, a respectable and honorable man. She could not, would not displace him from his new home.

It was time to leave Oak Meadow.

CHAPTER TWENTY

The warm, savory aroma of bacon cooking filled Brenna's nostrils and she opened her eyes, blinking against the sun's bright rays as they shone through the curtains in the living room. She sat up on the couch, surprised that she'd fallen asleep so quickly after her encounter with Tag earlier in the morning.

Did he say he was building a schoolhouse?

"You're awake."

Brenna glanced up to see the sheriff in the kitchen, a towel thrown over his shoulder as he chopped potatoes and tossed them in a skillet over the stove.

"Sheriff?" she said, surprised to see him moving about. "Should you be on your feet like that?" she asked as she pulled herself up and joined him.

"There was over a thousand dollars in that tin," the lawman nodded at the can sitting on the cabinet. "Along with a few expensive looking trinkets."

She nearly choked. "A thousand dollars?"

It was a hearty sum, but something just didn't add up.

"I've given it to Tag for safekeeping."

"Don't you think it seems a little odd? Peter obviously wanted everyone to believe he was dead. So, would a thousand dollars really be worth risking coming back for?"

"I've seen men do a lot more for a lot less."

"I suppose."

"Mornin', sis."

She whipped around. Her big brother sat at the table, devouring a plate full of breakfast potatoes and blowing over a cup of steaming liquid.

She hadn't seen him there before.

"Jeb," she squealed, rushing over to him and throwing her arms around his shoulders. "You are such a wonderful sight for sore eyes. You gave me quite a scare last night."

Her brother put down his food and turned to look at her. "Parker told me I missed quite a scene. He said that it was Peter who attacked me." He whistled low and long. "Are you all right?" he asked, concern lacing his tone.

"It's been quite a shock," she told him honestly. "Who's Parker?"

"That would be me," the sheriff held up a hand.

"I still can't believe that Pa was right about him. Peter really was no good. Wait until he finds out that you married a criminal who faked his own death."

That was something that Brenna hadn't considered. As if she needed one more thing to worry about. Her father had been against the marriage from the beginning, but she'd wanted to make her own decisions and prove to the man that she had grown into quite a capable young woman. How could she face him after this?

"It's funny," Jeb said, scooping another bite into his mouth. "Peter actually did me a favor, well, the second time anyway. I guess I really needed the sleep because I actually feel...rested and strong. And starving." He held up his fork, a large slice of salt-pork dangling from it. He nodded at the lawman, then shoved the food into his mouth. "He cooks a lot better than you, Bren," Jeb said between bites.

"Who doesn't?" She picked up a slice of cooked bacon from the plate in the middle of the table and took a bite, enjoying the salty meat.

"For someone who didn't even have coffee in her stores,

imagine my surprise when I found the salt-pork." The sheriff laughed, his smile reaching his eyes.

The kitchen door opened. Whoops and hollers sounded in the yard over the tapping of the rain and Brenna guessed the rest of the team had returned and were ushering their new herd into the fenced pastures. Tag stepped inside, followed by the doctor.

Brenna sat up straighter in the chair, set the half-eaten slice of salt-pork in front of her, and discreetly wiped the corners of her mouth.

"Oh, and I remember Redbourne," Jeb said, waving in Tag's direction. "At least the first couple of days after he arrived," he said with a shrug. "I'm still pretty foggy after that."

Tag nodded.

Gratitude filled her as the realization of what Jeb's regained memories meant—that he would be all right.

"That is wonderful news." Brenna glanced over to Tag, just to catch a glimpse at the back of his head as he closed the door behind him. Her shoulders slumped and she shoved the rest of the bacon slice into her mouth at once.

"I understand I've been missed," the doc said, pushing his spectacles higher on the bridge of his nose as he glanced around the room, presumably for his patients. "Now, son, let's take a look at that head." He reached over and started unwrapping Jeb's bandages.

Brenna excused herself from the table and walked over to the door. She pulled back the curtain covering the window to see Tag already mounted and riding out the gate to greet the onslaught of cattle and horses that were being diverted into the surrounding pastures.

Clouds rolled through the sky, intermittently casting shadows over the morning sun. A few droplets slashed against the windowpane as the rain started up again and within minutes another downpour had begun.

She leaned against the door and watched as the men

continued to work outside, unbothered by the weather. They corralled the horses into the small pasture closest to the house and the cattle were being turned out into the rest of the surrounding fields.

Brenna had been surprised when she'd learned of Tag purchasing two additional spreads to combine with Oak Meadow, but with the sheer number of livestock that were being driven in, and those that were sure to come, they'd need the space. She had a feeling that it wouldn't be long before he'd turned the ranch into something quite spectacular.

She let the curtain slip back into place. The children would be here for school in less than an hour and with everything that had happened over the last couple of days, she hadn't prepared her lesson plan. Luckily, she had done a brief overview of all classroom topics for the rest of the school year. However, as she reviewed the planned lesson outlines, none of them seemed to fit the day and so, reflecting on last night's storm, she decided she would talk to them about weather and its effect on every aspect of their lives.

With her elbows on her desk and her chin resting on her folded hands as she waited for the children to arrive, Brenna glanced up at the clock. School should have started half an hour ago. She stood up and walked over to the door, looking for any sign of her students, but the only movement in the yard belonged to the abundance of livestock that now adorned the ranch.

"No one is coming, Bren."

She glanced up to see her brother walking into her classroom, minus his bandages.

"Jeb, what did the doctor say?" she asked, making her way toward him.

"He said that I was lucky to have such an attentive sister." He chuckled. "He also said that it didn't hurt to have had the medical attention I received over the last couple of days." He sat on the corner of her desk and picked up the flint box that she'd left there. "He saved my life, you know. Tag, I mean."

"I know."

He set the wooden container back down and looked at her.

"Doc said the rest of my memory should return with time. He also said that I can get back to working as long as I take it easy."

"That's good news."

"You're telling me. I thought I might go mad if I had to stay cooped up in that bedroom even one more day."

She laughed, relieved to see Jeb acting like his old self. "It's good to see you," she said, wrapping her arms around her brother.

"I'm just sorry I haven't been more help to you over the last couple of days." He let go of her and pulled open the jar of licorice whips she had sitting on the shelf behind her desk. "I can't believe Peter got the jump on me. Twice."

"There is no way you could have known." She took half of the licorice sticks from her brother and returned them to the jar. "There was no way any of us could have. Peter is alive," she swallowed as she replaced the lid, "and I am going to have to deal with that."

"Honestly, I was kind of hoping that you and Redbourne..."

"Me too, Jeb. Me too." She dropped back down into her chair, leaned over her desk, and shoved her fingers through the front of her hair. "But, that's just not possible now." She fought the tears that threatened and the catch that sat like a lump in her throat.

"If I've learned anything about these Redbournes, Bren..."

She looked up at him, her hands still in her hair.

"...it's that they can accomplish the impossible."

She shook her head and opened her mouth, but was stopped short.

Knock. Knock.

The school door opened. Tag wiped his booted feet on the rug at the base of it and stepped inside.

Brenna shot up tall and smoothed her hair the best she could, managing a smile as she blinked away the wetness coating her lashes. Flutters surrounded her heart as she looked up at his beautifully chiseled face.

"I'm sorry to interrupt, ma'am," he said, his eyes piercing right through her, "but I've just been informed that the children will not be joining you today."

"Because of the rain? Did the cross-bridge flood overnight?"

"Well, yes, the rain did displace the cross-bridge. I have some men down there right now raising it. But, somehow, the town found out about the attack on Jeb and many of their parents are afraid that it may not be the safest place for the children to be around you until after the culprit has been apprehended."

She didn't blame them. The last thing she wanted to do was to put the children in danger. Their safety was paramount and admittedly, she was relieved.

"That's what I was trying to tell you," Jeb interjected.

"Do they know about Peter?" she asked. "Does anyone?"

"I don't know."

Jeb shrugged.

"I see."

"I'm sorry, ma'am." Tag placed his hat back on his head and turned to go.

"Mr. Redbourne?"

He paused.

"Yeah, I'm gonna…" Jeb pointed at the door into the house and left without finishing his sentence.

"Did you need something else, Mrs. Scott. I've got work to do."

"I hate this." She pushed herself away from her desk and started toward him.

The door flung open and the foreman grabbed Tag's arm.

"We've got a problem." Kade tipped his hat. "Ma'am," he

said in acknowledgement, then turned back to Tag. The hired hand lowered his voice and mumbled something that Brenna could not hear.

Tag turned to face her, shaking his head. "Mrs. Scott, I—"

"Go!" she told him.

He locked eyes with her for a moment before jumping down the few steps to the yard, following Kade. Brenna rushed to the open door and watched as Tag unstrapped the reins from the fence and mounted his horse.

"Be careful," she called after him, unsure whether or not he'd heard her.

It surprised her when several of the hands, including Cole, headed out behind them.

Peter?

She rushed into the main section of the house to see if she could find the sheriff, but it was empty.

"Sheriff?" she called as she ran to different corners of the homestead. "Jeb? Doctor?"

Where had everyone gone?

As she glanced around the place, something caught her eye under the hutch. She dropped down onto her haunches and slid her hand beneath the cabinet to sweep for the trinket, but she couldn't feel it, so she got on her hands and knees and glanced beneath the wooden furniture. There, situated up against the stout leg, sat a piece of jewelry that must have fallen out of the cocoa tin. She reached for it, her fingertips grazing the rough surface. She stretched just a little more until she could finally grab ahold of it.

As she held up the bauble into the light, she discovered it was a pearl ring, the top of which matched the clasp pendant on the necklace Peter had given her before the accident.

The accident.

If Peter hadn't died that day, then whose body had she buried a year ago?

Brenna closed her fingers around the ring. Maybe Peter had

come back for something more than the money, but this little bauble certainly wasn't worth more than the thousand dollars they'd found in the tin, so why did he want it or any of the other trinkets inside for that matter?

Maybe it was just all loot to him.

"Bren," Jeb burst into the house. "Brenna!" He started for the schoolhouse.

She shoved the ring into the pocket of her dress and pulled herself to her feet.

"I'm here."

"What in the world were you doing on the floor? There's a fire."

She ignored his question. "A fire? Where?"

"The orchard."

"What? No!" She ran to the porch, down the first couple of steps, and looked up at the swirls of billowing white smoke raising into the sky. The orchard was one of her favorite places here in Serenity Hollow.

"Lightning?" she asked, horrified at the thought.

Her brother shrugged.

"What do we do, Jeb?" she asked, twisting to look at him from near the bottom of the stairs.

"Redbourne and a few of the fellas already headed out there."

That would explain why Kade had come to get Tag, and why they had left in such a hurry.

"I'm sure they'll have it under control in no time," Jeb tried to soothe her.

Taking some comfort in the fact that rain still fell and could minimize the damage, Brenna wrapped her arms around herself.

"I would have gone to help," Jeb said, "but Parker went with the doc into town to try to gather up anyone who might be willing to join a search party, but with Peter still out there somewhere, Tag wanted to make sure someone stayed behind to keep you safe."

"But, you're still recovering. You should be resting, not standing guard."

"Well, that's why he left me here."

Brenna froze and slowly spun around.

Rafe Redbourne stood at the bottom of the porch stairs like a sentinel protecting the gates of heaven, a rifle in each hand. How had he approached without her hearing?

"They sure grow them big in your family, don't they?" she asked, still looking up at him even though she stood a step or two above him.

Rafe laughed good-naturedly. "Tag said you need to learn how to shoot. I figured now is as good a time as any."

"*You* are going to teach me?"

She swallowed the disappointment that rose in her throat.

"I've been known to hit my mark a time or two."

He had the same dimples as his brother and charm to spare, but there was something missing. He wasn't Tag.

"Now? In the rain?" She blinked away several drops. "Shouldn't we wait until it stops?"

Rafe looked upward, took off his hat, and allowed the rain to splash against his face, then he dropped his head to meet her curious gaze.

"This isn't rain. This is a light drizzle. And you, Mrs. Brenna Scott, are a mighty strong woman. Can't be afraid of a little water." He held out one of his rifles. "And besides, it will be a good opportunity for you to learn how to clean a rifle after it gets wet."

She self-consciously tucked a wet curl behind her ear, hesitating for a moment.

"The bad guys won't wait until it stops."

She considered that for a moment, then raised her chin with resolve.

"Give me the gun," she said, holding out her hand.

"You're a brave man," Jeb said to Rafe, chuckling.

"Very funny," Brenna retorted, narrowing her eyes at her

brother. She turned back to Rafe and nodded. "I'm ready."

White smoke rose in streams from the orchard, the mixed sweet scent of cooking fruit and burning wood filled Tag's nostrils as they approached the fire. He was relieved to see that less than half of the trees had flames licking at their trunks and branches. He'd never been quite so grateful for the rain.

It only took a moment before all men were down from their horses. Tag grabbed his saddle blanket, and marched to the creek where he soaked it in the chilly water.

As if he hadn't had enough to worry about between the storm, an increasingly restless herd, and two criminals both threatening the people around him, lightning sparking a fire on his land was just the cream on top.

A soft rumble cascaded over the ground and the sound of horse's hooves dancing in rhythm caught his immediate attention.

The wild horses were back.

With the herd they'd just driven from Austin to Oak Meadow, and with fewer resources at his disposal than he would have liked, the mustangs would have to wait for another day. It wouldn't be long before he could get the new fences built on the additional parcels of land he'd agreed to purchase from both Grimace and Mr. Cranston. He just hoped the wild bunch wouldn't startle the new cattle. A stampede was not on today's menu.

Today, there were more pressing issues. He beat at the flames that had jumped onto the tree under which he and Brenna had sat on their ride that had been so rudely interrupted by Tobias Pane and his boys.

CRACK!

Tag stood up straight, attempting to determine whether the sound was from a gun or a wave of rolling thunder chiming in with its opinion on his situation.

CRACK! Another shot split the air and he glanced in the direction from where the shot had originated, his jaw clenched.

It was a gunshot.

"Cole!" Tag yelled for his brother as he struck the base of the peach tree again with his sopping blanket, duly satisfied at the sizzle and the light rise of smoke that resulted as the flames were squelched.

"Did you feel that? I think the mustangs are back."

"And someone is shooting at them again," Tag confirmed. "Kade and I can take care of this," he said with another swing at the tree. "Take the others and find out who exactly is trying to pick off those horses."

Cole nodded. "On my way!" And without wasting a moment, he took Ben and Hector with him as they rode out toward the northeast border of his property.

He'd left four of his drovers back at the ranch to care for the beeves, along with Rafe to look after Brenna and Jeb, but after what had happened over the weekend, he hated to be too far away from the homestead for long while Peter Scott and Tobias Pane were both still out there, each a very real threat to Brenna.

The two men, Peter and Tobias, had obviously known each other, but Tag wondered if they'd been working together all along. He couldn't shake the feeling that it wasn't a coincidence they'd both come out of the woodwork around the same time—one looking for something at the ranch and the other wanting to claim it—though Tobias had seemed genuinely surprised that his promissory note was as worthless as the paper it had been written on.

After several trips to the stream and the better part of an hour, he and Kade finally had extinguished all remnants of the fire, and Tag hoped this was not what life on the ranch was going to be like forever. The cooler late April weather should not have sparked a fire in the healthy orchard. Lightning was always a possibility, but it was unlikely so many coincidences would occur so close together, which meant there was only one viable alternative.

Arson.

He'd been assured, mostly by his father, that Serenity Hollow was a small, quiet ranching community. From what he'd seen over the last week, he'd been grossly misinformed. So much for living a simple life. His adventure here had already proven much more complicated than he ever would have expected.

"Let's get back," he told Kade as he pulled himself up onto his horse. "Something's not right here. I'd also like to check on the injured mustang. There's no telling how she will react to being in the stable during a storm."

He'd stopped in the stable early this morning, but there hadn't been much he could do or see in the limited light and he'd been a little too distracted, so he asked Rafe if he would look in on her and attend to her injury. Rafe had a great sense of timing—showing up just when he was needed. His little brother had a real knack for that.

Tag glanced over the scorched orchard. Only five of the trees remained unscathed by the fire. They'd already been gone too long and he couldn't shake the feeling that something was wrong, but he remained conflicted. A part of him wanted to stay away from the ranch, from the beautiful teacher who'd bewitched him, but another part—the greater part—wanted to rush home to make sure she was safe.

Admitting his feelings to himself had been difficult enough, but actually telling Brenna had only made things harder. What had he been thinking? He needed to stay away from her, but the situation was making that increasingly problematic.

"You doin' all right, boss?" Kade asked, pulling up alongside Tag.

"I'll be doing a whole lot better when this whole Peter Scott mess is behind us."

"Are you sure there's not something else eatin' at you?"

Tag looked over at his foreman, his brow raised.

"I mean, it's a wonder that peach tree is still standing the way you were beating on it."

"It was on fire."

"I thought that maybe it had something to do with a certain woman."

Did everyone know how he felt about Brenna?

He had to admit though, it had felt pretty good to exert some of his frustrated energies on the trees.

"Come on, we've got a lot to do before the fellas leave tomorrow." He led his horse down the trail back toward Oak Meadow, thoughts of their encounter on the porch swing tormenting him. She'd looked so beautiful and had felt so right snuggled up against him.

He loved her. And, one way or another, he'd have to learn to live with that.

CHAPTER TWENTY-ONE

"Not bad for a novice," Rafe said as he took the rifle from Brenna's hands.

After an hour, she'd been able to hit several of the targets, albeit just a corner or an edge, but it was something. His lesson had proven to be quite educational, and she knew it was important to learn, but she'd been disappointed that Tag hadn't been the one to teach her and her heart just hadn't been in it.

"Thank you. At least I know how to hold the gun."

A couple of wagons pulled into the yard, followed by a few men and several women on horseback, led by Mae Taylor. Brenna wasn't surprised to see womenfolk there, as many of them had been forced to take on the roles of their dearly departed husbands, fathers, or brothers. Suddenly, she wished she'd been a more apt student for Rafe, so she could be more of a help than a hindrance in the search for Peter.

The sheriff winced as the buckboard hit a rivet in the yard and Brenna shook her head at his stubborn resolve. With new sutures, he should have been resting, not leading a posse to find Peter in the middle of a rainstorm.

"Mrs. Scott," Rafe said, turning back to look at her, "it appears that Hunt was able to get a few men together to go after that husband of yours." He took the rifle from her hands and held out an arm to protect it from the rain with his long duster jacket, then reloaded the gun. "I'm going to walk you up to the house, and then I'll need you to take this," he nodded at the weapon as he handed it back to her, "and then lock the door behind you."

"Is this really necessary?" she asked as they reached the bottom steps of the porch. "I can't imagine Peter would be senseless enough to return in broad daylight with so many men around the property." Though, most of Tag's hired hands had gone out with him to extinguish the fire in the orchard. Only a few of them had stayed behind to finalize their preparations for tomorrow's journey back to Kansas.

"Peter's not the only threat out there."

"You mean Tobias Pane? I truly don't believe that he wants to hurt me—especially now that Oak Meadow is no longer mine."

"He's already killed once, Mrs. Scott. There's no telling what he'll do. I've seen desperate men do some pretty desperate things and, from what I've heard and seen, he's getting desperate. It's better to err on the side of caution."

He was right, of course.

"Do not open the door for anyone until I return. Do you understand?"

She took the weapon, the bulk of it seeming a little heavier this time, and nodded. "Are you riding out with them?" She glanced up just as the wagon the sheriff drove disappeared around the back of the house.

"No." He chuckled as he shook his head in large movements. "Do you have any idea what my big brother would do to me if I left you here unprotected?" He leaned down to the door's handle, twisted it open, and waited for her to step inside. "I've been following Peter Scott for several months now and I've gotten to know his patterns pretty well. I want to let them know what they are up against. If Tag returns before they head out, I will join them, but for now, I'll stay on property."

"I guess that means I won't be meeting with Agatha Taylor this afternoon," she said more to herself than to him as she wiped a wet strand of hair from her cheek and tucked it behind her ear. She was supposed to meet with the cattle woman's daughter today to discuss the town's plans for the Founder's Festival. She regretted the need to inform her that a replacement for the committee would be needed.

"No, ma'am. I'm afraid no social visits until he's caught or at least until we feel the danger has passed."

"It must be hard," she said in a soft voice.

"What?"

"Tag told me that you've been after *him* for a while. I can't imagine you appreciate being stuck here minding me."

"Oh, Peter Scott won't get too far. Especially not bleeding the way he was," Rafe assured her. "If the sheriff is as good a shot as he's reported to be, it's just a matter of time."

His confidence offered some comfort.

"I'll be out in the barn. Then, after I speak with the sheriff, I need to look in on Tag's injured mustang, *if* she'll let me. I don't know anyone with quite the talent my brother has to get horses to trust him. Most would have put down any horse with an injury to the leg, but not my brother. No, if he can save them, without too much damage, he will do everything in his power to do it."

"He's a good man, that brother of yours."

"Yes, he is. You know, I have my reservations when it comes to women, but you are a good one Mrs. Brenna Scott, and my brother is lucky to have found you."

She stared at him for a good, long moment.

"You flatter me, Mr. Redbourne."

"Not at all. I say it like it is."

"Too bad the circumstances have changed." She didn't want to think about everything she was losing.

"I've found that the best things in life always find a way. For most people anyway." Rafe pulled on the door and took one step down before glancing back at her. "Lock it!"

"Please be careful," she whispered, peering around the edge

of the door as she closed it slowly.

"And don't open it for anyone until either Tag or I say it's all right. I've blocked the back entry with several pieces of furniture and have nailed most of the windows shut. The only way in or out of this house is through here."

"Is this what it feels like to be in jail?" she asked only half-jokingly.

"Depends on the jailer." Rafe winked at her. "Now, lock it." He waited until she'd closed the door behind her. And the lock clicked into place.

She glanced out the window next to the frame and Rafe still stood there, watching. So, she placed the plank across the opening and secured it in the hooks Tag had installed on either side. Then, she leaned up against the wood and exhaled.

It had been a long time since Brenna had enjoyed the indulgence of reading one of her favorite novels, so, if she was going to be stuck indoors without the children to teach and her trek to the Founder's Festival committee meeting cancelled, she found herself with some time. She sprawled across the couch and lay down on her stomach, the book opened to her favorite part.

She hadn't been looking forward to the look on Agatha's face when she told the ladies group that she would be moving back to Hillsboro shortly and could no longer help with the celebration. For now, she just wanted to get lost in her book. She turned the page, enjoying every delicious word. She needed something to distract her from the worry that seemed to well in the pit of her stomach.

Knock. Knock.

No! The hero of her novel was just about to save the heroine from a dastardly fate and she wasn't ready to stop reading. Wasn't ready to go back to reality.

Knock. Knock.

She glanced up to see an impatient Sophronia Miles peering in through the window.

With an exaggerated breath, Brenna snapped her book shut and pushed herself up off the couch and over to the door. She peeked through the window at the right.

"Sophronia," she called through the closed door, surprised to see the waitress from town holding out some sort of confection. "Thank you for coming out to help with the search party. I know the sheriff and the others really appreciate all the help they can get. Especially, on a dreary day like today."

"I know, can you believe this rain? When the sheriff came into town looking for volunteers to join a search party, but wouldn't tell us who, of course I had to be a part of it." She smiled, proud of her well-earned title of busybody. "I just have to know what's going on, though I'm not very keen with a weapon. You don't think they'll mind, do you?"

"I believe Sheriff Hunt and the others are out back in the barn," she yelled out the closed door. "If you want to know what's going on, I'm sure you'll want to join them."

"Oh, yes, but first…" The waitress pulled back the red and white cloth to reveal a large pecan pie and held it up to the window. "Mr. O'Malley said that I could only leave the restaurant to help if I brought pies for Cole and the other fellas to take with them for their trip back to Kansas. I'm guessing they're still leaving tomorrow."

Brenna was taken aback by the woman's familiarity of Tag's little brother, but she shouldn't have been surprised. Miss Miles knew everything about everyone in town. She was always abuzz with information.

"Is he around?" Sophronia asked, leaning sideways and attempting to peer into the house.

"There was a fire in the orchard this morning," Brenna said, realizing the difficulty of having this conversation through the locked entry, so she spoke a little louder. "He went with his brother to put it out."

"Aren't you going to open the door, Mrs. Scott? I can hardly hear a word you are saying."

Brenna thought for a moment, Rafe's words echoing in her head.

Don't open the door for anyone…

Certainly, he hadn't meant for Sophronia Miles. After another moment's hesitation, she lifted the wooden bar, unlocked the door, and opened it.

"Hello, Sophronia."

"You're locked up in that house pretty tight," she said, leaning to the right to look past her. "Is everything all right?"

"Fine," Brenna lied. "Cole and his brother went down to put out a fire at the orchard this morning. I'm not sure when they will return."

"Oh, no. A fire? You'd think with all these showers a fire would be all but impossible." Sophronia shifted on her feet.

"Where are my manners? Would you like me to take that? I am sure Mr. Redbourne and the others will be ever so grateful." She smiled and held out her hands.

"I would prefer to give it to him myself, if you don't mind. Though, I do have a few more in the wagon. May I come in and sit a spell?"

"It's not a very good time right now, Miss Miles. Maybe we can have a social visit another day. Besides, your other pies are going to be ruined if you leave them out in the rain much longer."

"There is a tarpaulin mat covering the back. The pies will be safe for a spell."

"Don't you want to go out and join the others?"

"Oh, I will, but I take my responsibilities at the restaurant very seriously." Sophronia pouted her lips and stared at the pie in her hands, "I guess I could wait out here on the porch for Cole to return." She glanced at the rocker just to the side of the door.

The last thing Brenna wanted to do was entertain the woman, but her upbringing wouldn't allow her to do any less. She stood back away from the door and swept a hand in front of her.

"All right, but just until they return." She glanced over at the barn where Rafe and the others were still meeting, then scanned the yard before turning back to her unexpected guest. "You are welcome to place the pie on the kitchen counter. I'm sure they will be back momentarily."

The waitress deposited the pecan delicacy as instructed, still covered with a small red and white checkered cloth. She looked around the kitchen, a scrunch to her brow.

"What are you bringing to Agatha's luncheon?" she asked.

Brenna swallowed as she reluctantly joined Sophronia in the kitchen. She wanted to get back to her book to help take her mind off everything, but instead, she sat down on the edge of one of the chairs at the table.

"Luncheon? I thought the committee was just meeting to discuss the Founder's Festival."

"Of course, we are. But, you know Agatha. She can't host anything without there being food involved." She leaned forward. "Much to her mother's chagrin."

Mae Taylor was as tough a rancher as they came, a regular force of nature. Nothing stood in her way when it came to running a successful and efficient ranch. No one dared cross her. But, her daughter was exactly the opposite—a spoiled, small-town socialite, who also happened to be one of the nicest people she'd had ever met with a real talent for organizing the town's functions.

It was hard to say no to Agatha—the one thing the girl had gotten from her mother. When she'd volunteered Brenna to be her co-chair, Brenna had, with wide eyes and a plaster smile, accepted the role, but now...now that her husband was no longer dead, there was little hope she would be able to build a life with Tag here at Oak Meadow.

As much as she'd tried to think of any way around it, maybe it really was time to go home to her father's house in Hillsboro. She hated to leave Agatha in a lurch, but finding out that Miss

Miles desired to be a part of the planning committee could not have come at a more perfect time. She hoped Agatha would see it the same way.

"I'm sure you've got something around here you can take," the young woman said, opening and closing several cupboards.

"I'm sorry?" What had they been talking about?

The meeting. Luncheon.

It's funny, Agatha hadn't said anything to her about food when she'd seen her last week in town.

Odd.

"I've heard you make some of the most delightful treats," Sophronia said as she continued to search through the cupboards.

"Miss Miles?"

Brenna had not shared her pecans or honey butter with very many people in town and she wondered who Sophronia had been talking to.

"Miss Miles?"

The woman's appearance was growing increasingly harried by the minute.

"Sophronia?"

"What?"

"Is everything all right?"

"Of course. Why wouldn't it be?"

"You seem a little…nervous."

"Do I? I'm sorry. I just really want to make a good impression on Agatha and I thought that maybe if I could convince you to bring some of your candied pecans, she'd be more open to let me be a part of the committee."

The last of Brenna's candied pecans were still in the basket from her picnic with Tag. However, if she started right now, she could probably have a loaf of bread ready to bake within an hour and combined with the two jars of her blackberry honey-butter out in the ice box she had left over from her last batch, Sophronia would have what she wanted.

"I'm afraid I'll be sending my regrets to Agatha for this afternoon's meeting. And, if you are joining the search party, you might not make it either."

"What about something to drink?"

It was as if the woman was too focused to hear what Brenna was telling her.

"Your cocoa maybe. I think that would be divine."

"My cocoa? How did...?"

"When that handsome sheriff came by O'Malley's this morning, he mentioned you have a special blend of cocoa that would beat any cup of coffee in this little town." She shrugged and tilted her head over her shoulder. "Maybe you could share some with us? With me?"

The hairs on the back of Brenna's neck stood on end. The sheriff never actually got to try some of the cocoa as it was missing from the tin, so how would he know it was better than his coffee? Besides, he'd gone into town looking for men to help look for Peter and with the few there were left in Serenity Hollow, she was surprised he'd found time to stop by O'Malley's to speak with Miss Miles.

"Normally, I would be happy to give you some of my hot cocoa powder, but unfortunately, it's all gone." Brenna didn't know where it had gone, just that it was, and it had been replaced by a small fortune in coins and bills. She glanced up at the tin, which still sat on the edge of the counter—though empty—still a reminder of everything that had changed just in the last few hours—let alone over the last week.

Sophronia's bottom lip protruded into an exaggerated pout. "Too bad. Well, I think I'd better be getting back. Mr. O'Malley will be wondering what has kept me."

"All right."

Something was off about Sophronia today and the oddity of her actions pricked at the back of Brenna's mind. She was glad the woman would be leaving. Her life already seemed a little chaotic at the moment and she rationalized that her suspicions stemmed from her anxious imagination. She hoped it wouldn't be long before some semblance of her life was back in order.

Brenna stood in the living area and waited for Sophronia to join her. It took a little while, as the woman lingered in the kitchen, but she soon followed.

"Do you think Cole has returned yet?" she asked as she finally entered the living room.

Brenna shrugged and shook her head. "I haven't heard them, but I've been inside with you the whole time. I'm sure we could go out and ask his brother."

"I thought you said Mr. Redbourne's brother had ridden out with him to put out a fire in the orchard." Sophronia squinted, her face looking more pinched than usual.

"Wrong brother." Brenna could see how it would be confusing and wondered how it would be to have all seven Redbourne brothers in the same place at the same time. "Rafe stayed behind to…to…"

What was she supposed to say?

"Oooo, wait, Rafe is the bounty hunter brother, right?" Sophronia reached out and grabbed Brenna's arms, squeezing, then letting go.

"Sophronia Miles, your ability to collect information never ceases to amaze me. Yes, Rafe is a bounty hunter."

"Is he as handsome as his brothers?"

"I suppose so. But, he's only passing through Serenity Hollow. He's looking for someone."

"A bounty? Do you know who?" She brought her hands up to her mouth. "Oooo…An outlaw maybe? Do you think it's anyone we've heard of? Is that why there's a search party?"

The young waitress seemed a little too excited—even for her.

"It's a long story." Brenna wasn't ready for the whole town to know her humiliation. If she told Sophronia that Peter was alive, it would only be a matter of time before she would become the object of dinnertime conversation throughout the community.

Of course, the sheriff had already been into town and returned with a couple of townsfolk to help track down her husband. It was curious that the waitress was trying to get the information from her instead of listening to the sheriff.

"Maybe it's time we go out and join the others," Sophronia said, grabbing Brenna's hand and dragging her outside.

"We?" Brenna actually liked the idea of helping in the search for Peter. If all those other women could help, then why not her? Sure, her husband had already tried to kill her brother, had shot the sheriff, and had threatened her, but that was only more incentive for her to find him.

When they reached the last step, Sophronia tripped, landing hard on the ground, her dress a tumble of pantaloons and petticoats.

Brenna hobbled to her side, still healing from her own mishap. "Are you all right?" She worked to right the woman and held out a hand to help her to her feet.

"Ow. Ow. Oooo. Ow." Sophronia limped to the steps with Brenna's help. "How am I supposed to help in any kind of search party when I can hardly stand?"

"You wait right here. I'm going to go get Mr. Redbourne. Rafe," Brenna clarified as she stood and started for the back.

"No!" Sophronia reached up and grabbed her arm. "I think I need to see the doctor."

"He *is* a doctor. Well, almost."

"I thought he was a bounty hunter."

"He is."

Sophronia's questions had started to get under her skin and Brenna was finding herself less and less patient in answering them.

"I don't understand. Is he a bounty hunter or a doctor?"

"Yes." Brenna tsked as she attempted to pull Sophronia to her feet. "Rafe went to medical school and now, well, he's…a bounty hunter. If you want more than that, you'll have to ask him."

She leaned up against the wagon and wiped her now wet hair out of her face. "I think I'd just like to go home."

Peculiar. Sophronia was usually one of the first gals to jump right in and get to know any new men who came through town as they were so few. Especially, when those men looked anything like the Redbournes.

"Will you take me?"

Brenna stared at the woman for a good long time and she wondered why she hadn't seen it before.

"How long have you known?" she asked solemnly.

"Known what?" Sophronia responded innocently.

Her behavior today made so much more sense now.

"How long have you known that Peter is alive? That he is who they are chasing?"

"Why, I'm not sure wha—Peter's ali…?" All innocence seemed to drain from the woman like water through a sieve and she stood up straight, all hint of pain gone from her face. "What gave me away?" she asked, her voice suddenly low and dripping with disdain.

"I thought it was strange that you hardly know me, yet you felt comfortable enough to scrounge through my cupboards. I have to admit, you are clever though, using Cole's leaving as an excuse. And Agatha's meeting. I think that was a little too contrived. We may not be friends, Sophronia, but even I know you couldn't care less what people think about you."

Something hard pressed into Brenna's side, but it wasn't until she heard the click of the hammer that she knew the waitress held a gun to her ribs.

"I really did want to help with the festival," she scoffed, "but Agatha chose you instead. What is so special about you anyway?"

Brenna didn't dare move, though she didn't believe that Sophronia would be stupid enough to shoot her with Rafe and a sparse wagonload of men just around back in the barn. Still, she didn't want to take any chances.

"What do you want, Miss Miles?"

"Peter."

"You can have him."

"Not until I get what I came for."

"And what is that, exactly?" Brenna's mind raced as she tried to think of something she could do to gain the attention of the newly formed posse. They had to be finishing up in there soon. They were wasting daylight.

What's taking them so long?

"Why don't we just go back into the house, nice and slow like, and you can show me where it is. The money, that is. Peter said there is enough there for us to start over someplace. We'll leave you alone and you'll never see us again." Sophronia nudged Brenna back toward the house.

"If you believe that's true, I feel sorry for you."

"No! You don't get to do that—feel sorry for me. Peter loves me. Always has."

"Then, why did he marry me?"

Out of nowhere, Sophronia backhanded her across the face, the force of it stronger with the weight of her pistol. Brenna's jaw flexed, her cheek smarting in pain, but she rose to meet the woman's bitter stare, returning one of her own. The heat in her face surged, the entire area throbbing rhythmically.

For the briefest of moments, Brenna thought she saw fear in Sophronia's eyes.

"Peter's wounded, Miss Miles," she tried to reason. "And, without seeing a doctor, it'll only be a matter of time before they catch up to him. To you. He's not worth it, Sophronia. You have to see it. You have to know he's not the kind of man who honors his commitments. I'm his *wife*," she said, leaning back, prepared for another attack which didn't come, "and he left me high and dry, believing he was dead. Believing I was a widow. Mourning him for over a year. What kind of a man does that?" She swallowed the anger welling up inside of her at the thought of it all and softened her voice. "What do you think he's going to do to you?"

"You're wrong," Sophronia responded with a little less conviction than before. "You're wrong."

"The money's not here."

That statement seemed to refocus Sophronia and she yanked Brenna's arm hard.

Brenna shrugged. The idea that Peter had been seeing Sophronia after they'd gotten married should have surprised her, but it didn't. The wool of naivety had been pulled from her eyes and she now saw her situation for what it was.

A sham.

She knew the sheriff had given the money to Tag for safekeeping, but she had no idea what he'd done with it.

"Sheriff Hunt is just around back in the barn. We could go and ask him where he put it."

Sophronia's eyes shot to the side yard and back again.

"We don't have time for this. Get in."

"Pardon?"

"You heard me. Get into the back of the wagon." Sophronia pulled a coiled rope from a hook near the driver's seat.

"You know where Peter is, don't you?" Brenna accused, whirling around to face the armed woman.

"You'll know where he is too, soon enough."

CHAPTER TWENTY-TWO

Tag's heart sank as he passed beneath the entrance arch into Oak Meadow to find a dozen or so cowboys and neighbors gathered astride horses and wagons, huddled in a make-shift circle.

"He's here!" one of them shouted and immediately the small collection of men parted to show Cole, standing in the center, a large burlap-wrapped bundle lying at his feet.

A body.

With his jaw pulsing and his teeth ground together, Tag braced himself as he dismounted and approached his brother.

"It's Pane," Cole said quickly enough to put him out of his misery.

Tag exhaled.

"Whoever made that shot we heard from the orchard wasn't after the mustangs."

"Have we found Scott?" Tag asked.

"Not yet. We were just headed out," the sheriff said, wincing as he moved the position of his leg as he sat in the driver's seat of the buckboard. "Nobody's seen nor heard from him."

A quiet murmur carried over the men—only a few of whom he didn't recognize.

"And, Brenna?" Tag searched for Rafe through the small crowd, but he wasn't there.

"Hi-Yah!"

The stable doors burst open and a mounted Rafe rode toward them. He met Tag's eyes and circled around, nodding his head in a gesture to follow.

"Brenna left with that waitress from town. I don't think it was by her own accord."

Tag glanced at Cole.

"Go!" his brother urged. "We'll be right behind you."

Without hesitation, Tag ran back to his horse, climbed up, and quickly joined Rafe as they headed north toward the Taylor place. His heart sped faster with each galloping step, his chest constricted.

Deep breaths, he told himself, though the action was harder on a quickly moving horse than he'd expected it to be.

As they crested one of the hills, a wagon that appeared to have only a single passenger could be seen pulling off the main road and onto a small trail through a meadow of wildflowers leading into a tall cluster of trees.

Rafe pulled his horse to a stop and dismounted.

"It looks like Miss Miles is alone. Are you sure that Brenna is with her?" Tag asked, pacing with his horse.

"Parker said that Miss Miles had agreed to join the search for Peter," Rafe squatted down at the edge of the road and peered down into the shallow valley, "but when they arrived at the ranch, she disappeared." He hung his head for a moment, then looked up at Tag. "When I went into the house to find Brenna, she was gone." He stood up. "Just gone."

Heat left Tag's face, but he fought to show strength in place of the fear that had gripped a hold on him.

"Now, that teacher of yours is right smart," Rafe said, as if sensing his dread. "I can't imagine she would have gone anywhere willingly without talking to me or the sheriff first. This Miles woman has to be the key."

Tag had learned a long time ago to trust his brother's instincts, but he couldn't just sit there.

"Head back to the ranch and get Parker and the others," Rafe said with an air of authority.

Tag raised a brow at his brother, his face unsmiling.

"No, you're right. Stupid idea. Of course, you're not leaving. You love the woman." Rafe pulled himself back up into his saddle. "If I know Scott, he's probably holed up in some hovel, drinking his whiskey, and lying low—though he's hurt and that makes him even more dangerous."

"Then, why are we stopping?" Tag asked. "If Brenna is in the back of that wagon—"

"We'll get her back, Tag."

Rafe started down the hill ahead of him, this time at a slower pace. Tag figured it was for stealth and he saw several other horses, all with mounted riders, dispersing over the mountainside, all headed for the same patch of trees. Sheriff Hunt approached from behind, while Cole pulled up the rear. The last thing they wanted to do was to spook the man. Someone could get themselves killed if they weren't careful. He pulled up alongside his brother.

"What I can't figure out," Rafe said quietly, "is why Peter would want to take his…" he looked up at Tag, "Brenna," he corrected. "He'd know that a hostage would just up the stakes for him—and he's generally the card-up-his-sleeve, not-taking-any-chances kind of ruffian."

"What happened, Rafe?" Tag asked. "I mean, how did this happen?"

"I waited, Tag, I swear, until I heard the door lock from the inside before I joined the sheriff and the others in the barn. She was safe. Secure."

Tag recognized the sting of failure in his brother's tone. As much as he wanted to blame Rafe for allowing Brenna to be taken, he knew it wasn't his fault. It wasn't anybody's fault, but the guilt that sprouted in his gut nearly killed him. He should have been there.

"It's not your fault, little brother. Who would have

suspected the waitress?"

"I should have. And the moment I saw that pie sitting on the counter in the kitchen, I knew. She was my responsibility and I let you down."

"No, Mrs. Brenna Scott was my responsibility, if anyone's. I should have sent her packing the day I bought Oak Meadow. That no good husband of hers would have never gotten to her then. And she wouldn't be in danger now."

"We still don't know for sure that Miss Miles is working with Scott."

"You believe in coincidences about as much as a worm believes in fishing."

Rafe chuckled. "You're right."

The mission would have been so much better under the veil of night, but as it were, there was not a lot of cover on the little trail. If they were headed into an ambush, they'd best be prepared. Tag reached down to feel the cool metal of the rifle slung against the horse's side, then rested a hand on his hip and unsnapped the leather strap of his holster.

SLAM!

Brenna jumped out of her skin. The old wooden door splintered open as it slammed up against the log walls of the tiny cabin at the far edge of the Taylor property.

Sophronia jumped.

Brenna held her breath and closed her eyes, releasing a sigh of relief when the gun still held to her side did not fire. Her jaw ached from the gag in her mouth, its knot pulling at the hairs at the back of her neck, and her cheek still throbbed with the sting of Sophronia's smack across her face.

"Let the girl go, Scott. There are lawmen and several newly deputized citizens encroaching upon this place as we speak."

Brenna's heart leapt in gratitude for the work-roughened

woman standing in the now open doorway—her long, gray-blond hair draping in sodden locks down the sides of her face, a weathered brown Stetson atop her head, and a rifle pointed in Peter's direction.

"Why, if it isn't the mighty Mae Taylor herself," Peter said in a low, unconcerned voice as he slid up against the headboard of the rusting brass bed until he was in a near seated position, the color all but drained from his face.

Mrs. Taylor narrowed her eyes at him and raised a brow as if daring him to make her shoot.

"I hardly recognized you without your crony, Pane, by your side." Peter clutched an old revolver in one hand while the other favored the side of his shirt soaked in various shades of blood.

"Tobias Pane will not be bothering anybody ever again." Sophronia leaned back, pushing the grime-encrusted curtains aside from the window, and wiped away years of filth and lack of care with the hem of her sleeve as she peered out, frantically looking from side to side. "It's true, Peter," she said frantically. "There's movement all over the hillside."

"I told you not to bring her here," Peter spat, "but you couldn't leave well enough alone." Coughs racked his body and fresh blood colored his lips. He quickly wiped it away with an old rag that sat on the edge of the bed next to him.

"Sit," Sophronia demanded and Brenna complied.

"What did you do, Sophie? Where is Tobias?" Peter asked, his eyes narrowing at her.

"Out near your old orchard last I saw him," she said innocently. "He was setting fire to several of the trees." She shot Brenna a knowing look and smiled smugly.

Brenna would have never suspected the waitress had a mean bone in her body as she had always been, if anything, overly friendly to everyone in town. It was a little disconcerting. As she sat on the dirt-riddled floor of the one-room building, Brenna realized that the rope binding her hands had started to come loose and she did her best to undo the knot with her fingers bent up at an awkward angle, but in a subtle way as to not arouse any suspicion.

Peter stared at her as if expecting something more.

"Well, I only brought her here because she wouldn't tell me where the money was," Sophronia whined, "so, I improvised." She looked back, over her shoulder, at the injured man. "Peter!" she squealed, rushing to his side. "You need a doctor."

The cloth the woman had used to gag Brenna tasted like sweat and she had to redirect her thoughts to prevent herself from gagging on her own vomit, as she tried to use her tongue to displace it.

"What I need…" Peter coughed again, sweat now dripping down his pallid face, "is to collect on an old debt."

"But, none of this will matter if you're dead. Or in prison. Come with me. I've got the wagon outside. Let *her* go," she said the last with an air of disdain, "and they might not come looking for you."

"Come on now, Mae," Peter said, ignoring the young waitress's pleas. "You're not going to turn me in. I know too much about the Taylor family secrets. And I haven't told a soul. You owe me."

The older rancher's eyes narrowed at him, then her gaze shot to Brenna.

"And she won't kill me neither," Peter turned his comments on Brenna, his eyes cold and angry, though beginning to droop, "will you, Mae?" he said without taking his gaze from Brenna. "Because, I've got something she wants."

"I'm tired, Scott. Getting older. Maybe it's time everyone knew my secrets," Mrs. Taylor said, a soft smile touching the corner of her lips.

"What is that supposed to mean?" For the first time since seeing Peter, the man's confidence faltered. His teeth ground together in a moment of obvious pain and he clutched the cloth at his side tightly as he hunched forward.

Brenna did not take her eyes from Mrs. Taylor. She had

grown to respect the woman. She'd admired her for everything she'd been able to accomplish, despite the odds. And she hoped now, that her admiration had not been misplaced.

Smart and savvy, with a keen business sense and a knack for a no-nonsense way of thinking, Mae Taylor had been a pillar of the small-town community of Serenity Hollow for two generations—her father being one of the town's founders. The man who'd started the Founder's Festival.

"Mae, don't be stupid. Your family's name. And mine. They'll be ruined."

Brenna stopped struggling against the ropes.

What would Peter's family name have to do with the Taylor's?

"Think of Agatha." Peter's voice had turned to more of a plea.

"I am." Mrs. Taylor stepped fully inside of the door to the small cabin, her aim never faltering from Peter, but she glanced over at Sophronia. "I think I am more disgusted with you than any of it," she said. "What would your ma have said about you carrying on with a married man?"

The younger woman stood up straight, her chin raised in the air as she opened her mouth, but it didn't seem that she had any idea what to say as she closed it again, folding her arms together and plopping down onto the bed next to Peter.

"Are you just going to let her speak to me that way?" she asked.

"See, Mae," he coaxed in a voice thicker and smoother than honey, "I didn't even tell little Soph here. Just think about what you are doing. This isn't what you want. It's not what I want either. I'm sure we can come to some type of understanding. All you have to do is go out there and tell them that you couldn't find me. That a racoon scared you into making that shot. You're well-respected in town. They'll believe you."

As Mrs. Taylor got closer to her, Brenna was unsure whether to be relieved or scared.

"That respect will be gone when everyone learns the truth,"

the woman said as she reached down and, with one hand, carefully pulled the gag from her mouth.

Brenna stuck out her tongue in an attempt to rid herself of the dank and salty taste to no avail.

"Thank you!"

"Are you all right, darlin'," Mae asked, her eyes still focused on the unlawful couple, as she slipped her hand beneath Brenna's underarm and helped her to her feet.

The tiny pearl bauble she'd discovered this morning fell out of her pocket as she stood, and her rope binding slipped to the floor behind her.

"Nicely done," Mrs. Taylor said with a hint of appreciation in Mae's voice.

With her hands suddenly free, Brenna bent down to retrieve the ring.

"Mrs. Taylor, you are sure a welcome sight for these sore eyes," she said, rubbing lightly over the angry red areas of her wrists, sucking in a breath as she grazed an open sore. "And a relief on my wrists."

It was no time to make light of the situation, but Brenna couldn't help it. She needed to focus on something other than her husband's complete betrayal.

"Thank you!" she said again sincerely as she moved behind the woman with the gun.

Peter was visibly growing more feeble by the moment, his hand too weak to support the weight of the pistol he held, but still, he maintained a controlled façade.

"What you got there, darlin'?" Mrs. Taylor asked, reaching out and taking the ring from her hand and turning it over to inspect the inside.

Brenna hadn't thought to look for an inscription.

"Where did you get this?" Mrs. Taylor asked, obvious pain in her eyes.

"It was in the tin where Peter hid the money he came looking for at my place. Why? Does it mean something to you?"

Mrs. Taylor handed it back to her. "Not anymore. It's over."

"Mae," Peter warned. "Don't. I give you my word, I'll let her go."

"And what good is that to me? Your word? The last time you gave me your word, I lost most everything—including my soul. And it's time to make that right."

Brenna glanced at the interior of the ring.

All my love, JS.

JS?

"That's just it, Mae. You may have lost all your money, your land, even your ranch, but your soul…" Peter slumped a little more, his color draining even faster than before, but he lifted his head enough to meet Mrs. Taylor's eyes. "Your soul is still…intact."

"Last I heard, killing a man, accident or not, was a sin against God."

"Don't you see?" Peter chuckled breathily, weakly. It was almost as if he knew he was on death's doorstep and wanted to get something off his chest. "He didn't die in that fall from your staircase balcony, Mae."

"What are you saying, Peter?" Mae took a step toward him, her gun wavering slightly, a desperate edge to her voice.

"I needed a way out." Peter's shoulders raised and fell in an attempt at a shrug, then licked at his blood-stained lips. His eyes sagged until they were mere slits. "He was alive when I took him from your place. I…I…" His head dropped and all went silent.

"No!" Sophronia yelled. "Peter, you can't leave me here. Don't go."

"You what, Peter?" Mae rushed to his side, her rifle slipping into a secured position beneath her arm, and she took him by the shoulders, shaking him. "You what?"

"Stop it!" Sophronia screamed. "Leave him alone."

Mrs. Taylor ignored the girl. She appeared more desperate than anyone Brenna had ever seen. She bowed her head, her voice choked with emotion as she whispered, "Peter Scott, what did you do?"

Peter moved.

"Mrs. Taylor," Brenna yelled in warning, afraid he might be bluffing, "look out!"

Mae jumped back away from Peter, whose eyes had re-opened, wet with death, and refocused her gun on him—not that it mattered in his deteriorating condition. It was clear now that the man would not be with them much longer.

Brenna struggled, knowing she should feel something, but she'd already mourned him—mourned the man she'd believed him to once be. And that was enough. Now, she felt…sorry for him. Sorry for the life he'd chosen to live. And sorry for the amends he'd never be able to make—not that he would have without coming to terms with his own mortality.

"I saved you. He died at my hand," Peter finally admitted. "I threw him over that cliff and saw it as my way out." He reached out toward them. "Your conscience can be clear."

"Why tell me now?" Mae asked, still keeping her distance.

"I lost." Peter forced a smile. "That's a risk every gambler takes."

"Peter," Sophronia stepped between them and the man, "do not give up, do you hear me? We can still find a doctor, someone to patch you up, and we'll find a way out of this mess."

"Sophie. Dear little Sophie. It's done."

"Not for me, it's not." She stood up, spun around, and with a quick snap of her wrist, raised the pistol still clutched in her hand toward them.

CRACK!

Without hesitation, Mrs. Taylor shot at the wood floor next to Sophronia, her rifle re-cocked in immediate succession, awaiting one more movement to fire again. The young, misguided woman screamed and dropped her weapon.

"I guess I lost too."

"Brenna!" Tag screamed as he ran his horse the rest of the way down the mountain through the drizzling rain and pulled to a quick stop in front of the small building, sliding off his horse, and headed for the cabin. "Brenna!" he called her name again.

He stopped short when Sophronia Miles appeared in the open doorway, her hands behind her. A moment later, she was thrust forward by a very formidable Mrs. Taylor prodding her out of the small house.

Tag held his breath, ignoring the soft tap of raindrops as they bounced off his hat's brim.

Where's Brenna?

He waited, trying to push all questions aside until he saw her face.

When she didn't appear immediately behind Mrs. Taylor, he prepared himself for the worst. He couldn't look inside. Couldn't see the woman who had brought so much light into his life in such a short time in the way he'd seen so many of his fallen comrades on the battlefield.

When a little splash of green peeked into the doorway, hope reseeded itself in his heart. The sight of Brenna, very much alive, emerging from the cabin filled him with an all-consuming gratitude that God had heard his quiet pleas to keep her safe.

He knew if he rushed forward, he would be unable to stop himself from pulling the married woman into his arms, holding her, kissing her. The hardest, but most appropriate thing for him to do would be to walk away. At least, for now. At least, until her marriage had been dissolved. Until she could be his completely and in every way.

It took every bit of restraint he could muster, but when he met her searching eyes, he simply tipped his hat, then forced himself to turn around.

One foot in front of the other, he had to remind himself how to walk as he headed toward his waiting horse—each step heavier and harder to make than the one before it.

"Is that the way you greet the widow who is madly, deeply, and completely in love with you?" Brenna yelled after him. "You just walk away like there is nothing between the two of you?"

He froze.

Widow? He didn't dare hope.

"He's gone, Mr. Redbourne," she said loudly. "Dead."

Tag spun to face her.

Did it make him a wicked man to want Brenna to be free of the bind Peter Scott held over her? If he found happiness in a soul's death? Relief?

His eyes locked on hers.

She nodded.

The clouds parted and the sun's rays shone down over the countryside, bringing its warmth and light to the people of Serenity Hollow. Within seconds, the area around the cabin was flooded with people, but Tag hardly noticed them as he purposefully made his way toward the woman who had captured his heart so completely.

As he reached her, it was as if his body had made the motions a thousand times as he thrust his arms beneath hers, wrapping them tightly around her full frame, needing to feel the warmth of her...to assure himself that she was no apparition that taunted him.

"It's over," she whispered with a squeeze.

"No," he said quietly as he released her, setting her carefully back onto the ground. "It's only just beginning." And he swooped down to claim her lips with his own, his arms wrapping once again around her, pulling her upward to meet his ardent kiss.

Brenna's passionate response warmed him to his toes as she twined her fingers into the hair at the back of his head and pulled him more tightly into her embrace.

When he broke their kiss, he looked down into her beautiful face, a pang of guilt tugging on his gut as he acknowledged the contusion just below her eye and he bent down to place a light kiss on the spot.

"I'm sorry I wasn't here sooner. I..."

Brenna shook her head. "Shhh...," she said, placing a finger over his lips.

Tag clasped her hands in his, kissing her wrists where the rough-worn ligature marks had cut into her tender flesh.

"I love you, Brenna Scott," he said, clutching her hands against his chest. "I can't deny it. I won't...deny it." He raised his head with a smile and yelled. "I love Brenna Scott!"

She giggled. "I love you, Taggert Redbourne!" And she raised her chin expectantly.

He did not want to disappoint, so he placed one light kiss, followed by another that lingered a little longer than the first before pulling away.

"Mr. Redbourne," she said all polite and proper sounding, "if you will just excuse me for a moment." She slipped her hands from his, lifted the hem of her dress, and marched up to a smug-looking Sophronia as Parker pulled the cuffs from his belt.

Without warning, Brenna slapped the woman straight across the cheek, eliciting gasps from several onlookers.

"That," she said, "was for holding me at gunpoint and then striking me in the face." She pointed to the bruise.

Tag was too surprised to move.

"Sheriff, are you going to stand there and let her do this?" Sophronia asked with affront.

Parker looked down at his bandaged leg and shrugged.

"And, this..." Brenna closed her fingers into a fist, and punched Miss Miles in the kisser, "is for partaking in sin with my husband." She turned to look at Tag over her shoulder. "Not that you didn't do me a favor," she said with a wink.

Dang, I love that woman!

CHAPTER TWENTY-THREE

Early August

Brenna passed the cordoned off section of the house for what seemed like the hundredth time that morning and the sun hadn't even been up an hour. The temptation to peek inside was far greater than she ever would have expected. It hadn't helped that she'd been forbidden to go in there while it was under construction. It had just made her even more curious than before and she had to find something productive to do that would take her mind off it.

It had been well over a month since Tag had moved out of the bunkhouse and into the small cabin at the edge of what used to be the Cranston property. She walked out the back door, sat down on the swing, and pulled her love's quilt up around her shoulders as she waited to see him crest the ridgeline on his way to Oak Meadow as he did each morning.

The kitchen door opened behind her.

"Would you like a peach muffin and glass of milk this morning, mum?" Thea asked.

It hadn't taken long for Tag and the others to learn that Brenna could not cook anything much beyond bread, so, shortly after Cole and the others had left for Kansas, he'd hired on an older woman who'd lost her husband and three sons in the war to prepare the meals and complete the housework.

Thea had been overjoyed with the prospect of cooking for a full house again.

Brenna felt like a queen in a castle that wasn't her own.

The Founder's Festival was finally upon them and Brenna looked forward to the evening's events and spending her first real leisure time with Tag in weeks. While they had shared a few stolen kisses, and had exchanged brief words of conversation, there was still a lot of work to be done and most of their time spent together was completing one set of chores or another— though, she'd learned way more about ranch life than she'd ever thought possible. The good and the not-so-pleasant.

The door to the bunkhouse opened and Kade stepped outside, pulling his suspender straps up over his shoulders. He nodded, then made his way over to the porch.

"The boss here yet?" he asked.

Brenna shook her head.

Kade pulled a watch from his pocket and clicked it open. "Don't you worry none, Mrs. Scott. He'll be along."

Just as he said the words, a wagon appeared on the horizon.

"Like I said." Kade placed his hat atop his head and tapped the front of it. "Ma'am," he said, then headed for the stables as more men began to trickle out of their sleeping quarters.

Several new hired hands had been brought on at the ranch—many from Georgetown and Austin and the last few arrived just a week ago from San Antonio.

Tag usually arrived on horseback, but as he pulled up into the yard, she could see why today was different. A huge, blanket-covered load sat in the back.

Brenna rose to her feet and stepped forward, hugging the post at the top of the stairs. It wasn't chilly outside, but she kept the blanket around her shoulders all the same.

"Good morning," Tag said with a wave, his voice full of energy and light-heartedness. He jumped down off the buckboard and within moments leapt up the stairs, taking two or three at a time, and planted a cheery kiss smack on her lips in front of everyone.

"Well, good morning to you too," she returned brightly.

"Come on," he said, reaching under the blanket and grabbing hold of her hand. "I have something to show you."

She giggled as the quilt dropped to the porch and she fluttered down the stairs behind him to the back of the wagon.

"Stay right there," he told her as he dropped the back latch and hopped up into the wagon's bed. When he stood up straight and faced her, a grin spread wide across his face and he reached down, clasped a handful of the blanket in his hands and pulled it off the cargo.

Brenna gasped. A large, white bathing basin with bright silver footings was now on display for her viewing. It was like looking at something from the Wheatley's trade catalogs.

"Tag," she said with awe as she closed the distance between them in a few steps. She reached out, running her hand down the smooth, cool, surface, delighted at the prospect of having the luxury of an indoor bathing tub.

He jumped down from the wagon and stood closely beside her.

"Do you like it?"

"Like it?" She wasn't sure what to say. "It's absolutely..." she searched for the right word. "...wonderful." She turned to face him. "It's wonderful," she repeated.

"Will you go on a ride with me?" he asked, his eyes alight with excitement.

"Of course," she said. "I just have to be back by ten o'clock, so I can go and help Agatha with the final preparations for the festival."

"I'll have you back in half an hour."

Brenna nodded. "Where are we going?"

"You'll see." Tag scooped her up and set her on the front seat of the wagon.

By the time he joined her, four men had already lowered the tub to the ground.

"We'll be back shortly," he told Kade.

"Oh, I almost forgot," the foreman said, "these came for you yesterday. The postmaster asked me to deliver this one to you in person and the other..." he glanced at Brenna, then back at Tag and cleared his throat, "came in last night." He handed Tag an envelope with beautiful script writing and a folded piece of paper.

"Thank you." Tag tucked them both into his shirt pocket without looking at them and snapped the reins.

The first few minutes of the familiar ride into town were in comfortable silence.

"Parker said that Mrs. Taylor confessed her part in Peter's little scheme. Turns out that Mae has been running a high-stakes poker game out of her house for more than thirty years. Peter found out that Agatha is Josiah's daughter and tried to blackmail her into giving him a stake in her ranch—only the ranch wasn't worth anything because Mae had lost everything, her ranch mortgaged, and her funds depleted. She was being hounded by debt collectors, one of them unfortunate enough to have been pushed down the long staircase at the Taylor homestead."

JS—the inscription from the ring--Josiah Scott.

That explained a lot.

Brenna didn't say anything. It seemed like so long ago. And she'd already learned much of the information from Agatha over the last month when they met about the Founder's Festival.

"I thought you might like to know that Miss Miles has been transferred to the Austin courts where she is going to be tried for Tobias Pane's murder," Tag said solemnly, his eyes on the road ahead.

"I still cannot believe that she was capable of doing so much damage. I'm just glad it's behind us now." Brenna actually felt bad for the young woman and the consequences she would likely be facing. "She's so young."

"When I thought I might lose you..."

Brenna placed a hand on his arm.

"It's over. Thoughts of them are ruining the mood. We cannot allow Peter, or any of them, to steal away any more of our precious time."

"Right you are, my dear," Tag said, leaning over to place a light kiss on her cheek.

Rafe had taken Peter's body to the U.S. Marshal's office in Austin before seeing that it was delivered to his parents for burial. Too little too late, his last act had been one of decency and that is what Brenna chose to remember about the man who'd shared a small portion of her life.

Tag pulled off the main road. As Brenna looked out over the countryside, a tall, beautiful white-washed building seemed to pop out from amidst a small cluster of trees.

"What is this?" she asked as they came to a stop in front of the edifice.

Tag pushed the brake into place, jumped down, and reached up for her.

The building was long with a protruding door column that extended upward into a bell-tower. They walked up the few steps to the front door and Brenna admired the beautifully ornate carvings around the window sills on either side.

"Did you do that?" she asked, remembering his love of whittling wood.

"Yes, ma'am," he said as he pushed the door open.

Brenna's eyes grew wide as she walked inside to find the children's desks from her school room inside, a new, large blackboard mounted to the wall, and shelves containing her vast collection of books adorning the area behind the wooden teacher's desk.

"You did this…for the children?" she asked, her hand at her chest.

"I did this…" he looked around the room, "for you," he said, pulling her into his embrace. "I love you, professor."

Any moment now.

She held her breath. She could feel a proposal coming.

Hoped a proposal was coming.

"And the teacher's quarters?" she asked, teasingly.

His smile faltered a little, but he recovered quickly. "We've built a small living space at the back of the building," he said, releasing his hold on her, "through here." He walked down a short corridor and pushed open a door to reveal a room nearly the size of hers at the homestead.

She glanced over at Tag who now avoided her gaze.

"Well, I promised to have you back within a half an hour. Best be leaving."

Brenna stopped him, her hand on his chest. "Tag, this is the most amazing thing anyone has ever done for me. Thank you! I just know the children are going to be ecstatic."

He nodded. "I hope so." His eyes still averted her.

"Are you all right?" she asked, concerned about the sudden change in his demeanor.

He smiled as he took her hand in his and raised it to his lips.

"If you're happy, then everything is fine," he said, finally meeting her eyes, searching them.

"I am happy when I am with you."

Tag bent down and placed a light kiss on the tip of her nose.

He looked like he wanted to say more, but didn't.

"We should go."

CHAPTER TWENTY-FOUR

Tag scanned the panorama of the land he could now call his own. The sun peeked over the horizon, casting beautiful shades of pink and orange like painted strokes against the canvas sky. He pulled Hannah's letter out of his pocket, grateful there was still plenty of light to read it.

Dearest Tag,

I first wanted to let you know that the Belgian's little filly and colt are both growing and getting stronger every day. Pa says it is a true miracle they survived, but even more so that they are now two of the healthiest little foals at the ranch. They are really fun to watch when they play with each other and their mother in the fields. Sally's kid ate the seat right off of Ma's rocking chair and she wasn't very happy about that, but other than a little discomfort in his belly, he is also doing well.

We all miss you and hope you are happy in your new home. I hear it is hot in Texas. I still think I should like to come for a visit in the near future. As for now, Raine is taking me with him to Granddad Deardon's place in Montana to spend the summer. I wish I'd been able to know him, but I am happy I'll get to know some of our cousins.

Please write soon. Cole has not returned home yet, so there is no word on your grand adventure. I love you, big brother.

Sincerely, Hannah

It seemed like living in Stone Creek at Redbourne Ranch was years ago. It was hard to believe it had only been a couple of months since he left. Oak Meadow was home now and he hoped he would be able to build the kind of life and legacy his parents had.

Tag patted his pocket where last night's telegram sat. It had taken a lot of doing, but he'd finally gotten a telegraph routed through the postmaster's office in Serenity Hollow and had requested a personal line installed at Oak Meadow as a surprise for Brenna—though Kade had almost given it away earlier in the day.

He'd been reluctant to read the contents of the telegram as so much hinged on its contents, but he took it out and slowly unfolded it. He glanced down, only one eye open, his head turned slightly to the right.

Dear Mr. Taggert Redbourne STOP After some consideration, my reply is yes STOP And, welcome to the family STOP Sincerely, Ezekiel Mallory STOP

Tag breathed out a sigh of relief and a happy chuckle escaped his lips.

YES! He screamed in his head, careful to not damage the relationship he was trying to build with his new mount. A grin spread wide across his face and his worry melted away.

Today's the day, Redbourne.

It had taken all the strength he could muster within him this morning at the schoolhouse not to offer Brenna a proposal of marriage, but he wanted it all to be perfect. And having her father's permission was paramount. When she'd inquired about the teacher's quarters, he'd frozen and had experienced a moment of doubt. What if Peter Scott had ruined marriage for her? What if she was happy with their current arrangement?

That was unacceptable for him. He wanted her, needed her, to be a part of his life, but he would not settle for anything less than being her husband.

"Come on, girl," he said as he patted the mustang dam's side. "Let's go home." The buckskin horse with the cream-colored mane was among the most beautiful he had ever seen. It had taken weeks to get her to trust him enough to guide her into the corral and another week before she allowed him to put a saddle on her back. This was the first ride they'd taken outside the ranch gate and he wanted to keep it short and easy.

The filly was healing, but it would be a while yet before she would be strong enough for a rider. He hoped that with the progress he'd made with the young mare and filly, he could show the people of Serenity Hollow that wild horses were worth more alive than dead.

He had more than he'd ever dreamed possible. Only one piece of his puzzle remained out of place and he hoped that tonight, the picture would be complete.

When he rode back into the yard, several of the new hands were just getting ready to head out and the mare's ears started swiveling rapidly. Her tail switched from side to side and she pawed uneasily at the ground. Tag cursed himself for having been distracted and hadn't anticipated a negative reaction around the other horses. He urged the mustang toward the field gate, away from the other mounts, but it was too late. The mustang pranced about wildly. Tag held on as best he could.

It would not be a good day to die.

He pulled his booted feet from the stirrups, preparing for the inevitable. The last thing he needed was to get a foot caught and be dragged for miles behind a wild horse. The horse bucked toward one of the men, then leapt forward in a jerking motion before rearing, tossing Tag like a ragdoll from the saddle, and bolting for the north meadow.

Thud.

Tag lay on the ground, attempting to catch his breath as he stared up into the slowly darkening sky.

"You all right, boss?" Kade jumped down off his own mount and rushed to his side.

All air had expelled from his lungs and he couldn't find his voice. He hit the ground with the palm of his hand and tried to pull himself into a sitting position, but the stabbing pain that shot through his chest prevented the motion.

"Tag?" The pitch in Kade's voice rose in alarm.

Tag closed his eyes and focused on his breath.

In. And out.

In. And out.

After several attempts, he was finally able to breathe in deeply and exhale.

"I'm fine, Kade. Just knocked the wind out of me is all." Again, he attempted to sit up, but found the motion difficult.

Kade took a hold of his hand and placed another on his back as he helped him up.

"Where's my brother when I need him?" he said jokingly, half expecting Rafe to emerge from behind a fence or the barn door. He was only moderately disappointed when it didn't happen.

It took several minutes, but he was finally able to get to his feet.

"Ow."

The men laughed uneasily.

"I think I'll take the wagon. Would you mind getting it hitched?" he asked the foreman.

"Yes, boss." Kade turned toward the barn, stopped, and turned around. "I'm glad you ain't dead."

"Aren't," Tag corrected and everyone laughed. "Stop. It hurts." He clutched his side, worried he may have broken a rib or two, but made his way into the house where he pulled a glass down from the cupboard and collected himself something to drink from the newly functioning water pump over the sink.

He smiled to himself as he thought about Brenna's reaction to the contraption once they'd gotten it to work last week. He liked making her smile.

The wagon was ready for him when he walked back into the yard. Kade had sent the others on ahead and stayed behind to drive into town with him. Tag stared at the lift for a moment, dreading the agony that would surely come from climbing up onto the seat, then straightened his back and pulled himself up.

As they pulled up to the meadow on the north end of town, it appeared as if everyone in Serenity Hollow and the surrounding communities from miles around had come to join in the celebration. Lanterns hung from tall metal poles, guiding the way into the festivities. Booths with fresh corn on the cob, pastries, and other confections lined the path. And folksy music was being played in the background. They had outdone themselves.

Tag scanned the crowd looking for Brenna.

"Nice to see you, Mr. Redbourne," Mrs. Taylor said as she approached him. "I would just like to thank you again for being willing to take on my mortgage. You have no idea what you have meant to me and this community."

"I'm glad I could help," he said quietly, "but, please, let's keep that little tidbit of information between you and me."

"Of course. Enjoy the festival."

"Ma'am," he said with a nod of his head and a tip of his hat as he excused himself and gingerly passed through the masses looking for Brenna.

He finally spotted her at the front, near the musicians, tapping her foot to the rhythm of the beat. He smiled, satisfied for the moment just to watch the delight on her face. She was the most beautiful woman he had ever seen and he longed to hold her, to kiss her, to make her his wife. He couldn't wait any longer.

"May I speak to you a moment?"

Brenna turned to face him, her eyes alight with the fire from the lanterns. "You made it," she exclaimed as she jumped to her feet, unknowing exactly how close he'd coming to missing everything. "Just look how beautiful it all is," she said with awe.

"I am." His eyes did not waver from her.

She turned to look at him, her soft, appreciative smile touching her perfect lips. "What is it?"

"Brenna?" he started.

Why did he feel nervous all of a sudden?

BOOM!

Splays of bright color shot into the air and burst across the sky in thousands of little twinkling lights and the crowd appropriately oooo'd and ahhhh'd.

The music stopped as the men turned in their seats to watch the show that hovered over the town pond.

BOOM! BOOM! BOOM!

Another round of fireworks dispatched and the chorus of people again oooo'd and ahhhh'd.

Tag reached down and took Brenna's hands and brought them up to his lips, pulling her close enough to hear what he had to say. His heart pounded. His chest swelled. And as he took in one more deep breath, his pain was momentarily forgotten.

"I love you," he said without reservation. "I love everything about you. I don't want you to move into the teacher's quarters at the school...because..."

"Because?" she repeated.

BOOM!

"Because I want you to stay...with me, Brenna." He swallowed hard as he reached into his pocket for the little trinket box he'd folded just hours before. "I am a better man when I am with you. You are a part of me now—body and soul—and I want you, professor, to be my wife." He held out the paper box.

Brenna giggled as she took it from his hands and the

fireworks seemed to blend into the background. "I thought maybe you'd changed your mind about me. That you'd indeed built that tiny little teacher's quarters for my accommodation."

"Forgive my stupidity. I wanted to ask you this morning, but I couldn't. Not until I had this." He reached into his vest pocket, removed the telegram from her father, and opened it for her to read.

She looked up at him in wonder, her eyes wide, and a grin shooting across her face.

"We have my father's permission!" Brenna jumped into his arms, the trinket box still clutched in her hands. "Oh, I love you, Taggert Redbourne. From the moment we met I knew you were something special. Yes, I will marry you. A thousand times, yes!"

Tag slipped his arms beneath hers, wrapped them around her waist, and pulled her in tightly, nestling his face in the crook of her neck. He pulled away enough that he could look down into her glittering eyes.

"You are the best thing that ever happened to me, professor."

"And you, me!"

He dropped his head and claimed her lips in a kiss that promised a lifetime of new discoveries, shared adventures, and love—a whole lot of love.

THE END

If you enjoyed Tag's story, please consider leaving a review.

To sign up to receive Kelli Ann Morgan's new release alerts and newsletter, visit www.kelliannmorgan.com.

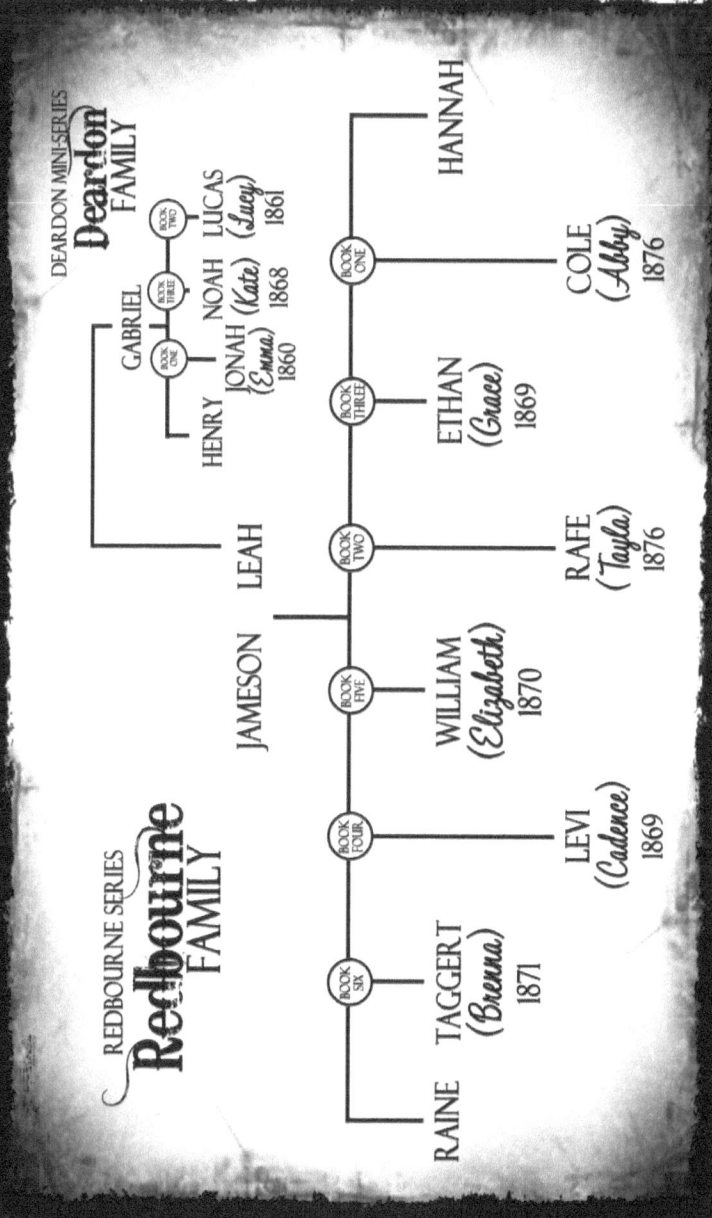

REDBOURNE SERIES
Redbourne
FAMILY

DEARDON MINI-SERIES
Deardon
FAMILY

GABRIEL

HENRY

NOAH *(Kate)*
1868

JONAH *(Emma)*
1860

BOOK THREE

BOOK ONE

LUCAS *(Lucy)*
1861

BOOK TWO

JAMESON   LEAH

RAINE

TAGGERT *(Brenna)*
1871

BOOK SIX

LEVI *(Cadence)*
1869

BOOK FOUR

WILLIAM *(Elizabeth)*
1870

BOOK FIVE

RAFE *(Tayla)*
1876

BOOK TWO

ETHAN *(Grace)*
1869

BOOK THREE

COLE *(Abby)*
1876

BOOK ONE

HANNAH

ABOUT THE AUTHOR

KELLI ANN MORGAN is a bestselling author whose western historical romance books have been downloaded over a quarter of a million times and maintain a better than four-star rating.

Kelli Ann lives in beautiful Northern Utah with her wonderfully creative and witty husband, her fun and imaginative teenage son, and two very playful cats. Before she started writing historical western romance, she worked as a photographer, jewelry designer, motivational speaker, corporate trainer and many other things, but has found fulfillment in living her dream of writing romance and designing book covers for herself and other authors.

She's passionate about creating stories with handsome, chivalrous men, intelligent, strong women, and in a world where there is always a happily-ever-after. Her novels are highly romantic and on the sensual side of PG—without all the graphic love scenes.

If you would like to receive new release alerts from Kelli Ann, please visit her website at http://www.kelliannmorgan.com where you can sign up for her newsletter.

FACEBOOK:
https://www.facebook.com/KelliAnnMorganAuthor

E-MAIL:
kelliann@kelliannmorgan.com

NEWSLETTER SIGN UP:
http://bit.ly/1iFvvwy

WATCH FOR

the
Lumberjack

REDBOURNE SERIES BOOK SEVEN
HANNAH'S STORY

www.ingramcontent.com/pod-product-compliance
Lightning Source LLC
Chambersburg PA
CBHW032145190626
46814CB00005BA/1837